ABOUT THE

Lindzi Mayann almost always has her nose in a book whether she is reading or writing it!

Lindzi loves to create vibrant, relatable characters, expose gritty truths, explore real life scenarios and use humour to create light heartedness.

There are plans for Maga High to be part of the Jodie Trilogy. A prequel is set to be released by the end of 2018.

You can follow Lindzi and stay up to date with book news:

Facebook & Twitter: @magahighmayann
Instagram: @Lindzimayann

Also by Lindzi Mayann

The Magaluf Series is available on Amazon- short side stories linked to Maga High. These are standalone and can be enjoyed in any order.

Maga High

By Lindzi Mayann

Published 2018©

Dedications

For those who believed in me. And for those who didn't!

Thank you to my chief readers; Ali, Jenni, Cat, Taz, Chloe, Sian and all of you fab ladies that have bought it so far! Charl, Hannah, Lou, Gilly, Dani, Stace, Shana, Bex, Marie, you know who you are too many of you to mention!

And thank you to my boyfriend Declan for always supporting me, never complaining that I've been on my laptop for hours on end and ultimately deciding not to read the Maga Series! Good call babe xx

TABLE OF CONTENTS

WE'RE HERE!

Who would have thought it?

I smile to myself and leisurely cast my eyes around the beach on which I am lying, propped up by my elbows. I relish the sensation of grinding them and my heels into the grainy sand beneath my towel. The bright yellow sun beats down from a deep, clear blue sky which rolls far off into the horizon meeting the equally blue line of ocean.

Next to me, Cassie and Alexa- oversized sunglasses, bodies exposed in tiny bikinis- soak it up lying flat on their own brightly patterned towels. I gaze around at the many other bare tanned limbs strolling along or reclining lazily on sun loungers- and amongst the huge variety of females and males I am particularly noticing the abundance of toned, tanned and muscular men! I literally have never seen anything like it.

Yes I've visited Spain before but this is my first time at a destination attracting predominantly people of my own age category, geared towards clubbing, dancing and generally getting trolleyed. And actually at 25 I feel a little behind in this experience, my younger brother George and his friends having been embarking on this type of holiday since aged 18.

Music dances in the air adding to the vibrancy of the atmosphere; we only arrived early this morning but I can already tell that Magaluf is going to be a thrilling place to explore during our 6 night break.

Who would have thought it? Only a few months ago I was still wasting my energy on that stupid prick! (That stupid prick being a paranoid shit bag that lied and cheated his way into over a year of my life.) Since I'd said goodbye to that toxic waste however, things have come good. I landed a new job- a complete change in profession too (waitress to teaching mentor). A total fresh start- stupid prick works in the kitchens of the same restaurant as I had; but I don't need to worry about any of that now.

The start date for my new position isn't until the new school year begins, late August but when I found out I'd been successful I immediately handed my notice in at the restaurant. Sunday marked the official start of almost 5 weeks without work. Chance to rest, recuperate and rebuild before embarking on my new career.

During a night out the holiday was mentioned and I got invited along. And although it was short notice; the timing- falling within my first week work free- I decided must be a sign it was meant to be. The next day, hungover and unsure I dared myself to use the small savings I have to book a place.

"It's amazing isn't it Jodie?" Alexa suddenly declares from my side bringing my attention back to the present; a fantastically wonderful and exciting present.

I take a deep breath of air, a warm and lingering combination of smoke, fried food, sun cream and salty sea.

"Just brilliant." I throw her an appreciative grin. "I'm so glad you invited me! Are you looking forward to seeing Tanya?"

"Oh I can't wait!" She exclaims dramatically throwing her arms around herself and grinning hugely. "I always miss her so much! But, look on the bright side- this is the second time I've been here this year already and it won't be the last holiday I have! I told you you'd love it and you haven't seen anything yet!"

Our chatter rouses Cassie and she stretches her arms skyward wiggling her fingers, a smile simultaneously stretching across her face.

"Can I just say how great it is to wake up from a little snooze and realise you're in fucking Magaluf!"

We laugh. The f-word doesn't belong with her petite, feline features but, well, what can I say? I fucking agree!

We're an unlikely trio considering Alexa is a friend of a friend- I know her socially and Cassie and I met only for the first time a week ago during a 'holiday planning' session. (Admittedly the necessities had already been decided through our WhatsApp group, the evening therefore rapidly descending into drunken chaos).

Tanya is our connection, mutual friendships with her binding us together. But due to her job as a rep with a big travel company I haven't actually seen her for almost 2 years myself!

Alexa has followed her from place to place since she started the job- being a self-employed hairdresser (relationship: serial man-eater) she has taken advantage of the plentiful opportunity for exotic mini breaks. There's a loose friendship between Cassie and Alexa although I'm not sure how, where or when they met. But there's no denying despite us not being traditional 'friends' it is a decent enough excuse to take advantage of Tanya's posting this season in Magaluf- or Shagamuf- as I've heard it numerously called since I booked.

I'm sure we'll all rub along nicely; we're here to tan in the day and party at night- that much we firmly know about one another.

"Who's up for a dip?" Alexa asks whilst shaking out her silky black hair and sliding her glasses up onto her head. "And then we'll get us a nice cocktail!"

"Sounds like a plan!" I agree my skin feeling as parched as my mouth.

My insides fizz with excitement. A dip in the sea and a cocktail at 2pm on a Wednesday! It is a million miles away from the monotony of back home. We bundle our belongings together into the middle of the towels before tip-toeing around the sunbathing bodies over the burning sand toward the sea.

"Oohya buggar!" I cry out as the first frothy wave rushes towards me and wraps like icy fingers around my ankles.

The sparkling allure of the sapphire water had me convinced I'd bound straight into the shallow waves without hesitation- relishing the cool, refreshing water and possibly even resembling a member of the Baywatch crew.

The reality however is a chilly shock and I stop dead for a moment; before resolutely continuing to stride forward- jaw determinedly clenched.

Yes I did notice that nearby group of lads watching us as we passed squealing girlishly and although I'm not going to check if they are still observing us I'm not about to make myself look like a wimp. Just in case!

"Woah! It's bloody freezing!" Cassie expresses my thoughts as she wades to my side and we push forward together wilfully until we're almost chest deep. Alexa has braved it and is swimming a casual breast stroke right through an all-male game of bat and ball to our left.

I pause to catch my breath and watch as she stands up allowing her shoulders and large boobs to break free of the ocean. Now that is a Baywatch move I think wryly. Water cascades from the huge curves glistening appealingly and the boys obviously think so too as they raucously catcall and whistle. Maybe the lads behind us on the shore are watching as well but I still avoid checking. These are Italian I guess, they're deeply tanned, thick dark hair and when one cries,

"Bella!" *Beautiful.* My guess is confirmed. I only know that because of my old assistant manage, Kate and the thought of her here makes me smirk. She'd look so out of place!

Alexa's lips smirk coyly as she glances back towards us; she makes a show of readjusting the glasses which are still perched on her head- and then her bikini top for good measure- before idly swimming back in our direction.

I laugh loudly admiring both her brazenness and the look of utter awe on the young men's faces.

Cassie shakes her head and murmurs. "I've got to give it to her, she's got fucking balls."

"Come on in girls." She purrs once she's a few metres away holding out her hands for us to take. The boys she intruded on have resumed their game but their eyes repeatedly glance over; tantalising smiles, teeth white against their dark skin. Acutely aware of the admiring looks Alexa has gained us, I brace myself for the refreshing sting of cold water on my hot upper body and take her hand allowing myself to be pulled deeper.

"I promise you ladies," she tells us in a low voice. "These boys are nothing. This is just the beginning." Her eyes glisten intensely like polished coal, flickering from mine to Cassie's and back again. I shiver with exhilaration; or perhaps it's just the nip that comes from being fully submerged in dense, cool water.

"Tonight, Tanya is meeting us at the Red Lion at 9." She continues. "She's hosting a bar crawl from there so we haven't got to worry about tickets for anywhere. We'll get to roll from bar to bar scouting for the fittest totty Magaluf has to offer! I have never been to a place like it; you're going to love it." Her smile is animated, the joy obvious- infectious- and I wonder if Cassie feels as excited and apprehensive as me.

I swirl my hands in the thick, salty sea relishing the feeling of the tiny bubbles tickling between my fingers and let Alexa's passion for this place sink in. The sun reflects brightly into my eyes from the rippling water's surface glinting sharply like shards of glass and I once again survey the enticing sights.

I note- again- the sheer volume of men. When Alexa says this is just the beginning I can only assume she is joking! The variety in my eye line at this moment alone includes tattooed, pierced, muscly, dark hair, blonde, shaved heads, long hair, dimples, bright eyes, loud laughs; despite myself, the saying a kid in a candy shop comes to mind.

Made ever sweeter of course by the dark contrast that has been the last 3 months- the last 6 months even. I shake off the familiar knotting sensation of humiliation threatening to take root in my stomach. Blinking my eyes, sore with gritty sea air I remind myself where I am now; and how far I have already come in such a short space of time.

"Magaluf, let's be fucking having you." Cassie yelps spontaneously and I realise she definitely is on par with my glee. "Shall we go for that cocktail?" She asks us slapping her lips to indicate her thirst. "My gob is like a feather pillow."

We're laughing hardily as we begin to slowly wade back to the beach, each taking in our own view and memory. This moment will last me a lifetime, I tell myself. It is a moment of pure happiness and promise.

From here I can see end to end of the wide cove, right to where the sand fizzles out to jagged rocks in the distance. We are roughly in the centre and beyond the beach near on 20 venues stand side my side, gaping open like mouths spewing music into the horizon- even from here I can make out the beats quite clearly as they compete for attention. The beach bars, I've noticed, all sport their own 'theme' (dark wood and ship-like to white wash with modern blue patterns and bean bags) in their attempt to win over custom.

Which will we choose? We push our way back through the receding tide and I dig my toes in to the soft sand below for traction. As my body begins to re-emerge I tense my stomach conscious of eyes unashamedly inspecting our every inch. Thank you heartbreak diet!

We stride as flippantly as sand allows back to our towels. Alexa shimmies her bottom and bust unabashed, Cassie and I glance at one another and she acknowledges the larger than life personality with a nod. Alexa is dominant and bold but her confidence is almost contagious. Feigning fearless and feisty I skip and trot over the sand beside them.

Reaching the towels we're in fits of silly giggles, our stream of banter happily flowing. I feel like I've gone from black and white TV to 3D overnight. I'm shaky, delirious, this whole place mysterious and so surreal.

"So girlies, which do we pick?" Alexa sweeps her hand along the row of beach bars like a gameshow host revealing our prizes. Which do we pick indeed! With our sandy beach bags hoisted onto our shoulders, Alexa overrides our suggestions and chooses the small bar painted completely black and upholstered in ethnic patterns of emerald and gold.

It's a choice that definitely seems to reflect her daring and alternative style and we step inside.

FIRST NIGHT; OUT OUT!

The walk from our hotel to the beach and main strip is only short, 10 minutes max each. We arrived back 2 hours ago, feeling light-headed from the sun and the mixture of strong cocktails.

Having grabbed pizzas from a takeaway reasoning we needed to eat something, we also picked up a bottle of vodka. Reasoning we needed to drink something too! I am not feeling that hungry, my stomach only consumed with giddy nerves and have instead spent a majority of the time dancing around the room with the same nibbled slice in my hand. But we *have* drunk over half of the bottle of vodka.

Now, 9pm and, deep breath, we are one corner away from arriving at the bottom of the strip! It's almost dark, the sky is smeared in inky stains above us and the air is cooler now making my baked skin prickle.

We're walking briskly, purposefully; unusually quiet as the eager anticipation builds between us. Snippets of loud music and unruly screaming plus the shouting and catcalling from balconies towering above us make up for our lack of words.

We're so close now! A few more steps and we'll be rounding the final building- we'll be coming face to face with the strip in its full glory. I don't know what to expect. My dizzy head is suddenly clear, my senses heightened, tingling with expectancy.

Oh wow! It looks like a riot has erupted! I look across at Alexa and Cassie who are both reacting; Alexa's lips have stretched into a bold, wide smile, her eyes focussed on the boisterous crowds of people up ahead. And Cassie reflects how I feel, mouth agape, eyes rounded!

How do we even begin to walk in that? Why would we even *want* to walk in that!

"Fuck me!" Cassie shouts and is still barely audible above the racket.

"This isn't even busy." Alexa states in reply.

Surely this is another of those comments she doesn't really mean!

My eyes are alive with the bustling picture before me, a river of bodies bashing and colliding flowing upstream into the distance, over a hump in the road and out of sight. Rows and rows of bars snake along both sides casting out colourful shards of light, smoke and music.

Alexa begins quickening her strides.

"C'mon girlies follow me. Don't let the P.R's get ya!"

She throws me an exaggerated wink. My heart flutters in a confused mixture of excitement and nerves and I instinctively grasp Cassie's hand as we reach where the colours and bodies begin to weave into denser and wilder crowds.

Bright, flashing lights change whole sections of my vision green, blue and red alternately and the music is so loud now. Speakers face the street from the train of bars pumping the air full of sound. Bodies jostle against each other, gyrating, stumbling, there are men in matching vests, women in fancy dress, jeering, singing, chanting; it is a breath taking clash of noise and light.

I can't afford to hesitate but my eyes snag on details; the scrawled signs (6 shotz 10 euros/ FREE clean toilet!), the skimpily dressed, heavily made-up girls holding trays of shots loitering seductively by the venue doors, the guy pissing in the gutter unaware- or unashamed- of the crowds circling by him.

White bulbs light up in succession snaking their way through pre-set patterns like puppies chasing their tails, sellers- African men ladled with watches, sunglasses and flashing charms waving their wares at drunken revellers.

"Evenin' gorgeous."

My free wrist has been gripped tightly taking me off guard. I stop and Cassie bumps into me.

"2 for the price of 1!" The cheeky looking boy says in his strong cockney accent- and then I realise he doesn't just mean the drinks offer as his beady eyes dart from me to Cassie. "Cam on beautiful, what dya say. I knock off at free firty we could all have a cheeky bang..."

Don't let the P.R's get ya! Alexa's voice pops into my head and he doesn't have chance to continue before, as though summoned, she swoops in cutting him dead.

"Do one short arse. We know where we're going." She tells him firmly and slaps the hand hard that's still holding onto my arm. He let's go smirking nastily.

"Fuck off you slag!" He retaliates and jumps immediately onto the next girls appearing through the human stream.

"Charming!" Cassie exclaims goggling and I begin to giggle in sheer astonishment, normal reactions numbed I absent-mindedly rub at the red marks left on my skin by the PR.

"They're an absolute nightmare." Alexa yells over the onslaught. "Ignore them. Just keep walking."

Easy to say but he had physically grabbed me! We continue and I keep my limbs close to my side, eyes peeled. I realise the PR's are fairly easy to spot- sporting lanyards, lots of bangles and wristbands, flat caps, bright vests, deep tans. Their eyes crinkled from squinting all summer scanning the crowds, quickly picking out targets to tempt into their bar.

"Buy one get one free baby." A Liverpudlian voice booms at me and I sneak a glance at the extremely good looking PR, I smile but hastily continue losing his face in the crowd.

"Free fishbowl and shots for you beautiful." Comes another from my left.

"Buy one get one free on cocktails all night!" A Welsh voice calls.

I feel like I have landed in a surreal auction. The PR's are majority male and are aiming their offers solely at the females. I feel hassled and yet oddly excited by it. Alexa halts turning to us with a smile. "We're here!"

A manicured nail leads our gaze to a huge plastic lit sign- Red Lion- it's a huge building and themed to look like a British pub only Pitbull is blasting out and the inside is lit only by strobes and spotlights, figures swarming tightly in the smoky darkness. We're pounced on- our hesitation making us easy targets.

"You're stunning." I'm told by a lad no older than 18, his baby blue eyes looking into mine as he snakes an arm around my waist.

"We know where we're going, thank you!" Alexa cries exasperatedly throwing herself at us. "Jodie, don't let him touch you like that babe. Who knows what diseases he's got!"

"What's the matter not getting enough cock love?" He asks brashly taking a step away from us. And before I can even register what he's said properly he literally whips his thingy out his shorts and starts swinging it around like a windmill. This causes the PR's nearby to jump into action, 3 more joining in with the sordid helicopter act.

Alexa claps her hands in glee laughing infectiously causing a ripple effect of laughter through the rapidly developing crowd and we take the opportunity to push our way free of the freak show.

"I love a good penis, I won't lie!" Alexa shrieks as we trip and skip towards the open glass panelling of the Red Lion giggling like school girls- and yet nothing like school girls I'd hope!

"But stay away from the PR's and their dicks Jodie for god's sake!" Alexa warns me knowledgeably. "They sleep with like, hundreds of girls every season. No wonder there's a clap epidemic back home!"

I laugh giddily unable to process everything at once. They're like a species- 'the PR boys'- operating as a pack of wild animals unafraid to do and say as they please. A Sir David Attenborough type voice takes on the description in my head ("...and here we have the PR boys.

Watch as they friskily take out their penises and erratically swing them, to gain the attention of passing party goers!") and I hoot tipsily.

The Red Lion is gloomy, packed and hot. The air is thick with dry ice, lasers slicing through it, strobes flashing bouncing off it, making everyone look like they're moving in jaunty, distorted movements. Dark, light, dark, light, dark, light. The whole scenario is wildly disorientating. With each flash of light my eyes meet another set of eyes, a different face, light, dark, light, dark.

"Where. Is. The. Bar?" Cassie hollers into my ear and I cast my eyes around. Finally the strobe takes a break and allows us to make some sense of the layout.

There's a bar to our right but it is jammed with bodies, a bar at the back plus another by the other entrance. Alexa beckons us close.

"We'll go back out. And round to that bar." She shouts the instructions signalling our suggested movements with her hand. A large ring catches a beam of light glinting mischievously.

We nod in agreement and nip back outside making our way through the crowded narrow outdoor space until we reach the next set of open doors.

Stepping back inside, the heat and blaring music immediately engulfs me once again. I find it comforting somehow like a hug from an old friend. The pushiness and sexism on the strip lingers in my forethought; but it feels dangerously inviting rather than intimidating and repulsive. This isn't how I should feel about it, I think.

"Tanya!" I'm aware of Alexa roaring- still only just audible above the volume of Wiz Khalifa. The besties are already embracing. Tanya's short, thick shock of sun bleached blonde hair bright against Alexa's shiny black mane.

Tanya pulls away and swoops onto Cassie and then me in turn.

"How lovely to see some familiar faces." She yells to us. "I'm so glad you decided to come along it's great to see you."

"You too!" We're both shouting loudly in return.

She looks great- I haven't seen her in too long but it's difficult when somebody spends most of their time abroad. Her skin is golden, freckles decorate her button nose. She has full lips stained pink and deep green eyes with rows of thick dark lashes.

"Drinks?" She shouts at us all now with her thumbs up nodding, a rhetorical question. And she turns away from us squeezing herself through the squirming mass of bodies. Alexa wastes no time reaching her hands up high, the ring once again shining like a star, and she sways her hips from side to side.

"Woohooo!" She calls to the roof engulfed somewhere up above by dry ice clouds and laser lights.

Tanya reappears clutching two huge spheres brimming with pink liquid, numerous straws surf the ice threatening to slip to the floor.

"Here." She thrusts one each at me and Cassie because Alexa has taken both hands of a tall blonde guy and is swinging him from side to side.

"Neck em." She instructs. "I can get you them free in here. We'll be moving on at ten."

She points to a huge clock hanging above the bar which I can vaguely make out and only now I notice a pair of girls in hot pants flinging energetically around a pole. I smile in recognition of the moves; I began taking classes this year. Just for fitness purposes mind but Alexa also attended the club and she is awesome like them. It'll only be a matter of time before she's bounding up there, shooing them away.

Taking long swallows of the strong, sweet drink my head tightens from the ice. I drain over half of it before tapping Alexa and offering it to her.

"Look!" I point out the pole once she's waved off the blonde guy and taken the drink from me. Whilst guzzling her eyes follow my finger and widen.

"Oh my god." She leans in shouting to me. "I came in May. It wasn't those bitches but I danced them off the pole." She spins around elegantly drinking from the straw simultaneously. "They were *begging* me to work here. You ask Tanya."

The music is thumping too hard for us to continue our conversation. I want to ask more, why didn't she take them up on it, then she could see Tanya all the time! Plus she would fit in perfectly.

She passes the almost emptied bowl back to me and as I finish it I watch her swinging her hair side to side, playful smile and narrowed eyes the music guiding her fluid movements. The girl does not give a shit- but then she looks great, she's having a great time, so why should she?

All around us groups dance and pump the air, foolish smiles and eyes full of spirit (namely vodka!) I can literally feel the electrifying energy pulsating in my ears and fingertips. The girls on the pole swing agilely in loops making effortless shapes with their bodies in perfect rhythm with each other and the music. Not having quite Alexa's level of confidence (or skill!) I certainly won't be taking these 2 on for a dance-off anytime soon!

A guy with a huge tray begins to navigate by us and I take advantage placing my empty bowl on top of his already teetering stack, I smile sweetly in sympathy but allow myself to dance now throwing my arms in the air like everyone else. Peering through the darkness I scan the sweaty sea of faces, it feels strange there being so many and yet recognising no one. It feels great actually!

Tanya is by our sides again now motioning for us to follow her. We push into the crowd immersing ourselves amongst clammy bodies and upon reaching the bar at the back of the club she hoists herself up onto its wooden top. We gaze up at her as she takes a bottle of tequila from the side.

I can't help but notice how at ease the barman is with a woman clambering onto his bar and kicking all the discarded cups and cloths onto the floor before marching commandingly up and down. Members of her team, recognisable by their huge lanyards with the large words 'BAR CRAWL', have been gathering others drawing them closer. When enough attention is gained Tanya takes the lid from the bottle and holds it up high like it's the FA cup.

The resulting cheer is certainly on par! It's then I hear the chant gaining strength;

'Get your tits out, get your tits out, get your tits out for the lads!'

Alexa looks elated as she joins in and I realise that as with most things I am experiencing for the first time, she's possibly not new to the scene.

Is she really going to do it? Actually get her tits out for the lads! Cassie and I mirror each other's disbelief as we exchange quick looks but I daren't miss a thing.

Sure enough Tanya finally puts her hands to the bottom of her vest enticing the cheers to rise to a ludicrous level. Faced with this scenario (if it was described to me I would surely be aghast) I'm secretly hoping she is going to do it. No not secretly, in fact, I'm chanting along with the best of them.

"Get your tits out for the lads!"

Suddenly her top flies up! A pair of tanned, pert boobs bounce proudly as Tanya jumps up and down. Everyone roars exuberantly and a wayward burst of pleasure prickles between my legs. In the darkness I blush looking around self-consciously but every pair of eyes is on Tanya's bust, obviously.

"Jodie!" Alexa barks in my ear. "Quick!"

Glad for the distraction I look only to find Tanya- topless Tanya- bending down to me with the tequila bottle.

"Open your mouth then." She laughs and I can't believe it's not already hanging open! Snapping my expression from what probably resembles that of an outraged prude into an 'I'm completely cool with this' smile I tip back my head and get ready to drink.

"Eugh!"

I've swallowed 2 large mouthfuls of tequila before what would have been a third sloshes all down my chin and chest. Saliva gushes from my lips which are recoiling in revulsion and I don't care about the smeared lip-gloss and soaking bra- just please don't be sick!

"Eugh!" I repeat and through watery eyes spot Cassie and Alexa howling with laughter. Alexa holds out a wedge of lemon which I shove straight between my teeth biting down releasing bitter juice. My face continues to distort in repulsion but at least it's quelled the urge to projectile vomit.

"You lightweight." Alexa teases gleefully going in for a slurp before Tanya moves away and along the queue of howling, leering men. She pours it into their eyes as well as their mouths and I think it's all strangely erotic.

"That's why I didn't have any." Cassie cries into my ear. "I wish I'd taken a photo of you!" She adds.

"I'm really glad you didn't!" I burst out laughing too wiping away what little eyeliner I'd bothered applying.

"You actually did really well there Jodes!" Alexa shouts to me now.

I was preoccupied wondering what my face must look like but Alexa's remark bolsters me. I don't care what I look like! Alexa thinks I did well enough to praise me for my crazy behaviour.

Here I am in Magaluf, swigging tequila from a bottle with a topless girl attached to it in front of a raging crowd of hooligans. I am nailing this.

We down another (and another) free pink fishbowl before we're being ushered back out onto the chaotic and unruly strip.

Cassie takes my hand again, Alexa marching at the head of our tribe with Tanya; the other reps swilling us past further clubs and bars. The strip seems never ending as it flashes by me. My ears ring and my stomach fizzles with the alcohol and anticipation. Where will be our next destination?

Another bar not quite unlike the Red Lion is the answer to that, this one called Ice. And another after that- Bounce. I am trying to understand my bearings- remember where we started, what we have passed to get to each destination. But not only is the strip fairly long there are a maze of side roads and alley ways; sprawling tentacles connecting again elsewhere or finally straggling away completely. The strip is firmly rooted into Magaluf's heart.

More loud music, flashing lights, faces, PR's, plus loads of shots and loads of fishbowls.

Make sure you drink plenty of water! My mum's advice rings in my head now that I have stumbled into bed at 3am. Belly sloshing with alcohol, and no mum, no water!

I feel a little sick, perhaps water wouldn't be such a bad idea, but I can't be bothered to move now. I'll wait until morning.

I'm so completely smitten. And not with any type of man this time but with Magaluf itself!

I lie awake long after Cassie and Alexa have fallen asleep smiling into the greyness at their drunken snores. My body vibrates and my mind races. And not for a change with anxiety and worry! No, it's with all the sheer gloriousness (what a wonderful word) that this place has turned out to be.

It would seem Alexa was correct with both comments; about the boys on the beach only being the start and it not being busy when we first hit the strip. Both of which continued to swell in proportion as the night progressed.

Tonight, I'm thinking, has already taught me a number of things: Number one; there really are *plenty* more fish in the sea! And that is a great thing to know! It's funny how a 'controlling' relationship can blinker your vision to one person who becomes godlike. And trigger you into feeling that nobody else will ever want somebody as flawed as you must be. But suddenly stupid prick has never felt more irrelevant and that feels amazing.

Number 2 and closely connected to number 1: Lots of people want to have sex with me!

Obviously I don't want to have sex with them. Well, not *all* of them anyway! I feel myself physically swoon at the memory of one guy in particular. He was tanned with brownie-gold hair and grey-blue eyes. Yum! And he *definitely* wanted to have sex with me. He told me so a number of times! But I was having *way* too much fun with the girl's to take him seriously.

And I won't be having *sex* with anyone anyway. Will I?

Why not?

Oh, hello inner voice Samantha, I thought you were being a little quiet! I smile again into the darkened room. Inner voices can be blessing or a curse; making me explore topics further, posing awkward questions...but on this occasion I don't mind pondering.

Well who knows, inner me, there is often more than one voice making comments. We'll have to wait and see!

This reignites the fizzing in my body and once again a surprise burst of tingles *down there*. It's nice to know I'm still working properly. Sex has been off the agenda for a few months now. Not that I'm saying it's back on the agenda or anything.

Lesson number 3: This place is hilarious and my memory is already filled to the brim with things I can't wait to tell my best friends, Leila, Cat and Micky. I want to type out texts now relaying everything but in this uncoordinated state it would take forever and then not make any sense. Tonight alone I've seen Tanya's tits, 6 PR's nobs (yes 6!), a wet tee-shirt competition and possibly a couple having actual intercourse on the street!

I am utterly convinced holidays are an absolute necessity and should be made law. *Magaluf* is an absolute necessity- but it should probably be against the law! I had no idea a place like this existed and I love it!

Number 4, off the back of number 3, life is made for living. I've learnt that just from watching Alexa today. I am channelling inner Alexa from now on!

And she is responsible for final lesson number 5- stay away from PR boys!

They are a species of their own. Arrogant, rude and unafraid to whip out their penises at any- and I mean any- opportunity.

'I'm gunna smash your back doors in.' Yep, that's right. 'I'm gunna smash your back doors in'- is apparently a go-to chat up line. Sounds more like a threat to me! But completely normal here! And seeing as I am so thoroughly enjoying the completely normal of here it's something I had better get used to.

Alexa has firmly warned me though noting my fascination with them. They are riddled with STD's apparently. 'So don't sleep with any of them!'

Without a condom.

That was a disobedient inner voice, speaking out of turn as usual. I won't be sleeping with any of them.

Without a condom.

Ok so they are attractive and their bad-boy vibe, no-fucks-given attitude is definitely appealing-

Buy some condoms!

Seriously now, you've been told- OUT OF BOUNDS.

Time to shut this wired and clearly irrational brain off! With images of the girl's faces amongst many others, sweaty, beautiful, unfamiliar, individual flashing through my mind I allow my aching body to relax into the mattress of my single bed. Dulcet tones from ongoing parties reach the window on a breeze and I let it lull me into dreams of confused craziness.

DAY 2
THURSDAY MORNING

I need a drink! Is the first thought to register when my eyes ping open.

It is 10am my mobile screen informs me. My mouth feels like a piece of old parchment and tastes like it's been used to wipe a camel's arse. My vision sways as I pad bare footedly over the square, tiled floor to the mini fridge in the corner extracting water.

I wish I'd bought something fizzy I curse my silly, excited yesterday-self, although mum will be proud. Better late than never!

"Grab me one please." Alexa rasps so I fetch 3, handing one to her and placing one on the stirring sheet covering Cassie. I clamber gingerly back onto my bed. My head is thumping and I gulp the cool liquid thinking it is the answer to all my dreams. The minute it hits my insides I propel myself toward the bathroom door and the swallows return to my mouth slimily. I throw myself at the toilet just as a huge muscle spasm takes hold of me but there's nothing to bring up except for more gritty liquid. I shiver feeling sorry for myself.

"You ok babe?" Cassie croaks from the other room. What a lovely sound for her to wake up to!

"I'm fine, thanks. Drank my water a bit too quickly." I feel stupid but already a little better. Alexa's voice says now.

"It's because you barely ate anything yesterday. Are you going to be sick again?"

I re-enter the room shaking my head. "I'm ok now, just needed to get the last fishbowl out." I'm too weak to laugh at my own joke but smile meekly sliding back onto my bed.

"A good breakfast will sort you out." Alexa nods and we set about discussing the events of the night before- that girl falling down the steps- oh my god, that guy dancing on the bar and flick through a number of photos I hadn't remembered being taken. Eventually we summon the energy to move.

We have our breakfast at a place Alexa found on her previous visit. She wolfs down a full fry up declaring it is the only way to recover alongside a cup of sweet tea. I opt for a pint of coke and a toastie- melted cheese being my hangover cure.

Tanya phones and invites us to meet her at the hotel she's stationed in today and we head there feeling more than ready for Day 2.

It feels deliciously naughty as we strap illicitly attained all-inclusive bands onto our wrists in the hotel lobby toilet. I giggle at Cassie. Alexa takes it all in her stride but I am on cloud 9 as Tanya escorts us to some plush sunbeds pointing out a bubbling hot tub and small bar complete with grass roof.

"Have fun girlies!"

"I need another drink!" Cassie smirks now, her pretty hazel eyes looking at us over her shades.

"Me too." Alexa chimes in. She places Katie Price's autobiography face down on the plastic table at her side.

Whilst reapplying my sun cream I have been using my shades as cover to assess the males present. A group to my left consist of 4 men who look like they in are in serious danger of bursting any moment their skin is so taut over bulbous muscles. If they don't use steroids, they definitely use sunbeds and pluck their eyebrows- all of which are a turn off for me.

And amid the couples and family groups, the only other set of potential male's (potential for what exactly Jodie?) is a huge group perhaps stag do or rugby tour- ages ranging from 18 to 50 odd. None are particularly attractive. Yes, a shallow judgement (their personalities might be great!) but currently easy-on-the-eye is the only thing I am interested in observing.

"Jodie?" Cassie addresses me shutting off my wicked mind. "Voddy-coke again?"

I nod smiling.

"Yes course, why not?" Not only are we on holiday but it's free!

I watch Cassie's retreating pert bum and slender legs- as do the bubble-muscle group. Their arms look like overstuffed sausages. Oily, brown balloons for shoulders squashing their round heads and making any turning of the neck look a taxing effort.

Beside me Alexa stands and stretches theatrically 'subtly' drawing the attention to herself- whether or not she finds them attractive or this just an instinctive reaction is unclear.

“I’m going for a quick dip.” She announces loudly ensuring I’m not the only recipient of the information and struts to the tiled steps that glide into the still water. Gracefully she sweeps down them, paying no attention to what is surely chilly water. I admire her audacious attitude- she’s never afraid or unsure.

As the water reaches to just below her voluptuous bust, she reaches up and ties her hair into a top-knot. The guys are watching her enraptured, as am I. I like my boobs- they’re more like Tanya’s I think and recall the image of her topless last night. But mine could never captivate all eyes like Alexa’s. And I could never just whip them out like Tanya.

Finally the boobs disappear into the blueness along with any booby related thoughts and she swims her signature, lazy breast stroke from one end to the other. I hear unabashed; ‘Fantastic pair of tits.’ ‘Get it all day long;’ Snippets of hedonistic wisdom drifting in my direction.

Cassie is back now, 3 plastic cups expertly clasped between her hands.

“Fishing again is she?” She comments loudly throwing Alexa a raised eyebrow.

Unfazed she purrs, “Darling, when the waters are so rich- eat.”

I giggle delightedly feeling like I’m in an episode of Sex and the City, the glee I felt yesterday rousing once again.

Alexa sidles back over to us now much to the disappointment of 2 of the men who have suddenly decided they needed to get in the pool. ‘Careful you don’t deflate!’ I want to warn them.

Her body glitters all over with sparkling droplets of water. She looks gorgeous.

"We need to take a photo!" I decide and rummage for my phone. Cue complete mini photo shoot. 3 way selfie, posed pics of each pair, lone shots taken by Alexa whilst calling out instructions.

"Now turn your back to me and look over your shoulder. That's the one baby, let's see you pout!"

There is a Jacuzzi after all! These will look awesome on Instagram!

As we prepare to undertake voddy-coke round 4 Alexa is explaining.

"The sun is just one of my favourite things." Whilst inspecting her rapidly darkening arms. "It makes me feel so sexual." She theatrically whispers now caressing her thighs.

Even under the heat of the sun I feel my cheeks get hot. It's having that effect on me too. Not that I'd brazenly announce it whilst stroking myself in full view of everyone but I nod in agreement.

"I definitely feel sexier." Cassie also agrees in her no frills, forthcoming way. "You 2 are ok, Alexa you're pretty with big tits and ridiculous confidence and Jodie your blonde hair and blue eyes are so eye-catching." I'm stunned at her evaluation, not shocked at Alexa's hers is utterly true. But me, eye-catching?

"What have I got?" She continues, "Boring brown hair and eyes that I don't even know what colour they are."

She laughs and my first shock is replaced by this second one.

“Oh my god, Cassie!” I exclaim. “You’re bloody beautiful! Have you not looked in the mirror recently or what! Your body is like a supermodel’s and your face is stunning; you have sexy, feline eyes.”

“*You* have sexy eyes!” She retorts. “You’re fucking stunning, your smile, everything!”

We’re giggling and blushing whilst Alexa watches on mildly amused.

“Oh honestly girls!” She purrs. “Let’s face it, we’re all different, but we’re all fit as fuck.”

This kind of talk is especially reserved for drunken toilet chatter between girls who barely know each other and don’t really mean a word of it. Or who are secretly guarding a raging jealousy and an urge to gouge out your eyes. But our exchange is warm and genuine. We could all feel a little jealous over something the other has, but there certainly aren’t any malicious feelings.

A combination of the heartfelt chat, sunshine and vodka is working to erase the last of any self-doubt instilled by the stupid prick. Certain events and situations had, I surely thought, damaged me beyond repair. But damage can and is being repaired just like in the aftermath of a hurricane.

Despite myself tears prick at the corners of my eyes and I gulp glad for the sunglasses covering this spontaneous leakage.

Pull it together I scold myself kindly, stop being daft. That’s all behind me now.

“Well, cheers!” Cassie offers raising her cup. “To being fit as fuck. And to Magaluf!” She laughs and we ‘chink’ our plastics calling. “CHEERS!”

Just then tinny music seeps onto the previously peaceful poolside. From the back of the hotel building appears a group of 4- two males and 2 females.

‘Tonight, I want all of you tonight, I want everything tonight.’ Lyrics escape the speakers of a tiny boom box. PR’s! I realise breathlessly. I hadn’t expected to see any out in the day!

My Attenborough voice rouses- ahhh, a small group of PR’s on the prowl for potential clubbers.

The group splits in a well-practised approach. The girls head for the bubble-muscle men and the boys pounce on the closest group of girl’s to them.

My attention is well and truly snagged on one of the guys. Woah! He is gorgeous!

Now, I’m sworn off men. Possibly for good! However, the arrival of this man affects me so powerfully I could easily scream ‘take me now’ before throwing myself panting to his feet.

It must be the sun. It must be the sun!

I watch them trying to chat to the girls but they are not interested and barely give them any attention. How can they not be interested in that divine being? But I’m so glad they’re not. I want them to hurry up and get to us.

I quickly check that the PR girls have no intention of approaching us first but they're busy writing details on tickets and handing them out.

He's looking now! He's looking over!

He's coming over! Oh shit!

"Afternoon ladies." He calls to us as they approach, a playful smile that reaches his eyes, lights up his face. I return the smile, agog, barely thinking. My palms are slick, my heart racing so hard I'm worried he can see it pouncing forward like a third boob between my small actual ones. Luckily Alexa suffers from no such afflictions in the face of such heavenliness.

"Well, hi!" She beams swiping up her drink and suggestively licking some condensation from the rim.

"And where are you suggesting we party tonight then?" She asks.

"Club Twenty One." The beautiful being who has disabled all of my senses says. "It really doesn't kick off till midnight. When I get there." He adds with a wink, the smile returning with force.

He holds out a card. I can see its logo imprinted on one side. Alexa, back arched steps up to take it and I hold my breath. There's no way I stand a chance now. Not that I really wanted a chance or anything.

"You're very quiet." She snaps the card from his fingers without meeting his eye and instead walks past him to his partner. "What's your role in all of this, are you going to be there tonight?"

I slowly let out the breath that I've held until my head spun daring a glance at Cassie. She looks… completely fine. Normal. Take note,

Jodie. I give myself an inner shake but to my horror he's stepping closer, sliding onto the sunbed next to me.

"Hey short stuff." He says softly. The world continues on; Cassie watches as Alexa toys with her meal, the other groups continue to chat. Mine has stopped- or sped up, I'm unsure.

"Hi." I return and can't fully meet his intense chocolatey eyes. Sitting this closely I can smell his sweet aftershave, see the black stubble along his jaw. "How do you know I'm short?" I ask. I wanted to say something better, something witty, but that's what comes out plus, anything, to make conversation.

He tilts his head back and laughs, dimples pressing into his cheeks. My breath catches; I get the feeling he's taking the piss out of me. Possibly, considering I've been reduced to a marshmallow. He's a PR boy remember, I mentally slap myself- they're untamed, unafraid, and also completely off limits, remember?

"Stand up." He commands getting to his feet. As he towers over me all I can think is, 'his penis is level with my mouth!'

I meet his eye properly now and get the distinct feeling he is thinking the same thing. Quickly, breaking the telepathic exchange I also stand and rise to the full height of his sculpted pecs. He is a head and shoulders taller than me.

"Aww shorty." He murmurs and leans back resting his forearms on my shoulders cocking his head at me. My knees want to buckle, and not with the welcome weight of his body but the contact sends sharp, intense pangs of desire right into my core.

"I could tell you were short by those tiny feet." He murmurs smirking and looks down at my feet, pale in comparison to his mixed race skin.

"Your tiny waist." He continues raising his eyes to my middle before finally meeting my face with an almost aggressive expression. "Your tiny shoulders. You're like a little doll."

I can literally feel electric shocks shooting from his eyes into mine, or are they the other way round? He knows what he's doing to me, there's no doubt about it.

Plus he's probably pulling this act at each hotel they visit, I reprimand myself.

"I don't fight like a little doll." I tell him in a tentative attempt to flirt.

"I like a fighter." He retorts eyes blazing still boring into mine causing an eruption of tingles in my bikini bottoms.

I smirk without meaning to and gather what scrap of composure has hung around before stepping away from him. He lets his arms drop to his side and I flop back to the bed feigning disinterest but feeling very hot and bothered, heart beating wildly. Grasping my cup I almost crush it and icy liquid runs over my hand. I swig it pretending not to notice as the cold drops hit my thighs.

"What's your name?" He asks still standing over me. His body blocks the sunlight out making my skin tighten in the coolness. "Shorty, what's your name?" He repeats and I look up at the gloriously cheeky smile that has returned and no doubt gets him whoever's name he wants.

"Jodie." I tell him and finish the rest of my drink for courage before asking. "What's yours?" But he ignores me instead looking at Cassie and flicking his chin upwards.

"Yours?" He asks her.

"Cassie." She responds. "And yours?"

I'm disappointed and pleased that he ignores her too. We're all looking at Alexa now who is mere millimetres away from his companion her long nails lightly brushing the obvious lump in his shorts.

"Alexa." She replies without needing to be asked. She might be staring squarely into boner boys' eyes but she isn't oblivious to us and our conversation. Poor boner boy; he's standing with his knees turned in and there's a crooked bend in his tummy, his eyebrows knitted together awkwardly.

I'm tempted to declare, 'and here we witness the rare occasion a PR boy meets his match. Observe his defeated stance as the holiday-maker torments him'.

Alright Jodie Attenborough, I think as I inwardly giggle, that is not going to make you seductress of the year!

"We'll probably have a much more fabulous party to go to than yours but thanks anyway." Alexa bellows assuredly finally taking a step away from her target and surveying him.

"Well, Jodie, if you want to find out my name." The PR says now pausing for affect. "And how I fight." He raises an eyebrow, one dimple showing- I'm going to die. "Then I'll see you tonight. After midnight. Come on."

Like a dog seeing its lead, boner boy responds immediately to the command. And I note the carefully placed hand guarding his crotch as they retreat to find the others in their pack.

Alexa lets out a tinkling laugh directly at their backs. "Did you see that guy's hard on?" She calls out gleefully and I flinch- he must have heard her- but then laugh despite myself. I'd certainly not been up to much in the girl power department after all.

There is no way Alexa will want to go to Club Twenty One, wherever it is. This is going to take some serious swindling if I don't want to come clean about my forbidden crush on a PR.

"What were you saying to him?" Cassie gurgles as a giggle spills out of her mouth. "I heard something about shagging in the waves!"

"Oh I was telling him all sorts." Alexa says matter of fact. "I told him I would squeeze his balls and stick my finger up his arse."

At this we all howl with laughter causing the PR group to take one more glance over as they exit the pool area altogether.

"Well, it's not like we'll see them again." She continues plonking herself beside Cassie and I feel my heart sink. "I'm sure Tanya said there was somewhere she wanted to take us later anyway. Silly PR boy, I wouldn't touch him with my arch enemies' fanny! They're a vile breed."

I'm laughing still but that doesn't disguise a stab of disappointment. I wouldn't have minded finding out his name- or how he fights as he'd put it. But then I cringe, Alexa has made it clear what they're like. They're off limits.

The business card is abandoned on the table and I pull it towards me with one finger, 'Twenty One,' bold red letters against a faded black background.

"Jodie wants to see them again." Cassie jibes fun in my direction and a smirk splits my face before I can control it.

"Shut up." I tell her lightly noting the curl of Alexa's lip. But I could use a condom! I want to shout at her, and then bite my own lip. Who is in control here!

"I need a drink!" I say instead.

We leave Hotel Aria around 5pm.

I feel a tiny bit guilty for my flash of happiness when Tanya informs us she's on an airport run this evening and so we'll be left to our own devices tonight.

So now all that's left to do is orchestrate us being at Club Twenty One after midnight. A mean feat when not only am I unsure where the club is but also face Alexa's overpowering will when it comes to making decisions.

All this Jodie, just to find out his name! Ahem.

On our walk back to our hotel I keep my eyes peeled and I'm elated to spot Club Twenty One on the strip. It's nestled between Cactus Jacks and Eve.

First obstacle easily overcome, I privately congratulate myself. Alexa next- and if I want to somehow trick her into going rather than just asking outright, I have a feeling this won't be as easy.

I lie on my bed back in the room. Cassie has gone off to make a call and Alexa is flicking through a magazine. We aren't rushing anywhere and I fall into a thoughtful snooze.

Maybe I could get her really drunk so she passes out and we drag her back to the hotel before... No, ok, that's a bit strong. Perhaps just so drunk that she doesn't care who chooses where we go. Yes, Alexa is wild. But one thing she doesn't seem to do is lose control of herself completely.

I could just ask her if we can go there. She won't just say yes though. She'll ask why or say no. And in either scenario I'll be all like, oh well I just really need to know that PR boys name- I think I recognise him as a famous footballer and my brother would really like his autograph.

Alright get a grip. But even if I was willing to admit I fancy somebody so badly I am willing to hunt them down- which to be fair she would most likely be up for- I am faced with the dilemma that he's a PR, and they're banned.

I don't want to lose the respect of Alexa and Cassie. I'm having the best time I have had in too long and to be honest I've lost enough respect from people recently to last me a lifetime, thank you.

PR boys are off limits and I won't be making the mistake of prioritising this man above the feelings of my friends. But, obviously, if the opportunity arises there's nothing wrong with double checking he isn't a famous footballer...

We're not even ready to leave the room until 11.30 but we'll be arriving on the strip really as it hits peak time.

Alexa wants to go back to The Sun Down, the third of the venues we visited last night but Cassie isn't so keen. She's complaining she wants to try out new places, it's her first time in Magaluf and she wants to check out the abundance of other bars. And I (cowardly I know) jump on her bandwagon instead of coming clean about where exactly I want to go.

As it happens, Alexa gets her way (surprise). She quite snootily I thought, and no nothing to do with my feelings about going elsewhere, airs her 'knowledge' on many of the bars on the strip (vile, dingy) and then tars everyone who dares step foot inside one with the same (trampy, cheap) brush.

Well that settles it then. If we want to remain one of the cool kids and know exactly where is best to go we must follow her lead. Of course, she has been here a whole once before us, making her clearly superior.

Meow, Jodie.

I'm pleased to see the strip has lost none of the riotous charm that I remember when we reach it. And we get to walk by Club Twenty One- it's just before midnight however and I don't spot potential-footballer PR in the crowd.

The Sun Down turns out to be better than I'd anticipated from my drunken recollections. A central bar; tables to the left, dance floor to the right. We're sat to the left, surveying the right.

"He is sooo my type." Alexa croons admiring a traditional tall, dark and handsome. "I absolutely love Italian and French men. They definitely make the best lovers. And are so much more sophisticated than English men."

She continues to stare unabashed stirring the straw of her drink. Maybe it's where I've been going wrong!

"Watch and learn ladies." She tells us suddenly and flounces off toward him.

Cassie shakes her head with a smirk as we watch the retreating swaying backside.

"I'd love to have her confidence." She remarks. "Even if she can be a bossy bitch at times."

I giggle, before attempting to reassure her although not really meaning a word of it.

"I'm sure we will be able to go to other bars one night!"

She took the earlier disagreement harder than me and has been openly huffy up until now. Life is too short to hold grudges though and holidays even shorter! Don't get me wrong, I want to see the PR again but it will cause unnecessary tension. He's only a guy. Plenty more fish and all that!

"Yeah." Cassie shrugs sounding as convinced as me. "Sure we will. Huh? Oh shit!" She exclaims and her eyes widen. I glance to Alexa and her Italian/ French target.

They look like they're having a major stand-off. Gone is the usual glamour-puss demeanour replaced by a warrior stance, hands on hips and eyes squared. Her mouth is moving quickly, lips forming solid syllables.

Currently wishing I could lip read and realising I can't despite my best efforts I look to Cassie.

"What happened?" I ask her. "Should we go over?"

I was so not expecting this outcome and I'm bowled over by shock.

"It's ok, she's coming." Cassie begins to stand as Alexa arrives at the table, face like thunder.

"Must be fucking gay." She announces to our blank faces. She follows it up with a laugh but the hollow tinkle doesn't fool either of us. Although her face is regaining composure by the millisecond her chest is still blotchy, a tell-tale sign of her distress. "Drink up girl's we're going."

Ironic!

"So is he gay French or gay Italian?" Cassie asks as we head for the doors.

"Oh fuck off Cassie." Alexa tells her narrowing her eyes but I can't help but giggle and Cassie smirks too. "He was bloody English ok. *And* gay." She adds pointedly but by now she's smiling too her regular bolshie manner returning.

I take a final glance at the gay English and note he is now chatting to a pretty brunette. Must be his fag-hag I suppose.

"So where to now?" Cassie asks. "Can I choose somewhere?"

Although this poses a really handy opportunity to suggest Club Twenty One, I know Cassie wants the opportunity to choose somewhere more than I do. I also realise Alexa was shaken by the clash, whether she'll admit to that or not. Whereas I have a shallow, selfish motive and it really isn't that important. I am going to do the right thing by my friends. Let Cassie choose the venue and make it a fabulous night still for Alexa.

Plus I'll be honest, seeing her get knocked back, or whatever had happened, has reminded me that the fish can sometimes be piranhas and I'm not ready to get bitten again.

I keep my fingers crossed that Cassie chooses well, for her own sake.

Out on the strip, we're easy targets being slow and unsure amongst the swirling crowds. PR's yell their offers like sellers at a market.

'2 for 1.' 'Free bar, 10 euros.' '5 shots and a fish bowl with your first round.'

I keep my arms folded, eyes averted but Cassie distracted in her task of picking a venue gets leapt upon and grabbed by the hand.

"Hey sexy ladies." A cute brown haired boy calls above the noise. "Aren't you the lucky ones? You've just found the best bar on the strip!"

His approach is refreshingly unthreatening and gives him more opportunity than any other so far.

"What's your best offer then?" Cassie steps up taking her responsibility seriously.

"Buy one get one free all night and a fishbowl." He says without hesitation smiling cheekily.

"And shots?" She pushes. I smile feeling proud of her, admiring Alexa's confidence indeed; it must be rubbing off on us all!

"For you 3 stunners of course. I'll join ya for one."

We follow the PR inside. The outside terrace is heaving with scantily clad bodies smoking and doing balloons of 'laughing gas'. Inside we manage to squeeze in at one end of the bar and he flags down a barman who pours us shots before taking our order.

"Cheers girls!" The PR takes one and necks it without waiting for us to follow suit before winking and returning to the street.

We have to down the fishbowl at the bar because we all have 2 drinks each to hold. And then with Cassie happy she has taken some control, Alexa's sparkle returned in full force we hit the dance floor to Lady Gaga's Born This Way.

DOUBLE HANGOVER FRIDAY

After another luxurious day spent at Hotel Aria, I give a gratified sigh as Tanya cuts the wristband from my arm.

"Thanks so much for getting them for us." I tell her genuinely. She won't be posted here again until next week when we have gone (huge gutted sigh).

"Perks of the job. There's got to be some because most of the time it's shitty." She says it with a smile on her face, knowing the perks also include the wonderful travelling opportunities. However there is no denying her hours are long. Tonight she's hosting another bar crawl and tomorrow a booze cruise.

"So tomorrow, meet me at Ocean café at 9.15." She's swooping in to peck my cheek, then Cassie's. "The boat doesn't leave until 10 but we can walk to the pier together and you guys can bagsy the best seats before it gets busy."

She swoops Alexa into a hug before adding.

"And get first pick of the totty. It'll be boys galore!"

Alexa claps her hands gleefully; last night's scenario well and truly swept under the carpet.

"I cannot wait. Will there be lots of disgustingly sexual games?" She asks animatedly and as Tanya nods laughing she cries.

"Brilliant. We can't wait can we girlies?"

"Well I'm not taking part in any fucking sex games!" Cassie says abruptly.

"Neither am I!" I add quickly, sex games! Of course I've heard about them but I didn't think I'd actually encounter one! I'd watched the wet t-shirt competition with perverted intrigue but I never imagined I'd be put in this position!

"Don't be silly Jodes, of course you will!" Alexa chides.

"I am looking forward to more free booze though!" Cassie continues not giving me the chance to oppose my participation in a sex game. "You've been a star Tanya; you've saved me a fortune."

I nod at this but not forgetting my dilemma whilst Alexa puffs up her chest, proud as if she were the one being praised.

"That's alright lovelies! I'm just glad you're all here!" Tanya tells us.

We leave her waving at the large glass doors and step into the warm, sunbathed street.

Following a day of drinking soft drinks we managed a cocktail each this afternoon. After waking on a double hangover this morning, nobody suggested alcohol at first, an unspoken mutual acknowledgement that we weren't feeling our best.

"So, I was thinking who's up for red wine and steak at the most beautiful roof top restaurant?" Alexa asks us.

I agree with Cassie's enthusiastic.

"Fuck, yes!"

It sounds an amazingly grown up thing to do (I think because of the red wine part) and just the tonic following our 2 heavy nights drinking.

BOOZE CRUISE SATURDAY!

I awake feeling fresh after last night's extremely chilled evening meal with extremely picturesque surroundings. Thank god for Alexa's Magaluf knowledge now!

I feel a little guilty for my thoughts on it. Had she not pulled Gino during her previous visit and been taken there for romantic, candle lit sluttiness (she pointed out the thicket of trees where she had given him a blow job after coffee) we never would have found it ourselves.

Thinking about today's upcoming Boat Party makes me tingle from my head to my toes. It's going to be another first for me but I am not completely naïve about what to expect. I already knew that the free booze and loud music resulted in rowdy behaviour and now thanks to Alexa I also know to expect sex games! I'm not even sure what a 'sex game' entails exactly! Surely not *actual* sex! Not that I'm taking part either way, but it will be interesting to watch.

Excitement and nerves swirl throughout my insides and I look over to see if Cassie and Alexa are awake purely for a distraction.

"Morning." I say to Alexa who is sitting upright at the desk in front of a mirror. Her hair is pinned up around huge pink rollers and I can see one closed eye in the reflection as she expertly applies fake lashes.

"What time is it?" I ask her a little panicked, I'm sure I set an alarm! I scrabble for my phone, 7.50. What time did she get up!

Cassie stirs as well. "What time is it?" She echoes.

"Ten to 8." I tell her swinging my legs from the bed, bare feet meeting cool tile.

"I'm going to take a shower." I tell them both. And think about what to wear!

There's nothing special to report about the big, white boat moored at the end of the pier. It's pretty standard looking and once Tanya leads us up the stairs to the top floor, I check out the silver railings and bench seats bordering an open central space.

The morning sun gleams from white plastic and metal. I have noted the chain blocking off a metre wide gap- presumably to allow people to jump off once we're anchored out at sea somewhere. My stomach clenches at the thought.

2 large speakers are rigged to the edge of the cockpit and there are four large blue barrels filled with ice and cans- the only indication that this might not be an ordinary boat after all.

We sit in the far left corner side by side and sip our chilled beers waiting for people to arrive. I spent the best part of an hour creating a 'casual' topknot and 'natural' looking make up. At least if some totty do turn up I can make a good first impression before sweat, sea air and wind take their toll!

I've managed to count the first 20 or so arriving (a few cuties but no 'worldies') but after that it becomes too crowded to continue with my tally. I'd guess there are 60 on board now and well over half are male.

'Magaluf, the party place, will make you want to get off your face!'

The stream of mantra continues above the loud level of crackly music- plainly demonstrating the nature of the party.

'We love Maga, we do! We love Maga, we do! We love Maga, we do! Oh Maga, we love you!'

I have divided the males on board into a number of groups. There are the skull heads: rowdy groups full of testosterone, tongues hanging out, clutching beers with burnt knuckles and goggling, glassy eyed at every pair of tits they spot.

The geeky guys: clinging together for safety, pale, twitchy and genuinely resembling spooked deer.

The posers: these exist in smaller groups or aren't afraid to stand alone. Ripped muscles, ray bans, diamond earring, generally well-preened.

Dotted amongst these are the guys that fall in-between categories. The in-betweeners! If I could create a type it would be one part geeky guy two part poser.

After an hour the boat slows down before coming to a stop in a crystal clear cove.

"Boys and girls we have arrived!" our host Eddie's voice crackles through the speakers. "Now the party can really start!"

The announcement is met by hoarse jeers and wolf whistles.

"We will start with some games to get us in the mood!" He continues and my throat tightens a little. "So what I'd like everybody to do is clear a little space at the front here, this will be our stage."

Bodies begin shuffling and repositioning to offer-up a rectangle slot in the centre of the floor around Eddie.

"Now the most important question. Have you all got a drink in your hand?"

"Yes!" Some people shout out as Eddie adds.

"If you haven't then sort your shit out and get yourself a drink! Now!"

"I'll get us one." Alexa tells us standing up and heading off into the slurry of bodies.

"Are you going to take part in any games?" I ask Cassie.

"Am I fuck!" She scoffs her eyes widening. "No chance! You should though, if you want to."

"I don't!" I tell her laughing but inside something stirs a little. As if to say, yes you do, just a little.

Alexa is back with warming beers- the ice in the buckets melted. She hands them out and plonks herself back down. I hold my breath waiting for her to broach the subject of participation and right on cue Eddie pipes up.

"And for our first game I need 4 sexy ladies and 4 very, very lucky men! Now don't all jump at once- but I promise you. You are in for the ride of your lives with this one!"

There is mayhem at the announcement and I try to peer through the tangle of torso's to see what is happening inside the rectangle.

"One ssseexxyy lady, two sexy ladies! Male player number 1 you lucky boy, number 2 and 3."

I am both relieved the spots are being rapidly filled and stunned Alexa has yet to breathe a word about entering. Maybe she is having second thoughts now that the opportunity is actually here.

"Third sexy lady, our 4th lucky man and who for our fourth sexy lady… Ah yes, you, you are perfect! Can we have a big round of applause for all of our beautiful contenders?"

The deck erupts in cheers and clapping, me because I am pleased to still be sitting here on the side lines.

"I know you're all dying to know what our first game is!" Eddie waits for the noise to die down. "But first I need our girls and guys to pair up. That's right, you with you, yes, that'll do."

Now that I'm safely out of the running I stand up to get a better view of what's going to happen. Tanya and 2 others have come along to help and when I catch her eye she winks cheekily at me nodding towards the mini arena. I shake my head laughing and look away back to Eddie.

"Ok, ladies and gents. I am going to set the timer on my phone to 60 seconds." He holds it up to indicate the clock feature. "And in that time you're going to make as many sex positions as you can!"

The roar is immediate and deafening and I'm squealing with curious delight.

"My wonderful glamourous assistants will be helping me with the counting. Are you ready? On your marks, get set, go!"

And just like that alongside the booming lyrics of, 'I'm horny; horny, horny, horny…' 4 couples begin simultaneously throwing and pushing each other into a combination of doggy, missionary, cowgirl and 69er!

It is hysterical to watch and I understand the popularity of these games immediately. The wet t-shirt competition had been a little seedy. Men leering at the girl's parading themselves on stage- one guy had even jumped on one contestant groping her roughly. Not that she seemed to mind but she was so drunk, it made me cringe!

The atmosphere here though is electric. Everyone cheers on their favourites and shouts out suggestions. By the time the minute is over and Eddie is crying;

"STOP!"

My face is wet from tears of laughter as I look across at Alexa and Cassie both also hooting with delight.

Once the scores are in, the winners are announced to rapturous applause and presented with a flower hula necklace each before being swallowed back into the crowd.

"Who's ready for game 2?" Eddie asks and he's answered by yells and whoops.

"This time I want 5, yes 5 females and 5 males!"

“Come on, we’re up!” Alexa tells me grabbing my wrist firmly and yanking me forwards. I trip to her side and look back at Cassie who smiles and shrugs.

“Sorry!” She mouths. But in her words, is she fuck! She’s just glad it isn’t her!

“Alexa.” I begin but it comes out in a pathetic sounding whiny voice and I shut my mouth again.

We’re being clapped and cheered and I’m a little overwhelmed, I can’t be a spoil sport and turn back now.

Tanya grins at us as we break free into the rectangle.

“And our 2 first seeexyy ladies are up!” Eddie booms as the crowd holler and whistle and I can’t help but enjoy the bubbles that burst in my stomach making my legs feel weak.

“Good girl, Jodie.” Tanya says in my ear from my side and the doubts are further snuffed out, this recognition encouraging me.

I can do this, whatever it’s going to be. Gulp!

Alexa is standing completely sure of herself and I mirror her. If she can be bold and daring, then so can I!

“Our third sexy lady and first 2 lucky, lucky boys, come on. You can’t be shy!”

Not for the first time these last few days I take a good look at the scene around me. I want to remember this and the emboldening feeling it has aroused forever.

Yes I feel as sick as a pig in anticipation of what the game will be, but Alexa is doing this, I can do this. And more importantly I will be able to say, 'I have taken part in a sex game'. Not exactly story of the year for any potential grandkids- or for an upcoming career in Education, I sternly remind myself and quickly scout the crowds for incriminating cameras.

"3 men! 4 sexy women! And our final sexy lady, come on which 2 of you guys want it the most."

This is so surreal it doesn't feel like it's really happening to me.

"And so we are ready!" Eddie announces.

Ok, it is happening to me, I tingle on high alert for his instructions. "This next game has 2 parts!"

My mind races, 2 parts? I think of the obvious 2 parts linked to sex and worry.

"But before I tell you what they are I need you to pair up!"

I cannot believe I hadn't thought about this sooner. I look up just in time to see one of my nicknamed 'Skull Heads' barrelling towards me.

"Mine!" He shouts snatching and raising my hand in the air. I think in 'normal' life I would have been offended, enraged even! But as it stands I find it utterly hilarious and burst into a fit of laughter.

"Mine?" I splutter and he turns to look at me innocently. His eyes are the clearest turquoise and it takes me by surprise curing my giggles, almost. "I'm Jodie." I say now instead because he is looking at me genuinely confused.

“Tom.” He tells me then looks across at another skull head; he is paired up with a blonde beside us. Tom begins directing enthusiastic thrust actions at my bum.

I try to catch the blonde’s eye for a shared eye-roll moment at the behaviour but she avoids it, choosing to pout and gaze into the sky instead. Ok.

Alexa has a poser of course. The only poser out of the 5 actually. Not surprisingly all 4 others are skull heads.

“The aim of the game...” He pauses and I am slightly worried now the moment is upon us. “Is to pop as many balloons as possible in 30 seconds.”

That doesn’t sound too bad. I begin to smile watching as bin liners of balloons are brought up the stairs.

“Firstly 30 seconds like this.” Eddie continues. Tanya is bent over in front of him holding a balloon over her bum. Eddie thrusts in eerie premonition to how Tom had been doing to me only moments ago. Then he grabs her hips and begins smashing his pelvis into the balloon, harder, harder until bang!

I am catching flies as the old saying goes. Shutting my mouth I glance at Alexa who is happily clapping and then, I begin to laugh too.

“And for the second part,” Eddie lies down on the floor placing the balloon over his crotch and Tanya stands over him. “You will do 30 seconds like this.”

She squats over him before dropping her bum 3 heavy times and the balloon bursts.

"Ooohhh!" Eddie coos above the screams and laughter. "It stings! Not really, don't worry boys, I'm just joking! You get to enjoy the view!"

Oh this is going to be fun! Whether I am being swept away by the crowd or delirious from the sun and booze- or a bit of all three, I don't care. I'm taking part in a sex game and it's going to be fun!

Tanya is responsible for passing us our balloons and I feel extra confidence for having her on our team. Tom has spoken 3 words to me.

"Get ready baby." Before speaking to his friend- loudly- about 'smashing pussy'. I have a feeling I'm in for a rough ride as Eddie counts down.

"Three, two, one..."

I fix my stance firmly holding one knee to lock my body as best I can, the other arm ready to take the balloon poised ready in Tanya's hand. As expected Tom has an iron grip on my hips and blasts his way through balloons as quick as I can put them there! My arse is going to be as red as a baboons at this rate mate, chill out! It is so funny I laugh the whole way through. My stomach muscles are crippled by the time Eddie is calling.

"STOP!"

We must have won that. I stand up to elated cheering, feeling dizzy and a little crazy, my face must be bright red and then I realise embarrassingly- I look like I've actually just been shagged! I turn to Tom, ready to congratulate him just as he high fives his mate and sings.

"Maga Shagger, Maga Shagger!" to the tune of Cher Lloyd's Swagger Jagger, whilst pumping the air.

"The scores after part one are as follows!" Eddie announces. "18! 19! 23!"

He's pointing out the associated couple with each score. Alexa's team is on 23 not that she notices, gazing seductively into the posers eyes instead. "23!"

She's joint top with Tom's friend and the pouty blonde. "And 25!"

As I suspected we come top! My turn now!

I'm actually pretty confident about part 2. I'm strong from pole dancing and I took on the '30 day squat challenge' once this holiday got booked so I'm well practised. Don't you just love it when a plan comes together!

"Gentlemen." Eddie croons. "Take your positions."

I meet Tom's aqua eyes.

"Get ready baby." I tell him smiling whilst taking my place over him and squatting down. I feel like a dominatrix, and honey this is going to hurt.

"3, 2, 1."

I manage to burst a majority of the balloons on the first or second attempt; not afraid to smash my bum down as hard as possible to achieve it. My strong steady pace ensures I'm popping balloons efficiently and halfway through Tom begins howling.

"Nooo. Slow down!"

I maintain my squat position and adrenalin taking over the 30 seconds passes quickly. Probably not for Tom.

I'm tempted to start singing:

"Maga Shagger!" But I know for a fact stuck up blondie will not return a high five and I can't see Alexa being all that willing either! She's far too cool!

"Come on, I reckon we've won!" I hold a hand out to Tom who is still lying on the floor. His mate isn't much use choosing to point and laugh.

"She was shit!" He shouts even though we're right next to him. "She only got 7! At least yours gave you a good ride!"

I feel sorry for the girl he has just humiliated but she just continues to stare off into the distance pouting more than ever. We could have just eye rolled this off and ripped into Tom for begging me to stop, if only she hadn't snubbed me in the first place.

Tom takes my hand and stands up laughing now good naturedly.

"You've got some fucking good technique going on there you know!" He finally takes an interest in me.

I just laugh some more because I'm not sure saying thanks is the right thing to do here. To be honest my legs have gone to jelly and I can't wait for the results to be announced so I can sit down and have a well-earned drink.

"Where are you staying?" He carries on. "Are you out tonight?"

"The scores are in!" Eddie calls thankfully now and I turn away from him. "With 30," Tom's friend. "32, 35, 45," that's Alexa, "and oh my gosh surely it's a record… 49!" He finally points at me and Tom.

"Yes!" Tom shrieks and abruptly punches his friend in the privates. "Nut shot!" He yells.

I openly laugh; he deserves that for his heartless comment earlier. I *knew* we were in with a chance! I feel stupidly happy about it. It's hardly worthy of the achievements section on my CV, what would my new boss Julie make of this! But it's a proud moment for now all the same, we won!

"Thanks everybody!" Eddie shouts. "Now we're going to turn the music up and open the platform so you crazy lot can start jumping in. Let's get wet and wild!"

Proudly adorned with my flower hula necklace I float (I think, because I can't feel my legs!) back to Cassie, huge beam on my face.

She has watched the whole thing and is laughing her head off as I reach her. We cling together because my legs really are useless now, spluttering and giggling.

"Well done Jodie, you smashed it!" Tanya is saying at our sides now too.

"Thanks! But I really need to sit down! Where's Alexa?" I ask taking a quick look around.

"Oh she's taking some time to get to know her partner a little better!" She laughs pointing to where Alexa is pressed against the poser their lips firmly attached.

"Well she wouldn't have taken part in the game if I didn't promise I'd convince him to as well!" She carries on.

"What?" I ask. "I don't understand?"

"Alexa asked which games we were playing so she could decide if she wanted to play. And then *begged* me to make sure I got him to play this one, he's called *Antonio.*"

She shrugs and I sit down; Alexa's behaviour is nothing new to her. And it shouldn't be a surprise to me really either.

"I'll fetch you both a beer." She says now. "I've got a twenty minute break, woohoo!"

I smile at her but I can't help but feel a little stitched up. I'm not *that* annoyed, I won after-all and her confidence (which I now realise was fake!) *did* help me to go through with it. But it does feel a little selfish on Alexa's part.

What if I'd been completely humiliated?

But I wasn't was I? Still though, I might have liked an *Antonio* rather than a Tom! Or at least have been given a heads up on the game, rather than being left to wonder.

"Did you know?" I ask Cassie curiously.

"No! I was just glad it wasn't me" She replies honestly. "I'm wondering when she even fixed it up? The girl is incredible."

Tanya returns with our drinks and I smile, what's the point in being bothered? Especially when it all turned out so well!

"So, how are you enjoying your holiday so far?" Tanya asks us plonking herself down between us and looking at Cassie then me questioningly.

"I love it!" I tell her truthfully. "It's crazy, but I love it!"

"Yeah me too. But I'm missing my dog!" Cassie laughs.

"Ahhh!" Tanya says. "And how's work going? Still at the same care home?"

"Yeah." Cassie replies and begins telling her how she's feeling fed up, looking for a change. I can empathise with that all right!

I run my eyes over the happy faces, a hubbub of chitchat, music plus the odd huge cheer then SPLASH! Those braver than me jumping from the unchained gap!

"How about you Jodie, what's been happening with you lately?" Tanya turns her attention to me.

Where do I start? I think wryly.

"I've got a new job!" I tell her.

"Ah wow! Congratulations. Still waitressing?"

"No, I'm going to be working at a behavioural school. I finished waitressing for good on Sunday! Then came here Wednesday!"

"That's brilliant, great way to celebrate! I'm so pleased for you, go girl! So when do you start?"

"Not until the end of August." I tell her grinning.

"So you've got a bit of a break! What's your plans?" She asks genuinely.

"Erm, well you know," I falter. "Resting, have a bit of me time!" I tinkle on knowing this sounds pathetic, self-indulgent at best. But I don't want to start going into the reasons for why I feel I need it.

"Oh. Well why don't you stay here?" She says now so casually; but the question resounds in my head like the gong of a bell almost knocking me off my seat.

"I can't stay here!" I titter. But already posters I hadn't registered I'd seen- 'workers wanted'- fling to mind. Haphazard but accurate thoughts, you don't have work to get back for, no rent to pay because you're living at home- you have no dog to miss like Cassie.

But I only have limited funds and I have family and friends who'll miss me!

"Of cause you can!" Tanya declares. "You could stay with me until you get yourself a room; there are loads of workers' apartments just off the main strip. And you'd find yourself a job easy. You're pretty, funny, more than confident enough to be a PR."

"A PR?" I laugh heartily at this. "I couldn't be a PR!"

"Why not?" She asks challengingly.

"Because," I flounder my mind racing through all the reasons I have tried to stay away from them. "Because I haven't got a load of STD's!" I say defiantly.

I actually know I haven't since facing the music and getting checked out. This tickles Tanya and she slaps my shoulder.

"Let me guess, Alexa told you about Jett giving her clap?"

"No! Clap! Who's Jett?" I ask.

"The PR from Tokyo Joes who she shagged in May? She wouldn't have come back if I hadn't told her that he left. I thought she would've told you, that's why she decided to visit again." She grins and I try to return it but feel completely numb.

"Oh right, yeah!" I hear my voice say faintly and she and Cassie begin gossiping animatedly about some of Tanya's saucy escapades so far.

I am unable to concentrate. My mind was already whirring at the idea of staying here instead of leaving on Tuesday but now this shock revelation has knocked me for six. Alexa slept with a PR! I hadn't even questioned her adversity to them, never mind her knowledge of them carrying diseases!

"And, for the final challenge before we return to shore." Eddie says. "The cannonball challenge!"

Who-can-cause-the-biggest-splash-jumping-from-the-boat competition is over. Part of me wanted to jump. If somebody had actually asked me to I think I would've done it. If nothing else, I need a splash of cold water to the face! The revelations about Alexa setting up the game, sleeping with PR's, Tanya's idea about staying…

Taking part in the sex game, yes it was a stitch-up, but it has given me a newfound bubbling courage I'm just daring myself to test out. Alexa has tumbled from the pedestal I'd placed her on and I realise now she's just a normal girl with flaws like me. She has at least taught me, I can do it! I can be confident like her.

As I watch the chain being replaced-I want to jump! I realise. But it's too late now, the boat is pulling away and I feel a tug of disappointment at not going for it. But there could be another chance, if I stayed.

Could I really be a PR?

Technically nothing stands in my way- Tanya has already said I can stay at hers and practically, nothing is stopping me. I'd be earning-probably not a lot- but surely enough to pay my way.

But enough of that for now, the thought beating consistently in my mind which I have been trying to ignore; I have disregarded no-name, potentially a footballer PR boy for nothing. Alexa might have made a mistake, but I am well and truly entitled to make my own. I want to (ok, I realise this with certain ferocity now) sleep with PR boy! And I have so far made zero effort to do so, a large part due to her influence.

I can't help but feel a little resentful towards her. The attraction I feel towards him is so exciting and I've continually shunned it in favour of appeasing her. But I hardly questioned her either did I? I know how judgmental she can be. And I was afraid she would judge me too if I went against her opinion.

I know her view has foundation and all evidence so far does weigh heavily against them, but I still determinedly fancy no-name PR boy!

And I want my own shot at catching an STD! Joke.

Alexa's actions, with the sex game and the PR hatred make me realise her intentions were selfishly motivated. And despite prior warnings, I've also realised it's OK to says, 'thanks for the advice mate, but I'm going to bloody well do it anyway!'

I am well and truly entitled to make my own choice *and* take the risk of making my own mistakes in the process.

God knows I have made enough so far already. What harm is a few more!

In a strange twist of fate, my mind is made up to get us to Club Twenty One that night, and then Alexa goes off with Antonio straight from the boat. Gleefully telling us not to wait up! Well now it's my turn.

MY TURN!

Cassie and I go for food before heading back to the hotel to get ready. Tanya tells us she will meet us at 11 at the Red Lion for a couple. She can't stay out for long because she is in charge of the emergency phone. It's a shame but it still gives me a chance to probe her some more about a potential job out here.

Club Twenty One will be an easy task with my fresh confidence, yes and without Alexa around to call the shots!

"Hey!" Tanya joins us a table outside. "I'll just get a drink."

"No it's fine! Here!" I slide her one of mine over. We took full advantage of the PR by feigning uncertainty about whether to come in here or not; pushing his offer to 5 drinks each plus the obligatory shot at the bar.

"Making the most of the drinks offers then?" She laughs accepting it. "Cheers!"

I must say the naughtiness of Magaluf is sweeping me away. Taking the piss out of PR's and their ludicrous offers to get girls inside, whatever next? Shagging one? Becoming one?

It doesn't take long for us to clear 10 drinks between us and we get a round of fishbowls next. If I'm going to Club Twenty One I'll still need a dose of Dutch courage!

Back out on the patio I eye 3 girls loitering by the door with trays of shots in hand.

"Are they selling shots?" I ask Tanya dumbly but not knowing how else to approach it.

"Yeah, overpriced and probably watered down." She smirks grimly. "Shot girls." She quotes it.

"Are they paid to do it?" I ask running my eye over their scanty outfits and make up. Could I be one of *those*?

A PR *or* a shot girl- I'm not sure which one scares me the most.

"I'm not sure." She replies her forehead creasing. "I think they're paid commission- you know for how many shots they sell or something?"

We all turn to stare for a second before Tanya adds.

"They'll wait for the boys to get drunk then do whatever they can to get sales."

Oh-kay!

Maybe this whole idea isn't so simple after all. Could I honestly be a PR or a shot girl? This world that I am uncovering piece by piece is so surreal and enticing but have I really got what it takes to stay and work here.

"I've got to go after this fish bowl." Tanya announces interrupting my thoughts. "Where do you think you'll go next?"

Now is my chance, I realise!

"Well, I wanted to go Club Twenty One," I glance at Cassie to see how this information is received. Her face splits into a wide grin.

"That's the place that PR works at isn't it? Who came to the pool the other day. You little fucker, I knew it!" She blurts and I cringe at the mention of my PR crush. What will Tanya say about it?

"Ooh Jodie, you saucy minx!" Comes her response. "I wonder if I know who it is? What does he look like?"

I realise suddenly, how silly I've been. I have blown this completely out of proportion! Why was I so worried about what Alexa and everyone else thought about it? All that matters is what *I* think about it!

"Tall, gorgeous, mixed race, beautiful smile." Cassie takes the words right out of my mouth and I laugh despite of myself. This is the first time I've even heard her talk about a guy I realise, plus I had no idea she thought he was attractive too. I have been completely blindsided!

"Dimples, six pack, shaved hair and a bit of stubble." I add to the initial (and very accurate) description. It feels so exciting to be talking about a crush like this- it hasn't happened in, well at least a year!

Tanya rolls her eyes now but she's smiling.

"Justin? He's been working out here since May. He slept with 2 girls from my original team. One went home and one has been transferred since. Nothing to do with him!" She adds quickly.

Oh, I hope not! But I quickly brush that aside. Justin! His name is Justin.

Now I don't even need to go there, I tease myself, now you know his name. But I know from the jealous clench in my tummy, that I also want to have slept with him, like these 2 girls from Tanya's team. Thanks warped brain!

And yes alongside all of the other girls he will no-doubt have slept with already. But I wouldn't say no to having a go in a used Ferrari would I?

So, that's it then, there's nothing really stopping me. Except, of course, for him!

"Well, it's a shame you can't come with us Tanya." Cassie says slurping at the last quarter of her fishbowl.

"I know." She sighs. "You'll have lots of fun without me though- I'm just a tired fart all of the time! We still have a few days to get together yet!"

Another tummy clench. I really don't want to go home yet. I think about that feeling on the boat earlier when I realised I'd missed my opportunity to jump. I don't want a repeat of that. If I don't at least try, will I be left regretting it?

Perhaps Justin can help me find a job? A barrage of thoughts accelerates through my mind- we could work together, maybe even live together! Woah, Jodie, learn from past mistakes!

We say our goodbyes to Tanya before jumping into the ribbon of bodies making our way further along the strip until Club Twenty Ones red letters come into view. I am physically shaking in the cool, night air, a mixture of excitement and nerves giving me the jitters. It is gone midnight, closer to one; let's hope he work's every night!

"Cassie! Slower!" I shout to her breathlessly as we march. "So we can see… if he's there!"

Delicious pins and needles nestle in my crotch at the tantalising thought of what could occur. I scan the crowd. And sure enough there he is. He's wearing a long baggy white vest, it scoops low revealing sculpted pecs and I sizzle with lust. He has a wide smile on his face, dimples on full display and as we walk towards him he turns and looks straight at me.

This could be a moment from a film! Fireworks erupt in my brain (is a mind orgasm possible?) as he locks eyes on me lowering his head a little, smirking sexily.

"Shor-tee!" He catcalls.

I feel like I have died and gone to heaven. Cassie let's out a little excited squeal from next to me.

"He recognises you!" She hisses.

I giggle gleefully, although this nickname is probably standard issue because I did tell him my name before and he's obviously forgotten it!

Assuming a suitably shocked face I reply. "Why hello!" And glance up at the bold Club Twenty One sign for good measure. "So *this* is where you work?" I continue with my 'surprised to see you' act.

I hear Cassie let out a snort of laughter and hope the blush I feel creep across my cheeks goes unnoticed.

"You didn't come the other night." He raises his chin challengingly but his eyes don't leave mine.

“No, we had another party to go to.” I lie echoing what Alexa told him at the time. “And anyway, your name was easy to find out. You have quite the reputation.”

“Been asking about me then?” He responds immediately and I notice the fire dance in his eyes, his dimples indicating he has suppressed a smile.

I shrug, “my friend works out here.”

I note the smallest change in his expression; this information has given me the upper hand. I smile sweetly as he continues to stare.

“So come on then, what drinks offers have you got for us?” I feel as confident as ever- my flirting has gone down a storm!

He looks at Cassie and then over my shoulder.

“Wasn’t there 3 of you before?” He asks. He obviously has a habit of ignoring questions. And I’m glad he doesn’t remember Alexa’s name either.

“Yeah but she pulled.” I tell him bluntly hoping he picks up on the suggestion that we’re not afraid of this situation.

He claps his hands once grinning broadly.

“Well isn’t that the turn up.” He comments before turning and scanning the crowd swarming around us.

“Ben! Ben!” He shouts to the back of a broad, blonde haired guy. Ben turns and I realise it isn’t boner boy, who I was expecting. He leaves the girl’s in front of him to scurry away and ambles over.

"Ben's my roomie." Justin says winking throwing an arm around him and I understand in an instant he's thinking of this as a 'double date'. Will Cassie take the bait? He's cute! I don't even know if she's got a boyfriend, I realise.

"Hello Ben." Cassie says from beside me. "I'm Cassie and this is Jodie."

Now that there, is a wing woman!

"Be a gentleman Ben." Justin directs him mockingly. "Get the ladies a drink."

I get the same impression as before that he's taking the piss. But this only adds to his dangerous allure. It couldn't have gone better so far!

We dutifully follow Ben into the comparatively small club and become instantly engulfed in the pumping music, dry ice and lights.

We're handed a pink plastic wrist band- free bar Ben tells Cassie who relates it to me. And he doesn't charge us anything!

"We're well in there!" I squeal thanking the music for being so loud because regardless my voice was coming out at that volume. "Do you *want* to be in there? Do you fancy Ben?" I ask now regaining some composure.

She shrugs and I fleetingly wonder if Justin will still sleep with me if Cassie won't sleep with Ben. Her eyes cloud over a moment as if in deep thought and I feel instantly bad for willing her to do it.

"It doesn't matter if not. You don't have to do anything you don't want to!" I shout reassuringly.

"But I do want to!" She contradicts and raises a hand to her mouth as if trying to catch the words. This reminds me of how I have felt since arriving in this fabulous place- thoughts and feelings running amok.

"Well what's the bloody problem then!" I laugh giddily happy at the way things have turned out. "Your life has to be lived by you! If you want to do something, go ahead and do it, fuck what anyone thinks! Come on, what are we waiting for? Let's get some drinks!"

Cassie looks satisfied by my little speech. *I'm* satisfied by my speech and we turn our attention to the bar man waiting to serve us.

Its 3.30am now- Justin and Ben finish at 4. I feel considerably drunk but also high on the elixir that is J. Yes, J. He told me to call him that. I am not holding back on the feeling he has awoken in me and I think he can read my eyes like an autocue giving away my lustrous intentions.

The thought of having sex with J causes my body to vibrate with a thrill that verges on violent in its potency. The knowledge of what is going to happen between us- in about an hour's time- tears through me like a hurricane of desire.

This will be the first person I have slept with since stupid prick- and just fucking look at him. What a beauty. Well played, Jodie well played.

By 4.15am the 4 of us are walking back to J and Ben's apartment. I am having to clench my fists in an attempt to quiet the excited tremors in my arms and chest. Our conversation still consists of flirty suggestions, back and forth banter not amounting to much other than the shared knowledge we are going to have sex. No chance has arisen to question job opportunities- and anyway I have *far* more pressing things on my mind.

We arrive in the dingy, orange foyer of a tall block of flats. I have to seriously suck up my dislike of lifts when J pulls back the rattling metal gates of a contraption that looks at least 80 years old. I wouldn't be surprised if we have to use a rope and pulley system to heave ourselves up the floors.

I watch as his slender, brown finger pushes the number 4 anticipating the feel of him caressing my body. Silence descends on our group as the lift climbs. I wonder what Cassie is thinking and if she is going to sleep with Ben? It would seem so!

The door to their apartment is heavy, worn, dark wood. Justin pushes it open, leading us inside and keeps walking until he reaches a room at the end of the long narrow corridor. He switches on the light and it illuminates him a soft yellow.

"Come on." He tells me.

I walk towards him. Is it his and Ben's room? Where is Cassie going to go?

As soon as I step foot into the room he slams the door shut behind me and pushes me up against it.

'Divide and conquer' comes to mind as concerns over Cassie's whereabouts promptly fade away. I am pinned by his warm chest, looking up into his gorgeous face, his dark eyes staring intensely into mine.

Click. He flicks the light switch and plunges us into near darkness. My eyes, already fully dilated, quickly adapt to the milky light from the window giving the room a dreamlike glow.

Everything falls into slow motion as J's face comes towards mine; his full lips meeting mine, his tongue gently searching for mine. I feel his hands at the waist band of my shorts, realising they're elasticated he forces his whole hand down, fingers stroking and probing through my knickers.

Feeling how wet I am (I think I was from the moment I spotted him earlier) he works my pants aside and begins slipping his fingers across my throbbing clit and in and out of me.

The sensation is an absolute eruption of pleasure as sharp as splinters. I have never been this turned on and I gasp, clinging to his shoulders for support. My legs are going to melt from under me.

Without stopping and whilst placing kisses all over my mouth and neck Justin guides me to the edge of the bed. One hand plucks the straps of my top and bra from my shoulders and he yanks both downward. Boobs freed he dips his head down to begin licking one nipple then the other. This is so nice it hurts. I can't handle it and yet I don't want it to stop. Ever!

I search his own shorts and find a huge, rock hard cock waiting to be unrestrained. I tug them down a little, find the waistband of his boxers and pull both down to his knees. The now free boner boings impressively between us and I pull him by his shoulders down onto the bed; I need to feel his weight on top of me, his massive dick inside of me.

He gladly takes me up on the invitation and kneels between my legs, guiding himself in without any difficultly; thanks to the puddle I've been reduced to. I gasp; and again as he lies forward his body pressing down on mine. Delicious tingles make me feel like I'm made of nothing but white noise from the waist down.

J's heaviness, his hot, damp body and cock feeling intrusively large adds to the ferocious intensity of my excitement. I can feel an orgasm that keeps building before ebbing away as he pounds into me urgently.

And then with a guttural groan his whole body tenses up.

"Fuck!" He exclaims and pulls out leaving hot cum to dribble across my thigh. "Sorry." He laughs self-consciously. "I think I got it out in time."

He passes me a roll of tissue and I unceremoniously wipe myself off chastising myself for being an idiot, why didn't I use a condom? Conception isn't a risk due to my pill but another trip to the clinic? Great!

In the pastel light he smiles at me bashfully and my worries quiet. I got carried away. I'll be more careful next time. If there's a next time? I hope there's a next time!

"Are you kipping?" He asks me and I realise after all the exhilaration I feel completely spent.

"If you don't mind." The walk back seems too long to contemplate now and it's almost 5am. Surely Cassie will do the same, wherever she is- I've got my phone if she needs me.

"Course not. I'm going to have a fag on the balcony. Do you want some water?"

"Yes please, thanks." The bed could be made of concrete but to me it feels as soft as cotton wool and I curl up under the thin sheet blissfully happy (despite the condom slip up) awaiting J's return.

I barely register him clambering onto the bed beside me, an arm snaking around my waist. He spoons me tenderly and in my sleepy haze I grin with delight.

SUNDAY SURPRISES!

I awake with a jolt. The room is unfamiliar and smells funny; stale sweat, I think. I wrinkle my nose and stare at the bed opposite me; scruffy blonde hair peeking from beneath a grubby off-white sheet. In one great whoosh the events of last night flood my mind and I become aware of Justin's steady breathing behind me.

There isn't a sound from the flat and I realise I have no idea who or how many other people live here. And, more pressingly, where's Cassie?

I sit up giving myself a clear view of the bed opposite where just Ben sleeps. Then scrabble around for my phone. It's half ten and there are no missed calls or texts from either Cassie or Alexa.

I am a confusion of hangover, joy and concern and find it a nauseous combination. I pick up the water J has left by the bed and sip it carefully.

Next to me he stirs.

"You ok?" He mumbles but before I can reply his breathing becomes heavy and I realise he's asleep. I scramble about self-consciously trying to cover my naked body- aware that Ben could wake at any moment. Pants, bra, top, shorts, shoes- all located I apply them as quickly as is possible. My body is so strained from yesterday's squatting but once this is accomplished, I take a moment to appreciate the bedroom properly.

There's nothing magical about it this morning, I note grimly. On the floor discarded clothes, towels, food cartons; no-doubt complete with congealing leftovers and lots of other random tat.

To the left of the window a St. George's flag is pinned limply and to the right promotional posters and flyers haphazardly slapped in a display of Magaluf's finest venues and events. I note BCM Dance Planet, Mallorca Rocks amongst others.

Both of the beds look grimy. Sheets and pillows that were once white now a patchwork of cream and brown shades. Eugh!

Amongst it, J's beautiful sleeping face, and I take a last gaze wondering if and when I'll see it again (not counting the amount of Facebook stalking I'll be doing! Yes, I did get his full name) before silently opening the door and slipping into the corridor.

Tiptoeing with ninja stealth I pass 5 closed doors. Even if one is the bathroom, one a kitchen and one a living room that still leaves 2 rooms unaccounted for. Potentially 4 or more people who could appear at any moment, or is Cassie in one of them- sleeping in a spare room?

As I reach the heavy front door I press call on Cassie's number straining my ears for a ringtone. I don't hear anything and she doesn't pick up. Finally I let myself out into the main hallway. She must have left already, but why didn't she wake me? Before this question can consume me however, where are the stairs because there's no way I'm going into that lift again!

The walk back to the hotel isn't comfortable for 2 reasons.

At just past half ten, there are lots of people around. And not just the earlier risers of my own age-group (that's bad enough) but families with children, middle-aged and older couples, large groups- lots of people!

I've taken off all jewellery in an attempt to dress down but I still feel like my outfit is tell-tail 'going-out' attire. And a quick look at my face in reverse camera mode reveals a creased cheek and congealed mascara. I also have bed hair, no brush or hair bobble- so have to make do with a quick head shake and some strategic patting.

In short: I am obviously doing the walk of shame. And everyone who looks at me is noticing it.

Reason number two. I've tried to ring Cassie three more times and she doesn't answer any of them. I send a text, 'R U OK?' and try not to worry; I'll be back in less than 10 minutes.

At least her phone is on. Surely that's a good sign? I gulp, more curious stares coming my way and scuttle a little faster.

What was it that Cat said before I came out here? A random thought begins to swell in my mind and I let it glad for the distraction.

'The Stride of Pride!'

Yes, that was it! And it's what I should be doing now. Just look at Justin; I wanted this after all! I slow my pace trying to look inconspicuous. If only I'd used a condom though, I scold myself again. Then I really could be proud without that niggling fear of chlamydia or worse. I'll make another appointment when I'm home. I'm not sure I can use the excuse of a cheating boyfriend for a second time but nothing can be done about it now. I'd rather regret *doing* it, than *not* doing- like the jump from the boat, I realise dryly.

Home. The thought of a potential STD makes me think of home.

Mum, George, Leila, Cat, Micky and Grant. I already have so much to tell them (not everything to all, namely mum!) But wow, when I tell Leila, Cat, the others about J! I could be making more memories yet though. With him? With other people? Maybe I'm not done creating these crazy stories of my own just yet- home can wait a little longer, surely.

I cannot believe I have done exactly the same as Alexa, my mind backfires. Minus diagnosis of course (fingers crossed I'm lucky). Fair enough wanting to have my own experiences; but by not learning anything at all from her mistake I have now put my own health at risk. I've gone from one extreme to the other!

I'm turning the corner of the final street now. There aren't anywhere near as many people here and I relax a little. There's nothing I can do about it now, I tell myself again. And add firmly, definitely buy some condoms! Just in case. I should have done that the minute my inner voices piped up instead of trying to ignore the whole situation.

I thought I'd already decided to always listen to my instincts, since, well since then. And I resolutely decide never, ever to ignore it *again*. I'm sorry gut instinct!

I'm almost at the room now. And hopefully Cassie will be there!

One worry is replaced with another and I physically cross my fingers hoping she is safely tucked up in bed.

Ok, so I am instantly aware of Cassie's presence, yay! But I realise with horror what I can hear, is her crying. My heart sinks to the absolute pit of stomach- it's got to be something to do with Ben! What has he done to her? I begin to feel horrible guilty responsibility.

"Cassie?" I say softly.

She immediately stops and I find her in the bathroom burying her face in tissue trying to wipe away any evidence.

"Cassie?" My heart hammers. "What's happened?"

She splashes cold water over her face and pastes on a tight, false smile.

"I'm just hungover Jodie. Missing home, you know being silly!"

The untruth of this statement fills the room awkwardly and I stare at her baffled.

"Did you sleep with Ben?" I ask her assuming he must have something to do with it and puzzled at her clear lie.

She lets out a huge huff and looks to the ceiling, jaw set.

"Yes I did. But that's not the problem." She clips and my confusion continues.

"So what is then?" I have no idea what the hell is going on. For one instant I was desperately happy to find her here and now I'm completely racked with panic.

"Jodie. I never wanted to hurt your feelings in all of this. I feel so guilty!" Her tears have dried now, *she* feels guilty, what for? I have no further time to question this strange statement before Alexa appears beside me.

"Alexa!" I exclaim jumping, have I woken up in an outlandish, parallel universe?

"And so you should." Her voice is dangerously low making me realise this is unfortunately very real.

I have no idea when she snuck in but she seems to understand better than me whatever is going on.

"Are you going to tell Jodie why you feel guilty or shall I?" Her voice is cold, oily, oozing slick tension into the room.

I feel dizzy. What the fuck is happening? I was on cloud nine after sleeping with J and now my mates are recreating scenes worthy of Hollyoaks!

"I've got a boyfriend back home." Cassie says now standing up straight staring at Alexa, not me and despite the nonchalance in her voice, shame pours from her.

"*Her* boyfriend is *my brother's* best friend! I introduced them. He's like a brother to me. And you've cheated on him!" Alexa fires off and I'm stunned this has never come up before. Why would it have, I'd never thought to ask and Alexa spends a majority of the time talking about herself.

"Oh." Is all I can say realising at once why she acted so bizarrely last night when I asked if she fancied Ben. A million things buzz through my head paralysing each response as they form. 'So what?' 'You only live once.' 'He doesn't need to know, if it was a mistake.' 'I was cheated on.' 'She's done what he did.' 'This is nothing to do with me.'

The silence hangs loudly in the room and it feels like forever that I stare dumbly from Cassie to Alexa, unable to think clearly for the profound hush that has descended around us.

"Are you not going to say anything Cassie?" Alexa purrs in a sing-song voice not one to shy away from drama.

Cassie looks briefly at me, then back to Alexa who's staring her down intensely.

"I'm sorry! I'm sorry I have done this to him. Look I've never done anything like this before in my life. I just got carried away."

"You've made a mug out of him Cassie! Getting carried away isn't a good enough excuse!" She's shouting now, eyes narrowed but Cassie isn't backing down either and only seems to become angrier.

"It's nothing to do with you Alexa. You don't know anything about my relationship. This is my mess, you need to stay out of it!"

They stare at each other, whilst I stand motionless and helpless in the crossfire. I just want to be out of there.

"Erm," I croak because I was going to say something wise about giving advice, support, not judging etc. except the sentences won't form. All I manage to do is bring the attention to myself.

"And what about Jodie? How do you think she feels hearing this when *her* boyfriend cheated on *her*!"

"I was just about to tell her when you burst in. Don't you think I already feel bad enough?"

They're rallying about me as if I'm not standing right there. I want to tell Cassie it's alright, but I don't know if it is. And I want to tell Alexa not to use my situation as an excuse, she already has her own which is good enough- she doesn't need to use *me* as a point scoring pawn. I've had enough of that thanks!

"Look guys, I'm going to go for a walk." I tell them rationally trying to hit the pause button in my brain. My head beats with pressure. "Let's take some time to cool off and hook up again this afternoon. When we've had time to think."

How very grown up, I applaud myself weakly, but I just cannot think straight in here. I need to get out. I need space to digest what is happening. And a part of me just wants to escape into daydreams about J.

"Fine by me." Alexa stomps to her suitcase and uncharacteristically drags on the first bikini and outfit she finds. In record time she shoves a towel, sun cream and book into her bag and grabs her sunglasses from the side as she flounces from the room.

I have been almost as quickly doing the same, eager not to be left in this room sticky with unease; but equally not wanting to leave with Alexa. I need some fresh air but I don't want to look like I'm taking sides.

The door slams by which time I am standing up with my bag packed, also ready to leave.

"Look Cassie." I begin but I don't know what to say. "Call me in a bit yeah. Decide what you're going to do."

I'm lying on my towel, on the beach- just as I had on that first glorious day. In one respect it feels like a lifetime ago, in such a short space of time so much has happened. But then on the other hand, it feels like it's going to be over way too soon. How is it already Sunday?

And what of Alexa and Cassie's friendship. And mine with them?

How do I feel about Cassie cheating? I had wanted her to sleep with Ben after all! But had I known she was in a relationship I would never have put her in that position. Did I put pressure on her? No. She didn't have to do anything did she? I even told her that. She made the choice to cheat.

So have I got any right to feel anything about it? I barely know her and I don't know her boyfriend. It's not my business. I, too got carried away last night, surely I can understand.

But then I am here following the shitty humiliating months after being cheated on. Picking up the pieces of my shattered self hasn't been easy and cheating isn't something I agree with, at all. Did *he* get caught up in the moment? Did *he* feel guilty?

My mind rakes over the painful conversations I've had only months previous. Like hot coals the more I turn the pieces the more it burns.

I'm angry that this has put me back here, deep in those horrible moments. I physically shake my head, snapping myself out of it. The only heat I can feel is from a blazing hot sun in the Magaluf sky I remind myself. It's the here and now that's important.

I won't go there. My experience is nothing to do with Cassie, just as Cassie's is nothing to do with me. Didn't I literally yell at her in

Club Twenty One last night that everyone has to live their own life and make their own mistakes?

Alexa feels hurt by this betrayal, it's natural considering the connection and so do I because of the rawness of mine.

But ultimately Cassie did what she wanted to do, for reasons I might never know or understand. It isn't Alexa's or my right to judge her for that. She was right that it is her mess and right now I'm sure she is making some serious decisions about how to clear it up.

This brings me to my own serious decision.

Could I stay? Yes I have established I would miss those at home. But it would only be for 3 more weeks or so, it's hardly forever. My mum wouldn't be best pleased, the worry-pot that she is but I have my phone, I can call daily if she wants me to. I feel like this is the break I need. Not wallowing at home, not hiding away from the shame. Nobody knows me here, nobody knows my backstory.

I have a place to stay, Tanya's. I'd have to find my own place though and the worker's apartment I saw this morning was disgusting! Surely they're not all that bad plus I can keep my room tidy, it's not a huge problem.

Could I be a PR or a shot girl though? I can't believe I am going to say this but I think I'd be better off as a PR. To be a shot girl I'd have to embrace my inner Alexa- and then some.

Plus I know J and Ben now, and Tanya. I'd get to know others on her team plus make new friends on the strip. I could be whoever I wanted to be out here, newly confident Jodie with added spice.

These thoughts are all a little overwhelming and I sit up scanning for any sign of Alexa or even Cassie. Although I suspect Cassie has stayed in the apartment and Alexa possibly gone to meet Antonio or Tanya.

I've missed out on all of the juicy gossip about Alexa's night of passion and I haven't been able to relay any of my own either. If I can just mediate between Alexa and Cassie this afternoon- perhaps I can get this holiday back on track ready for the last stretch.

I feel fresh hope as I fish a battered book from my bag and roll onto my front, losing myself in somebody else's drama for a change.

When my phone tinkles a while later I am surprised to see its Alexa who's calling first. I assumed she'd gladly keep silent until one of us contacted her.

"Hey." I answer putting a smile into my voice.

"Hiya Jodes." She says sounding deflated and I can't help but feel sorry for her compromised position in all of this.

"You ok?" I ask her frankly.

"Yes, I'm ok." She snaps sounding a little more like herself already. "I just can't believe she's put me in this position! It didn't even cross my mind it might happen. I mean, how? How did it happen?"

A flash of blame falls into my lap. If she hadn't been a wing woman for me, I mean I was rejoicing that she'd taken on the role so willingly.

"Look, where are you? Let's go for a drink and we can talk properly."

I come clean to Alexa over stiff Long Island Ice Teas- my crush on Club Twenty One PR, Justin, about us meeting him and the double dating scenario, how Cassie had reacted when I asked if she fancied Ben, how I felt some responsibility for her getting carried away.

When Alexa curls her lip and begins spouting obscenities about PR's I bite the bullet and call her out on Jet. Well, now all of the cards are on the table!

"Tanya told me accidentally, she thought I already knew."

Alexa looks for a split second like she's been slapped but then blinks and replies.

"Yes, well I won't be making that mistake again." She says firmly.

Me neither! I could share but currently I want to take this secret to the grave. Instead I say.

"Cassie did what she did. And however we might feel about it, it is up to her to deal with it."

Alexa exposed of her own blunder, nods slowly. Any remaining feelings of resentment I harboured toward her slip away. She is selfish sometimes and probably always will be, but she is learning valuable lessons as she goes along, just the way I am.

"What do I do now though Jodes? I can't lie to him, or my brother!" She says finally.

"I guess we need to hear from Cassie and what she wants to do about it. Shall I call her?"

"Oh this is so horrible." Alexa says nodding her head, agreeing. I feel like I am looking at the real version of her for the first time, underneath all the flashy bravado.

"I know. It is. But a lot worse for Cassie. She obviously feels terrible."

Speak of the devil and all that, Cassie is calling me as I retrieve my phone. I show it to Alexa before answering with a fake cheery:

"Hello!"

"Hey. Where are you? Are you with Alexa?" She says sounding very glum and I can't help myself, I feel sorry for her too.

"Yes. We're in Ocean Café. Come down to us, we want to check you're ok?" I hope she picks up on the mention of 'we' because she must be feeling proper grim.

"Ok. Ok." She responds after a long pause. Then asks, "Does she want to kill me?"

I laugh at this and Alexa eyes me inquisitively.

"No." I tell her. "She doesn't want to kill you."

Alexa jokingly, I hope, runs a finger across her throat and smirks. We'll be exchanging sex stories in no time at this rate! Well, not Cassie really. But Alexa and I can!

LAST NIGHT OUT, OUT!

We have completely messed up what should be our last night, out out! Tomorrow night it will be praying on our minds that we have to be up and out for the airport by 9am.

Cassie turns up, tail firmly between her legs. (Shame it wasn't there last night I inwardly joke tipsily!) But then she tells us some of the problems in her relationship and it goes some way towards explaining her actions; and finally relieves me of any feelings of responsibility.

Cassie had ultimately succumbed having felt stuck-in-a-rut with her life; boyfriend and work not fulfilling her any longer. My mind rewinds to her conversation with Tanya on the boat- I hadn't even bothered listening properly and if I had paid more attention to her maybe I would have known she had a boyfriend! Perhaps all of us are guilty of being a little selfish at times.

She tells us she's going to end it the moment we arrive back in England. That she will be using the excuse that the holiday gave her chance to think. Judging by the arguments she has described it won't come as a complete shock to him- and this way his feelings are somewhat saved too.

"Will you please keep quiet?" Cassie asks Alexa.

To my relief she agrees and they hug it out.

Over umpteen cocktails we begin to forget about the whole issue. Cassie drowns her sorrows whilst Alexa divulges explicit details about her sordid evening with Antonio. My tale of passionate, missionary sex that was over a little too quickly pales in comparison to her 6 times over, 6! Chandelier swinging included… (Ok, slight exaggeration)!

Its 8pm we're still in our hastily chosen daytime outfits, not a scrap of make up between us and completely sozzled. But friendship is restored, lessons have been learnt and all is well in the crazy, alternative world of Magaluf.

Well except that I don't want to leave it behind!

Alexa's usually flawless complexion is waxy under the orangey outdoor lights. We've made our way down to Mulligans, the complete opposite way to Club Twenty One, understandably, and we're stood outside around a sticky bar table.

Eyes heavily hooded Alexa slurs. "Do you know what men tell me? That I'm too full on!"

"Don't be silly!" I smear my words in return. "Men love that don't they?"

Alexa is opening up about her altercation with gay English. I am all ears. Up until now it's all been glitz, glamour, extravagant and positive encounters with a touch of filth. This is the real dirt that I suspect she would never usually open up about was it not for the alcohol loosening her poise.

"Nooo!" She hisses and we lean forward, our foreheads touching conspiratorially. "Men are intimidated by it! They don't like women who are too confident! Honestly, that was his problem. I in-tim-i-dated him!" Alexa emphasises the word. She leans back to take a drag from the cigarette that she has acquired.

I wonder if you can ever really win with men. I have spent my holiday striving for Alexa's confidence and now she's telling me it's the reason for her downfalls?

"Well I like it!" I jolly her encouragingly. "I think you're *well* sexy!"

Who cares what men want, it should be about what we want! She carries on cheered by my assurance.

"He told me. Piss off you tart!" She exclaims her eyes widening but failing to focus on me. "*Piss off you tart*! That's what he said! He doesn't even *know* me!"

She looks from me to Cassie shrugging, puffing some more. The irony is not lost on me, Alexa on her high horse over being judged. She's the queen of it! But there is no denying it's harsh. No wonder she reacted the way she did that night, there was no need for it.

Like the typical Brits we are, we sniff out a takeaway, purchasing kebabs (meat: god-knows-what but who-cares!) and cheesy chips before stumbling back to the hotel.

I messily devour my food- the only thing I have eaten all day- and I'm so glad as I trip into bed that our fractured group has reformed, stronger it would seem than before. Today has been based on real emotions and honest feelings, being supportive and sucking it up. That's what friendships are about.

STAY, STAY, STAY!

Waking up the next day my mouth feels like it's been pasted shut with garlicky glue. Vile! Through squinted eyes I feebly reach out for the coke can I have left by my bed and take three swallows of the flat liquid.

I feel awful, my bloated stomach feels like it's filled with concrete and my head is pounding. I go back to sleep.

Waking up the second time isn't much better but I can hear the shower running. I look over knowing already it will be Alexa that's up. She will be gutted if she misses a moment longer of our last tanning opportunity.

Everything hurts at the thought of our flight tomorrow and it has nothing to do with the hangover. I want to stay!

Is that really what I want to do? Gut instinct, is that you?

It turns out it was actually only half 8 when I awoke the second time. Rather embarrassingly we were in bed by 10 o clock last night! Party animals or what!

And now here we are enjoying our last Magaluf breakfast. Not my last, I dare to hope. Bubbles of anxiety burst in my already delicate tummy.

I keep my eyes peeled as I pick at the toastie- spotting at least 2 girls doing a 'walk of shame/ stride of pride'. I wonder who Justin went with last night. The jealousy is only superficial, of course. I am under no allusion about what his nightly antics consist of. But it only serves to further fuel my craving to stay. I wouldn't say no to round 2; with or without condom if I'm honest!

As the morning drains away and the afternoon begins to follow suit, I start to feel overcome with the urge to make a decision. I hear what my instinct is telling me loud and clear.

Stay, stay, stay!

I am filled with a different type of excitement to the easy-going buzz I have become accustomed to. This is an intense, nervous and thrilling apprehension; all-consuming as I sit on my towel, decision made.

"Girls? Alexa, Cassie?"

They turn to look at me quizzically and I feel the sensation of time slowing down.

"I don't want to go home. I want to get a job out here and stay a little longer." I gush quickly. There! I've said it!

"I would never do that." Alexa promptly declares. "I have far too much going on at home to stay here."

Cassie sits up and intervenes.

"I couldn't either! I wish I could! But that doesn't mean you shouldn't Jodes." She says this more to Alexa before adding encouragingly. "Tanya already said you could stay at hers!"

I nod glad to have her assurance because I am already trying to quell a number of restless uncertainties threatening to take root.

"When did she say that?" Alexa snaps looking put out and I realise she hasn't been present at either of our Magaluf working related conversations.

"On the boat. We were talking about how I haven't got work for a few weeks…"

"Oh well, what's stopping you then. Of course, I would if I wanted to! But I don't." Alexa continues with her tirade and I wonder who she is actually trying to convince here.

"I need to find a job." I tell them both feeling oddly focussed now that the decision is made. "I'm going to have a look. Ask about. This afternoon. Now!"

So with my heart in my dry mouth I'm rolling up my towel and repacking my beach bag ready for mission: find a job. Before I can change my mind!

"Are you sure you don't want us to come with you?" Cassie asks again gazing up at me. I want them to, I'll admit I'm so scared my palms are sweating and my heart is pounding but,

"No thanks." I tell her resolutely. "I'll be fine."

If I really have got the bottle to stay, I have to start by doing this alone.

"I'll call you and see where you are when I'm sorted." I tell them with much more confidence than I feel and smile before marching as best I can over the sand and toward the strip.

Where to begin? I suppose I need to go straight into the bars and ask them outright.

I cut through an alleyway and find myself part way up the strip. There are numerous bars dotted amongst the souvenir stores and tattoo parlours, stretching both to my left and right. Club Twenty One is just over a hump in the road to my right, and I'll be heading off to the left to get back to the hotel later.

It'll be a long and disappointing walk home if I'm not successful. A painful pang of longing reminds me how important it is that I at least try.

I start as I mean to go on and dip straight into the first bar, Ruby's it's called and the whole bar is themed red and black. It looks tacky in the daylight, is eerily still inside and smells fusty.

A bored, young bar man reads a newspaper, only looking up when I nervously clear my throat. This is it!

"I'm wondering if you've got any jobs?" I ask him assertively, my voice too loud and echoing in the quiet room. Well at least it all came out in the correct order, the question made sense, I congratulate myself feeling proud already.

"Come back at 9 tonight when the manager is here." He tells me then looks back down at the paper.

"Oh, ok! Thanks." I cheerily tell him. Surely that's a good sign then, there must be jobs going?

I head for the next bar a spring in my step. There are some people drinking on the sunny terrace and I smile gamely as I pass them finding an old, tanned man drinking a half at the bar.

"You ok?" He asks me gruffly but he has friendly blue eyes- just smoked too many cigarettes.

"Yes, I was wondering if you have any jobs going?" I ask him with a grin. It's never too early to make a good impression.

"Ahh. You'll have to see the manager. He'll be here later." He nods and looks over my head at the approaching customer. "Same again pal?"

"Ok thanks!" I call out brightly but he isn't listening and I return to the street.

This pattern continues as I work my way up the street and way past Club Twenty One. Justin isn't there- I suspect he's promoting somewhere else; it would have been so cool to casually bump into him, let him know about my plans to stay. But now is not the time to distract from the task in hand.

The bars on the strip aren't very busy. Some have captured a few shoppers; some lucky enough to have attracted a large, rowdy group- stag do or something.

In near enough all of them only one or 2 people are working. Those where I have found a PR posted outside, I speak to them instead.

But they all say the same thing. You need to talk to the manager, come back later, around 9pm.

It isn't completely hopeless. I got asked if I wanted to 'spoon' which is an improvement on declarations of a desire to 'smash my backdoors in!'

I'm trying to keep myself upbeat as I head back the way I came. After passing Club Twenty One again- still no sign of J- I nip into a souvenir store. They wouldn't say to come back if the answer was no, would they?

I browse the trinkets on offer thinking perhaps I had better pick a few bits up now- just in case I really do have to go tomorrow.

It's strange how quickly 'going home' has replaced the allusive idea of staying. I really want to stay now. Going home does not feel like an option.

I hope Alexa and Cassie are up for coming out with me at nine tonight to hunt down these prospective managers. I have a feeling seeing 3 girl's dressed up will work to my advantage when conveying the sassy PR girl act.

But then, regardless, they go home tomorrow- and with all of the drama of yesterday I can't see either of them being in the most vibrant mood of the week.

I choose a shot glass for my brother to add to his collection and a magnet for grandad to add to his, pay for them and leave the shop. Taking out my mobile I call Alexa to find out where they are.

"Hey darling. We're just packing up to leave the beach. Did you get a job?"

"No." I say trying not to feel gutted. "Everywhere said to come back later, at nine'ish- to speak to a manger."

"Oh." She isn't forthcoming with an offer to join me so I continue.

"I'm walking back towards you guys now, I'll meet you and we can walk together."

"Ok!" She trills. "See you soon!"

It'll be ok. I did this part on my own; I can come here at 9pm alone too if I have to. I'll make an effort with my make-up and outfit too. And I'll find myself a job. I can do this.

I am Jodie who makes her own, possibly crazy, decisions I think rebelliously and I *will* do this!

"Hey girls!" I overcompensate for the creeping disappointment at not yet being successful.

"Hello." Cassie waves, I can tell she still isn't herself but she's trying to be positive for me and I'm thankful for it.

"I'm sure you'll find a job Jodie." Alexa says practically as we fall into stride together. I can tell she's a teeny bit jealous at the thought of me staying, I can see that now. And I appreciate her effort to think of me instead of herself.

"Thanks!" I smile and really, really hope she is right. We retrace my steps through the alley way this time turning left and heading toward our hotel.

I glance at Mulligans on my left and Cocoa on the opposite side amongst numerous others continuing to stretch down the street. There are so many we haven't even been in, I realise! I feel positive, hopeful for my quest later on.

Up ahead a dark-haired girl steps onto the street. She has a deep tan and a deeper voice.

"Ladies!" She bellows and holds up her palm in a 'stop' gesture. "Do you want a drink? Happy hour starts now!"

The small bar with wooden veranda is called Blush. Alexa and Cassie make to side step her shaking their heads but I instantly retort.

"No, but I want a job!" And laugh at my serious joke.

She grins at me and looks at a guy sitting on a close by table.

"Jamie!" She thunders even though he's right there. "I think I've found an answer to our little problem!"

She beams and reaches out to grab my wrist, as boisterous as the PR lads at night. Everything is happening so quickly I have barely registered what is happening. Alexa and Cassie observe from the pavement as she hoicks me toward Jamie- is he a manager!

"This girl here wants a job!" She roars laughing joyfully in a strong Northern accent. "How great is that!"

My head is spinning, is this really happening? The adrenalin rushing through my body is sending me giddy.

"Want a job do you lass?" He is a broad Londoner with blue eyes, fair hair and a customary tan. I'd guess mid-thirties, with boyish charm looks; he would have been better looking if not slightly leathery.

"Yes, yes I do." I say enthusiastically. "I've been looking today, already. Everyone has told me to come back at nine."

Please don't tell me to come back at nine!

"No need." He says reading my mind as a grin creeps across his face. "Do a trial run with Heather this afternoon and I'll see how you get on."

"Ok!" I agree my mind on full speed. A trial run! "I'll just tell my friends!"

There's no need, they've heard everything and tell me to come back to the hotel when I'm done. When I've done my trial run!

I have never felt so daunted in my life. Even my recent panel interview doesn't begin to compare. But the timing! It must mean it's meant to be!

"Do you want a drink?" Heather booms from my side. She isn't as pretty as the shot girls I've seen but what she lacks in looks, she makes up for in loud bolshiness suiting her PR role.

"Erm," I glance at her hands for a clue, what is she drinking?

"Voddy and coke?" She asks.

I nod happily, could this really get any better? I'll neck that and get to work. I have got to try and attract at least one customer in to impress Jamie!

Voddy and coke half gone (it was way too potent to neck!) and we're on the empty street. I take the opportunity to ask Heather more about what the job actually is. You know; the important stuff!

"PR 12 'til 8." She replies. "50 euros a day. Every day. The girl who was doing it back-doored it this morning."

"Back-doored it?" I enquire.

"Yeah, didn't turn up, has left the flat! Probably got a flight home in the night."

"Oh! The job that bad is it?" I jest but Heather gazes at me evenly.

"It isn't an easy job. I see girl's turn up all season, get a job thinking it is will be all fun and games! Back door it after 2 or 3 weeks. It does my fucking head in!"

It sounds like she's describing me! I'll be leaving in 3 weeks! But I'm not scuppering my chances now. The hours are good even if it is every day! The money OK and honestly Heather intimidates me. I won't mention it yet, after all I don't actually even have the job yet.

"I'm a shot girl." Heather continues unfazed. "I was just helping Jamie out. And then you came along!"

A shot girl after all! I try to hide any surprise; I can't imagine her flirting, fighting more like! But at least I've gained brownie points already; I've saved her working double shifts.

3 guys amble toward us, they look burnt and drained- surely a cold, refreshing pint is in order.

I jump into action aware that Heather has stepped back and Jamie is probably watching me. I have seen enough PR's in action to know what to do. Taking a deep breath I throw myself into the role.

"Afternoon boys!" I step into their path. "How about a cold pint!"

The two either side step around me and I create an awkward 'let's dance' situation with the middle one purposely blocking him.

"We're hanging!" He tells me desperately trying to side-step me.

"Hair of the dog!" I respond. "It's the only way!"

But he is round me and I'm shouting the last part to their retreating backs.

I look at Heather and shrug. I don't look at Jamie- I'm disappointed, but I want him to see that I'm not fazed. I'll try again.

And now, a group of girls round the corner to my left and begin walking up the strip. They're on the other side of the street and I ask Heather.

"Can I go over to them?"

"You can only approach people from this point," she toe pokes the edge of the wooden veranda- "and that point there. Where that shop ends. If somebody walks up the road this way"- she sweeps a hand arching right to left, the way we had walked earlier and the guys just now- "you can approach them regardless of the side of the road they're on. Until they come level with Chrissy's, over there. And then, if they're on that side, you gotta leave em.

But, if they're walking up from down there-" she thumbs over her shoulder to our left. "You can only approach them if they are on this pavement." She stamps her foot indicating the tiled, white path beneath us.

Wow, glad I asked! I recite the rule in my mind mapping out the area she has indicated as our territory. The girls walking up from our left aren't on this pavement- so they're not fair game!

"Does everybody have sections like this?" I ask and she nods.

As a tourist it all looks completely chaotic. I love finding this out, a secret code for PR's to abide by keeping the system flowing.

"Also PR-ing is illegal. The bar gets fined if they're caught using workers without a work permit. If you see the Police- the ones in black, there are 3 types. Well anyway, any police, Guardia whatever you need to sit down, get inside the bar, play on your phone. Don't let them catch you in the act."

"What happens if they do?" I ask horrifying scenarios blooming in my mind.

"The bar will say you're a weirdo; that they don't know who you are!" She breaks into hearty laughter so I join in. She continues, "They aren't gunna get fined for a poxy worker so that'll be *you* sacked. And you better hope the other bars don't hear of it cuz *nobody* wants to hire a sloppy PR. If you're good, they'll sort you a permit!"

There's no time to really digest all of the information now as more people begin approaching on both sides of the road- from the right. There's no police about, so until they reach Chrissie's opposite they're all ours for the taking.

"I'll get those, you grab these?" I suggest to Heather and she nods. Together we try to accost a pair each. Heather's style is loud and boisterous, mine chatty and playful.

Neither of us are successful and the time after that when we take on a group of 4 lads together isn't either.

I've almost finished my second drink now, I must've been here for over an hour but I daren't check my phone because it's in my bag right near Jamie. I'm beginning to feel uneasy about what he is thinking. I haven't managed to get anybody into the bar- the small comfort being Heather hasn't managed to either- but how long is he going to keep me here? Until I get somebody in? Until I give up?

Another group of guys appear heading my way and I think, 'this is it!' Last chance saloon! I need to get these in here.

Confidently stepping out onto the strip I try to pick out who I suspect might be the leader of the pack and stare squarely into his eyes.

"Fancy a drink?" I ask him in a flirty manner.

"Are you buying love?" He asks to the raucous laughter of his gang.

"Maybe I'll let *you* buy *me* one, we'll see!" I retort saying whatever is needed to engage him.

"Dream on love." He replies to more wild laughter and they keep walking leaving me outside Blush alone.

I've fucked it.

"Oy, girl, come ere will ya?" Jamie calls out to me now. I stroll over to him refusing to hang my head- I've given it my best shot!

"Where are you staying?" He asks catching me off-guard.

"I have one night left at Sol Wave and then my friend says I can stay with her until I find somewhere. She lives over there." I tell him pointing in a vague direction.

"We've got rooms. Are you starting tomorrow?"

I nod blankly wanting to answer but my mind has gone into overdrive. Rooms? Start tomorrow!

"Are you prepared to chat that shit with the lads every time? Day in, day out?"

I nod again eagerly not taking time to think. Right now I'd do anything! Almost anything!

"Ok, bring your case with you and I'll hook you up. What's your name again?"

"Jodie."

"Well Jodie, welcome to Blush. Be here for half 11 in the morning."

"Ok." I turn to leave my mind whirring, skin like popping candy. "What should I wear?" I ask him suddenly wondering if there is a rule for uniform.

He looks me up and down and smirks. "A bikini?"

I am unable to tell if he is joking and flounder for an appropriate reaction.

"Ok, shorts and a bikini top?"

Ok, so he wasn't joking.

"Erm, yes, fine. See you tomorrow."

I'M STAYING!

I jubilantly announce the news to Alexa and Cassie that I have got a job and a place to stay, sorted!

"I'm fucking staying!"

Then I make a phone call to dad- 'I'm staying!' and mum- 'I've got something to tell you…' Well, as anticipated it went down like a lead balloon and then she starting crying. But she's ok now! And finally I send texts to a handful of friends:

You'll never guess what…

Let them guess the news!

I cannot wait for this to trickle through the grape vine and reach stupid prick! This will be the definitive message I wanted to send, that the Jodie he knew is long gone too!

In the hotel room we're all packing our suitcases ready for tomorrow. Except I'll be unpacking mine again tomorrow evening in a real workers apartment- because guess what? I'm a real worker!

A majority of my friends know now, I've been rapidly replying to a flurry of texts. And I gleefully pick out my sunset bikini top and denim hot-pants to wear 'for work' tomorrow and an outfit for tonight.

We're meeting Tanya for a nice meal and a few cocktails to toast the holiday. I can't wait to tell her the news! I'm staying! I'm actually fucking staying!

WORKING LIFE: DAY 1!

I wave goodbye to Alexa and Cassie in a taxi early this morning. I don't have to be out of the room until midday which works perfectly. They are going to let the airline know that I won't be turning up for my flight.

I cannot believe I am doing this! And yet I know I am being driven in this direction, like a moth toward a flame.

At 11.15 I set out for Blush and wonder what passers-by think of the girl in the make-up, bikini and hot pants pulling her suitcase along grinning ridiculously.

At 11.30 I arrive to find only a Spanish man at the bar- his English is good and his accent strong. He introduces himself as Don, gives me a bottle of water and tells me the others won't be around until 2.

I don't know who he means by the others but check I can leave my suitcase behind the bar before happily taking my position on the street. There are no police and enough people about for me to my smile at and ask if they fancy something cold. I have been trying to pick out those I think are other workers. There's just something about their look. They have a confident strut, duck and dive in and out of bars, greet each other noisily. I watch out for Justin, but I don't see him.

It's a hot day and I sizzle on the pavement drinking 2 bottles of water before 2pm arrives. So far nobody has come into Blush for a drink. Jamie turns up first on a battered moped. He smiles, twinkling eyes crinkling up.

"Had many in?" He asks and I shake my head. There's no point lying, Don knows there has been nobody. "Shit season." He tells me. "Too fackin' quiet."

It doesn't seem quiet to me! But I suppose he would know. He has barely disappeared into the bar before another boy and girl arrives, followed by another boy and girl. They walk straight in, not even looking at me, swarming around a table chatting amiably. Another girl and 2 more guys join them too.

I am watching the group as casually as I can. They aren't paying any attention to me but I'm self-conscious all the same as I continue to pounce on passers-by. If I could just get some customers in I could at least relax a little.

Jamie is chatting to the group, he hands something out to them and they start standing, ready to leave in pairs.

"Our Jamie says you're looking for somewhere to stay lass?" A skinny guy with a cute face addresses me.

"Yeah, I'm Jodie." I introduce myself.

"I'm Carl. We're off to PR at the hotels but when I'm back I'll take you over with your case and get you a key sorted n that." He tells me in his scouse twang. "There's me and Andy living there already," he stops to point out a short, squat guy. "He's the DJ. We have a room each. You'll have your own."

"Ok, cheers." I tell him merrily. My own room, I thought I'd be sharing! "What time will you be back? I don't finish until 8." I remember suddenly.

"We'll be back about 4. Jamie won't mind you nipping over, it's only down there." He points to an alley a little way up from us and towering above the bars are plenty of high-rise buildings. I wonder which one is my new home!

Everybody leaves to 'PR at hotels' except for Andy, and Don who sits behind the bar reading a book. Andy goes into the small DJ booth, puts on a pair of big, black headphones and begins blasting out some music.

I happily scan the street noting a group of boys ambling towards me. Slapping on my best smile I start towards them.

"Nooo!" One of them eyes me cautiously. "Stay away from me!"

I laugh glad he is chatting to me; even if he is begging me to leave him alone.

"Oh come on, you don't even know what I'm going to ask!" I tease him and they slow down a little. "Come in for a drink. Keep me company for a bit!"

Mr 'Nooo' becomes Mr Yes! As he looks to his 3 friends saying, "Shall we? Have a quick beer before home?"

"Go on then." Mr Spotty agrees.

"Yaay!" I show my first customers to a table and Don is out within seconds to take their order.

"You want one Jodie?" He asks me.

"Go on then, a voddy and coke?" I am celebrating after all.

He nods and returns inside.

"I'm Lee," aka Mr Nooo/ Yes tells me and this is, "Timmy, Josh," (aka Mr Spotty) "and Frank. How long you worked here?"

"It's my first day," I admit. "You're actually my first customers!"

"Ah well! So what's our prize?" He quips grinning. "A cheeky snog?"

"The privilege of talking to me!" I retaliate giggling; I can see what Jamie means about having to chat shit!

Don returns with the drinks and Lee raises his pint. "Cheers Jodie, well done!"

Having Lee, Timmy, Josh and Frank to talk to helps the time to pass. The drinks flow and I don't have much chance to dwell on what my new quarters might look like. When the music abruptly stops and Andy heads 'home', I watch him cut into the alley which leads there, curious and excited.

I manage to get 2 girls to come in too, and together we all banter and joke. The boys are taking great delight in imagining me as a 'sexy teacher' since I told them about my new job! Before I know it Carl returns with his PR buddy. Jamie and a man I haven't seen before also come along. Then in dribs and drabs the other PR's return too.

I'm so pleased they have come back to 6 whole people on the terrace and glow as Jamie introduces me to Tony- the co-owner. He's huge with stern, slate grey eyes that he runs over me before nodding bad-temperedly and marching inside.

"Jamie, I'm gunna take Jodie over to the flat now with her case. Then I'll send her back, so she knows how to get there when she finishes." Carl tells him.

We collect my case and head toward the alley and I feel like I should pinch myself to check it's all really happening.

"I haven't got you a key sorted yet Hun. Andy's a lazy fucker and will never do it. Even though he tries to lord it cause Jamie's his brother."

"His brother?" I exclaim. They are so unalike looks-wise!

"Ha ha!" Carl catches my drift. "I know right, short changed or what! But yeah he's rented it off Jamie since he got here so he acts like it's his flat. But I will sort it." He tells me as he walks quickly. I do my best to keep up with my suitcase in tow. "It's £250 a week. It's alright. If you can put up with Andy that is! I just can't work him out do you know what I mean?"

As he gossips away he leads us into a gated yard, and we enter the main doors of an apartment block.

"We're fifth floor." He says by way of explanation as he steps into the lift. I know I am in for a good work out the next few weeks because I'll be choosing the stairs every time going forward!

Carl slides his key into number 502 and I begin to feel a little nervous- please don't let it be horrid. He said it was 'alright' though didn't he.

The door opens to reveal a wide L shape hallway. There's a huge overcrowded shoe wrack, a shelving unit piled with bedsheets and a clothes pole filled with t-shirts lining the walls- like a jumble sale. And this is just the hall?

Stepping inside we turn the corner and straight on is the living room. I see double patio doors presumably leading to a balcony, and the edge of a coffee table and sofa.

To my left 3 doors and to my right- just one.

"That's yours." He pushes it open revealing a large bedroom with 2 single beds, a dark wood wardrobe, drawers, desk and chair. A narrow window lets in some light and on first inspection it looks quite nice.

Opposite me is the bathroom, down the corridor Carl's bedroom and then Andy's. The living room is open plan and attached to a small kitchen space.

I will have a good look round later because right now I have got to get back to Blush.

"I work from 8 so I'll see yous in a bit!" Carl tells me when I make to leave. "Andy starts at 9 so he'll be here to let you in when you get back. We don't finish until 3 or 4 so if you go out you'll have to come and fetch the key off me, ok?"

"Yeah ok, bye!" It's annoying about the key. I'll get a pizza when I finish, eat that in my room and once Andy goes off to work have a proper snoop around the place. I probably won't venture out tonight- I feel like I need time to adjust first!

Back at Blush the afternoon creeps slowly by and into the early evening. The girl's had gone when I got back, Lee and his cronies leave not long after telling me there'll pop back tomorrow.

There is only me and Don as I continue to plead people to come in for a drink. I manage to catch a couple in their 40's who are visiting Magaluf for the day. In-between approaching passing tourists I talk to them about the infamous nightlife here and the much quieter resort they are staying in half an hour away.

By 7 they've long gone too and I'm really bored. I can't wait to get back to the apartment to have a nosey about.

The street has virtually dried up and I suppose a lot of people are taking siestas or getting ready to come out later on. Don comes out for his twenty-fifth cigarette and I talk to him about the other Blush staff. He lists off the names of the PR's and tells me about the 5 shot girls, including Heather, who I have yet to meet. The shot girls start at 9pm- so I doubt I'll see them tonight. I'm drained from today, and can't wait to settle in at 'home'. But I'm looking forward to meeting them, maybe tomorrow night I'll come and could potentially make a friend or 2!

By the time quarter to 8 rolls around I have pulled 1 more couple into the bar but they have left now too.

Carl returns ready for his shift indicating mine is almost over.

"You had a good first day?" He asks me.

"Not bad." I reply. "It's really hard to get people to come in!"

"Argh you'll get used to it. It's a quiet season. You gotta be pushy. Use your looks- that's what the others do."

"Yeah I've heard it is. I'm sure I'll get used to it."

"Competition is high. Use whatever you can, girl."

"Ok, thanks." I tell him wondering what he is suggesting I do! "I'm going to get some food and head back."

"Yeah, Andy is still in. Do you think you'll be coming back out tonight?"

"Probably not to be honest. I'll probably just chill out."

"Well there's a Sky box in the living room so plenty to watch on the telly." He cheerfully informs me.

"Great! Ok well, I'll see you tomorrow! Do I need to tell anyone I'm leaving? Don?"

"If Jamie or Tony was here you'd wanna tell them but," he shrugs. "If they said to finish at 8, I'll let them know you were here 'til then. No point telling Don anything, that old stoner won't remember anyway!"

"Stoner!" I exclaim.

"Yeah, he loves smoking the hash!" He tells me gleefully looking round for him. "If you ever fancy a toke, he's your guy!"

"Brilliant. I'll bear it in mind!" And with that I happily trot off in search of the closest takeaway, feeling like I have already gone someway to making my first friend.

Back at the apartment I jog the first 3 sets of steps and wearily climb the last 2, the pizza box hot in my hand. By the time I reach our door I am lightly panting and try to steady my breath whilst waiting for Andy to answer my loud knock. I rap a further 2 times before he finally opens the door- my heart rate and breathing firmly back to normal.

Andy stares at me with none of the natural friendliness that Carl has or his brother Jamie.

He steps aside to let me enter, his eyes don't leave mine and I have to look away because it makes me uncomfortable.

"Just having a pizza, I'm starving!" I try to fill the awkward gap and walk towards my room feeling him watch my every step.

"If you need a key tonight come to me because Carl will be busy outside." He says finally to my back and I remember what Carl said about his self-appointed role as landlord.

"I don't think I will be." I tell him breezily and enter into the safety of my room.

I put the box on the desk and pull up the chair. As I munch my way through the first slice my eyes roam around the room uncovering the truth behind my initial assessment.

Both beds look unchanged and dingy. I saw sheets in the hallway I will do this once I have eaten. I wonder about the possibility of them renting out the other bed. I'll ask Carl tomorrow- landlords (*real* landlords!) must make an absolute fortune! I bet Andy *wishes* it was his flat! I already know I'll be staying out of his way as much as possible. He's a little creepy.

Along the skirting of the room are receipts, tissues, cotton buds, a food carton and even 2 discarded condoms! The more I notice the muck and filth, there are crumbs and dirt on all surfaces, the floor thick with dust, fluff and hair, the less of an appetite I have.

I need to sort this shit out! Is this a sign of growing up? Wanting to clean and tidy my surroundings. But as I gaze at the crap around me I realise it's just survival instinct speaking! Closing the box- good job I like cold pizza- I pick up a plastic bag and toss all of the rubbish into it. I use tissue to pick up the rubber jonny's! Next I strip both beds and fetch a pile of sheets from the rack outside my door. Both changed and looking suitably brighter I decide I'll need to wait until Andy leaves before hunting for cloths and a broom.

I busy myself by checking if the drawers and wardrobe are empty. They are and so I unpack my suitcase realising how little I actually have to wear. There are plenty of shops selling clothes- I'll perhaps treat myself to some even skimpier outfits to suit my new role.

I hear heavy footsteps pass my door and a slam as the front door closes behind Andy. I'm relieved and offended he doesn't care to say goodbye. Carl is easily my favourite of the pair already.

Now it's time to explore!

I to the bathroom first… it's disgusting! I want to wash my hands but I can't believe the state of it! The sink is filthy; grime getting thicker and darker as it rises out of reach of the running water. There's toothpaste stains *everywhere* yellow, even green and fresher ones bright white and foamy.

The shower cubicle looks muddy it's so caked up with brown gunge. The tiles are mouldy, a rotting shower curtain hanging limply open. And the toilet! I suppress a gag. How can I wash in here! I feel dirty just looking at it. I am definitely going to have to wear flip flops in the shower- it's just grim.

Next I go to the living room. In here it's scruffy but not as foul as the bathroom. There are 2 large sofas, one of them covered in more t-shirts, newspapers, an ashtray and empty cigarette boxes. There's an overcrowded glass coffee table, empty fruit bowl, cards, change, lighters etc. A large TV sits in a massive wooden cabinet which is overflowing with DVD's and books.

It looks like people have been slowly filling this apartment for fifty years, nobody ever taking responsibility for a clear out and deep clean.

I dread to think what the kitchen is going to look like but I go to investigate all the same. It is as horrific as the bathroom, probably worse. Moulding plates are stacked high filling the sink and surrounding area. The free surfaces are stained and sprinkled with sugar and coffee granules. It looks like somebody has attempted to mop the soiled floor leaving swirly patterns in the dirt.

That must mean there's something around to sweep my own floor with and I open a few cupboards in search of any cleaning products. There isn't anything- not even cloths and washing up liquid. There's a washing machine but no sign of any detergent or fabric softener.

I'll have to wash my knickers in the shower with shower gel! I realise. Unless I can find somewhere to buy more!

I open the fridge which is sparse and also unclean. A bottle of milk sits in the doorway, alongside a pot of mustard. There's some cheese and butter on the shelves but I wouldn't like to think how long any of it has been there for. There is an oven that I'm not even going to look in, a kettle and a microwave. I think I'll just steer clear of this whole area.

Finally I step out onto the balcony.

I've purposely saved this until last, holding out hope that it will face the sea! And now I'm so glad I did because I need to breathe some fresh air after witnessing this squalor.

Wow! The view is as I hoped; fantastic! The balcony itself is square with a plastic table and chairs in the centre. There is a drying rack full of stiffened clothes in one corner. I sit heavily in a chair drinking in the scene in front of me. As I suspected I can see the shoreline and horizon stretching all along to my right hand side, small boats bobbing out at sea. In front of me there are glimpses of the strip between buildings, I can roughly make out where Blush sits even though I can't see it but I can clearly make out the roof of the Red Lion and even further up see the top of Club Twenty Ones red sign.

From this high up I can see across miles of rooftops, hotels, other high rises, until they separate out eventually being swallowed up altogether by greenery that looks black in this light and rising into mountainous hills. The sun is almost completely set, it's dusky and cool and I sigh contentedly, I can put up with the vile flat for the sake of this extraordinary view.

Sitting outside I type out messages to those closest to me letting them know I have settled in to an apartment and that all is well. I include Cassie and Alexa in the texts checking they got home ok and feeling a teeny pinch smug that I'm still here.

I notice a sweeping brush propped by the doors and take it along with some damp tissue to my room, attempting a clean-up as best as I can. Once this is done the room looks much more inviting. I feel my hunger return slightly and decide to finish my pizza whilst watching some TV.

Despite the unkempt state of the place, the act of watching television shifts my experience of Magaluf from being a holiday to an everyday living arrangement. *Home*, of sorts! I realise I probably won't be out every night- for one I won't have the money (I'll have 100 of my wage left over per week after rent) and 2 I don't have anybody to go out with!

That's fine though, I'm just happy for the extended break, somewhere that nobody really knows me. And I'm pleased with myself for being so daring and taking the plunge on Magaluf. Look how well everything has turned out so far aside of a few hiccups.

Take the good with the bad! I smile to myself and sink into the sofa. I've got such a positive feeling about this. Had I not shut *particular* doors this one could not possibly have opened!

At 1am I take myself to bed. The strip is in full swing and I can easily hear the music, voices and DJ's filling the night air with party spirit. This kind of noise doesn't bother me, if anything I enjoy the constant reminder that I am far, far away from the everydayness of my tedious village.

BCM BANGING

I wake up to my alarm at 10. I didn't think I'd actually sleep up to it but I feel like I've had the best night's rest despite a strange dream that I was being chased down the street by a possessed mattress!

I decide I have to bite the bullet and take a shower. I do so trying my best not to touch any part of the tiles and wearing my flip-flops, it's the quickest shower I've ever had. There's no sign of Carl or Andy- I suspect with hours like theirs they don't rise until midday- later even.

I get dressed for my shift relishing in the feeling of being out the ordinary. I mean, boob tube and hot-pants for work!

The shift follows the same pattern as yesterday. Don is there when I arrive, I don't manage to get anybody in before 2pm when the PR's arrive and Jamie; this time minus Tony. They head off for the afternoon and I carry on trying my best to chat up strangers and entice shoppers into the bar.

4pm comes and the PR's return from their rounds. Carl finally introduces me to the girl he pairs up with, Amy and another of the guys, Sam. They aren't interested in me and talk about going to the beach as they leave together.

"Any drinkers?" Jamie asks me and I'm disappointed to have to shake my head.

"Fack sake." He tuts and stomps off to his moped. Surely I can't do much more than what I'm doing already? It isn't my fault if it's a quiet season plus I'm hardly working during peak time!

I'm relieved when true to their word Lee and friends turn up.

"Hey Jodie!" Lee calls to me as they walk down the road towards me. "Told you we'd come back!"

"Yes you did, a man that keeps a promise!" I tease him.

"Ay!" He feigns hurt. "We're not all the same you know!"

They sit down on the table closest to me and Don comes straight out to take their order. Today he doesn't even ask but brings a voddy and coke for me alongside theirs.

It's amazing how having a set of customers makes attracting others a little easier. Whilst we banter and flirt, 3 groups come in for a drink and leave again.

"What you doing tonight?" Lee asks me now and I hesitate. I hadn't thought about it. I still don't have a key I realise and make a mental note to ask Carl at changeover time.

"I don't know!" I answer honestly. "Why?"

"We're going to a foam party at BCM, hitting a few bars first. You could join us?"

I think about it as though I have lots of options to consider and quickly decide;

"Yeah that'd be brill! Shall we meet here?"

"Yeah at, say 10?" He suggests.

"Fine!" This gives me a great opportunity to meet the rest of the shot girls too.

My shift ends finally, the last hour dragging by. I have kept up with the vodka drinks, taking advantage of anything free and I'm feeling tipsy and excited when home time arrives.

Carl says he still hasn't got me a key cut but that I can share his for now. This isn't very convenient at all and I think about Andy warning me to only borrow his key.

As before, I'm banging on the door for almost ten minutes before he comes to let me in.

"Can't you hear me knocking from your room?" I ask him frustration getting the better of me.

He shrugs and doesn't answer. I'll take that a yes then. Carl said he was lazy! But then I get the impression he's doing it purely to piss me off. I don't bother trying to make awkward conversation today. And I'll be using Carl's key later, thank you Andy!

At ten o clock the tepid night air makes my skin bristle as I stroll to Blush. I will soon be rocking the traditional workers tan!

I can't see the lads on the terrace yet, perhaps they're inside but I spot Heather instantly. She's standing with 2 other girls- both slimmer and prettier- the traditional shot girl image that I have become accustomed to.

As I approach she spots me, taps the others and points at me. I give them all a friendly wave and go up to meet them.

"Jodie!" She booms. "How's it going?"

"Yeah good thanks!" I reply.

"This is Gemma and this is Beth. Jodie's the new daytime PR."

"Hiya!" We all greet each other.

"I didn't think they were bothering with a daytime PR anymore?" Gemma enquires and Heather shrugs.

"They'll see how she gets on." She says matter-of-factly. Unsettling nerves flutter- my job is by no length secure then.

"Who you out with?" Heather shouts.

"I'm meeting some lads who came in for a drink today. They invited me to a BCM foam party." I tell them. "I don't think they're here yet though unless they're inside."

"Well go get yourself a drink and have a look!" She orders me, so I do as I'm told.

I have never seen Blush busy and the atmosphere is completely different to the lull of the daytime. Due to its compact size the bar and dancefloor seem crowded but there are only around 12 people at each.

Behind the bar are 2 people I haven't seen before a guy and girl. Jamie walks through now and slaps my bum playfully.

"Nice to see you sexy!" He cries cheerily above the thump of music. He strides up to the bar calling something into the mystery man's ear before pointing to me and saying something with a crude smirk on his face.

The guy meets my eyes and beckons me over. He is covered in tattoos; from what I can see the artwork looks unusual, not a bog standard design. He has dark hair but wears a cap and up close I can see thick, dark lashes and green eyes flecked with brown. He's good looking, around 30, and when he leans over to ask me what I'm drinking is voice is sexily husky.

"Vodka-orange." I shout to him, fancying a change.

The girl behind the bar is working fast to keep on top of the customers. Her naturally attractive face is virtually free of make-up and she has honey coloured hair swept into a loose ponytail.

When I reach for some money to pay for the drink my hand is shooed away and he moves onto the next customer. I don't get chance to ask him his name but as I can see no sign of Lee or friends in here I head back outside.

Only Heather and Gemma are here now, Beth off to make a sale. Gemma has thick, loosely curled blonde hair, full lips painted bright pink and huge fake lashes. She is very eye catching with large boobs spilling out of her tiny top.

"Free drink!" I indicate the glass to start conversation.

"It's poison." Gemma tells me and I look to her slightly confused. Doesn't she drink? "The vodka," she elaborates. "It's poison. Haven't you noticed everyone's voice? That's what it does!"

Come to think of it everyone does seem to have gravelly, husky and deep voices. I take a sip all the same; it tastes just like every other cheap vodka- acrid.

"So, what are the bar staff called?" I ask now not wanting to look too specific.

"Max and India." She tells me. Are they together? I'm about to pursue when Carl comes tumbling off the street,

"Hey Jodes!" He greets me and he has Lee, Timmy, Josh and Frank in tow. Lee smiles at me soundlessly following Carl into the bar- I suspect they've played the same trick Cassie and I had to ensure discounts are still offered.

"He liked you!" Gemma comments now.

I look into her deep, blue eyes and tell her. "That's who I'm meeting!"

"Well he *definitely* likes you!" She giggles girlishly. "There's a bang in it for you, if you want it that is!"

I laugh a little shocked but instantly I'm intrigued at the thought. It hadn't even crossed my mind about 'banging' Lee.

"I always stick to banging tourists. I don't get involved with the workers!" She informs me before adding conspiratorially. "You don't want to complicate relationships out here."

I think about Justin; he has been a great way to end the drought, a great start to my singledom. And I've already been with him so surely he wouldn't count as 'complicating' relationships if I went there again? But could I bang Lee, just like that? Just because I can?

He reappears now and I look at him in a totally different light- he looks fresh in a white t-shirt- he certainly isn't unattractive. Does he fancy me?

Heather and Gemma exchange a look and Gemma stalks away. Heather grins and in her manly voice makes Timmy jump by demanding,

“Get yer wallets out then gents come on. This gorgeous lady has been waiting for you! She wants one too.”

Timmy looks helplessly from Frank to Lee.

“What are ya, man or mouse? Get your fucking wallet out!” Heather drops her tray of Jagerbombs onto the table and marches toward him patting at his pockets.

“Here, love, I’ll help ya.”

I observe all of this in awe- so that’s how she does it! Well I’ve never seen anything like it! It’s funny and yet takes any harassment I’ve experienced to the next level!

“Lee!” Timmy pleads. “It’s your turn! I bought them all last night!”

“Give over!” Lee replies but takes his wallet out anyway. “I’ll pay darling, how much?”

Is he paying to impress me? I think as he gives me another smile whilst extracting the cash.

“20 euros.” She barks holding out an expectant hand. “Chop chop else I’ll make you buy me one too!”

He sighs and smirks; used to the forceful nature of Magaluf workers and obviously also used to these prices- 4 euros a shot! It’s in direct opposition to me having virtually drunk for free all holiday!

He gives her a twenty and she swipes it stuffing it into the money pouch around her waist. She leaves us alone after we have drained our cups, piling them back onto her tray and going to loiter with Beth and 2 other shot-girls I've yet to be introduced to.

"She is a grenade!" Lee exclaims the moment she is out of earshot.

"A grenade?" I query.

"A girl who just explodes, like what the fuck just happened! She's so loud!" He explains laughing; a 'grenade' doesn't seem an unfair description.

They are an easy bunch to get along with, I knew that from before, but now freshly fuelled with alcohol they regale me with some of their tales so far.

Frank got pickpocketed by the 'prostitutes' on the first night. I hadn't taken much notice of the small, African ladies I'd sometimes seen scuttling about in groups of 3 or 4, late at night. But, I am told, they call themselves prostitutes, crowding around a lad and offering sex. Whilst they distract him by pinching his willy and pulling at his shorts another sweeps any possessions from his pockets!

I am stunned but a little amused. It is utter madness.

Gemma approaches us now singling spotty Josh out as her target, bless him. Her selling style is completely different to Heather's.

She uses her prowess; eyes hooded, biting her lip, trailing a finger across her breast. God, even I'm a bit turned on. Poor Josh is rendered helpless!

Her shots some green, some red are in large plastic syringes, they're 3 euros each. She insists on squirting the shot into each boy's mouth, one by one. She lets me do my own. It's bizarre but I suppose its quirkiness is the selling point.

We stay at Blush until midnight.

"What should I do about a key then?" I ask Carl before we're swept away by the strip.

"I'll be here until 3ish. Take my number and call me if it's later."

We swap digits and I skip away in the direction of the BCM Bar for more pre-drinks. I'm so pleased Lee invited me along because I had wanted to try out a foam party- I'd seen them advertised on the internet before we came. Alexa had insisted it would spoil our clothes, hair and make-up and that was that, obviously!

I miss her and Cassie being here with me. Well, I miss Leila, Cat and the others too- how they'd love this!

The realisation just makes me ever more grateful for the experience. Even if my job isn't permanent and I'm on a flight home by Friday at least it's happened.

BCM Bar is an outdoor venue alongside others on a large concrete expanse behind BCM nightclub. This is the first time I have even seen this part- we are right at the top and just off the strip. As I take my seat I count 6 rectangle sections, each plot a themed bar. They all have at least 1 podium dancer and the music which blasts around the whole area is what the DJ is playing inside the main club behind us.

This is also virtually the first time I have had to put my hand in my pocket for a drink! Although it would seem buy-one-get-one-free is a bog standard practise- I still end up with 2 drinks at a time.

Having stayed at the bar outside until gone 2 we finally head for the doors to pay for entry to the club.

Lee insists on paying for me and I realise perhaps Gemma is right. There's no doubt about it he has switched up the flirting notch. I noted him clearly taking a role that placed him as potential suitor- pulling out my chair, offering to buy me a drink. The effort he's making is nice. A little bit more subtle than the PR's!

Once inside we are met by a huge expanse of bars, stools and tables, dance floor and podiums. A DJ booth adorned by 2 pole dancers is just visible through the fog of dry ice, flashing lights and lasers.

I am filled with new exhilaration reminding me of how I felt when I was just a tourist pulling back the curtain on Magaluf for the first time.

I never would've thought I would be here in this massive, crazy club- as a worker! Complete with random, new friends that I've only made because I have stayed here! It's all too much to comprehend.

Meeting Heather, Beth and Gemma, India; Max! Knowing there's a Justin somewhere! Andy, Carl, Don, Jamie and Tony. And now what about Lee?

What about Lee?

Yes, he's cute and funny. He's flirted and been a gentleman. Does that mean I can just *bang* him? Gemma seems to think so- and as long as I play safe, where's the harm? He's no wow-fuck-me-Justin, but he could be just-a-bit-of-fun!

"Come on!" He shouts now grinning lopsidedly and takes my hand, guiding me toward a stair case.

Frank leads the group; Josh, Timmy, Lee then me down the stairs. As we descend, music from the awaiting downstairs swallows the music from the floor we leave behind. We arrive directly beside a bar and I look out across a sea of heads stretching in an oblong toward another DJ booth at the far end. There are no poles or podiums down here though. Instead 3 huge grey tubes hang from both walls and as I watch they begin oozing foam onto the crowd below.

At first foam covers their heads and outstretched hands like snow but as the pipes continue to gush, it quickly fills up parts of the crowd causing mini white mountains.

Bodies and hands quickly disperse the mounds slapping it into the air like clouds.

I stare open mouthed. I cannot go in that! Alexa was right!

It's only now that I begin to notice people around me are wet and slimy from being engulfed in the foam. Long hair in rat tails, shirts see-through. I wanted to do this! The google images looked so fun! It's surely an experience worth having still, you only live once right?

"Shall we go straight in! Before we get a drink?" Lee calls in my ear laughing he's still holding my hand. I look at him grinning at me.

"What are we waiting for?" It can't be as bad as jumping off a boat after all!

I let him weave me into the crowd and as it becomes denser my feet begin to slide on the foamy residue on the dance floor. I'm glad for his strong grip tensing each time he feels me slip. The music becomes thicker and I look up to see a gaping hole almost right above me; any minute another bubbling fog is going to come tumbling out and engulf me! It is excitingly frightening.

I find Lee's eyes and mirror his smile and raised hands; enjoying David Guetta's 'where the girl's at' we energetically move our bodies to its rhythm. I am really finding my stride when; IT'S SO COLD! The foam tickles my outstretched fingers, tingles my scalp and then icily seeps its way into every crevice!

For a split second everybody around me is coated in white. And then it becomes completely white! I can't see a thing! All sound has become muffled. Where *are* the girls at? I am completely disorientated and I feel the thrashing of bodies as they throw themselves into the foam determined to smash it apart! And my head if I don't get out of the way rapidly!

It is great fun for about 3 seconds before it has become wildly alarming! My arms thrust out in front of me I shove into and around other heads before feeling cold, foam free air on my hands. Brushing frantically at my face I clear my vision and continue to move in one firm direction- back toward the bar.

That was mad! I'm still covered in foam, it's everywhere! At least knee deep still all around me.

How am I ever going to find Lee in this! I can barely see a thing as I weave along and finally the crowd begins to thin. I pause to look properly for any sign of Lee or his friends.

I'll just have to walk home alone, I think practically and I recognise that this feels like a disappointing result.

"Jodie!" I hear now vaguely over the music. "Jodie, over here!"

I turn and face a tall, frothy snow man. It's Lee! I'm shivering from head to toe laughing shakily. I am freezing and he looks hilarious!

"Well! That was fun wasn't it?" He cries sarcastically and I giggle some more as he tries with no avail to wipe the foam from himself. "This stuff is mental!"

"You just have to wait for it to melt!" I try to tell him giggling.

"What?" He calls bringing his smattered head closer.

"I said, you have to wait for the foam to melt!" I can barely hear myself over the music but he catches my gist and puts his thumbs up grinning. The bubbles are already dissolving, soaking his clothes in darker wet patches.

"I'm freezing!" He says leaning in again close to my ear.

"Me too!" I call back, close to his.

He turns his face holding my eye and for a moment I think, he's going to kiss me!

"I don't know where the others are!" He says instead losing his nerve and shrugs as if all hope is lost.

Are we going to 'have a bang'? I laugh out loud at my unspoken question and luckily he takes this as an answer.

"Shall we get a drink?" He points to the bar. I nod and we head over together.

We join the back of the queue and I wrap my arms around myself shuddering. I'm glad to be knitted in so tightly with everybody else. We're trapping our body heat like penguins.

"Are you cold?" Lee asks when he feels my body shivering against his side.

"Yes!" I say. He puts his arm awkwardly around me and I lean into him further. Old school move! But it works.

The queue subsides slowly. I don't even want another drink now, I realise. I'm at peace with my decision that I'm going to do it, if he wants to that is, I'm going to have a bang!

And, you know what I'm going to make the first move too. I suspect he has been daring himself to do it for some time now anyway. What's the worst he can do? Turn me down like gay English?

"Shall we go to mine? Dry off." I say. I am a fearless, fearsome Magaluf PR with intimidating confidence, we'll see if he likes it or not!

"Yes, come on." He answers without hesitation. Yes, I thought so.

He is pushing me quickly through the throng of bodies. Oh my god, here we go again, my *second* shag since stupid prick! This so much *fun*! And actually so easy!

I wouldn't dream of acting like this back home. Making the first move like that for a start! But this type of information would be round like wild fire in our tight-knit community. Prying eyes and rabbiting mouths. But I don't have to worry about a reputation here. Nobody will ever know!

Except for Carl it occurs to me now. We're exiting BCM Club after no more than 30 minutes. He will still be on the street working it isn't quite 3 and so will Jamie and the others.

Suddenly people *will* know about my night time activities.

I'll make Lee wait in the alley way for me. Like a sneaky teenager!

I definitely feel like I've reverted to a teenager- breaking the rules with gusto!

As we walk we talk casually and I find out he goes home not tomorrow, the next day. (A bonus if this turns out horribly because I don't ever have to see him again). Now I get it Gemma!

He lives with his mum and sister, drives a supped-up Focus; we talk about his work as a mechanic a little more. And then the biggie;

"So, do you have any condoms?" I ask him bluntly as we make the final approach to where Carl should be working still.

"Erm, yes." He says losing characteristic coolness for a moment.

"Good." I throw in a cheeky wink, kind of proud of myself. Dummy here still hasn't bought any yet! But I never thought I'd be having sex again so soon if I'm honest.

"I've got to grab the key from my flat mate." I tell him now as we make our final approach to Blush. To my relief I see Carl, crowds have thinned and he spots us.

"Have you pulled our Jodie!" He catcalls loudly and everyone it feels turns to look at me and Lee.

My relief quickly changes to embarrassment. So much for those prying eyes!

"Jodie's banging!" He cheers and they all join in clapping and guffawing.

"Ah don't be nervous girl!" He chortles. "We all do it. You'll be wanting the key then!"

Oh my god. I want the ground to open up. It isn't the reaction I'd get back home though and I have to smile at this thought. 'Jodie's banging!' cue rapturous applause!

I wonder how Lee feels, surely appalled. I take the key from Carl's outstretched hand avoiding Lee's eye wondering what he's thinking.

"I'll leave it on the latch." I tell him and scuttle away quickly.

"Sorry about that!" I say to Lee suddenly feeling sober. What am I doing? You're having another one night stand, an inner voice gleefully answers. But should I be?

"It's ok!" He laughs gaily. "I don't mind the whole strip knowing I'm gunna bang the fittest girl in Magaluf!"

"Shut up!" I punch his arm but there's no denying it, the comment makes me glow on the inside.

"What. It's true!" He insists.

I don't care if it's an exaggeration, it makes me feel good, fuels my ego.

We cut through the alleyway and head to my apartment block. Butterflies begin to take hold now. He's nowhere near as fit as Justin, but that doesn't mean I'm not still a bit nervous about getting naked in front of him. Or doing something wrong!

We enter the dark flat; I flick the catch on the lock of the door and head to my room. Switching on the light I realise it's too bright in here as we stare at each other only inches apart. Lee smiles and puts his arms around my waist pulling me closer. Should I turn the light out? This is all happening very quickly. But what did I expect, a game of charades first!

Lee kisses me with an open mouth and pushes his tongue in a little bit too far. My own mouth is forced pretty wide and within moments he has become a washing machine.

Perhaps we're playing charades after all? This isn't a great experience and with the amount of alcohol I have already consumed I'm worried I'm going to gag.

Pulling back slightly makes it more bearable but now there's an uncomfortable bend in my neck from leaning my head so far backwards. He begins passionately moaning now, something I'm not accustomed to at all and I wonder, should I do it in return? Men like that don't they?

Who knows! Alexa?

I'm thinking all of this whilst Lee is whimpering and moaning snogging my actual face off and suddenly he breaks away. I gasp for air whilst I have the chance.

He takes this panting as a good sign and jumps on me again almost immediately.

Bloody hell!

He's pushed me onto the bed now and he's on top of me, I can't pull my head away from his tonsil tickling tongue. His groaning is incessant and he thrusts his hard penis against me whilst we're still fully clothed.

I think I'd quite like the humping if it wasn't for the shit kissing and off-putting moaning!

"I want you so bad Jodie!" He whispers breathlessly in my ear. "From the first time I saw you, I wanted you so bad!"

Oh god, go back to the whimpering!

If I wasn't so glad for the break from the kissing, I think whilst sneakily wiping slobber from my mouth, I'd probably be a lot more embarrassed at these vocal declarations.

"Do you feel the same?" He asks now continuing to kiss me frantically all over my neck and chest. "Tell me you want to feel my cock inside you!"

Oh shit, now I'm put on the spot. I open my eyes and stare at the ceiling, my own voice sounding very awkward in the brightly lit room.

"Yes, I, erm, want to feel your… cock inside of me." Suppressing a giggle is difficult but Lee is completely overcome with lust and doesn't notice my gurning.

"Do you want to ride me Jodie? Do you? Tell me you want to ride me like a horse!"

It's too much to hold in this time and to my horrified amusement I let out a small snort of laughter.

I have to cover my faux pas so I quickly please him by muttering as seductively as I can.

"I want to ride you like a horse Lee!" I pray to anyone listening that, well, that nobody *is* listening. If this got out, I would book a flight home tomorrow!

Lee rolls onto his side now and begins tugging his trousers down.

"I'm ready for you baby!" He tells me and grabs hold of a long, thin, red penis.

"Condom?" I manage to choke out and he tuts but fishes around for his pocket, extracts his wallet and slips out a foil package. He rips it open with his teeth- I'm sure Sex Ed tells you to not to do that- but then hey, at least I'm using one!

Seconds later his penis is lime green and covered with rubber bumps. I'm pleased to see it's a 'dotted' condom (designed to heighten pleasure!) because it might help with the, ahem, 'pencil dick' situation I am faced with here.

Am I really going to ride that? I'm possibly as dry as bone down there still! I find there's nothing quite so mood dampening (excuse the pun!) than bad kissing. And now a pencil dick!

But even so, he *is* a nice guy, he's made me laugh- it's just a bang! A bit of harmless fun!

I climb aboard and think of England, well in all honesty I think of Justin, and begin to bounce up and down keeping myself firmly upright and therefore lips determinedly out of reach.

This helps, as does the dotted condom and I begin to rather enjoy myself.

Oh no. The moaning has started up again.

"Take your top off." He instructs me. I do this and he continues. "And your bra."

I expertly undo my bra 1 handed exposing boobs; light in comparison to my brown body. I feel quite sexy.

"Ah yeah baby!" He gasps in-between his porno style lady cries. "Uh! Ughh. Yeahh! Touch your tits!" He tells me now.

Well, in for a penny in for a pound, I tell myself and begin to rub my boobs.

"Ooooh, Ahh, yeah. That's right!" He is thrusting his hips into me now and the intensity of how much he wants me causes clouds of tingle to form in my pelvis. We're really going for it, Lee is howling like a strangled cat and through my rising pleasure I really hope no one is home yet- they'll think it's me!

With sweaty palms he grabs hold of my hips smashing me onto him harder, faster. The cries are coming rhythmically now- uh, uh, uh, uh- his back arches, and head rolls back.

I must say it is a real turn on and I almost fully orgasm from seeing this man completely lose all control because of me and my body.

"Jodieeee!" He squeals and the thrusting becomes less powerful before slowing to a complete halt.

"Wow!" I say being completely misinterpreted by Lee who grins like the Cheshire cat and replies.

"Wow indeed!"

He pulls me down onto him and gives me a hug. Nice touch!

We complete the awkward dismount and he redresses- I put on a comfortable, dry t-shirt and shorts. Lee looks around for a bin, neatly tied jonny in his hand.

"Just put it on the floor by the desk. I'll sort it."

He looks at me bemused but does as I say, placing it gently against the skirting board. I realise he has no idea I moved in to find 2 already on the floor hence it seeming a rational suggestion to me.

"Look, Jodes." He says looking wary and I panic- please don't be something awkward or embarrassing!

"I'm going to have to go because my phone's dead and my clothes are all wet, honestly, it sounds like I'm making excuses- but I haven't got a key or any way of contacting the lads- so I'm gunna have to go now." It flows out of him but I am honestly relieved. I've had my bang! I'm more than happy for him to leave.

"It's fine!" I reassure him laughing. "Honestly it's cool."

"I'll come see you tomorrow though!" He tells me. "And we could y'know swap numbers. Or add each other on Facebook!"

Oh society's calling card. I don't mind being 'Friends' we live 3 hours' drive away in the UK, a repeat performance is unlikely.

"Yeah cool. I'll see you out. I don't know if anybody is in!"

We walk to the front door and he gives me a kiss, just a peck thank goodness. I swing open the door and almost jump out of my skin. Andy and Carl are both there.

"Hey Jodie! That was quick work!" Carl jokes.

Andy stares at me lip curled. Because I've used Carl's key instead of his? Or because of the terribly indecent act I have just committed!

"Well! We'll leave you to say goodnight in peace!" Carl titters idiotically and they go off inside leaving us alone again.

"Bye then." Lee says to me.

"Bye then."

"I'll see you tomorrow."

"Ok Night."

"Night then."

"Night!" I trill and shut the door on him because he still doesn't turn to leave. Then creep back to my room hoping Carl doesn't come to quiz me. Andy will be too busy judging me from his room. But I don't care, he isn't my friend. If he is bitter because his brother is so much better looking and so much more successful, let him wallow! He isn't going to cramp my style!

I retrieve the condom, wrap it in tissue and put it in a bag I've saved for rubbish. It's the first thing to go in it. I wonder if it won't be the last of its kind.

That definitely was not the best sex I've ever had but it was certainly the most unusual. I have *never* done it with a guy who's made so much noise before. And despite his awful kissing being reminiscent of my teenage years- there's a theme here! It doesn't put me off the idea of having more casual sex. It's rather an intriguing business!

I lie on the other bed because Lee's wet clothes have dampened my sheets. More than his foreplay did for my mood! But despite the sex being odd, and the kissing downright awful I like the fact it's brought about (another) new experience.

Does it make me a slag wanting to sleep about? Erm, unfortunately, possibly yes it does. But then I'm away from home, what goes on in Magaluf stays in Magaluf; other than entertaining my chosen few with the experiences I want to share!

I've come this far by making my own choices and I'm not just talking the trip to Spain. I've had to disregard what others think about my decisions and just go for it in the past for better or worse! And people who I care about a lot; so I certainly won't be fazed by the likes of Andy!

I already feel different. Like the old me and a new me all rolled into one.

I set an alarm on my phone and decide to call Leila tomorrow- I have got to tell at least her about this strange groaning business. I have a second sex story to tell her already. And I must admit, I like it!

THE VISIT!

I feel sluggish and have a faint headache when my alarm sings its head off at 10am. I snooze it and drift back off into a restless sleep.

2 more snoozes and I decide I can't ignore the pull in my stomach telling me to get up, have a shower and buy something to drink and eat.

I'm glad I bite the bullet because by quarter past 11 I'm sat on a bench staring across the golden sand and out to sea. There are plenty of people already about, sunbathing, strolling along happily and a teeny part of me is gutted I have to work. But then I wouldn't still be here if I wasn't working!

A bottle of water, crisps and fruit sit beside me and I begin munching pieces of watermelon whilst scrolling for Leila's number. England is an hour behind so she won't have started her pub shift yet.

After three rings she picks up crying out my name. It's so good to hear a familiar voice and I experience a tiny pang of homesickness.

"Hey!" I greet her. "How are you?"

"I'm fine silly, how are *you*? Is it crazy fun?"

"Mate, you wouldn't believe!" I laugh and trap the phone between my ear to open the crisps. "Get this; I had sex with a guy last night who made these noises all the way through!" I dish the dirt lowering my voice- you never know, he could be around.

"No way! You had sex, again!" She's in awe. I knew she would be!

"Yep. With a tourist guy called Lee!"

"A tourist, oh Jodes, listen to you. You're a proper worker! Have you seen much of Tanya?" She enquires now.

"No actually but she's so busy with shifts and I'm working every day too. I must text her though. It's so nice to hear a familiar voice!" I admit.

"Are you missing us all then?" she probes.

"Course I am! Tell Cat I miss her!" I say genuinely. "Ay, you should come out here and see me, you'd love it."

The suggestion comes suddenly and even as I say it the idea flowers. It would be so easy. "Oh my god, yes, Leila you should come and visit!"

"How! No, yes! But how though!" She cries.

"Leila listen. You get Sundays and Mondays off right? See if you can get a shift covered either side. Book flights. You can stay with me. I have 2 beds in my room even!"

I try to say all of this slowly so she can process it. Please say yes! I want to rush her but know I can't! She's my bestie I know how she works.

"Oh god Jodie. I want to say yes, could I really? Could I come and visit you!"

"Yes! Yes, get on it now. Look at your rota first. See what you can do I'll be here for almost 3 more weeks."

"Ok! Ok."

It's going to happen I just know it! Leila might be a little more hesitant than me but I can tell she wants to and perhaps she is ready to take this step now. It's her time to venture from the nursing pool.

We ring off even more excitable than we started. I eat my food and drink my water and my hangover completely lifts. Leila is coming! Well it isn't set in stone, but still it's worth getting excited over. I'm raring for my shift at the prospect.

Just wait until she sees this place!

The strip is busier today as I work within my designated area, more holiday-makers ambling, striding, stumbling by! The odd coach rumbles past, taxis and mopeds. I spot a girl, no joke she looks well frankly rough! Tall, skinny, limp white hair and a face that is literally haggard. She has no shoes and darts from alley to alley. I see her 3 times in total. It's impossible to guess her age; somehow she looks youthful beneath the dry, lined skin. I'm guessing she's a worker but I feel sorry for her- she looks homeless.

For the first time there are customers in the bar when the PR's arrive at 2 and I have failed to spot the old woman girl again. Jamie gives me an approving nod buoying my great mood further.

Carl delightedly tells the whole group I got banged last night and even this doesn't knock my spirits. This kind of gossip is welcomed here and not judged by formal standards. Plus I feel like one of the group, everybody, except for Amy smiles at me and I join in with the crude talk agreeing that tourists here love getting 'banged'.

They file out and I'm back out on the strip wearing my proverbial PR hat with pride. Nothing is out of the ordinary, my wonderful new ordinary and I squint as I scan the street for potential punters.

A group of four is striding in the distance toward me, 2 girls, 2 boys and there's something strikingly familiar about the guy on the right. His muscular build, soft brown skin.

It's Justin!

My heart begins to pound. He hadn't even occurred to me today. There is just so much going on all of the time, I didn't think. Oh my god, he's looking!

I'm as proud as a peacock to have people actually drinking on the veranda- I look good at my job!

He spots me and I see a glimmer of recognition cross his face. His chin drops and his eyes burn as he strolls towards me.

"J." I greet him as casually as I can.

"I don't remember every slag I fuck but I remember you, *Jodie*. You must've been good."

He smirks and I hold his eye as he walks past me, catching up with his clan.

He said my name! I know that shouldn't be my first thought but it is! And he said I was good!

He also called me a slag! Finally that part gets through!

I know I should feel completely mortified but actually *it is* a compliment after all albeit back-handed. And wow, he's good looking.

But then he also called me a slag. *And* compared me to other girl's *he's* slept with. How hypercritical! We're *both* slags, not just me! Well, I am being a 'slag' aren't I? Not that I'm justifying his comment-compliment! I should have just realised that whether home or away labelling still applies.

I still get the impression he wants to see me again. He wouldn't have spoken to me else, would he? But then that's what bad boys do isn't it, string you along?

I wish I could talk it through with Leila or Cat or any of my girlfriends. I know I could call them but they're not here and up-to-date on everything as it unfolds; how can they even begin to understand.

'Oh he called me a slag but he did say I was good!' It would go down like a storm of shit! How do I then begin to explain that I probably actually still fancy him and it seems quite reasonable enough to forgive and forget?

This is most definitely a 'break' in its most extreme form. It's just me here from my world, I can only convey so much to those who are not here experiencing it. Hopefully Leila will change that! But for now I have stepped into this alone. Everyone I have met so far is unique to this experience of illegal working in Magaluf. Except for Tanya who exists on the side which is above board; Yes! I'll message Tanya! I wanted a break, and she suggested this! I've most definitely found what I wanted- even though I didn't know this was it. And I am glad to have her here, the one link to my other world.

I extract my phone to text Tanya and quickly check I'm not going to miss out on any potential customers. My heart jumps to my mouth; a Police car has stopped just up ahead.

Wow, I'm so pleased I pulled out my phone at that moment because I concentrate on the screen now and oh-so-casually stroll to the Blush veranda.

I fall back on the acting skills gained through waitressing but still feel like a sign flashes above my head screaming 'illegal worker right here!'

I daren't even lift my eyes to look at the car again- but it was definitely a police car of some description. I was the only PR out on the street right then I must've stuck out like a sore thumb.

"Drink?" Don is at the table now happy to roleplay that I'm a customer.

"Yeah, please. Vodka." I smile. That was too close for comfort. I was so distracted I have no idea how long they sat there before I noticed them.

Don returns and stares at the cop car, giving them a long, slow smile completely unfazed. He must have his permit, he's safe.

U working later?

I type out to Tanya trying to forget the loitering threat of law enforcement. It does give me a nice impromptu rest. After twenty minutes I begin to wish I had a book. A half an hour passes, the car still hasn't moved and finally my phone pings.

Finish at 9. Early start tomo but come mine for some food?

I'm so pleased. A night in at Tanya's discussing the feeling of being far from home sounds just the tonic. She's used to it all by now, but at least she understands.

Yes, call me when ur done.

I reply eagerly and signal Don to bring me another voddy-coke. It's a bit cheeky, I know, but apparently it is cheap poison after all and there is literally nothing else to do.

Half 3 comes and goes and finally at 4 o clock the car rolls away. Don is out immediately.

"Stay seated." He tells me firmly. "They might go round the block and come back."

I nod and he goes back inside. Carl returns with the others. Jamie looks at me frowning as he marches into the bar and after a moment I hear him shout;

"FOR FACK SAKE." I flinch but nobody else is bothered.

Andy trots up the strip now too and also heads inside. He doesn't bother to look at me- judgementally or otherwise and I don't take his dismissal to heart.

15 minutes later it is just me and Don once again and he pops out to say;

"The coast is clear Jodie."

Jamie didn't ask me why I was sitting down before he'd left- I can only assume Don filled him in. It would explain the shout. The Police have certainly managed to scupper my chances of helping the bar gain trade this afternoon as the street is virtually clear now.

I turn to look back up the street and there's Lee!

Shit, I'd virtually forgotten lasts night prolonged farewell- he'd said he would come. He's on his own as well.

"Hiya!" He greets me in his friendly manner.

"Hi!" I return it. Maybe I should try and stick to nice boys. Even if they are bad kissers and have pencil dicks! He self-consciously plants a kiss on my cheek.

"The others didn't want to come. They've gone back for a 'nap'." He quotes the last word rolling his eyes. "I'm on holiday with a bunch of grannies!"

I laugh. "So are you staying for a drink then?"

"Of course I am! I'll be gone tomorrow! And then, well you know, you'll be gone."

He giggles bashfully and I realise this is so much more than just a bang to him. I feel a little shamefaced for discarding him as just-a-bit-of-fun! But he's leaving soon anyway. It's the perfect set-up, no opportunity for an awkward 'I don't like you in that way' conversation.

Don takes his order of a beer and fetches us both a drink. I receive a free drink almost every time a customer buys one. I'm not complaining but it means I end up drinking every day.

"Are you out tonight?" He asks hopefully. I feel guilty for being relieved that I can reply.

"Sorry, no. My friend works here too and I have plans with her. It's been arranged for ages." I add for good measure.

Lee's been a temporary pal useful for his good company. He is a lot more into me than I am him but he'll be gone tomorrow, back home getting on with his life. And I'll just be a distant memory- some bird he pulled on holiday.

After Lee orders his second pint conversation begins to dry up and I find myself standing out on the street more and more.

Eventually he senses there's nothing really left for us to discuss and he stands up getting out his phone.

"Type your name into Facebook." He tells me. "I'll add you!"

"Ok!" I reply. I hope he doesn't drag this out- but I've got a feeling he will!

"And you know, I'll message you!"

"Yeah ok." I smile. Like a modern day pen pal.

"It's been great to meet you!"

"You too!"

"So, I'll seeya then."

"Safe journey!"

"Speak soon!"

I don't reply and just wave trying to create the impression that the short distance he has put between us is way too vast for my voice to carry.

"Bye!" He calls again.

I'm tempted to mouth, "Bye!" to continue with the allusion but decide against doing anything other than carry on waving.

Why are there no customers right now, just when I could use the distraction? At last he turns around and I also turn-around just in case he keeps looking back.

LIKE THE OLD DAYS

When I finish at 8 I'm dismayed to be told Carl still hasn't got me a key.

"Andy's just making it really difficult." He says pathetically using Andy- yes he's rude to me but how exactly is he making it difficult for Carl to get a key cut!

"How?" I push him to explain

"Well he wants us to wait and see if you last a week. Says he doesn't want too many copies of keys being cut. I don't see why- and what his problem…" Carl babbles but I only hear the first part- last a week? Are they going to get rid of the daytime PR position?

"I'll ask him again, I will. You can use mine again tonight?"

I nod and leave thinking I'll ask Andy myself.

After waiting for the obligatory 10 minutes for the door to be answered I agitatedly greet him with;

"When am I getting my own key?" I wait for an answer, standing my ground and ignore a glint in his eye.

"Please." He adds quietly and I stall, I was expecting him to slap his one-week-trial clause in my face. Now *I* feel like the rude one, how out of the blue this must feel to him. He probably isn't even aware of Carl telling me everything- and that's if it's even true.

"Sorry," I apologise feeling ashamed of myself. "I've been waiting on a key and Carl said you were involved with the delay."

I sound like I've applied my 'telephone voice' and he shrugs giving nothing away.

"I'll ask him to do it soon." He tells me unhelpfully.

"Great! Thanks." I force through gritted teeth.

I have a shower and throw on the tracksuit bottoms I travelled in with a strappy top and wait for Tanya's call.

"Do you want food picking up?" I ask her when the phone finally rings.

"I've got us some Chinese." She informs me matter-of-factly her natural organisation in full force. "And I've got us some weed."

"What?" I exclaim shocked.

"Yeah, thought we could have a smoke on the balcony like old times." She tells me breezily. "I'll meet you just past Burger King, there's a supermarket? Mine's not far from there."

"Yes, ok."

We ring off. Just like old times? I rake sludgy memories, getting high over the years on random occasions, was Tanya there? Yes, on some of them she was. But there were definitely no balconies. And no Magaluf. No ludicrous tales to tell. I thought I was a colourful character back then! Little did I know that was tame in comparison to this.

I trot to meet Tanya a skip in my step. I'll admit it I'm excited! I'm going to get high like old times sake!

Everything here is so ordinarily out of the ordinary. It doesn't even feel odd to be making decisions that I probably wouldn't consider back home.

Tanya looks tired but beautiful as always when she meets me at our designated spot. Her apartment is a short walk away and on arrival I observe *so much* nicer than my own.

Clean for a start! But also decorated and homely; I tell her about the squalor in which I live and she laughs before entertaining me in return with stories about the passive-aggressive tourists she's had to deal with today. It reminds me of dealing with customers when I was waitressing- but it is a million miles from this- literally.

I watch as Tanya expertly builds and rolls a long slim joint. The balcony we're sitting on is so much more comfortable than at mine. These are proper wooden chairs with cushions! And there are trailing flowers from plant pots and hanging baskets. It's enchanting. But then it's also no sea view.

"I'd love you to see the view from my balcony." I tell her dreamily. "Maybe you'll get chance to pop round- and I can show you the kitchen too!"

"Are your flatmates cool?" She asks and I think about how I should answer.

"Yes and no." I say eventually. "2 guys. Carl seems nice enough, And Andy." I pause. "I'm not sure I like Andy much, he makes me feel uneasy plus they haven't got me a key sorted yet and Carl's blaming Andy. But then I don't think Andy likes me anyway! So it could be true."

She lights up and blows sickly, fragrant smoke into the night sky.

"Just one of those things mate. Not like home where you move in with a friend or something. You haven't got to put up with it for long. That's shit about the key though! Are they getting you one?"

"Apparently!" I say and take the joint from her.

"But are you enjoying work and, you know, being out here?"

"Yes, oh yes definitely! I was thinking earlier I should thank you!"

"Thank me! Thank me for what?" She exclaims.

"Giving me the idea to stay!"

She laughs loudly. "Jodie, I only suggested it! I've suggested it to Alexa before- and other friends, do you remember Cathy?"

I nod my head. "Yeah I remember her. So am I the first to actually do it?"

"Yes! I was kind of surprised at first, but then I remembered you have always been the ballsy one!"

"Ballsy!" I shun the estimation but I like it. I'd have described Alexa as the ballsy one and yet in Tanya's opinion my actions warrant the title- Alexa didn't stay when she had the chance, and I could tell she'd felt peeved when I decided to. "I get free drinks all day!" I switch the subject.

Tanya sighs. "There's definitely perks to the work you do Jodes."

Insensitive topic change; Tanya's schedule is non-stop and barely allows her to join in the fun. But then she has a contract and job security. She must have her own fair share of stress and worries but I doubt they are anything like mine.

"One of the girls said the alcohol is poison- you know the vodka; I don't know how serious she was?" I trail off but before I can wonder if I sound deluded she says.

"Mate, all the alcohol sold on that strip is dodgy. Just like this whole place! It's run by gangs and cons; profit is the only language these businesses understand."

"Bloody hell. But it isn't that bad for me really is it?" I ask her and take note of how husky my voice is becoming.

"Everything's bad for you!" She giggles soothingly. "Stop worrying."

I think it's the weed making me paranoid. I'll be back drinking it tomorrow!

"I don't know how permanent my job is either!" I confide allowing another developing concern to escape.

"How come?"

And I go on to explain about the comments so far about the daytime PR role plus the appearance of the police scuppering today.

"Well, plenty of people change job out here. You'll see that I'm sure. You found this job, you can find another." She has a sure confidence that this is the case and she was right about me getting a job in the first place. I'm comforted by her reasoning for now.

"And what happened with Justin?" She asks now.

"Oh god! Well, I did sleep with him." I begin and she's laughing animatedly.

"So tell me more!" She pleads. "He is seriously hot Jodes!"

We pass the spliff back and forth as I explain about him and then about Lee in comparison.

"I saw Justin today actually!" I refer to the incident which inspired me to reach out in the first place.

"He told me 'I don't remember every slag I fuck, but you must've been good *Jodie*' or something like that!"

Tanya's eyes widen. "What did you say?"

I burst out laughing. "Nothing!" I croak and manage to splutter. "But I am a slag aren't I!"

And that's it, Tanya laughs at my giggles and the fit worsens.

"Don't say that!" She tells me off and I can't catch my breath to explain it's alright, I'm not criticising myself.

"But I am!" I squeak eventually. My stomach muscles ache and my face feels all scrunched up like it is stuck in that position. Finally the giggly feeling leaks away as quickly as it came. I am able to explain myself properly.

I accept that being labelled a ‘slag’ is just the way it is for girls. He’s a twat for saying it obviously but I won’t be changing my ways because of him. I love the newest opportunity I have stumbled upon, casual ‘banging’.

Another joint and plenty of chatting shit later Tanya suggests we eat our food. What a delicious, yummy idea!

My stomach groans forcefully as we wait for the microwave to ping. I hadn’t realised I was this hungry. We wolf down our food in contented silence and to my extremely stoned delight she then makes us a hot chocolate and gets out the biscuits.

We have covered a wide range of subjects including where else Tanya has worked, her travelling experience in Thailand (she showed me her traditional bamboo tattoo), how we think the Earth will end, if aliens do really exist and what we envision for our futures.

Tanya bridges a gap between home and here- and inspires me about the routes I could take in the future. She combines an understanding of my feelings with advice fuelled by her own diverse experiences. I feel inspired and extremely content and all I can think about is closing my eyes.

“Tanya can I stay here tonight?” I ask her drowsily having stuffed 7 biscuits into my already bulging tummy.

“Course you can babe.” She replies eyes mere slits in her face.

“Great! I need to go to bed!” I tell her and she shows me to her room. It is pretty in here, smells nice and I lie down on the closest side of her double bed without pulling back the covers or undressing. I am so happy and full up I barely have time to worry about getting into the flat in the morning or anything else before drifting into a blissful sleep.

When Tanya's alarm begins to repetitively bleep it is barely light. What time is it? I wonder and check- to my horror- 20 past 5! I've been more used to getting in at this time than waking up now!

"Ohh." I groan realising Carl will probably be in a club somewhere and I've got to go and meet him for the key.

"Shhh. Let yourself out when you're ready Hun. It was great to see you." Tanya says in a hushed voice.

I don't know how she does her job with its early mornings and endless responsibility. I'd take creepy housemates and drinking poison daily.

"Thanks. You too." I say drowsily and fall back asleep happily.

When my alarm sounds at 10 I'm dizzily disorientated at first. I stare at a photo of Tanya and Alexa on the bedside table and realise not only where I am but that I actually feel quite refreshed. Not just thanks to a satisfying, deep sleep but also because of the good old chat we'd had last night.

I send Carl a message.

Hey I need to get in before 12 to get changed. Ring me when you get this ☺

If I don't hear anything by 11.30 I'll start ringing him! Otherwise I'm going to have to go to work in trackies! I can always try banging on the door if needs be. Although I hold no hope of Andy answering, maybe Carl will hear me?

In the meantime I'm going to treat myself to a proper breakfast somewhere maybe on the beachfront. Tanya wouldn't take a contribution towards the food last night so I still have money in my purse.

THE ARRIVAL

2 o clock arrives and Jamie looks me up and down but doesn't comment on my less than revealing outfit. Carl's phone was off when I decided to ring. And needless to say banging on the apartment door at 11.45 had been fruitless. Don looked none the wiser when I tried to explain my predicament on arrival.

"Jamie," I approach him now to explain. "Andy and Carl, they haven't sorted me a key yet so I couldn't get in this morning to change!"

I am hoping he will pull his weight and push his brother into action.

"Out shagging again you filthy bitch!" He growls smiling and the others overhear.

"Fuckin hell Jodie, you don't mess about do ya!" The lad I have overheard as Ryan comments.

My cheeks smart. I hadn't even thought about the natural conclusion he would come to. Especially after they all witnessed me with Lee.

"No, I," I begin to tell them about Tanya but they don't care and are already chatting to each other about somebody else.

"Go get changed!" Jamie snaps noticing I'm loitering and points out of the bar. "I'm paying you to *attract* the geezers in!"

I turn to see Carl has just entered and his cheery smile instantly annoys me.

I march up to him.

"I need the key." I hold out my palm.

"Ah yeah, sorry, I'll definitely get it sorted today! Here." He gives it to me and I want to retaliate;

You'd better do! But seriously, what would I do? The job and apartment come hand in hand and I need both.

Stalking home I take some calming breaths. At the end of the day, if he doesn't come up with the key and soon (ish) - or if I lose my job for turning up in trackies- I'll book a flight home. It's fine.

Ok, despite what I initially thought, it doesn't feel fine; but it will have to be.

I get back to Blush in less than 15 minutes- somewhat defiantly still choosing the stairs over the lift. Everybody else has gone other than Carl and his PR partner Amy.

"Please get me a key sorted!" I shamefully beg as I place it in his hand.

"Getting in the way of your banging!" He teases me but I'm not in the mood after Jamie's scolding and scowl at him. He pushes my shoulder. "Chill out, chill out, I'll get it sorted."

“Thank you!” I say prematurely. I won’t believe it until it’s in my hand.

I smile at him, then at Amy who smiles in return but it doesn’t reach her eyes.

At 3pm I’m horrified to see a Police car crawl into view and park up in the same place as yesterday. I don’t know if it’s the same one as before but chances are it is and if so there’ll recognise me as being here *again.*

Oh no! I’m so going to get caught and then I will *have* to get a flight home. Nobody likes a sloppy PR, that’s what Heather warned me.

I step onto the veranda and sit down. Because she also said as long as they don’t catch me in the act, I’m ok.

“Fucking Policia.” Don says from beside me now and he fiddles with his rolling backy making himself a cigarette. “Always on the make. The government is.”

I once again can do nothing but sit soaking up the sun, a little bored after constructing a text message to everybody I know.

Just then a taxi rolls up to the curb and out hops a girl even smaller than me, big round boobs and shiny chestnut hair in a high ponytail. She slides large sunglasses onto her dainty round face and looks up then down the street. The taxi driver heaves out a suitcase, places it on the pavement beside her and drives away.

Looking straight at me she heaves her case up the 2 steps and approaches me.

“You don’t know of any jobs going do you?”

I’m pleased it now looks to the officers as if I was waiting for someone all along and tell her to sit down. This is just how I was when I was first looking for work- although she looks like she has come straight from the airport.

“I’m Jodie!” I introduce myself.

“Stacey.” She says. “You will not believe what has happened to me today!”

Don comes out momentarily interrupting her and she orders a ‘large’ gin and tonic- although all the measures out here are large!

“My friend was working at Ice- do you know it?”- I nod and she carries on- “She was all like come out, I’ll get you a job, you can stay at mine! Great I thought, just what I need! I’ve just split up with my boyfriend, you know!” – I nod again dumbly- “And guess. Where. She. Is?”

“I have no idea?” I reply earnestly. Could be anywhere doing anything- it’s Magaluf!

“She. Has. Fucking. Gone. Home!” She cries each word her eyes as round as 10ps and I can’t help but laugh a little at the absurdity.

“Gone home?” I echo.

“Yes! Gone. Home! I landed about- oh 2 hours ago now. Turned my phone on and- BAM- voicemail! Sorry Stacey I’ve had to go! What. The. Actual. Fuck?”

I nod in agreement. That really is crappy. “So, what are you going to do?”

"I. Have. No. Idea." She slurps the drink Don has placed in front of her.

"Maybe you could stop with me." I tell her. "I'd have to ask the landlord, but you know?"

"Maybe they take her as a shot girl." Don suggests now too.

"Yeah!" I smile at her reassuringly. I hope so, I like her!

Carl and the other PR's return; he's got me a key! Great news and even better it could be a sign that I'm deemed likely to last the week! Or maybe Jamie did get on to Andy's case. Either way no more worries about being locked out!

Stacey is a larger than life character, despite only being pint sized and I introduce them after sliding my metal prize into my pocket.

"This is Stacey." I tell him. "She needs a job and somewhere to stay. I thought she could stay with us tonight?"

He runs an eye over her and nods approvingly.

"She can stay but only if she gets a job. Meet Jamie tonight? See what he says."

"Well I haven't exactly got anywhere else to be, have I?" She retorts playfully and I think she has confidence beyond her years. She looks younger than me and childishly I hope she will be my friend.

"The Police have been here all afternoon again." I inform Carl now and he eyes where the car is still parked.

"Aye. It's what Tony's been telling Jamie will happen. But Jamie was insistent a daytime PR would help us make money." He leaves us to it.

So, there we have it my fears are founded. And still relevant! My job is on tenterhooks, not helped one iota by the police keeping watch.

I take my mind off any impending doom and get to know Stacey a little more. She is here running away from an ex she cannot stand to be around any longer- not all that different from my situation then.

We agree she will come home with me at 8, leave her case, change into her 'best' (aka sluttiest) outfit and return to woo Jamie into giving her a job. We swap numbers. She's going to call me with the verdict- I assume she will have to work a trial like me- and then we're going to hit the strip together. Exciting, like old times!

Stacey is filled with unabashed excitement for her new surroundings reminding me again not to take them for granted- it won't be like this forever!

At 10 that night my phone pings with a text from Stacey- she is on a trial until midnight. Then we're free to roam if I'm up for it?

My response; *Yes* ☺

Feeling like the opposite of Cinderella- maybe the bathroom would be cleaner if she was around! I get ready for midnight.

"So how'd it go?" I ask Stacey enthusiastic for success- meaning I have gained a roomie and potentially a Maga-bestie!

"Yeah really well!" She squeals bouncing beside me. "I got the job, and I'll be living with you! I'm selling laughing gas!"

This is new to Blush- but I've seen it being sold in plenty of other venues.

"Did you try one?" I ask her curiously.

"Yeah!" She nods energetically. "I wasn't that keen." She wrinkles her forehead. "Made me feel sick. But oh well! I'm selling em not doing em!"

I wonder how long it will take Stacey to get herself a key as we're swept along the strip and when I notice Club Twenty One's signage coming up I hold my breath. I'm going to see Justin again!

Ben stops us in the crowd and I hastily scan the area for J.

"He's not here!" He tells me and I cringe at being caught out. "Had a massive argument with the manager last night. Got a new job today." He shrugs like it isn't a big thing but to me it feels huge. I thought I'd always know where to find him. Not that I *need* to find him, so it shouldn't matter! But it does, I'm so captivated by him.

"Who's this?" He smiles coyly at Stacey who grins girlishly in return.

"Stacey. She's working at Blush now too."

"Is it your first night Stacey? Come on in for a drink. Maybe we can get to know each other a little better!"

He is full frontal charm offensive and Stacey is putty in his hands fresh to the PR's flirty ways. Ben perches us on one of only two outside tables and fetches us a fishbowl to share.

"So how do you 2 know each other then?" Stacey looks from me to Ben.

"Oh we don't really, just you know, workers!" I reply lightly sure he won't want Cassie bringing up when he's so obviously trying to get into Stacey's knickers. Best to avoid the whole subject!

"Oh, I know Jodie very well!" He drawls smirking and I think here we go; he's going to lift the lid on my encounter with Justin whilst keeping his own behaviour out of the lime light. I hope Stacey won't label me as well.

"I've seen everything." He continues in a theatrical whisper and really rouses Stacey's suspicion now. Where exactly is he going with this? That we all slept in the same room, did my sheets slip off in the night perhaps?

"What?" Stacey probes further. I'm confused too and look at Ben questioningly.

"Oh, my flatmate Justin," he tells her. Here we go! "He takes photos of the girl's he sleeps with. Well, you know *their bits*! Whilst they're asleep!"

I'm stunned, sickened. All of the things he could've said. I actually feel like I could fall off my stool. A horrible image conjures in my mind of Justin and Ben standing over me whilst I was asleep-photographing… *it*!

Ben laughs none the wiser to the discomfit he's caused. It's everyday business to him and he disappears within the swirl on the street. Stacey is smiling but still looks a little nonplussed her cute head cocked to one side.

"He didn't mean that did he?" She says to me now and I just continue to stare back at her my mouth completely disconnected from my brain. "Surely he couldn't have meant it?"

My thoughts exactly! Surely *nobody* would stoop that low, even in Magaluf! Justin is mean but that's just plain weird. But then making it up is even weirder! All of the criminal TV shows I like to watch spin through my mind, are these people even safe to be around? If me and Stacey are both running from failed relationships what are *they* running from? And what have we ran in to? There could be wanted criminals, dangerous murderers lurking around every corner!

"He's just winding me up!" I tell her falsely before I fail prey to manic theorising. "Justin is obnoxious and rude. But he wouldn't do that."

Would he?

"Eugh. Well make sure you point him out. I'll stay away from him just in case!"

Yeah I'd better too, hadn't I? There's hardly the most positive picture forming of him. I should do myself a favour and shut all thoughts of him off. From now on! Maybe those girls left Tanya's team because of him after all! Maybe he took pictures of them too and they found out.

Not wanting to put a downer on Stacey's first night I store the revelation away. I don't even know if it's true but I'm sure I'll have to deal with it later- probably relentlessly mull it over with my inner voice stating it's ultimately my own fault for putting myself in that position. But I mean since when was this ever a normal concern to have. 'I'd better make sure I'm neat down there, just in case he takes photos whilst I'm asleep!'

It's ridiculous and disgusting but I can't be a party-pooper over something so disturbing it's probably untrue.

After the fish bowl we agree to leave weirdo Ben and continue our stretch up the strip. We come across Tokyo Joes next. Ironically this is where Alexa's clap PR worked- I don't want to think about her PR guy warnings now. STD's seem the least of it!

Tokyo Joes is a long skinny upstairs bar. It's busy in here and between us we attract plenty of attention from guys.

"I love this place!" Stacey calls to me giggly, her eyes alive with the strobe lights. "Remind me why I wasn't single sooner!"

I laugh and agree heartily when at that moment a guy barges into us 'accidentally'.

"Oh sorry girls!" He fakes an apology. "I'm Face. Cuz, you know, I'm the Face of the Magaluf strip! Everyone knows me here." He's rabbiting on animatedly and I want to laugh, Face! What is this an amateur Mafia set up! Well Tanya did say the place is run by gangs and cons.

"Let me give you my number." Face tells us. "If you want *anything* I'm your man. Weed, coke, pills, you name it, I can sort it! Where do you work?" He asks us now with his phone out; a battered black Nokia with green screen- completely 'retro' I observe, it must be an original model! "You must be new I haven't seen you before."

"Blush." Stacey tells him adding, "I'm new, how long you been here Jodes?"

"2 weeks?" Before adding proudly. "I was here on holiday but then decided to stay!"

"Ooh, get you! Congratulations. I've not been home in 4 years! I'm going on to Thailand from here. I've been saving all season!"

"Nice!" I say genuinely. I almost wish I hadn't got a great new job opportunity to go home to. Not been home for four years though, my mum would have kittens! And I think I'd definitely be homesick by then.

"So what's your number?" I ask getting out my own phone realising he isn't going to shift else. He reels it off to me and I type it in.

"Give it to your mate yeah. And if anybody needs owt," he winks, "you send then my way! Nice meeting you girls!"

He glides off and I think he has been testing out too much of his own stock judging by the torrent of talk and sweat patches on his shirt.

"Thank you Jodie!" Stacey calls to me now. "You know, for taking me under your wing! I could've ended up alone out here! Nowhere to stay! I'm so glad I met you!"

She's thanking me now like I thanked Tanya last night!

"I'm glad I met you too!" I call back genuinely because not only does it feel good to be sharing it with somebody but also she referred to me as taking her under my wing! And that feels good too, filling me with confidence that I am doing something right out here at least!

Even if I am the subject of a lewd photo shoot and at risk of losing my job any moment!

We finally roll in at half 4, drunk, firm friendship forged.

"You're my Maga-bestie!" Stacey murmurs sleepily in the darkness of our room.

"You're my Maga-bestie too." I reply.

My mind tosses around thoughts of Justin; what my photographed fanny might look like, fears surrounding my security in general- Face and other Mafia wannabes, potential murderers, before succumbing to an agitated form of sleep.

EARLY NIGHT

I won't lie, I feel like dog shit.

I sleep right up until 11.30 before finally dragging myself to the bathroom. A face wash and gag-inducing tooth-brushing session later I'm pulling on some shorts and a bikini top with bleary eyes.

I am hungover and tired and stop to look at Stacey fast sleep- she doesn't start until 9 tonight- bitch, I'm so jealous right now!

But when 8pm painfully crawls around I am so glad it is my turn to crawl into bed.

I go to the closest convenience store when I finish and pick up all my favourite goodies before heading home.

Stacey looks fresh, recently showered she's still in her towel.

"Hey babe!" She greets me and it is nice to find a friendly face waiting for me.

"Hi Hun." I croak and without a care strip off changing into my baggiest shorts and top. "I am hanging!"

Lying on my bed, bag of crisps, sweets and pop by my side, phone and book nearby I let out a huge relieved sigh.

"You have no idea how good that feels!" I tell her. "It has been a long day! Aren't you hungover?"

"I was!" She tells me wryly. "I didn't even wake up until gone midday. I went to the beach with Carl for a bit and met a few of the others- Gemma, have you met her? I liked her and her friend Stevie." She mentions a few more names some I've heard some I haven't. "They went off to work and I sunbathed until they came back. I feel great now, the sun sorts everything out."

Usually it does but today it has beat down on me relentlessly whilst I've slogged it on the strip, my whole body aching. The police didn't come so I at least kept myself going by chatting to those would pay me any attention and observing other worker's as they went about their daily business.

Andy came to do a sound check half way through which was about the most exciting thing that happened. When the PR's were around Carl comments about Stacey;

"She's nice isn't she!" And I'm glad we agree. She *is* nice! She's a lovely little surprise!

"Carl told me about Andy and the key situation. Did you find it difficult to talk to get one?" Stacey asks now whilst strapping up her sandals. "He said it's been a nightmare. But he's going to sort it. I'm going to stay away from that Andy he gives me the creeps." She adds innocently and takes a final look in the mirror.

"Yeah he told me he can be a bit… awkward." I reply. "I found it hard to get a key too. But I don't know which of them was to blame for that really! They both kind of blamed each other."

I try to balance it out because I can't help but feel some sympathy towards disliked Andy. Maybe it's the hangover talking but he doesn't stand a chance with Carl, who's so much easier to get along with. Although, he's not really helped himself to convince me otherwise!

However, I've said my bit; I've tried not to influence her on the subject. She can make up her own mind; as will I.

"Do you want to take my key?" I offer. "I'm not going out tonight."

She glances at the door pausing before replying. "It's ok, Carl said I can use his. I think I'm going to go out with him and the others when I finish."

A romance blossoming maybe? They do look very cute together both being small and with attractive happy faces.

"Andy told me I have to use *his* key!" She says more quietly now.

"Yeah me too!" I tell her.

"I'm staying away from him, he gives me the creeps!" She repeats shuddering dramatically and I can't help but giggle at her ways. Her mind is definitely set. Maybe Andy is one to watch, who knows!

I say goodbye to Stacey and cuddle the thin sheet slowly munching my way through everything I have bought. It's the first time I have eaten and it feels good to finally settle my churning stomach.

I've been thinking about Justin and the apparent photos on and off all day. I was on high alert that I might see him again. But he didn't pass- or he stayed away. Perhaps Ben has told him what I know.

I'm disgusted at the thought but as I suspected I am angry at myself for putting myself in that position. It's not a usual concern when you go home to sleep with somebody- but still if I hadn't have done it- if I hadn't been a *slag*. And who knows what other more dangerous situations I could encounter? Perhaps I should always bring them here- and kick them out again after. And keep a knife under the bed!

I think I saw the old woman girl again though but I was busy with a customer and couldn't afford the distraction. I want to find out more about her but I don't know who to ask, I'm curious plus want to check she's ok! Maybe she's in the same boat as Stacey was!

Not that I can imagine Andy being so hospitable if I came home with another waif or stray! And it's ruthless to acknowledge- but especially one looking like that. It's going to be a task getting him to sort a fourth key I suspect, not that Stacey seems to mind.

But I do hope old woman girl is all right. She sure doesn't look it.

I also recognise a lot more faces now- even seeing Face from last night a few times! He'd waved at me cheerily and it feels nice to be making alliances. It's like being at home and seeing a neighbour or regular from the pub. Familiarity *is* pleasant. One lad in particular blows me a kiss each time he passes by. I have no idea who he is! But I like it.

I didn't expect to miss Lee and really I didn't. I hope he's home safe by now and has a lovely, happy life! He had, not that I realised at the time, played a significant role in taking my thoughts away from Justin. But then perhaps finding out last night that his actions might not always be forgivable hasn't helped. I have *got* to forget him now, he's *obviously* bad news.

Work worries were at the back of my mind today. Carl's comment revealing Tony never wanted to hire me in the first place make me accept that if the police *do* keep coming or trade continues to be unpredictable I really might well lose my job.

And then I'll most likely lose my bed here too, and my new Maga-bestie!

But at worst, I get a flight home early; it isn't the end of the world. It seems like it is- I don't want this world to end so soon but worrying won't change anything.

I've told myself that enough times already and I decide to wash my hair. A long, steamy shower is just what I need and then I'm going to watch telly and snooze for the evening. I can't afford another night out and my liver will be glad for the break!

LEILA IS COMING

The best thing has just happened! Leila called and she is coming to see me!

Stacey has now taken the spare bed but we'll share my single that's fine!

3 whole nights- it'll be like a whole new holiday. She lands late Saturday but will be here on the Magaluf strip before midnight. I'm *so* excited!

My bouncy mood helps me to continually approach the flow of potential customers. Their knockbacks don't deter me and through my jolly persistence we've had one table at least almost all day! I have roughly totted up what people spend and I'm rapidly coming to the conclusion that even with my best efforts yet it does not cover what they are paying me to try.

I have got to keep going until Leila has been and gone! Else she'll be in a similar position to Stacey when she got here on Friday- I'll be on a flight home- sorry Leila!

Except I would never abandon her! If all else fails we'll sleep on the beach if we have to! But, then we'll be like old woman girl, shoeless and dishevelled!

I can't help but laugh at this and even though it's a bit mean I make a mental note to include Leila in the joke when she arrives.

If she doesn't arrive to a failed attempt at becoming a Magaluf worker! Because then it won't be a joke after all. Egg on my face!

Sigh.

Thinking about egg makes me think about food- regular foods that I haven't eaten in so long it seems.

It's a Sunday and in my old working life I'd have been serving roast dinners today to a busy restaurant. Now I'm trying to sell moonshine by all accounts. I must say I suspect there is some truth in the rumours about the alcohol being dodgy. Despite looking slimmer and more toned (a combination of running 5 flights of stairs and diet of mainly fruit and sandwiches), I don't *feel* very healthy. It probably shouldn't come as a surprise that the constant drinking is having side effects. But I am waking up daily with a sore throat, sensitive gums and a deep aching in my gut.

By the time I have a drink alongside the custom I pull in the less I notice it.

If the vodka is poison, then it is the cause but also the cure!

My stomach groans now thinking appreciatively of vegetables and other things that are good for you like gravy and stuffing! Having an out-of-action kitchen has removed many foods from the menu. I'm relying on the convenience of shop bought prepacks and the odd take out (which I can no longer afford).

Stacey pops in when the PR's return at 4. There's talk of Blush having a lock-in tonight which I agree I will be coming to. I tell her ecstatically about Leila's visit before she leaves with Carl to head back to the beach.

I wish I could go with them! I feel left out as I watch them walking away together- but then being careful what I wish for I scan the road for the police and wonder whether they'll make an appearance today. I hope not because I do want this job! Even if I can't go to the beach! Plus if I was to have the same hours as Stacey I'd have to sell shots or laughing gas which I'm not sure I'm cut out for.

The police don't turn up which adds to my high spirit and I manage to become quite friendly with a couple around my parents age. They gasp in horror when I tell them about failing to return after what only started as a holiday. Mother hen Julie clucks about what she'd do if their daughter did the same, she's 21 and at university studying media. The dad, Dave physically pales at the thought!

By 6pm they have gone on their way and the bar and street is dead again. It's mad how it can do this when there are so many thousands of people here!

2 hours shouldn't take too long to trundle by. These lulls never last for long and sure enough 2 guys have appeared strolling towards me.

They look like they have come straight from LA, Miami- somewhere glam like that. They're both black; one is tall with huge thick dreadlocks swept into a high ponytail, the other short, topless and a striking triangle shape! His shoulders, chest and arms are so muscly in comparison to his tiny waist he doesn't look real!

They walk with style, glisten with expensive jewellery, I part expect a camera crew to come running to catch up with them. They are the coolest motherfuckers I have ever seen in my life!

"Hey," the short one greets me and he is American! I feel star stuck as though they are actually famous, I don't think I've ever even spoken to a real American!

He has the widest, whitest smile which I can't help but return.

"Hi!" I half yelp. "Are you stopping for a drink?"

"I sure wish we were. You're a little cutie!" He continues to smile widely and the tall guy whoops with laughter at his friend. I wish I could slide my sunglasses onto my face these characters are too vivid for my eyes.

"Do you work here every day? What's your name?" He's paying me more attention than I expected. I thought I was the one in awe but he hasn't taken his eyes from me and licks his lips at me now suggestively. "I'm Nathan."

He's not much taller than me but more than 4 times as broad! "Have you ever seen a black cock?"

At this his mate howls with laughter and opens his eyes wide in delighted shock.

"Come on man, leave it out!" He jumps to my rescue and I try to laugh it off thinking does Justin count? Because if so, then yes Mr I have! I also see at least 1 cock a day. I wish I could tell him that too- your cock isn't all that special love!

"What's your name?" He asks me to my relief all the same.

"Jodie." I tell him. "What's yours?" I ask the tall guy inviting him to join in the conversation.

"Zion." He tells me and his voice is so deep in comparison to his laugh it takes me by surprise. More than Nathan's question about black cocks!

"So, have you seen one of these before?" Nathan has actually got his black cock out. My eyes ping wider than Zion's were and I have to tear my eyes away from it. "What do you think?"

He replaces the member and grins expectantly.

"Yes, it's erm, great. Very, erm big!" This is just about the most bizarre exchange yet. He nods proudly. "Sooo, are you having a drink?" I chance it.

They amiably decline and carry on their lazy stroll. I wonder who else he will see fit to introduce to his dick!

I decide to take a nap when I finish (not because I'm a granny!) But I want to make sure I'm ready to party until the early hours. It will only be starting at 4am! And I still barely know the team I work with. Stacey knows more about them than I do and she's only been here for 2 days!

THE LOCK-IN

I arrive at Blush around 2.30am it's busy and I stand at the end of the bar ready for Max to serve me when he gets a chance.

Yes I came to this end on purpose; what's wrong with that? And anyway he's a barman, not a PR, maybe they're different!

Andy flicks between the eras of RnB which really puts me into the party spirit; maybe I could like him purely on account of his taste in music!

'I don't see nothing wrong, with a little bump and grind' R Kelly croons and I dance happily on the spot, I agree Robert, neither do I!

I look up and catch Max's eye. Now that's the kind of attraction I'm talking about. Physical chemistry that makes my pulse race- he has that bad boy aura about him like Justin and I bet he's a good kisser too.

"Vodka?" He asks me and I nod. He pours an extra-large amount before topping it up with orange juice and passing it to me. I check if he wants payment but he shakes his head.

"Only when Tony is looking!" He leans over the bar to shout to me and his warm breath on my neck makes me shiver.

I look around, Tony isn't in sight but I spot Don at the other end of the bar on a stool. Outside I find Stacey, Heather, Gemma, Beth and the other 2 shot girls on the veranda.

"Hiya!" We're all greeting each other, Stevie and Jess are properly introduced and in-between chatting, dancing and drinking I observe them all working their magic with the punters.

Each have a different style, Beth is slinky and mysterious, Stevie girly and cute and Jess is smoky, sex-on-extremely-long-legs.

They skilfully convince drunken lads to part with their cash, going back to the bar when their tray is empty for a refill.

"So how does it work then?" I ask Heather when she is by my side. "Do they pay you hourly?"

"No, no! We get a tenner a tray- plus tips. My shots are 4 euros- because I'm the best at it! The other girls can only push 3 euro shots!" She declares loudly not caring if she's overheard. "We pay up after every tray. They make 20 for the bar, *I* make *30*."

She says smugly.

"So that's how it works!" I say and she eyes me now suspiciously.

"There's no room for more shot girls here!" She tells me possessively mistaking my general curiosity.

"No! I couldn't do it! I wouldn't know where to start!" I assure her. That would mean selling 5 trays to make what I'm earning per day. I thought PR-ing was tough but watching the girls as they beg, steal and banter makes me realise it's definitely the favourable option. Even if I do have to enviously watch the others walk to the beach every day.

"How many trays do you usually sell?" She's happy to answer this, giving her another opportunity to boast and make it clear she is queen bee around here.

"Oh it depends but usually 10 or more. On a good night I can get rid of 14!"

I'm surprised, that's pretty good money but actually thinking about her savage selling style it adds up. She virtually steals the money from their wallets- forcing sales to happen. She's a grenade!

Suddenly she bounds off and true to form begins brutally driving 3 boys to buy a Jagerbomb.

Stevie, Gemma and Stacey are back now.

"I'm going to take advantage of Heather's sale!" Stacey informs us and skips over to join in.

"Why don't you all end up doing that?" I ask Gemma suddenly realising this is the first time I've seen any of them work together.

"Oh, we're not allowed to. Stacey is ok because she isn't in direct competition- but she's still got to wait for them to buy from Heather first, she can't just take the sale." Gemma explains to me.

Just like with PR-ing, there are some rules at least. A system allowing the girl's to operate without complete carnage breaking out.

"Yeah, if I was making a sale," Stevie joins in now. "I could say to Gemma, come here, if I'm happy with what I've taken from them already. You know, we're not completely selfish." She smiles sweetly, she seems like a nice girl and I wonder how she ended up here!

"Not *all* completely selfish!" Gemma pipes up now and runs her eyes pointedly over Heather and then Jess as well.

"Yeah well, we wouldn't want to be friends with them anyway, would we?" Stevie grins at Gemma.

I learn they came out together at the start of the season. After Gemma got made redundant from the call centre she worked at and Stevie split with up with the 'tosser', Gemma convinced her to take the plunge and work a season. They share a room and have bounced around a few jobs each before coming to Blush.

They tell me Ryan and Bex (both PR's) are in a relationship- apparently they both left partners behind, Ryan's with a baby! It's dawning on me that everybody here has history- something they are escaping or running from.

"Is anybody else in relationships here?" I pry wondering if Max is in fact with India. It wouldn't surprise me, how could any man look at her and not find her attractive! To be honest a majority of people working here are attractive- it's a predominantly good looking workforce. And those who aren't are bolshie and commanding to make up for it.

"Nah. Most people here just wanna fuck. I think Kristie- out there," she points to a girl on the strip, "she's seeing a DJ, he works at BCM doesn't he Stevie? We don't see much of her."

"Erm, Gemma just cuz all you want to do is fff- have sex, doesn't mean we all do!" Stevie cries looking embarrassed.

"Don't act like you're virgin bloody Mary!" Gemma teases her and nudges me.

"Well. We don't all want to flaunt it, do we?" She retaliates and looks to me for help on the situation.

I laugh and shrug, "whatever floats your boat!" I say sitting firmly on the fence. I wish there was an in-between!

Gemma and Stevie are completely different from each other but their close friendship is obvious. I like them both they're poles apart (opposites attract I suppose!) nice in their own way.

4 o clock creeps round and other than fetching more drinks I've been outside chatting to mainly Stacey, Gemma and Stevie. I follow them inside now and watch Max as he takes their final payments. The music which has been easily audible outside is turned down now and the lights above the bar go out. India begins ushering everyone out and I feel fantastically 'involved'. I'm one of the in-crowd!

Despite it only being staff we are a substantial group for a small bar. Tony still hasn't made an appearance, but Jamie is here his wife Maria, Max, India, Andy, Ryan, girlfriend Bex, Carl, Amy, Sam, Kristie, Heather, Stevie, Jess, Stacey, Gemma, Beth, Don and me. I'm chuffed I finally know and can recall everybody's name.

The doors have been locked, blinds drawn and the music given a little boost. A bottle of vodka and gin is placed on the bar and we're told to help our self. I take a look at the label on the vodka bottle- Rushkinoff. Are you making me ill? Don lights up a spliff filling the air with the all too familiar smell of weed. Everything here is bad for you, Tanya said that and I'm not too naïve to realise it.

Relax, look around; my new world!

Kristie sits chatting to Bex but within minutes she's leaving, perhaps meeting speculative BCM boyfriend. Bex now fervently begins snogging Ryan and so I don't try to speak to them. It might look a bit weird!

I know Stevie said they didn't want to be friends with Jess but I try to talk to her anyway determined to remain non-judgemental. She is indifferent to my small talk and looks at me with cool disinterest as I slowly trail off about Blush seeming like a good place to work.

"Jamie!" She interrupts me and intersects his stride past.

"I need the loo Jess!" He tells her but she is not deterred.

"No. Jamie!" And she darts off leaving me loitering alone by the bar. Well at least I tried! Miserable cow!

India is sitting at a table close by and I approach her now not put off by dismissive Jess. And I'm so glad I did! She reveals she's a seasoned worker having done the Magluf season for 3 years running; as well as travelling Asia *and* doing volunteer work in Africa. I am completely taken with her stories. I want to be as interesting as her! I felt like this when Tanya was telling me her about her experiences too; minus getting a traditional bamboo tattoo- I want to be more like them.

"How old are you?" I ask her. God, I've been so sheltered! Just meeting American's on the strip felt like an achievement to me.

"29." She smiles. "I'll settle down when I'm 30!" She adds with a wink.

Well 30 is still 5 years away for me I think positively. Plenty of time for more daring adventures yet! When I came away I felt like I had spent a lifetime with the stupid prick. Yes I wasted too much time on him but it's nothing in the grand scheme of things! In some ways he is responsible for setting off the chain reaction of events which have resulted in me being here.

Wow, I never thought I'd say this, but thank you stupid prick!

I love it when Stacey comes over and asks me if I need the toilet- definite Maga besties! And I can't wait to introduce her to my original one when she gets here on Saturday! I ask her if she's spoken to Jess much but she shakes her head.

"She doesn't speak to me so I don't speak to her!" She tells me and shrugs. "Nobody likes her. Gemma said so."

Back out in the bar we head over to Gemma and Beth with Stacey. To my delight Max comes to join us. I have been consistently meeting his eye whilst he spoke to Amy and I chatted to India. And Amy comes to stand by his side with us now too.

Max gently flirts with us all. Gemma takes it all in her stride, bantering with him but keeping a clear, firm distance between them. Amy isn't so subtle and I get the distinct feeling she's becoming more and more agitated by the attention he pays to us.

This seems to only spur Max on as he cruelly shuns her advances but continues to give me a steady longing stare. Jess stomps out of the bar dramatically momentarily distracting me and I wonder what conversation she's had with Jamie.

"So is that your girlfriend or something?" I give Max chance to explain the behaviour when Amy finally scuttles away to join Andy.

"No!" He appeals holding up his hands but his smirk suggests there is more to it. More fool her for hanging around and allowing him to treat her that way!

Don't overcomplicate your relationships, I tell myself remembering Gemma's clear advice. But he smells so good and without the bar separating us I can't help but want to be in his personal space.

"You said that a little too quickly!" I tease him before adding. "Don't worry, I'm used to Magaluf by now, I know what goes on out here!"

"Oh, you do, do you?" He asks prolonging his gaze into my eyes. I notice they look darker now as though the brown flecks have expanded, almost blotting out any bright green from before. "And here was me thinking you're a good girl."

"No way!" I disagree although by Magaluf standards I'm positively an angel. I don't want to be seen as a 'good girl', I realise and narrow my eyes in what I hope is a seductive manner. "Would a good girl stay here and work instead of going home with her friends?" I retort challengingly.

"Hmm well. Either a very bad girl indeed. Or just downright stupid!" He is joking but the comment resounds with me. He's got a point.

When I clock the time is gone 6am I make up my mind to go home. I have had my fun and haven't made any stupid decisions- like sleep with Max in the cellar. No, honestly I haven't done that. Yet!

"Stacey, I'm gunna go Hun. You ok to walk back with Carl because he's got the other key?" I check with her. There's no way she'd consider walking back with Andy so no point mentioning him.

Thanks to her start time being a lot later than mine I sincerely doubt she will want to leave now and I am right.

As I call my goodbyes to India, Gemma and Beth, Max looks for a moment like he's going to offer to walk me home- or come home with me- but I don't get the chance to find out because Don sidles up to me now.

"I'll walk you back Jodie. I'm leaving now too." His gruff voice rumbles above the music which is still pouring out- the party in full swing.

"You really don't have to!" I tell him. "It's only up there!"

He is unmoving though and nods to the door. We leave and step out onto a trashed street lit by pale sunlight. And head in the direction of the alley way.

"You have to keep your wits about you." He warns me in his strong Spanish accent as we walk doing our best to step round litter. "Especially at this time when nobody else is around."

"Oh ok! Thanks." I reply hesitantly and shudder, wrapping my arms tight around me. I know about the prostitutes targeting drunken men but I hadn't given serious credit to the dangers which could be lurking for me.

Psychos, murderers, stalkers, weirdos and robbers too!

We reach the apartment block and Don gives me a farewell nod returning to the alleyway to make his own tracks home. I wonder where he lives as I wearily climb the stairs to my floor. I can't imagine him sharing a worker's apartment- I assume he is a local being Spanish. He could have a wife and kids at home- or he too could be running from something just like everybody else seems to be.

I set an alarm for 11.15. 4 hours and 52 minutes my phone informs me spitefully and I console myself, it's almost 5 hours, I'll be fine.

IT HAPPENS

Surprisingly I wake up 10 minutes before my alarm and even more surprisingly I don't feel like a badgers bum. Stacey is snoring profusely beside me. For something so tiny she can certainly rock the room- perhaps that's what's woken me!

I take a shower and sift through the outfits I have already worn. I'm out of clean underwear and could do with some other new clothes too! Pay day tomorrow so I'll pay my rent and treat myself- I can get by barely spending anything living on crisps and free drinks.

I can't believe I've almost been doing this for a week! I've been away for almost 2.It feels a lot longer!

I sit at the desk and take a long hard look at myself in the mirror and realise I actually quite like what I see. I look different. A little tired yes but I *feel* different too. (And I don't just mean from the *Rushkinoff*!). Perhaps the most significant change is how I actually feel about myself.

"How you feel Jodie?" Don asks me when I arrive at Blush and I smile telling him.

"Good thanks," I don't feel like I can truthfully declare bloody fabulous actually, never better! Instead I ask for a bottle of water.

“How do you ask ‘how are you’ in Spanish?” I query now and he smiles kindly making me pleased I asked.

“Que tal.” He tells me. “Or como estas? Bien is good, no bien is bad.”

“Ok!” I smile brightly at him I remember now. I took Spanish at GCSE but I’ve forgotten a lot of it. “Bien! Can you ask me in Espanol manana?” *Spanish, tomorrow.*

I remind myself of Del Boy (Only Fools and Horses- family favourite!) and his tragic attempts at French.

“Of course! Si!” He laughs nodding.

Nothing wrong with learning a little of the local lingo!

“Gracias!” I pick up my bottle. *Thanks.*

“De nada.” He states. *Your welcome!*

The sun is shining as it always is and a T-shirt I saw a guy wearing once in Greece, ‘Sun is happiness’ springs to mind. I was only young but I always knew it was true to me- perhaps I was always destined for this.

It is quieter today and I stroll back and forth. Andy comes to do a sound check, acknowledging me with a grunt. Honoured! At 2 o clock the PR’s turn up, Ryan and Bex first, Amy who completely ignores me, Carl who tells me he’s completely hungover, Kristie and then Sam.

Everybody talks about last night and I join in with their chat. It turns out they went back to Ryan and Bex’s place- the party hadn’t finished until half 8 this morning. It is obvious they are feeling the consequences because despite usually being rowdy they clearly lack the energy.

Jamie arrives late and looks an absolute state.

"Here he is!" Carl jeers but without his usual vigour. "True what they say then once you're over 30! Look at him, he's a mess."

"Shut it." He growls and Carl's mouth actually snaps shut. A silence descends on the group. "Tony found out about the party last night. He's faking fuming."

With this he stomps off leaving it to resonate that his foul mood is more than just a hangover.

"Tony didn't know?" "He'll be docking wages." "Heads are gunna roll!"

Whilst speculation forms I wonder if I'm in danger, I was there after all will I be due punishment for my participation? As if in symbolic warning I spot the police car rolling into the position it had taken up before.

Double fack!

Jamie reappears. It looks like he has been to splash water on his face in the toilet. Not a good sign.

"Well, come on then!" He barks. "You know the drill. Get out there and work your arses off." He marches towards the veranda stops in his tracks. "For fack sake!"

He spins around and stamps his foot looking like a snarling bull and locking his eyes on my face. "When did they turn up?" He asks exasperatedly.

"Just now!" I say defensively as though I'm personally responsible for conjuring them.

He throws his arms into the air plainly agitated. "Great! Just facking great."

I stand in the bar after they've all gone except for Don and Andy. I look at Don who shrugs and then Andy who smirks seemingly enjoying every moment of his brother's and my distress. Cheers *mate*!

Despite wanting to get away from him I also don't want to go out onto the veranda. What if it's the same Police? What if they recognise me as the same girl here again? If I get the bar a fine my time here will be terminado! *Finished*!

So I loiter inside instead awkwardly and wish Andy would put some music on like he usually does. If he did I could at least pass the time asking Don for more revival lessons in basic Spanish without feeling self-conscious.

Barely 10 minutes has inched by, they've been long and silent. I've sat, paced and looked at my phone screen intently and still no music comes on. Tony marches into the bar suddenly and I take an audible sharp intake of breath.

Don looks up and obviously Andy's sound check won't start now. Tony and Don begin talking rapidly in heated Spanish and I wonder if Andy can understand them. I have no hope of interpreting the quick exchange.

Even if I'd started Spanish lessons with Don last week I would still be nowhere near able to eavesdrop and I feel silly for my 'learn Spanish' crusade.

The conversation is serious, but I don't hear any mention of fiesta *party* in relation to last night. I do hear *Policia* repeated by Tony a number of times and I begin to realise the likelihood of this directly affecting me.

Tony rounds on me now and I'm physically intimidated by his huge stature. No wonder Jamie was so shaken after having a ruckus with this beast of a man.

"Jo-die we no need day time PR." He tells me bluntly and my heart instantly sinks through the floor.

I have to fight a severe urge to cry, my mortification that Andy is watching the whole thing, becomes the motivation not to do so.

I thought I had accepted it might come to this! Had reasonable doubts and tossed them aside thinking I'll deal with it *if* it happens. But now it has I am so bitterly disappointed. I have literally just made friends! Leila has booked to come at the weekend! Will they let me stay if I can pay my way? But would I really want to! Living in the shadow of my former and more successful work mates... becoming haggard old woman girl!

"Jamie pay you later." He continues. "Go home, Jo-die. Bastard Policia here all the time."

"Ok." I hold back tears, avoid Don's eyes in case they're kind and tip me over the edge. And Andy's because I know he'll be watching me intently. I feel sick. I thought I had it so good.

Well there'll be no 'como estas' tomorrow morning will there? Muy no bien! *Not good at all.*

By the time I take the steps from the veranda to the strip emotion really hits me and hot frustrated tears arrive fast and heavy.

I want to walk home with my eyes shut- refusing to look at what I have to leave behind. It was only just getting started. I just want to get inside so that I can really let my grief go. A good old fashioned cry is in order.

I'm pleased that Stacey isn't here. For a solid half an hour anything and everything that has happened over the last fortnight adds to my unharnessed emotions. I cry for my lost job and I cry over Justin, memories of the holiday, my enlightening conversations with Tanya and India. I cry for myself, for the poor old me and the shit she'd put up with, who came here so completely unaware of the 'me' she'd be introduced to.

And finally my tears are no longer sad; or bitter sweet. They stop and my eyes are refreshingly wet. I feel determination seep calmly over me.

I can get myself another job. It happens all the time out here. I can stay, I'll find a new apartment too if needs be.

I pad to the bathroom and look at my puffy reflection in the smattered and smeared mirror. It's a far cry from the girl looking back at me this morning. She will be back soon enough but until then I cannot go out to look for a job like this!

I fetch my flip-flops and have a soothing (trying to ignore the grime) shower. Do I want another job PR-ing? Chances are a lot of day time PR's are in my position especially with the 'government on the make' and it being a 'quiet season'. So that'd mean PR-ing at night! There aren't many girls who do that. And Heather who I thought would suit the role turns out to be top shotter! That's the level of competition. Being a shot girl is hardly an option is it? She already warned me of her feelings about an extra shot girl at Blush- the only place I'd perhaps dare to try it out- no room at the inn. I'm looking very short of options, I realise as I shut off the water.

Wrapped in a towel I lie on my bed completely glum and exhausted. I can't even settle on *what* job- bar crawl rep, ticket seller, pole dancer? Perhaps I took lessons in pole dancing for a reason? But no the idea cannot even sprout. I'm just not good enough and nowhere near as confident either.

I should at least go to the beach and enjoy my day. Ironically it's what I wanted only a couple of days ago but now I can't bear the thought of seeing Stacey and the others. I feel feeble from the energy spent wracking my nerves. I continue to lie on my bed staring at the ceiling. I am safe in this box. I don't have to worry about telling anybody just yet; including Leila. There's really nothing to joke about now.

I nod off and dream that Magaluf is actually an active volcano… which is erupting. You can't go there, my dream self is telling me from where I hover above the sea watching the carnage unfold. You can't go there now.

I wake up realising there's a tapping on my door. Oh no, who is it and what time is it? And what must I look like!

"Hello?" I call out when the door taps again.

"Jodie?" Carl says softly. "Jamie's here to see you. Can he come in?"

I'm naked in bed in the middle of the day having virtually cried myself to sleep- no, he cannot come in.

"Hold on Carl. Can he wait in the living room, I won't be a sec?"

"What you doing, frigging yourself?" He asks and I have to smile. I'll even miss the crudeness.

"Don't be daft," I shout in reply. "I'm just not dressed!"

"He won't mind that." The voice continues from behind the door and I laugh again glad for the distraction. This is going to be an awful conversation; one of many when I have to start telling everyone.

Jamie is sitting on the sofa when I emerge and I try to paste on a smile over my sadness.

"Hiya Jodes." He addresses me smiling. "Here's your wages for the week." He hands over a wad of cash and looks altogether pleased in the face of somebody else's shit situation. Maybe he and his brother share some qualities after all.

"Cheers!" I take it from him and turn to leave.

"Jodie wait!" He says now and I stop dead tiny seedlings of hope shooting into my chest. "I've got an offer for you?"

I stop and turn reserving judgement waiting for him to continue.

"Jess has gone." He says bluntly. "So how do you fancy your chances at being a shot girl?"

"What?"

A shot girl! Jess has gone? Did she get the sack too? Because nobody likes her, or something she said last night perhaps.

"Yes or no Jodes, come on?" He's standing now looking impatient.

"Yes, yes of course!" I say before I can fully think it over and before he can change his mind! Faced with no job or a job this is an easy contest. Heather was my only concern but if Jess has gone there's no problem!

"You'll have to do 2 hours in the day still- say 4 till 6? That's when those pigs seem to fack off. Then 11 till 4 in the bar, at night?"

I nod in agreement. The hours are hardly negotiable. And this way I can join in with Stacey and the other's when they stay out late or go to the beach! And at least I've still got a chance at a job. I mean, shot girl?

"Start tomorrow night. You look like shit!" He tells me and marches out. But I don't care! I don't feel like shit! I feel amazing!

I go back to my room feeling overwhelmed. Today has been a complete emotional rollercoaster. When one door closes, another opens- that's just the way of the world isn't it! Becoming a shot girl must be my next way in this world then. I lie back thinking over the prospect, I can't believe my luck! And on the other hand I know I need more than just luck on my side now.

FUCK YOU!

I've called Leila and explained the changes. I completely played it down to her as though I'd taken the role change in my confident Magaluf stride! Still dazed at the idea of coming over she isn't fazed when I say she will have to stay at work with me all night every night! I think she's actually a little relieved. She could even prove useful- 2 for the price of 1!

I also call my mum to check in- obviously I tell her all is going well and don't bother to mention the drama in my work life. I think of mother hen Julie, she'd made me realise just how frantically concerned mum will actually be- and she needn't be. Yesterday was emotional, and the whole experience so far has challenged me in a number of ways but I've emerged victorious, ready to fight another day.

I drop Tanya a text;

I've changed role, I'm a shot girl now!

She will understand the trade I am embarking on, appreciate the specifics of the role. The initial conversation we'd had about me staying had blown my mind. A PR! A shot girl? It had seemed so ludicrous.

I've been through my outfits deciding what will be suitable to wear as a 'shot girl'. It's the complete opposite to sorting out clothes that are suitable for a teaching assistant- not short enough, not low cut enough.

If I'm taking my lead from what Jamie wanted me to wear as a PR and the girls already doing the job then the more revealing the better.

After selecting 5 or so outfits which fit the bill I decide to go and find a few more items to add to the collection.

Nobody else is awake yet and I quietly let myself out of the flat. I assume Stacey will have heard about my change in job but I can't wait to see her reaction.

After a morning shopping I return to find her getting ready to go out.

"Oh Jodie!" She squeals- it's almost midday- usually I'd be rushing off for 8 long hours of PR-ing. "I heard about your job! What the actual fuck!"

"I know, but now I'll be working with you guys!" I exclaim.

"So you're ok about it?" She asks.

"Yes! It was a bit of a shock at first obviously! And I hope I'm going to be ok at it!"

"Of course you'll be ok at it! More than ok! Just look at you, you sexy bitch!" She laughs happily. "So are you coming to the beach?"

"Yes, why not!" I cry out gleefully. She called me a sexy bitch! Nobody has ever called me a sexy bitch! "Do you want to see what I've bought first?"

I swing 3 plastic carriers onto my bed.

"Duurr! Yes!" She demands.

After gaining approval for all of my new slinky garments- things I wouldn't dream of wearing at home- we head off in the direction of the beach. I take Stacey's lead because she knows where we're headed. On and across the sand we go until I spot Gemma, Stevie, Beth, Ryan and Bex in the distance.

We wave when they see us and plonk ourselves down amongst the group.

"You're joining us shot girls then?" Stevie asks me once we're settled.

"Yes, I'm looking forward to it!" This is a bit of a white lie because although I am, every time I think about the actual selling part apprehension bristles. 10 trays Heather had said!

"Yeah we are too aren't we?" Stevie grins at us all and they nod.

"I'm just glad they got rid of Jess. She was stuck up!" Beth adds.

"Yeah but she was fit!" Ryan chimes in. Bex slaps his arm but she's smiling at him gooey-eyed.

"So is Jodes." Gemma coos.

Ryan shrugs, "yeah I suppose. But we already have a load of blondies don't we!"

"Oy!" Bex warns him now; she has black hair with striking blue eyes. She pouts her full lips eyeing him more sternly.

"I'm just saying babe. Variety is key in life! You'll always be my number one girl, you know that!" He mumbles the last sentence into her neck and they begin kissing passionately.

I look away and find the others with their eyebrows raised exchanging smirks.

"So why did they get rid of her?" I ask out of interest.

"Jamie was pissed off that Tony got rid of you but he said someone had to go." Gemma tells me. "So he told Jess to fuck off!"

"Isn't it great?" Stevie grins kindly.

"Nobody liked her anyway." Gemma continues. "And Jamie says she was always complaining about Tony."

"Oh, ok!" I reply and the chat continues. She hardly made it easy to be liked, so perhaps Gemma is right about 'nobody' liking her. I'm trying to kick the habit of taking everything at face value but it makes me feel better for feeling so happy about it all! I feel bad for her job loss- particularly if it's at the gain of mine- because if Jamie did drop her for me, that means I've got to do at least as well as she was doing. Tony will be watching me like a hawk and I wonder what complaints Jess had about him. I decide to set myself a target of 6 trays. One over what they saw fit to pay me during my PR shifts.

Randy tales from Gemma, Beth and to Bex's distaste Ryan are shared over the afternoon. The melting pot of UK accents fixates me. I look at each person as they talk, they're still new to me but I can find similarities in all of them from people I know back home.

It's like a parallel universe but this version is so much hotter and more vibrant.

Carl lollops along at almost 2 and he and Ryan talk animatedly as they stroll away from us, with Bex trailing behind.

"God, I feel sorry for her!" Stacey blurts once they've walked away.

"Me too." Stevie agrees.

"I don't!" Gemma declares sounding heartless but Beth agrees with her. The 3 remaining faces look at her questioningly and she elaborates. "Well! She knew what he was like; I mean he left his girlfriend and baby to be with her for a start! If you lie with dogs, expect to catch fleas!"

"Did he really!" Stacey exclaims and I giggle at the expression. I know it's true!

"*Apparently*!" Stevie balances the situation. "We don't *know* that!"

"Cause we do. Ryan told Carl and he told me. Lads don't twist things like girls!"

"You'd be surprised!" I can't help but joke at this. Now I am the one faced with questioning faces, wanting to know more. I proceed to tell them a little about my experience of stupid prick.

It was always *my* fault when he behaved the way he did. His web of reasoning never failed to snag me, and quickly wrap me up into believing he was right, as usual.

This opens up a whole can of worms with Stacey telling us more about her commitment-phobe ex and Stevie divulging a little about the tosser- with Gemma topping it up, a lot.

Poor Stevie! Turns out the tosser was just that- a complete tosser to her! He had openly flirted with other girl's and treated her like a complete doormat. At least stupid prick bothered to try and charm me at times!

"Well I'm proud of you!" I tell Stevie full of warmth. "I'm proud of us all. We're here, giving all of the negative people from our life a huge middle finger!"

I prod my middle finger into the open air to demonstrate the gesture.

"Well, fuck you!" Gemma laughs and also puts up her middle finger.

"Fuck you all!" I join in laughing heartily now.

"Fuck you!" We all cry together giving each other the finger. I'm sure I still hear Stevie say 'F' you instead; she has somehow remained unaffected by Magaluf and I like her even more for her rare shyness.

4 o clock comes around a lot quicker than I'd anticipated and I ask Stacey what her plan is for after 6 when I'll be finished again until later.

Nerves flower in my stomach- later when I'll be a shot girl.

"You can come to ours for dinner if you like Jodie?" Stevie asks me now and I look at the smiling faces. "We'll walk up to you at 6?"

"Brilliant ok. Thanks! See you soon."

I feel like I could float like a butterfly. The afternoon has been such a giggle and it has helped me to appease some of the worry about tonight- at least I'll have the girl's around to support me. I mean, Stevie has busted out the word 'team' twice and we even have a private joke! (The 'f you' middle finger has already appeared a number of times during our conversations).

2 hours should fly by. Then I'll be having dinner with them and get the chance to scope out their living arrangements. Then with the

time I'm left to kill I intend on practising some pouty poses in the mirror. Sad I know, but necessary I feel.

When half ten rolls around my stomach is churning with a torrent of adrenalin. I have been applying make-up for almost 40 minutes- my eyes extra dark and lips bright pink (the exact same as I did for *his* birthday night out!) and spent time assembling my hair carefully so that it tumbles around my face.

I vainly amaze at how well applied make-up changes everything! I think I could rate as a firm 8 at least and I feel ready to conquer anything!

Tanya said the girl's prey on drunken boys and I've witnessed for myself the types of tactics employed. I've practised pout perfection and how to narrow my eyes to convey sex-goddess, so now, bring on the sales!

This is it! I leave the apartment and strut to Blush.

FUCK ME!

"Fuck me Jodie!" Carl yells when he spots me 10 metres away.

Jamie and Ryan turn to look and their mouths hang open. This is an extremely good sign! I won't lie; their reactions cause me to tingle happily all over.

"Fuck me!" Jamie echoes. "Where *you* been hiding!"

I notice Amy scowling from where she's bartering with a group of guys. But I'm bolstered by the feedback from the boys and smirk at Carl before climbing the steps to Blush, waving at Gemma and Beth as I pass them.

Inside I don't need to signal Max he spots me instantly eyes burning intensely.

"Wow." He says simply.

"I'm working as shot girl now!" I call to him over the music.

"I can tell!" He raises his eyebrows. Then smiles, "You look good though. Hold on I'll sort you out."

He makes me a drink and I sip it watching as he grabs one of the large trays from under the bar and begins arranging 10 small shot glasses around the edge. He pours something into them all and I'm wondering is it Sambuca perhaps, when he places a salt pot and plate of lemons in the middle.

"Tequila!" I gasp. There's no way I can sell tequila! Who even likes tequila? I cast my mind back to glugging it from a topless Tanya. I am *not* resorting to that! Talk about give me a hard sell; I'll *never* sell 60 of these!

"3 euros a shot. Let's see how good you *really* are!" His grin is lizard like- his eyes challenging and brighter green. He holds out a money belt and I strap it around my waist, tightening it which makes me feel pleased. I take the tray from him and look at his expression wondering if how he treated Amy should serve as a warning. But his cockiness is still attractive. What can I say I'm a sucker for punishment!

Ok, this is it. And I have no idea where to start!

There are a couple of people inside and I begin by doing the rounds in here.

"Fancy a shot?" I'm shouting in their ears but to no avail. One guy nearly smashes the whole tray out of my hand! I grab it though avoiding too much spillage- that would've been a great start! Lesson learned.

I go outside to join the others. Gemma is standing with a group of four guys spurting shots into each of their mouths in turn.

Stacey, Stevie, Beth and Heather are leaning on a table looking bored.

"Alright girl's. Been busy?" I ask them conversationally.

“Not really.” Beth tells me. “It’ll get busier though. Midnight onwards.”

“I hope so!” I reply.

“What you got?” Stacey asks me eyeing the salt pot. “Tequila?”

I nod glumly, the distaste on her face reflecting my own feelings.

“They’re testing you.” Heather tells me. “If you can sell them, you can sell anything!”

I feel happier that we’re in agreement that selling these shots won’t be an easy task. But that isn’t going to make me my money- or keep me my job. There’s no doubt about it, I have got my work cut out.

Midnight comes and goes and finally there is a regular movement of people into the bar.

“Evening lads.” I greet a group of 3. I am aiming for a style in-between Gemma’s foxiness and Stacey’s playful girly act. “You look like the kind of guys who can handle a shot of tequila!”

One looks away disgusted.

“No thanks!” He tells me stubbornly I’m not giving up that easily though and continue with my reverse psychology.

“What’s the matter can’t you handle it! I had you down as being more of a man than that!” I continue pushing, if I can convince just one of them I’m in with a chance. “Only 3 euros, come on and you even get free salt and lemon!”

At this 2 of them laugh and I can feel my first sale edging tentatively toward me.

"Well it'll make a change from shots of peach Archers." One of them shrugs referring to the bog standard freebies. And a firework of achievement explodes prematurely inside of me.

"Go on!" I encourage him. He reaches for his wallet and passes me a ten. Yes!

"Keep the change." He winks removing 3 from the tray. "Here we go lads."

"You can have mine." The disinterested third tells me. "I really can't do tequila."

I look over my shoulder seizing the opportunity.

"Stevie! Come here." I call over to her. "I'll do the tequila but you can buy one of my friend Stevie's shots. That way you won't miss out."

He gives me a lingering look knowing I have set him up. Stevie grins at me realising I've thrown her a sale. Hopefully she will return the favour later.

"Pink or black Sambuca?" She smiles sweetly. "I'll have a pink one. 6 euros please."

He rolls his eyes but not wanting to lose face and perhaps charmed by Stevie's natural innocence also reaches for his wallet.

To my first sale! I think as I tip some salt onto my hand and raise the yellowy shot. If the vodka is poison then this is probably petrol. The salt barely disguises the disgusting taste and I ram the lemon into my mouth. Bitter relief floods my tongue and throat, quelling the burn in my tummy.

The lemon makes its ok. If I have to do another, I'll use even more salt; great make it taste like sea water, yay!

3 shots down, 7 to go! 57 to go actually I remind myself but with fresh first sale confidence I head back inside to track down any boys drunk enough to part with their cash for tequila shots.

4 boys are dancing wildly around a tall table and I decide they look crazy and therefore potential customers.

Placing the tray on the table and out of the reach of their flailing arms I grin to them and switch between gesturing a shot technique and thumbs up.

"What is it?" One leans in and asks; his English is heavily accented he sounds Swedish I think.

"Tequila!" I tell him. He nods approvingly. I was right to judge them as crazy! He hands over 12 euros and I wait for them to neck them before stacking the miniature cups back onto my tray. Only 3 to go! It's been almost 2 hours though let's not get too chuffed.

It takes another 40 minutes of alternating between the veranda and inside to get rid of my last 3. I triumphantly take my tray to the bar and Max checks an imaginary watch on his wrist.

"Took your time didn't you?" He teases me with hard green eyes and begins refilling the tray. I'm determined to make him take me seriously as a shot girl! I grit my teeth in determination to sell this one faster.

"20 euros Jodie." He charges me for my first tray leaving me with my wage so far of 11 euros. 1 extra thanks to the first guy telling me to keep the change. I get another free drink for my efforts though and I need the alcohol to further fuel my courage.

Outside Heather is making 3 men in their late forties buy from her.

One of them hands her a twenty for 3 cups after refusing to buy her one. She takes it and hands out the cups. Once they have finished the shots she stacks the cups and makes to walk back to us.

"Ay!" The paying geezer calls to her. "You haven't given me my change!"

"What change?" She booms staring at him. "I don't owe you anything."

"Bitch you owe me 8 euros!"

She shrugs unconcerned and picks up a Jagerbomb cup holding it up in salute and then necks it before calling, "So complain to the boss!"

I am stunned. She just full on robbed him. I look around to see if anybody else has witnessed it.

Gemma is returning from making a sale but has missed it all.

"Heather!" I gasp when she also comes to us. "You just stole from him!"

"Argh, tight bastard should've bought me one then." She says it like its standard practise and Gemma doesn't look fazed chiming in now;

"Jodie, you *always* have to get something extra out of it. Always take one for yourself and charge them for it!"

"*And* keep the change!" Heather adds.

I look at my fresh ten shots and think of the 11 euros I've made so far. Even if they let me keep my job I can hardly live on that earning! I'd drink all 10 if somebody else paid for them!

Another influx of customers hit the bar and I get back to work. I find a group of 6 surrounding a small table.

"Tequila anyone?" I ask brightly and flash a grin.

"How much?" One asks. He's interested. I narrow my eyes for good measure hoping I resemble the minx I saw in the mirror earlier.

"3 euros!" I try to say as lightly as possible as though it isn't extortionate for a thimble of petrol.

"3 euros! You're having a laugh aint ya!"

"It's probably rocket fuel." A different voice comments reading my mind.

"Good way to get your night going!" I joke. "Maybe I should charge double."

This gains me a laugh and I realise I'm close to getting rid of 6 in one go. Well 7 if I follow the shot girl advice and get them to buy me one.

"Come on Nick, get your dough out." One of them chides cue: argument about who should buy.

Nominated guy, Nick, begins to sift through his pockets.

"Twenty 1," I tell him. "The rule is you've got to buy me one too."

"Is there also a rule that I get to lick the salt off your tits?" He quips back to a rowdy eruption of laughter.

I feel my cheeks blush at the suggestion. As if!

"I'll pay extra!" He jokes now. Who is selling to whom here!

"No, no, I couldn't!" I back out realising he's serious. "I'd get told off."

This is a blatant lie because I'm pretty sure the bar will welcome anything I can do to bring in the cash. Although I'm not sure how it sits with the shot girl rules!

"Ok, well how about I take the lemon out of your mouth?" He continues to push his luck and I feel the sale slipping away.

"Ok, ok." I agree laughing. "But you'll have to pay 25."

His eyes widen. "Wow, you're tough. Fine."

I take the notes and place the rind of lemon between my teeth ready for him to take it from me.

He necks the shot and lunges forward throwing his lips round the lemon slice and engulfing me in a clumsy kiss.

I feel hard, sharp bristles on my mouth and I release the lemon recoiling. He's old enough to be my dad and it makes me feel a bit weird.

The group cheers and I rearrange my face into a smile- I have just made a bulk sale after all.

"Had to get my money's worth!" He tells me brazenly licking his lips and I can see lip stick has transferred onto his face. I can't help but shudder and wipe my own mouth. It must be in the same smudged state after the impromptu kiss.

"You should buy another for that!" Gemma snarls as she brushes past to meet another group. He laughs and begins nodding.

"I will buy another," he tells me slowly now gazing at me. "But only for a proper kiss."

I stare at him for a moment feeling queasy from how he is looking at me. But then this is exactly what I was aiming for, wasn't it? Sexual attention that would ultimately help me to sell my shots?

I lick my lips and swallow making a decision.

"Twenty euros." I tell him firmly. "The last 3 shots and a kiss for 20 euros." Even as the words hang between us I still can't quite believe I've said them. I haven't done my shot from the first round and neck it bravely without the salt then realising my error gag into a slice of lemon.

"You're on." He claps his hands not noticing.

I quiver nauseated but excited. He's so easily taken the bait! I mean, what's a quick kiss, it's not like I've got to see him again!

I stuff his money safely into my pouch. He holds a shot out to me and I decline thinking if I'm sick now I'll have to hand the money back and that just cannot happen!

Technically I've already kissed him once. And I'm not going to use my tongue! That's just gross.

Nick leans in and his kiss is quick, dry and hard- over in seconds. His friends cheer and I quickly scan my tray to check I have the glasses, salt and lemon back on my tray. Mission accomplished- tray 2 done!

"Don't tell the missus!" He squawks excitedly to his mates. And I return to the bar trying not to overthink the comment. I've sold another tray, yay! And I've made tips! But I did just sell a kiss to a possibly married man. I can't help but feel a little sordid.

If I'd known he'd got a partner I wouldn't have done it. I didn't even think to check for a ring!

"Good girl!" Max calls to me now loosening the chain of thoughts tightening on my heart. I smile feeling a little triumphant noticing his eyes have darkened slightly. I've impressed him.

I watch him fill up another ten shots and think, next time I'll look for a ring! And then I catch myself, next time? It's not exactly a realistic selling technique is it?

I do have a job to do though. And as I've also been regularly told, you gotta use your looks; do what you need to do!

I could offer to hold the lemon in my mouth as a unique selling point. After all Gemma uses her syringes to her advantage and Beth has funky looking test tubes which help her to sell. It isn't too risqué and if it makes money quicker then so be it.

"Get em tiger." Max growls over the music as he slides the third tray over. I flush. Is his attraction to me based purely on my success?

I determinedly swig the drink he's given me. If it wasn't for the ice I could've done it in one, but it takes 3 separate attempts before it's all gone.

After my not-so-bad-girl display I march straight over to an inside group of 5 by the door but as I can open my mouth to speak one shouts.

"Fuck off will you!"

So I skirt round them and go back out on the veranda.

"How many you sold?" Stacey asks me when I join her and Stevie.

"2 trays." I tell her. I won't explain about me exploiting myself to achieve it! If I carry on with *that* behaviour it'll only be a matter of time before she sees anyway.

But I'm still not ready to admit to myself that not only have I done it, I'm considering doing it again.

"Here we go, we'll get these together." She tells me excitedly pointing to a group just settling around a ledge.

I let Stacey take the lead, offering the group balloons first.

"Come on ya wimp!" She heckles them giggling. "I want one too and so does Jodie!"

Do I? I think trying to catch her eye. I thought she said they made her feel sick!

"And you've got to have a shot of tequila if you're having a balloon!" She continues finally looking and I smile now gratefully. "We want one of those each as well, don't we Jodes!"

I grin ruefully, no! But if she's prepared to do a balloon *and* tequila to gain the extra sales! Well who am I to judge?

"So that's 30 for the balloons," she continues her barrage holding out a tiny hand and I realise she has rounded the cost up. "And, babe, what's yours?"

"25." I give them a big grin hoping they don't do the math.

"We've barely sat down!" One of them laughs grinning but he's already opening his wallet. It's amazing what pretty ladies can achieve here!

"Well you get enough free drinks for coming in don't you!" Stacey shrugs and begins stretching out colourful balloons one at a time and lying them on the table.

Am I really going to do a balloon? I must admit I wouldn't mind trying one to add to the ever extending list of new experiences. But if I throw up, collapse or something else horrid that will not only be my job down the drain, but shit, poor mum! I shake away pessimistic thoughts. Surely a few little puffs can't hurt?

"Let's do the tequila first shall we!" I buy myself some time and look at each of the lads. "So who's paying for these?"

My eyes snatch on one of their faces. He is hot! And he returns my gaze evenly.

Moments later I'm gasping from my shot- they're getting better I think or I'm getting drunker. Boom, 7 empty! But, before I can get too happy about that it is balloon time!

With a click and whoosh Stacey inflates the first balloon. She drops the metal bullet onto the table and reloads her canister, click whoosh over and over until we're all holding one. My heart races with anticipation. Smoking weed the other night with Tanya was one thing,

I've done that before. I already feel close to a heart attack should I really do it?

I'm overreacting, surely. I watch as the others take the neck of the balloon into their mouths and begin to breathe in and out, in and out. I follow suit and breathe a little bit in, hold it and breathe out. I feel an instant head rush but I feel that with smoking. I breathe in again a little more deeply now and woah! The head rush expands engulfing my whole face. I instinctively let the remaining gas escape, my ears ring. Alarmed I look around but then momentarily feel overcome with a great whoosh of euphoria!

Then as quickly as it came on, the affect sweeps away again. I am left feeling completely normal within about 10 seconds.

2 of the lads are still going, puffing in and out. Hippy crack, that's what I've heard it called.

"Thanks lads!" Stacey says now that all deals are complete.

"Yeah cheers!" I also tell them and we leave them to their evening with lighter pockets and even lighter heads.

"That laughing gas is strange!" I conclude.

"Told you didn't I! I don't even do it I just let it go down!" She divulges letting me into another trade secret.

"Like Coyote Ugly!" I comment thinking of the scene where the girl spits the shot back into the bottle. She just looks confused and I remember she's younger than me. "What about the tequila, did you drink it?" I clarify.

"Ah course don't be daft Jodes, I did that even if it *does* taste like shit, free alcohol babe!"

4 o clock is closing in and I am on my fourth tray. Not only am I two trays short of the target I set for myself but I have 3 shots remaining and I'm desperately searching for a group I haven't asked yet. Tony is sitting at the bar, his presence intimidating as he stares at us whilst we try to work.

He'll have seen me passing the lemon over with my mouth numerous times and I wonder if he judges me for it. Tanya said businesses here speak strictly profit. I suspect he doesn't care how I sell, as long as I do. I notice Andy watching with contempt from within his booth and remember his face when he caught Lee leaving that night. I don't need his approval though.

My search for custom is completed to no avail and I realise I'm going to have to pay for the last shots myself, taking a chunk out of my wage.

"There's literally nobody left to ask!" I complain to Stevie and Gemma who have both finished and are waiting for Beth to cash up.

"We'll buy one won't we Gem." Stevie tells me encouragingly and Gemma rolls her eyes at the kindness.

"Don't be daft." I tell her. "I'm not going to take your earnings!"

"No it's fine honestly. You gave me that sale earlier." She says fairly and Gemma adds;

"Well I certainly made enough to afford it."

Talk about rubbing salt in the wound!

I do a shot with them (we toast 'fuck you!') and finally I'm paying for the last tray- shift over. It would seem I still have a job because nobody tells me otherwise, I'm so relieved.

Stacey tells me there are workers parties sometimes but she isn't going to one tonight. And to be honest with my earnings I can't afford to be splashing out- even if the drinks are cheap!

Stacey and I head back to the apartment together. Carl disappeared a while ago and Andy stayed behind talking to Max and India. She still hasn't got a key; but between me, her and Carl we're getting by sharing 2.

"I'm going to take a shower." Stacey tells me when we're home and I climb into bed in a pensive mood.

Being a shot girl isn't going to be easy. I can see how Heather remains top dog with her *ways*. Guys were hardly interested in buying tequila. *Without* the extra offers that is! So it's either that; or rob them like she does!

I'll have to up my game tomorrow. 4 trays are not going to be enough to keep me my job. Reinforcement needed!

THE HARD SELL

I wake up much later than I have been used to thanks to my new working hours. I set an alarm for 2pm, luckily because it's that what rouses me.

Stacey isn't there so I send her a text and take a shower. By the time I'm done she's replied, beach- same place as always. I take a stroll to meet her before heading to Blush for my daytime shift.

When I get to work at 4pm there's no Don. To my pleasant surprise Max is there instead making my heart bounce appreciatively. He greets me his eyes like mood stones always presenting me with a new combination of green-brown. Do I get cold or warm Max today?

I ask him for a bottle of water and he rolls it along the bar looking at me broodingly.

"If you want to sell shots Jodie, you gotta do what the other girl's do. Use what you've got; you know your looks, tits, all of it!"

Ok so he is more to the point than Carl but I already got that vibe. He senses me stiffen.

"Thought you was a *bad* girl!" My own words are used against me and I'm drawn in by his arrogant smile.

"I wasn't sure how bad I could be!" I hint towards the idea of kissing people to gain an extra sale here and there.

"I want to know how bad you can be." He retorts.

Of course nobody cares if I kiss every client who crosses the threshold as long as they all buy a shot! And Max seems to be getting some kind of kick from pimping me out.

His eyes flash. "You gotta do whatever it takes. That's what *they* do… the ones who make it."

I want to be one of the girls who *makes it*!

I go out onto the street. PR-ing doesn't stress me out anymore- it is no longer the defining point of my success. Selling shots is. However I can!

"Alright guys!" I approach a group of 4 lads. "Fancy a beer?"

"Yeah why not?" One steps forwards taking control of the decision. Well, that was easy! I show them to a table and Max comes out to take their drinks order.

Jim, Joe, Bobbie and Shaun are from south London; today is their first day of 5.

"So can you be our personal tour guide tonight?" Shaun asks with a mischievous glint in his brown eyes and I'm disappointed to have to tell him it won't be possible.

"But you could come here to see me?" I grin at him making it clear I like him too. "I work as a shot girl from 11."

"A shot girl, ay! Sexy!" He shoots back at me.

Between flirting with Shaun and Max the 2 hours fly by. The girls are off out for dinner but I decline the offer- thinking again of my money situation. I'll have supermarket sandwiches. Yum!

The kitchen being a health hazard is an annoyance. I've seen Gemma and Stevie's, theirs is ok, and they managed to whip up chicken fajitas for us yesterday! But even just a microwave meal would be nice. But there is no way I'm risking it. I haven't even ventured back in there since my first night and I don't intend to- other than to show Leila!

As I stride to Blush again later that evening, I wonder if I will still have to sell tequila and whether Shaun will stick to his word and come back to see me. Max arranges my tray as before, yes tequila, and I get to work.

Following last night's pattern the hour before midnight is slow. Once it arrives however custom steadily increases and I make my first few sales.

"You can take the lemon slice out my mouth?" I offer once again when the answer is initially no. Deal completed I'm scouting again when I hear;

"Jodie!" Shaun followed by his friends comes onto the veranda. Being fresh to Magaluf they haven't cottoned on to tricking the PR's to gain a huge drinks offer and I make a mental note to enlighten them.

"Hey! You made it!" I greet them pleased. "You can start by buying a shot from me, I need to get rid of these last 4!"

"I think you might be taking advantage of me!" Shaun flirts smoothly.

"I think you might want me to!" I reply without missing a beat. He is fit but I also know that flirting significantly improves my chances of selling.

Final 4 sold I strut back to the bar and evenly meet Max's eyes. As soon as my tray is replenished I go on the hunt for my boys again, not wanting them to be cajoled by any of the others before I've had a chance to rinse them.

They've made their way to the dance floor and I signal for Shaun to come over.

"My tray is full again!" I shout to him. "So you can buy me one now!"

I must admit I like the pushy, audacious me and I like it that it works in my favour even better!

He digs about for his wallet and pulls out a 5. I shake my head and pull out my practised pout.

"No, no, you've got to have one as well! And your friends! Come on it's your first night!" I smile sweetly staring right into his eyes and he starts to shake his head but then rolls his eyes. I can tell I'm making it impossible for him to say no.

"How much will that be?" He asks.

Do I dare round it up to 20? No, that's taking it too far, he is buying me one after all and I do fancy him a fair bit too.

"15." I truthfully say instead.

He pays, we do the shots and I thank him, telling him I'll catch up with him in a bit. Then I slip away looking for more sales.

Outside I come across 3 rowdy, young Spanish lads.

"Chicken nugget!" One yells gleefully into a cheap, plastic loudspeaker. I have seen the lucky, lucky men selling them, and saying the same thing. Chicken nugget!

"Ah, beautiful girl!" The closest to me states and I can see he is extremely drunk.

"Chicken nugget!" The other shouts again.

"Fancy a shot?" I ask him, his eyes barely focussing on me.

"Noo! I have no money!" He laughs stumbling to one side. It's pointless pursuing this conversation and I look to see if they are all this drunk. To my left, he doesn't seem too bad.

"Do you have money?" I ask him forwardly.

"For a shot? No! For sex? Yes!" he slurs.

"No sex, but tequila?" I try for the last time.

He shakes his head shrugging and they carry on speaking in Spanish apart from the odd call of 'chicken nugget!'. I cut my losses and move on to the next group.

I encounter one pointless seedy conversation after another, manage to force a few sales using the lemon in lips offer and finally there's nobody left to ask.

Nobody tried to kiss me like Nick from last night. But there are a few I wouldn't have minded trying! And a few I think would gladly take me up on the offer! I'm mulling this over, waiting for a new influx of faces and I wonder, can I go back to Shaun and seduce him into buying again?

It seems a little harsh but I really need to make the sales, one way or the other! And I do fancy him so it gives me the perfect excuse to talk to him again.

He appears now and spots me heading over.

"The answer to my dreams!" I greet him unashamedly.

"Really." He enquires and follows it up. "You must be the beautiful nightmare!"

I smirk happy with the witty assessment.

"We're gunna head down the strip for a bit!" He says now.

"Not until you buy another!" I push it and I can see in his eyes that he knows I'm taking the piss. "Come on, I'll make it worth your while!"

"How?" He retorts instantly and I realise even I haven't figured that part out yet. Yes Jodie, how exactly?

"5 shots plus a kiss, 20 euros." I answer with a grin decisively.

"How can I resist that?" He grins. "Lads, there's a shot here for you!"

He hands them out and we all follow the salt, shot, lemon ritual. He looks at me coyly now. He's gorgeous and yet he's nervous about kissing me, I can tell! I feel a thrill of naughtiness at being so *in-tim-i-dating*!

It isn't that bad because I'd kiss him anyway, it's just a necessary bonus!

It's a shy kiss which is nice but doesn't give way to throes of passion thanks to his mates ogling us intensely.

"See you again hopefully." He tells me afterwards. I hope I do!

"Wow, you've pulled a hottie there!" Stacey sidles up beside me. No need to tell her it was part of the sale!

"Another tourist bang!" We giggle together and I tell her I'm going to restock. I know that Max is impressed with my pace tonight. He doesn't say so but his eyes say it all.

Outside I am greeted by the very drunk Spaniards shouting me to come over. The loudspeaker lies forlornly on its side.

"How much, for a shot and a kiss?" The extremely drunk one slurs and blinks his eyes as if trying to clear his vision. He must have seen me kissing Shaun!

Shit, but I wanted to kiss Shaun! But then I also want to make more sales and quickly!

"Well, er," I flounder for a response but they're so drunk they don't notice.

"Twenty euros?" He clumsily flaps a note around now. "A shot for me and my friends. And a kiss."

I thought you were out of money, I think but don't say.

Well this is very tempting indeed. 3 shots would be gone just like. And with my own personal cash flow dwindling I can't really afford to refuse him.

"Ok." I take a deep breath. He's too drunk to kiss well. I know that.

His intoxicated friends count us in. "Uno, dos, tres!" And he swoops in to embrace me. He's rampant and horribly slobbery. If the experience with Shaun convinced me, this completely puts me off!

I wipe my mouth. I hope he doesn't have a cold- or something else contagious! It isn't that bad really. It's over so quickly and more sales are achieved. But not only is not a maintainable tactic- it isn't very responsible either.

"Jodie, did you just snog him!" Stacey cries.

"Yes!" I tell her indignantly. I knew the time would come that my secret would be out and I am not at all sure how she- or any sane person- will react to it! "Well Heather virtually steals from her customers!" I remind her.

She's laughing though not bothered. Anything goes in Magaluf right? It's hardly the worst thing I've come across. Maybe in the top 5, but not the worst!

It seems the kissing went quite the opposite of unnoticed by more than just Stacey. A guy appears at my side now.

"Did you just sell that guy a kiss? Because I want one!" He tells me eagerly. He is short, chubby and burnt across his turned-up nose.

“He paid 20 euros though!” I tell him apologetically. If he hands that over I’ve got shots in hand for myself; or a big tip! I feel a slight twinge of guilt when he nods willingly.

“That’s ok!” He says and instantly takes out the cash handing it over. I notice his hand shaking and feel a pang of pleasure witnessing this effect I’m having on him.

I feel like a goddess!

Once the money is away he virtually launches himself in for the kiss with zest. It’s all I can do to swing my tray out of the way and steady it one handed as he latches his lips onto mine. I let him jab his tongue into my mouth 3 times before extracting myself and giving him a big smile.

“Shot time!”

I think he’s forgotten completely about the shot he just stares dreamy eyed for a long moment. I am beginning to worry I have triggered a seizure when he snaps back into the present.

“Oh, yeah!” And he does the shot without any salt or lemon and not even a flinch. “Thanks!” He says and returns to the one friend he has left behind who’s starting at us agog.

“You’re on to something there Jodes!” Stacey says from my side witnessing another illicit sale.

“But will I get in trouble?” I ask looking around for the others. How will they feel about their co-worker using this underhand tactic to win sales?

"Nah!" she swipes an imaginary fly. "Tony's desperate. Blush hasn't made anywhere near what it did last year. And anyway," she adds conspiratorially. "I've heard Gemma and Beth both show their privates for money."

I splutter into laughter. "Don't be ridiculous!"

That is absolutely the most absurd thing I've heard! Let me guess Carl told Ryan who told Beth who told Stacey!

"No honestly! Stevie told me because she was a bit freaked out by it. I believe her!"

Funnily enough, I'm shocked yes but I'd believe her too. And Gemma did make that comment last night about having earned enough to buy a shot, I wonder now with a strange awe. Plus Max insisted that all of the girl's do whatever it takes to sell.

He told *me* to do whatever I had to.

Did Jess get the sack because she had limits to what she'd do?

I have 6 left and I manage to finish selling my third and fourth tray without any more kissing- but I do have to resort to the lemon form lips trick a few times.

I have surpassed last night's record holding my fifth tray now and have way more in my pouch than I should thanks to the tips I've swindled. This tray is proving more difficult to shift. It's approaching 3 o clock now; I only have an hour left.

I spy a large group in the corner- 8 men. I definitely can't kiss all of them! And passing the lemon over with my teeth is tedious. It isn't the most time efficient!

How can I make tequila more attractive? Topless Tanya parading the bottle during the bar crawl springs to mind again. Is that a worse act than kissing somebody for money?

Use your tits, Max explicitly said that. And I've had my boobs out before as a topless sunbather- it's no different to that.

My mind fuelled by petrol and poison races as I approach them.

"Evening!" I announce putting one hand on my hip and trying to look as lusty as ever. "I've got an offer for you."

"What's that then?" One asks bored. He thinks I'm talking about a drinks offer.

"10 euros each gets you a shot and I'll show you all my boobs. But only if you all buy one!"

There's an intake of breath and I realise I have managed to shock them more than I have myself!

"You'll flash yer tits?" One cries out gleefully and is already grabbing for his cash. It doesn't take long for everyone to follow suit. I can and I can't believe it. Men really are such simple creatures.

I do a shot with them and then decide to do the remaining one for good luck- it's not like I can't afford it. Isn't that just what Gemma said last night? Well now I know why!

And I bloody well need it to get over the fact that this is just part of the life.

With 10 empty shot glasses back on my tray I get ready to lift my top. I'm reluctant to admit it but the rush is extremely liberating. Perhaps Education isn't my calling after all! But now is not the time to be thinking about my new job- and the possible consequences of doing something as outrageous as this.

Tada! I want to call because they look suitably impressed with my trick. My bare breasts feel cold and I hope my nipples have hardened because I always think they look so much better like that!

The group cheer and I quickly return my top feeling embarrassed somebody might see, which is ridiculous! Somebody might see who hasn't paid for the privilege!

"Thanks girl!" One of the men puts his thumb up.

"No problem!" I laugh at the unbelievable scenario.

Flashing my boobs turns out to be a resoundingly successful technique! It suits me better than selling a snog. That requires actual contact, worry about cross contamination and bad kissing! A flash is quick and simple in comparison. I turn in my 10th tray at 4 and I haven't even kept a count of what I've earnt in extra tips!

"Good job Jodes. I knew you'd work it out." Max praises me and I glow. He isn't bothered, the girl's aren't bothered- Stevie is probably a bit shocked and Stacey doesn't seem likely to succumb to the tactic anytime soon. Gemma and Beth already do it and Heather hardly has any moral high ground to preach from!

"What does chicken nugget mean?" I ask Max now as I hand over the cash for the last tray of the night. He looks at me with his dark, deep gaze and smiles slowly.

"Cheap white meat, Jodes."

Ah, ok!

"Oh, right!"

"English girls. They're talking about white skinned English girls." He clarifies what he doesn't need to. I'm shocked and probably more so because I think, is that what I am?

Do I feel like cheap, white meat!

"Night Max." I walk over to where the girls are waiting for me.

I'm just doing what it takes to sell. And actually the buzz from flashing for cash is hypnotising, I don't care, I want to do it again. I want to *make it* as Max had put it.

We're going on to a worker's party- I finally feel flush enough to afford it. And as we make our way down the strip I grin when I hear;

"Ello, chick-en nugg-et!"

THE GOING RATE

Well that escalated quickly! My mind rakes through the events of the evening before. Who even am I?

I have a dry mouth which no amount of old, warm water from the accumulating bottles by my bed will quench and my head thumps as I count 170 euros from my bag- and that was after paying for my drinks at the after-party.

I drag myself to Blush for dead on 4 finding Max is there again instead of Don. I'm glad but in my surprise yesterday I didn't even ask why this is the case. I hope my glee is not at the misfortune of him.

"Is Don ok?" I check.

"Yeah, he's gone part time." He replies and I can't help but wonder if this is voluntary or something else to do with the flailing business.

The shift drags as I knew it would. The sun always goes someway to perking me up and I decide in light of last night's success to treat myself to a pizza when I finish.

Tonight, I'm going to try and earn even more than last night!

Just before 6 o clock arrives, Shaun and cronies turn up. They have a beer and convince me to stay for one with them. I ask Max for a lager needing a change from spirits and one beer turns into 5.

I'm jealous to hear the guys are off to see Dizzy Rascal at Ibiza Rocks and I briefly wish I had my old job back meaning I could go with them! You just can't please some people!

By the time we part ways at almost 9 o clock I am tipsy and happy from more flirting with Shaun. He tells me they'll be back tomorrow to let me know how the gig is and I tell them sulkily I don't want to hear about it! But really I am already looking forward to seeing Shaun again.

I arrive to find Blush absolutely heaving! And despite this all of the shot girls stand on the veranda choosing not to interact with the crowds.

"What's going on?" I ask them, it's never like this before 12 at least and why aren't they getting stuck in there!

"Pub crawl." Heather answers in loud monotone.

"Pub crawl? That's great isn't it?" I'm confused.

"They get a free drink on entry and told its unlimited shots- which is actually just the host pouring it into their mouths randomly."

Sounds familiar! But I still don't understand what the problem is.

"They don't bring any money with them. They never buy a drink never mind a shot. It's a fucking joke." She booms disapprovingly. "Tony said we had to take them. Every Thursday and Saturday from now on. Completely pointless if you ask me!"

"Oh right." I peer between the milling bodies and see it's as busy inside as out here, I can make out numerous jiving silhouettes.

“They’ll be gone in an hour. Chill.” Gemma chides and I decide to go and fetch my first tray, investigating the bar crawl for myself.

Max greets me with the same grin as earlier and loads me up. His look is positively sexy as he pours out tequila, again!

I don’t mind so much anymore though- I can sell anything! I turn to look around the small, stuffed bar now that my eyes are more suitably adjusted to the light.

I wonder if I can teach Heather a thing or 2 and induce a sale using my barefaced, no sorry, bare-chested tactics.

Oh. My. God. I feel like the wind has been knocked out of me. It’s Justin. Like, standing right there. Justin!

Has he come to see me? I hopefully marvel. He spots me looking and I close my gaping mouth looking away pointedly. The last time I saw him he called me a slag. And if I can forgive that then don’t forget the info divulged by Ben! Stay strong. There’s Max and Shaun to have fun with now!

“Shorty.” I look up into huge liquid chocolate eyes and curse myself for fizzing lustily at the sight of him.

“Fuck off J.” I manage to say against all will.

“Ah Shorty, come on.” He calls into my ear and I can hear the smile in his voice, visualise those dimples denting his cheeks.

“Thanks!” I tell Max who looks at me inquiringly but I turn away, strapping my money belt on. I need to get outside, away from J and his delicious smell and even more appealing face.

He follows me though, obviously. He's like a predator playing with its prey, enjoying the thrill of the chase.

"What are you even doing here?" I crossly ask him when we're on the veranda.

"I run the bar crawl now." He tells me his toned pecs lifting with pride and I feel stupid for thinking he was here to see me. Of course he isn't, he didn't even know I'd changed shift. "I didn't know you'd be here! Added bonus." He disarms me by reading my desires and I try to shake off his charm.

Tell him you know about the pictures! No, actually no, don't look at his gorgeous grin!

"I think we should hook up again." He says to my further delight but before I can relish in the words I'd secretly longed to hear he adds. "But not tonight. There's a little hottie in there wants to suck it right off!"

My stomach clenches at his lack of tact. How can I let him treat me this way? Like his silly plaything.

"No thanks." I say much more firmly than I feel and turn to leave. He grabs my upper arm and pulls me into him. I steady the tray before glaring at him.

"I will have you again. Shor-tee." He says almost nastily and I'm ashamed of myself for enjoying it. The same rules don't apply as at home. I feel like Magaluf well and truly has me now.

I'm pumped with scratchy adrenalin from the exchange and his presence torments me. I try to avert my eyes every time we're near to each other but they continually wander in his direction against my will. Stacey and Heather watch me.

"He aint giving you trouble is he?" Heather shouts as Justin retreats inside and I shake my head quickly wanting to silence her. The last thing I want to do is rock the boat for the Blush/ bar crawl relationship.

"No, no it's fine." But then when her attention strays for potential custom I hiss to Stacey. "That's him, Justin! The one who apparently took photos of my… you know!"

"Oh wow!" Stacey whistles. "He is fucking gorgeous Jodie!"

I mistook her initial exclamation as one of shared horror but now I realise it's a shared attraction.

"Stacey!" I scold her and she giggles feigning innocence. The last thing I need right now is encouragement!

When the bar crawl filters out Justin seeks out my eye and gives me a big wink. I note the tiny blonde with huge hair and huge eyes attached to his side and shudder at the thought of what huge thing she'll be attached to later.

I can't help but let it get to me. How can I possibly still want him after what Ben told me! I don't even know that it's true, I appease myself. He is selfish but not twisted. Or maybe I am being completely taken in. Again! I just don't know what to think.

I can't let him take my mind from the job in hand. Look what happened last time I was enthralled in thought over him, I almost got caught by the cops! Let mission: make money, commence.

"So lads, I've got an extra special offer to make to you tonight." I'm busy selling my third tray. "You get a shot each and a flash of my boobs for twenty euros."

It's another easy sell, another wicked rush of exhilaration from capturing eyes how I never believed my own boobs could!

By 3am I have lost count of my trays- I think I'm on 10- or even 11 by now! The standard refill of voddy and coke every time I go back for another tray is taking its toll- topped with the numerous shots of tequila I wangle for myself. I am a tequila convert!

"Jodie the shot girl." Max gives me a lingering look when 4 o clock comes round and he takes note of my full tally. "12 trays! You really are a bad girl."

I stare into his mesmerising eyes and feel my body swaying with an intoxicating mixture of pleasure, accomplishment and alcohol. He's impressed by me. *I'm* impressed by me!

It's strange how quickly this has all become normal. And not just *normal*! I baulked at the idea of exposing myself and now I'm doing it, I actually like it!

"What you doing now?" He asks taking me off guard.

"Erm, I don't know?" Is he going to ask me to go to a party with him?

He turns and says something to India who is putting the last tray of glasses away. She nods and I long to know what he's saying! But in all honesty, it could be anything, I don't care; I'm a bad girl now.

“Come on.” He takes my hand and leads me from the bar. I just have chance to throw a shrug at Stacey before we step into the gaggle on the strip. The PR’s are long gone, she’ll have to find Carl for the key she’s spent enough time with him recently.

I wonder how Amy will react if we turn up at the same party!

But Max doesn’t head either way along the strip instead pulling me through a jitty heading shore side.

Are there any beach bars open at this time? Well he would know.

“Where are we going?” I slur barely focussing in the darkness.

“Shhh.” He soothes me. “Just a minute.”

I simmer with anticipation. We’re leaving the noise and light further and further behind us. Is he safe to be coming down here with? I refer to my list of potential dark characters I have conjured so far.

Surely with all the gossip I hear I’d have been warned if he is a robber, stalker, serial psycho killer! I’ve asked after him twice- he must be ok!

We hit the sand now and he continues marching decisively dragging me unstably as grit fills my shoes.

“Why are we…” but I trail off. He wants to have sex with me? He wants to have sex with me!

“Here.” He finally speaks. We have reached a lifeguard hut.

“What?” Are we doing it up there?

“Climb the steps Jodie.” He instructs me. Yes we are!

I turn, trip, he catches me and I giggle trying to focus on him in the silvery moonlight. He isn't smiling though instead his intense eyes bore into me.

"But, I can't, we can't," I stumble again laughing nervously. I'm far too drunk to climb this ladder! It'll be worth the view through, in more ways than one! I snigger again feeling shy and silly.

"You'll be ok." He takes my face into his hands. "I know you want this Jodie." He soothes and kisses me deeply.

Well, yes, when you put it like that, I do want this!

He's a worker, but he's not a PR! I won't be falling asleep here so there's no chance of nude photos being taken. If Amy had been friendly towards me girl code would have formed but he's told me already she isn't even his ex. No worries there.

I fall into his arms (literally) and allow reservations to scramble. As though in a trance I climb the ladder and take a deep breath of damp wood. It's completely bare inside and I wonder how many other girls he's bought up here before me. I wonder if he bought Amy up here!

Once Max has also made the ascent there's no foreplay on offer. He literally whips out his cock, already erect and expertly rolls a condom onto it.

"Bend over." He commands me and I do as he says unbuttoning my shorts. I hear him spit on his hand- classy- and feel the cold wet saliva between my legs and he roughly inserts 2 fingers into me.

I take a sharp intake of breath but before I can steady myself he shoves his dick right into me. Pounding harder and harder I soon realise there is nothing more to this than him getting his end away and my mind casts back to Tom on the boat bursting balloons on my ass.

But if you'd told me then, I'd be here doing this now I would've laughed in your face!

It isn't exactly the traditional sense of pleasure but my face is hot, my legs numb and his fingers dig into my hips vehemently. It's another bang after all, because I can! I think it's going to take a while before some men realise it isn't about just getting *their* end away but I'll take what enjoyment out of it I can for now!

It's funny how I always have this dialogue running during sex. But it's hardly worth clearing my mind for because barely a minute later he is grunting and the deed is done.

Feeling unsatisfied but not unhappy I turn up my nose as Max tosses the condom into one corner. It's one thing throwing it into the corner of my own room but quite another here!

He avoids my eye, hurriedly pulling up his jeans and tightening his belt. I wonder if he'll help me down the ladder and I busy myself with my attire feeling growing concern at the thought of getting down!

Is he going to say anything? I realise awkwardly. Should I say something?

Thanks, it was great. Because it really wasn't!

The sky is inky shades of blue as the night gets set to give way to daytime. Max fiddles with his pockets. He throws something at me, I follow it as it glides to my feet and squint, is it his number? A calling card? It's a brown and white rectangle.

"It's the going rate isn't it?" He snipes quietly and before I can register what is happening he is making his way out of the hut.

I look down again realising I should have kicked him straight in the face because it's a ten euro note. I begin to shake all over, he's disappeared out of sight and I hear a thud as he jumps the rest of the way to the beach below. I weakly slide to the floor and hug my knees to my chin in utter shock.

How can I continue to be so shocked!

Cheap white meat!

I can't believe this has happened. I don't want to believe it's happened. So I certainly won't be trying to convince anybody it has! My mind flits to Stacey who saw us leave together and will want to know the gossip… I will not be sharing!

I sit very still for a few minutes concentrating on dissolving into the panelled walls. Maybe I can evaporate myself home. But which home? Here in Magaluf with snakes like Max? I'd take Justin any day over this!

But perhaps that is just the problem. Flitting from one guy to a next! But then they do it don't they; have their cake and eat it.

I should've already learnt my lesson about workers! And I should've learnt that here or away differing rules for genders still apply. It's the slag situation all over again- earlier I readily took dosh for deeds at one end of the scale. But thanks to this sick and cruel prank I feel used. In hindsight I probably should've felt that once or twice already. But they were all a choice.

This *was* a choice, it's not like it is rape. But Max lured me into a false sense of security. He encouraged this behaviour, made a purposeful move on me and threw said antics back in my face.

I'm upset and angry but perhaps not as much as I should be. Or would have been back home. Or even would have been a year ago- before the stupid prick taught me that some people are just vile.

Light is beginning to replace dark and I realise the sun is going to be imminently rising. I need to get home and get some sleep. There's no way I want to see Stacey now! I can only hope any of my flatmates are back and asleep or still out.

The ladder looks steep from up here and I feel sickly drunk peering down at the sand below. I can see the tracks of out footprints leading here, only Max's leading away.

I don't regret selling my shots in that way. I regret having sex with Max, but that's the risk I took and now I'll have to live with it.

Carefully I descend. Feeling each rung solid under foot and gripping the rough wood tightly. Ultimately, tonight I felt proud, liberated and in control. Max might have momentarily stolen that from me but he won't be damaging anything further.

Fortunately one thing I have learned about is damage control. Dwelling on things, wishing they could be different and relentless questions is helpful to nobody.

Stacey is still out and I climb into bed completely drained. As long as it doesn't get out this episode can be forgotten. I'll have to make something up for Stacey's benefit and sweep it under the carpet. Like Alexa did with gay English. Perhaps this is an example of a man lashing out because he feels intimidated by my confidence. Wanted to bring me down a peg or 2 as the saying goes; well that won't work I'm afraid Max. I don't care what you think. Just like I don't care what Andy thinks about me either!

THE RUMOUR

Today I try not to feel anger towards Max. It's a wasted emotion! But how dare he use my behaviour against me like that? If I was more... sane... I might have been on a plane home in the night!

It was Max who surmised I could be a bad girl- or I could be a very stupid one! He's succeeded in making me feel stupid and I realise, I don't want to be a bad girl. And I also don't want to like bad boys anymore!

I want to *make it*. In my own mind that is, not his! I'm not ready to jack it in yet- for as long as I have a choice in the matter I will exercise it. I am Jodie the PR-come-shot girl, I am proud of myself and I don't need anybody to accept my choices. I have another notch on my bed post and do I dare joke, an extra tenner to boot!

I'm going to blag to Stacey when she asks that I went for a beer with Max and then he walked me home. Let's just hope he doesn't extend the humiliation by enlightening anybody else.

It's in moments like this when I miss my friends, the ones back home. Stacey is lovely but I wouldn't confide something this serious in her. Whilst I'm just sitting quietly doing so much deep thinking I realise how much I would usually vent for support.

I have got Stacey if I *need* her. But the gratifying thing is I don't feel like I do. I feel strong enough to deal with these hurdles alone. But I do miss my friends.

If the Justin's and Max's create the darkness in Magaluf, Stacey and the girls are certainly the opposing light.

I take a deep breath from where I am plonked on a towel on the beach. Stupid prick was just a warm up it seems. I am destined, unfortunately to meet many more stupid pricks in my life time. I just need to get a bit better at recognising them!

All this high drama has certainly given me perspective. Life is well and truly what you make it. And if I want to continue to explore opportunities- most of which aren't available back home I've got to expect some turbulence along the way.

I am tougher now than I've ever been before, resilient to influencing factors around me.

I close my eyes and raise my face to the sun. Leila will be here tomorrow. I have *so* much to tell her, how do I even begin!

I've spent the whole day on the beach alone with my thoughts and my book. I am almost in need of new reading material and decide to send a quick text to Leila asking her to bring something with her.

My afternoon shift approaches. Despite having a blissful day refuelling and taking stock I am acutely aware of a nervous drone starting up in my ears. I have no idea whether it'll be Don or Max working when I arrive but I am dreading it being the latter.

It's neither! I spy Tony behind the bar recognising his huge hulk. It hardly conjures any feelings of relief. If it had been Max I wouldn't have gone in but although I'm terrified of Tony I decide I should poke my head in and say 'hola!'

Ok, no I don't quite dare greet him in Spanish.

"Hiya!" I call out meekly. His stone grey eyes find mine and his face breaks out into a smile which unexpectedly changes his face.

"Jo-die! Come in, come here." Is he drunk?

I feel oddly paranoid. First Max switching back and forth now Tony following suit! Well one thing's for sure, I resolutely won't be sleeping with Tony!

"What do you drink?" He asks raising a thin empty glass, my newly grinning boss.

"Erm," this must be a set up? Tony is renowned for being tight. "Erm, coke?" I venture.

"*Vodka* and coke?" He corrects me and sets about making the drink. "Jo-die, you are very good shot girl." He passes me the glass and I look into his face which is weathered like a rock face. He looks gentle somehow, a friendly rock face. "Cheers."

He holds up his half lager and I meet it with mine. "Cheers!"

The drama is definitely getting to me! Every situation I encounter now I'm going to be expecting smoke and mirrors. Magaluf and its offerings have been disconcerting so far to say the least, but there's no need to be on high alert all of the time! It's a compliment from the highest source, take it, you've earned it!

"Keep up the good work." He tells me in his deep voice. "And don't let any of these," he wafts a hand about as if looking for the right word- "boys, distract you from the job. You know who I mean."

His eyes twinkle but without resentment and oddly I feel like I've received a hug from my dad; maybe because like my dad- nothing slips under the radar. Tony has a close eye on his staff keeping productivity healthy amongst all of the unhealthy goings on. I'm glad it is Tony standing knowingly beside me, and not my dad though!

I go out to the strip with renewed resolve and a wiser still attitude. I have come this far, and made the right people happy. Me- and the boss! And that's all that counts right now.

Oh and Leila! Who will be so overcome with this place! I can't wait to show her all the sights- her best friend flashing for cash and willy wielding PR's!

Andy is marching towards Blush now bringing me out my reverie.

It suddenly occurs to me I ought to mention about Leila coming to stay, you know out of courtesy, not because he's self-appointed landlord. With my shot girl success I suspect I could pull weight with Jamie even if Andy chooses to be awkward about it.

His piggy eyes flit between me and the veranda steps.

"Hi!" I say almost sarcastically. He doesn't return my greeting. "My friend is coming to stay tomorrow." I add and he focusses on me finally.

"As long as you don't keep us up all night fucking." He spits crudely and I laugh gleefully at the joke.

"No, she's a girl!" I cry hoping the misery guts might actually smile now. It must be tiring being so rude all of the time.

"Yeah?" He shrugs. "Everyone knows you're really a dike Jodie! I know your type."

Turning on his heel after 'triumphantly' blowing my cover he stomps inside.

Type! However he has categorised lesbians I don't know- but it's wildly off the mark. I'm still erupting in silly little giggles when snippets of music blast from Andy's sound check inside. Sound-check! The guy needs a reality check!

Out of all the things the rumour could be about- and he picks this! Is he trying to offend me? I don't know his motive but it just goes to show that opinion out here is so wild it's hard to know what's true and what isn't! If Max *does* spill the beans I'll just deny all knowledge!

And what of the photos J supposedly took? What if that is all an elaborate rumour too. But what if, exactly! I must forget about him too, especially if I am to follow Tony's advice and not become distracted by the boys!

I slowly pace backwards and forward patrolling my territory like a lion. I feel mighty, courageous, transformed from the pussy cat that first arrived! And speaking of pussy, a lesbian indeed!

I can't wait to tell Leila. And Stacey and the others! No chance, the way I've been going on! I'm still finding it hilarious, it couldn't be further from the truth!

Shaun and gang begin ambling towards me and I run an appreciative eye over him. Aflame of lust licks my pelvis, you'd think

I'd been burnt enough already! But when you're thrown from the saddle, you just have to get right back in it.

He's a tourist after all!

"Don't tell me, I don't want to know!" I stick my fingers in my ears referring to their experience watching Dizzy Rascal.

"We won't rub it in *too* much!" Jim grins remembering I am a big fan like him. "I won't tell you about how he smashed it with Bonkers, Holiday. *And*, I Luv You."

"Shut up!" I cry laughing as instantly the tracks play snippets in my mind.

"Well, we only came to tell you that." Shaun reaches out to lightly jab my arm and catch my attention.

"Yeah I bet you did!" I look into eyes that are telling me he wants so much more.

"And to say, we're going to come here again tonight. To see you." He adds.

"Ok." I smile in return. How will he react when he sees me lifting my top to sell my shots? Tony wasn't talking about him when he said not to become distracted from the job in hand- but the message remains the same. 'Keep up the good work'.

"So, I'll see you later?" He says looking unsure. I've hardly been forthcoming I realise.

"Yes, yes, that's great. I'll see you later."

I watch them walking away and Shaun turns back to give me another wide smile. I can't afford to let it interfere with my selling tactics but I can't see how I'm going to get around it either!

DARK VERSUS LIGHT

I might have avoided Max today but I know as I head to Blush that night there will be no avoiding him now. I've made an extra, extra effort! It's a while since the 'fuck you' middle finger has been busted out. It's time to revive it!

The effort is partly to show Max exactly what he's missing but also partly to show Shaun exactly what he's getting. And obviously it all goes to aid my persuasive ability with the customers. I'm wearing a new simple boob tube dress- making it even easier to release my boobs whenever is necessary. Tony is happy with my efforts and I intend to keep it that way.

I nod to Max in greeting giving nothing away. He doesn't speak to me and I watch him deliberately as he sorts my tray and pouch.

"Voddy and coke?" I prompt when he slides it toward me. He slams a glass down, sloppily glugging vodka into it and then the mixer. I suspect he thought I'd be awkward and upset but he's only succeeded in spurring me on! Fuck you, silly boy!

I'm in a great mood and whilst having fun with the girls I easily get rid of my shots- with and without added extras. Stacey wants to know what happened with Max last night and I feed her the rehearsed line before jumping straight to the revelation made by Andy earlier; that I'm obviously gay. This does a fantastic job of derailing further Max questions and highly amuses us all.

Gemma insists I keep the joke going when Leila arrives, maintaining an allusion that we're lovers! I can't see Leila being at all up for it, but it's an entertaining idea and we laugh at all of the scenarios we could produce.

At around 2.30 Shaun and the others turn up partly scuppering my selling tactic which was going so well. Luckily it works out fine and alongside the numerous sales I make from him I sneakily flash my boobs to groups whilst he's inside!

I am on my ninth tray already!

Stacey hits it off with Jim who is suddenly partial to laughing gas and to my delight we're deciding to head out with them once we finish.

At 4am I'm paying for my twelfth tray- on par with last night. And I know I can do even better tomorrow without Shaun hindering me.

Max glowers, put out by my continuing confidence and Stacey stands beside me. He won't say anything incriminating in front of her.

"Enjoy your night girls!" He sing-songs sarcastically staring at Shaun and Jim waiting for us on the veranda.

"Oh we will!" I chirp.

"He. Is. So. Jealous!" Stacey hisses as we swagger away and I realise she is probably right. But I don't care, my bag is stuffed with notes from another good night selling and we're hitting the strip with our tourist friends!

"Let's go to Crystals." Shaun suggests and we join the babble of bodies navigating the strip heading upstream. We pass the black and red bar, Ruby's, past the Red Lion and find the door to Crystals tucked away inconspicuously.

Inside it's loud, hot and busy and we push and shove our way toward a lit bar at the far end. The DJ in here favours base laden beats and my ear drums vibrate along with the floor.

It is impossible to hear each other in here and I let Shaun take the lead ordering us drinks. I take a swig.

"What is it?" I shout up at him pointing to the drink. My voice is instantly swallowed by the music.

He answers but I don't hear him, instead I lip read- Andy? Oh, brandy!

I actually quite like it, it's a welcome to change to vodka and tequila which I'm mildly concerned is corroding my insides.

We stomp our feet to the music, take it in turns to invent new dance moves and drink 3 more brandy's in quick succession. I haven't had time to discuss with Stacey about what exactly the plan here is- are we taking them back to ours? Even though we share a room? Will we both go back to theirs- or will we split?

I gaze at Shaun; he is conventionally attractive with dark and handsome features. He's a darling, like Lee, but so much sexier. I'm looking forward to another bang!

Stacey pulls me off to the toilet. Now is the chance to confirm our plan.

"I think we should go back to theirs!" Stacey proposes. "That way we can have some fun and then go home! I don't like sharing a bed!"

I laugh because she is so tiny she barely takes up any room on a bed! But I'm happy with this call.

Joe and Bobbie stay at Crystal's and Jim and Shaun lead us back to their hotel.

"We're going to go out on the balcony." Shaun tells me with a wink. "You ever done it on a balcony?"

No! But does a lifeguard hut count!

Their hotel is not too shabby, with a large pool and wide corridors decorated with gummy green plants. In stark contrast their room is a complete mess. There are 3 single beds side by side and a camp bed running along the foot. Clothes, sheets and towels literally cover every surface and I have no choice but to traipse over shirts and shorts to reach the sliding patio doors.

I take a seat in a plastic white chair and wait for Shaun to bring a beer out to me. Stacey and Jim get the main room and as Shaun comes out to me he slides the doors closed giving a cheeky grin to the occupants.

"I keep meaning to tell you," I tell him conversationally aware that any moment we could be undressing. "You should take advantage of the PR's at night! Don't just walk straight in. Pretend you don't know where you're heading and you'll get even better drink's offers!"

"Argh check you out Miss Scam-Queen, you know all the tricks don't you!" He teases good-naturedly. I feel at ease in his company and joke;

"Well, at least if I'm going to take all your money for shots you get plenty of free alcohol from the bar!"

He laughs at this and moves his chair closer to mine taking a deep breath. He's going to kiss me! But then;

"To be honest, money isn't really an issue." He says it sincerely his eyes penetrating me.

Alright show off! I want to quip but he isn't showing off and I don't want to offend him. Plus if he's rich this could be even better than I already thought!

"My dad has a boat. Him and his girlfriend are moored up somewhere nearby but they're coming to get us Sunday and we're heading to Ibiza! You ought to come!"

What! What? WHAT. I can barely keep up with what he's saying- it's bizarre enough to be fiction. Is he a fantasist because he didn't need to make up this elaborate story to get into my knickers- I was already going to let him!

"I mean it!" He continues. "If you want to come and leave all this shit behind, you could fly back to England from there instead!"

This causes a whirlwind of desire and it's completely unrelated to my increasing attraction to him. I would absolutely bloody love to! Can you imagine that announcement, I have left Magaluf aboard a boat, destination: Ibiza!

But not to mention how highly risky it would be- he could also be amongst other things a pirate; snatching vulnerable girls to trade in as sex workers!

Leila comes tomorrow however. And, no, I am not disappointed about this.

Ok, so just a little, but still the decision is made for me.

"I would absolutely love to!" I tell him honestly. "But my friend comes out tomorrow to visit me and she's staying for a few days! Maybe next time though." I add hopefully.

Just because I can't go this time doesn't mean I can't ever! We could keep in contact, arrange it properly.

"Ok, yes maybe!" He smiles.

I want to burst with excitement. I decide then and there to kiss him. I'm getting good at this 'first move' malarkey! I lean over, placing my hand on his knee aiming for his parted lips and he reciprocates. I swell in the knowledge that my confidence continues to billow. I never imagined I would have so many new experiences and I easily could have been put off! But I've succeeded in satisfying my decision to do otherwise, the potential opportunities so worth it!

We have sex in about 5 different positions, switching and changing to accommodate rising aches and cramps. Me, reverse cow girl on his knee until my thighs burn from the quick repetitive squatting; doggy with me clinging to the balcony rail for support- until somebody wolf whistles and it puts Shaun off his stride.

Against the wall until Shaun's arms ache with trying to lift me, cursing my short legs we finally succumb to the cold tiled floor. Here everything is uncomfortable, the hardness grinding on knees and spines- it's the kind of sex which is funny and still raw and passionate, easy in each other's naked presence and yet not so easy to execute.

In the end, panting we decide to give up.

"Sorry, I've just drank so much and I can't relax properly!" He explains chuckling. I pull my knickers back on; I didn't have to undress further thanks to my dress.

"You don't have to apologise! It was… fun!" I laugh reassuring him.

"Fun! Well, I must say I think that's the best feedback I've ever received!" He jokes with me easily.

"Fun's good!" I assure him whilst he taps on the patio window. I check my phone to see it is almost 6. The sky is pale blue becoming yellow with the newly rising sun.

"Do you have Facebook?" I ask him. I intend to orchestrate further contact if possible, this one ticks some serious boxes and I wouldn't mind trying sex in a bed!

By the time he has written his name into my phone Jim has appeared at the door. He's topless and grinning broadly and Stacey appears by his side, her hair ever so slightly bigger than usual.

"You ready?" She asks me.

I go inside and Stacey snatches a plump pillow clasping it to her chest.

"Grab one Jodes! I think we deserve some new bedding!"

"Stacey!" I chastise giggling. "We can't do that!"

"Of course we can! I've got the complimentary shampoo and conditioner in my bra and a toilet roll in my bag!" She gleefully informs us all. "Sorry boys!" She says to them playfully. "Thanks for having us! Jodie come on, don't you want a nice soft pillow?"

I think about the flat, doughy excuse on my bed at the apartment. Of course I do! Shaun can afford a fine after all! He said himself, money is no object!

I laugh out loud and grab one for myself. "You'd better get to bed before Joe and Bobbie come home and claim those!"

I point to the 2 remaining and throw a lingering smile in Shaun's direction.

"Take em." He laughs. "I don't care. I might see you tomorrow!"

"Yes brilliant, bye!"

We step out into the maze of white tiled corridors searching for a stair case to lead us toward reception. We manage to emerge pool side but its ok we spot the exit straight ahead.

Giggling furiously we dramatically sneak along the edge of the large oval pool, our stolen goods clearly on display. There is no way of hiding the bulky clouds of bright white!

"Shall I try and stuff it up my top?" Stacey is spluttering in-between laughter and begins attempting to pull it under her tight strappy vest. The pillow is much longer than her torso and has no chance of being disguised. I'm laughing even harder now.

"It'll stretch your top!" I gasp between cackles.

Suddenly up-ahead a security guard steps into view. He's on the opposite side of the pool, slightly ahead of us, closer to the exit but not looking our way.

"Oh no!" Stacey squeals and points. In slow motion his eyes swing round before coming to rest on the 2 workers trying to leave with a huge pillow each. The hilarity of the situation overwhelms me and all I can do is roar with laughter as Stacey crouches down, completely pointless because there's nothing to crouch behind, and begins scuttling furiously towards freedom.

Simultaneously the guard scurries along his side of the pool in order to block off our escape. The look of shock on his face is tickling me and I can barely keep up with Stacey who continues to dart as if we have a chance of dodging him.

We are laughing so hard we're crying when we come face to face with him- for a split second I think Stacey is going to attempt a quick dash around him (I understand her temptation, I've become attached, I was looking forward to sleeping on this so much!) but she gives up breathless from the laughter.

"Sorry!" She cries thrusting her goods at him. "Here you go, take it back, room 207!"

I am hysterical, the guard still unable to articulate a response his expression remaining one of comical surprise. I pass him my pillow as well and he takes them both mutely. As we retreat howling with laughter he calls.

"Don't come back. Thieving whores!"

This only adds to our continued humour and we head back toward the strip which will take us home. Stacey slept with Jim. She tells me excitedly he is her first since her recent break up. He was crap by all accounts but she's enjoying telling me about it all the same.

"I finally feel like I'm back in the saddle! You know, forget everyone else, live fast, have fun, die young! Whatever the saying is." She's babbling.

Sounds familiar, I muse. It is completely deserted this end, bars shut down, street strewn with litter and bodily fluid. Clean up will start very soon and by early morning order will be restored. You would never know it had been so trashed only hours before.

Up ahead I note a group of men filter from an alley way. They spread themselves out across the road making our only choice to walk straight through them. An icy sensation seeps from my head through my core. I feel a heightened state of pure terror that I have never felt before in my life.

We're going to get raped. Is my first thought; or robbed- my second. I feel sickening fear to the pit of my stomach and instinctively reach out for Stacey's hand. Don't be paranoid. It'll be fine.

"Stay by my side." I instruct her quietly. "Keep walking, don't stop."

As we get closer the line begins to curl at the edges enclosing us loosely in a ring. Is this what Don meant when he walked me home that night? He was worried, and it was around this time too! My heart pounds so fast it's making my breath shaky. I don't know what is going to happen but it isn't good. I'm lightheaded with terror.

One of them begins talking in Spanish, another joins in. They're closing in on us. One takes Stacey's arm and she screams.

"Fuck off!" She hollers loudly yanking her arm to her side. They don't get any closer but move with us, encircling like a pack of rabid street dogs. The one that focusses on me is deeply creviced and yellowing, Stacey's rich brown like a conker; they continue to intimidate us snarling, saying things we can't understand.

"Just keep walking." I'm repeating under my breath like a mantra. "Don't act scared. Just keep walking."

There's a 24 hour shop up on this corner- if we can just make it to that.

My arm is grabbed now and I abruptly side-step smashing into Stacey knocking her off balance. The guy most central to us steps closer and tries to push himself between us. Something inside of me knows if we're separated its game over and I resist the attack forcefully pulling myself back to Stacey's side.

"Just fuck off will you!" I yell loudly panic flaring inside of me. I bunch my free fist anticipating ensuing violence.

"Fuck off!" Stacey desperately choruses. "Fuck off, fuck off!"

Wild eyes, fight or flight fully triggered our aggressors hesitate slightly, their formation loosens. We march forward, slamming between 2 of them and they begin laughing harshly.

Perhaps they were just trying to scare us. And I am scared. Truly shitting it! Or perhaps they were concerned our shouting might cause attention.

Either way they are behind us now. We've broken out into a wobbly jog- adrenalin coursing through our bodies causing high pitched nervy laughter. Nothing like to how we had been laughing only moments before.

I can see the alleyway up ahead, through which home and safety lies. I take a cautious glance back to check they aren't following us but they've gone completely. I'm not sure what is more disturbing and I bat away visions of them stepping out again ahead of us.

"That was bloody scary!" I dare to exclaim finally as our tower block looms.

"Mmm, hmm!" Stacey's eyes are wide, lips pursed. She's usually so bold and positive but now she looks serious and frightened. "I thought, I thought…" She tries, "I don't know what I thought!"

No I don't want to voice my fears either and although we are no longer in danger my face prickles with what could've been.

We'd been so caught up in the merriment of being silly and stealing pillows it hadn't crossed my mind we could be in danger! I'd taken Don seriously at the time- but then hadn't heeded the advice when it was necessary.

"Probably best we don't dwell on it." I say.

I lay on my bed, body alive with hormones released by my distressed brain, rushing through my body equipping me for action. Sleep is not on the horizon now, my senses are far too amplified to relax and I listen to Stacey's steady breathing suspecting she is awake still too.

I was paranoid earlier around Tony's uncharacteristic behaviour. Worried my experiences had tarred my naturally trusting nature putting me on 'high alert'. But not only I am I right to be on guard, tonight has proven irrefutably that Magaluf *is* dangerous, not in a thrilling, glamourous way, but like really dangerous.

I'd been thinking of the dark and light side of Magaluf in comparison to the people I have encountered. And now tonight has proven the startling contrast yet again in the form of events. One minute we had been laughing our heads off and the next…

No point dwelling on what could have, but didn't, happen! I put a halt on the train of horror before it can leave the station. We're safe now. No more wandering about the strip when it's closed and no more sleeping with workers. Bear advice in mind, I've been told to do this before, but take opinions with a pinch of salt.

Clean up begins on the strip in the distance making it a safer place once again. The mechanical whining, screeching and clanking of the rubbish truck doing its business lures me into restless dreams involving an out of control bull.

I wake up several times throughout the morning and early afternoon. Each time I do it resonates with me that Leila is coming today- TODAY! I hear Carl angrily yell 'just fuck off' before slamming a door but I still smile to myself contentedly. I'm safe- minus the treat of a fluffy new cushion; I have survived another day, more experienced than ever before.

LEILA'S FIRST NIGHT!

Don is back at his usual post this afternoon. I wouldn't have cared less if Max was there anyway, nothing can squash my spirit. Leila comes tonight!

I learn that Tony cut back on Don's hours because he pays him more than the others- being an old acquaintance and Don isn't happy about it. His wife doesn't work through illness and I'm sad to hear he's looking for a new job.

It shows how desperate Tony is! Savagely saving money despite old loyalties and trying new ways to make it.

Don's back-story includes much heartache of its own; a different kind to mine and many of the co-workers. And he is suffering far more than I will from the backlash of losing this job.

Mine would mainly be a sting in the pride!

I am safe for now though because Tony himself virtually told me so. As long as I don't get distracted; which I won't!

I think I balanced last night fairly well. But then I think of one of his money making tactics- the bar crawl- it will return tonight. And Justin will return along with it!

But the thought of him is becoming less and less of a distraction in my mind; how different can the real thing be?

At least I can point him out to Leila and bask in the glory of her admiring his exquisite looks. I wouldn't want it to go amiss how gorgeous he is despite turning out to be an absolute twat.

Leila has text:

In taxi!!!!xxxxxxx

I am all alone in the apartment and bounce on the spot trying to expel the excited energy. She'll get here just moments before my shift starts. I've told her to get her taxi to as close to Blush as it can get amongst the night time crowd- I'm going to march her here so she can leave her suitcase and then throw her straight into the thick of it!

"Jodie!"

"Leila!"

Her familiar bright red, curly mane encases my face as she wraps me in a tight embrace. Wow, that's the first (nonsexual) hug I've had in ages, I didn't realise how much I'd missed this type of contact.

"Oh my god, Jodie!" She remarks eyes wide drinking in my appearance. "You look so different!"

"Come on, we've got to be quick! I'm meant to start in a minute!"

"You sound so different as well! Your voice is so husky!" Her observations continue.

"That'll be the vodka!" I remark wryly. "I've drank enough it!"

"So have you drunk every day? (YES!) I bet it's been one endless party? (SOMETIMES!) Have you slept with anybody else? (YES!) How much do you earn? (ENOUGH!)"

The questions come thick and fast and keeping up with the answers means the subject chops and changes, things being mentioned and not explained.

"Let me just tell you the rules of being a shot girl," I begin to rapidly fill her in on what I think she should know first. We're hurrying to Blush ready for my shift. "Now I've found some, um how can I put it, unique ways to sell the shots. It's difficult you know, I'm selling tequila."

"Eugh!" She crunches her nose up repulsed.

"Exactly, so to convince the punters I sometimes offer to, erm, flash them my boobs." She starts to laugh when I pause, surprised at my revelation. "And erm, maybe a kiss too! For extra money of course!"

"Jodie!" She shrieks. "No way! Who are you and what have you done with my friend! Well, you *have* always been a bit crazy."

I look at her affronted. Flash my tits crazy? I thought she'd be horrified!

"And I can't *believe* how you look; you're so brown and toned! Have you lost weight?"

She reacted more disgusted at the thought of tequila than her best friends' minor prostitution!

The incessant chat continues as we pass the PR's. There's no point me trying to point out who is who now. Leila's eyes are glazed with the sights around us.

I don't get chance to fill her in about Max or tell her Justin might be here before we're entering the heaving club. The bar crawl revellers collide and I scan for J but I'm disappointed to find he isn't there.

Max holds up a queer looking cup, like an upside down light bulb.

"Tony got these." He shouts by way of explanation. "You're selling cheeky vimtos now."

He divides 3 bottles of blue WKD between the 10 before topping them with port. They look brilliant- and I love Cheeky Vimto so I know they taste yummy!

"Yay!" Leila claps happily by my side. This should make selling so much easier! It takes away my extra offer involving the condiments but surely more people will be interested in these, and I might not have to resort to flashing after all!

"4 euros." He tells me. "And Tony says to charge you a euro for any lost cups so don't lose 'em."

There's always a catch, 4 euros! Only Heather's are 4 euros and that's because 'she's the best at it!' I should take it as a compliment! He thinks I am capable of rivalling her ability to turn in the sales.

Have I become a top shotter? Have I made it!

But I also realise I would be stupid to think I am immune to Tony's ruthless cost cutting- if I don't do well, 4 euros! I'll be gone no doubt about it.

"This is my friend Leila." I tell Max and he gazes at her his eyes a mixture of green and brown- impassive tonight.

"Hi Leila. You gunna be helping Jodes?" He queries and I think to myself how dare you shorten my name as though we're friends!

Leila none the wiser beams enthusiastically. "Yes of course!"

"You drinking voddy and coke too?" He asks her taking her answer for granted but I already know what she'll say.

"Actually vodka and lemonade please?"

"And I'll have brandy and coke." I intercept. Don't act like you know me, you don't know me at all.

I turn to Leila poised to divulge a little about Max whilst he's busy making our drinks but she's staring over my shoulder agog.

"Oh, my fucking god!" She rasps and I recognise the raptured look in her eye. It's Justin, I know it. She's spotted Justin.

I turn, following her gaze and he's looking straight at us smiling brazenly.

"He is gorgeous." She hisses not taking her eyes from him.

"That's him, that's Justin!" She doesn't even know the half of it and she grips my arm tightly.

"Jodie, you lucky girl!" She squeals swept away with herself. He is upon us now and without missing a beat reaches out unbuttoning the cleavage of Leila's tight shirt. She lets out a girlish cry, eyes gooey and cheeks flushed.

I want to tell her to pull herself together! Especially as Justin relishes in it flaunting the attention she's giving him. Yes I wanted her to agree that he's beautiful but not fuel his ego even further.

“Who’s your friend Jodie?” He asks, the eye contact causing a jolt of electricity to run the length of my spine.

“Leila, I’m Leila.” She spurts.

I give her a subtle nudge hoping to bring her back to her senses.

“Come on Leila, we’ve got a job to do.” I resort to when it doesn’t and I don’t want to witness J coming onto her anymore. I push her toward the doors forcing her to tear her eyes away. J slaps my bum.

“See you soon,” his voice says into my ear but with my tray in one hand and Leila’s shoulder in the other I keep my eyes fixed firmly ahead.

“He is sooo fit Jodie!” She cries exuberantly once we’re back out on the terrace.

“He’s also a complete dick head!” I retort. “Honestly, you wait until I explain. He’s arrogant and rude. He’s so mean!”

She looks at me in utter horror and for a moment I think she’s interested before she gushes;

“But Jodie, look at him! What was he like in bed, was it- you know, big?” She can’t keep a straight face and I rib her. Wait until I tell her about Nathan!

“Ay, hoes before bros, don’t you forget that! And yes, it was.” I divulge before reeling off the afternoon I met the Americans.

I begin introducing Leila to the girls as they drift over. I give her quick low downs on each of them when possible, repeating the snippets of information I have been told by the others. I then point out each PR on the street filling her in on what I've heard about Ryan and Bex and how he treated her at the beach.

She is suitably enthralled by my gossip- hanging on my every word in between thirstily looking around at this new environment.

Cheeky vimtos prove to be tempting. But the added euro does its job in deterring as many people as buy. I will still have to resort to flashing- because I want to sell these quickly. I want to prove I'm top shotter! To myself but to Tony as well; and the others, I want to impress Leila too.

At one point I was scared she wouldn't have a worker friend to even visit- and now I'm up there with queen bee, selling the most expensive shots on the strip!

Having Leila around makes work more fun than it's ever been. And in between chatting, drinking and making sales using conventional tactics she doesn't even witness any lewd behaviour until gone 2.

We've been hitting on a stag do for a couple of minutes. The banter is deteriorating by the second as is my patience.

"You can have the tray for 60 euros and I'll show you my tits!" I offer shamelessly and I see Leila in my peripheral observing me intently.

"I want to touch your tits!" One response.

"I want a photo!" Comes another.

"A 3 second flash." I ignore the comments. "No touching, no pictures. 3 whole seconds of looking."

"Come on you fanny." One of the blokes challenges another. "You put thirty in and I will. Let's treat em, some of these sad fuckers aint never seen a pair of tits."

They all laugh jovially and I politely join in. Just hand over your cash and let me craic on!

I reveal my chest and give them a jiggle- more for Leila's benefit. Her eyes look ready to pop from her head as she witnesses my party trick for first time and I relish in her astonishment. I'd felt the exact same when I saw Tanya do it! And I'd sworn I'd never partake!

Tray empty we once again head back for more.

We're getting sloshed on freebies and with Leila's help I'm pulling in the custom more quickly. She is having a whale of a time, finding the life as riveting as I first had, listening to my tales with enthusiasm and throwing herself into having fun.

"Shall we go skinny dipping?" She suggests drunkenly to me Beth and Gemma as the bar approaches closing time. She's just finished drunkenly snogging a really goofy boy with bright yellow hair. I always tease her for having the worst beer goggles in history and yet again they haven't let me down. She is trolleyed!

"Noo, no!" Gemma tuts waggling a finger. "I know soo many people who have been robbed whilst they're skinny dipping. Don't do it!"

"Well at least not when you've got any valuables on you!" Beth prods Gemma's shoulder. "Ay! Remember when we went?"

Her eyes cloud over as she recalls the memory no doubt full of sordid and sexual activity.

"Oh, yes that *was* fab! But there's loads of jellyfish this year. I've heard loads of people have been stung!"

I nod in agreement. I too have heard that through eavesdropping on plenty of conversations daily.

It's enough to stopper Leila's excitable disposition and she rapidly drains of colour looking serious all of a sudden.

"Are you ok?" I ask her concerned. Does she have a phobia of jellyfish I don't know about?

"I'm going to…" before she can finish her sentence a stream of orange sick evacuates her mouth and lands on the wooden floor between us.

I can't help but laugh- well it is a little bit funny seeing Gemma lurch out of the way, the animated look of shock on Beth's face.

"Shit, sit down babe." I guide her to a stool. "Are you going to be sick again?"

"I don't know!" She tells me frantically.

"Come on. Let's go to the toilets."

I guide her down the stairs at the back of the club which leads to the cellar and the dimly lit, stuffy toilets. There's an attendant and he raises a hand in greeting acknowledging that I am a worker and therefore letting me have toilet paper for free. Cheers mate!

After Leila has been sick twice more we head to the bar to get her some water and I tease her that the thought of jelly fish made her sick. Luckily my shift is almost over and I plonk her in a corner on the veranda to recover whilst I finish selling my last tray.

This has been fun. Even with Leila vomming, poor thing! Cheeky vimtos tie in nicely with the cheeky shot girl demeanour I have created for myself and although the price is tricky I haven't offered to kiss anybody. There wasn't anybody I wanted to kiss, I might add! But the odd flash was more than encourage to sales!

I finish on 13 trays. My best so far!

I won't boast like Heather did though! Power and control here should never be taken for granted. I look around for her- *we're* top shotters- but only catch sight of her retreating back as she flaunts out.

The excessive alcohol and exhilaration has gotten the better of Leila whose arm is looped around my neck and we head back to the apartment. She isn't used to my rampant lifestyle and after the day's travelling combined with heavy drinking she is a goner!

I just get her to the bed and we both collapse exhausted.

"Jodie?" Leila whispers into the dull room.

"Yes?"

"Why are there so many clothes in this flat?"

I begin to giggle at her observation. Of all the things she could have said!

"I don't know!" I laugh remembering my own curiosity. It's become a far less important part of the scenery and I've never thought to question it. She sighs before slurring.

"This is all so cool Jodie. I'm so proud of you!"

"I'm so glad you came Leila." I tell her but I think she's already fallen into a drunken slumber.

CHRISSIE'S

I wake up clammy and hot from sharing the small bed. Stumble dizzily to the window and flinging it open I realise I can't even offer Leila a tea. That is the one thing she always craves when she's hungover and oh, she will want 2 cups today!

"Morning." She stirs groggily when I clamber back beside her.

"Morning! How are you feeling?" I ask in a hushed voice not wanting to disturb Stacey.

"Hungry!" She replies smiling weakly with her eyes still closed. "The last time I ate was in England! And my mouth tastes like shit!"

"Welcome to Magaluf!" I joke and she shakes her head.

"Mate, it's crazy, I love it! I don't want to go home already!"

"That's why I didn't!" I jest.

"I can't believe I was sick!" She grumbles.

"I can't believe you've got a phobia of jellyfish!" I tease. I'm so glad to have her here! "And you had your beer goggles on!"

She death-stares me, warning me off the subject and I abide, for now! Instead, we hurriedly dress and go in search of breakfast. I want to show Leila the disgusting kitchen but not until she's had something to line her tummy in preparation. I'm not sure she could cope with it in her current state!

Over sugary tea, a pure orange juice, more tea and then finally a bacon sandwich attempt, I tell her about Andy. How he's apparently difficult and obviously rude. Carl; his crude but friendly comments, the bars rumoured flailing turnover, and my rumoured sexuality! How insecure mine and everybody else's job actually is, the full truth about Justin *and* Max. The fear I'd experienced with Stacey on encountering menacing street urchins. And I must admit it feels really good to get it all off my chest.

I need her to understand it isn't all fun and games. Come to think about it now that I'm sitting opposite my best friend from home I realise how lonely this has really felt at times.

But keen to show how the pros far outweigh the cons I tell her about Shaun- his dad's boat and the Ibiza offer, me and Stacey stealing the pillows! Face, the workers parties, daytimes lounging on the beach. The guy who blows me a kiss every time I see him, the rude propositions I receive on the regular and endless opportunities for people watching! I talk out loud for the first time about old woman girl and tell her my plans for us sleep on the beach with her.

"I hope we see her!" Leila enthuses with perverted intrigue.

Following breakfast we take a stroll along the strip and I point out the different venues I've visited. We keep our eyes peeled but don't see old woman girl- nor any of my other 'regular' faces. I text Tanya and find she's stationed in a nearby hotel so we drop by for a quick visit.

By the afternoon we're strolling the length of the lovely beach and covertly eyeing up men.

My phone ping's and to my delight Shaun has sent me a selfie! Aboard his dad's boat! I show off to Leila having earlier admitted my reluctance to take him for his word.

So the Ibiza offer was for real! Not that I'd wish Leila hadn't come now! I wouldn't trade her remedial company for anything.

But that means in the future, it could be on the cards!

If any teeny cracks have begun to appear in light of the darker experiences of Magaluf then having Leila here pastes over them. Its ability to go from hilarious to horrifying in a nanosecond has been proven. For all the many positive experiences there have been negative ones. But I want to continue avoiding potential risks as best I can and carry on learning and growing.

"Well I definitely want to go out tonight when you finish Jodes!" Leila tells me undeterred now we're at Blush. "I bet your friends think I'm a right idiot after last night!" She prattles whilst scanning the veranda for any remaining orange stains.

"It's ok, your jelly fish phobia is safe, I won't tell them!" I rib her yet again and she laughs it off.

We've been here for over half an hour, nobody has come in yet but Don has given us both a free drink.

"This is going down well!" She remarks happily.

"Plenty more where that came from!" What she's seen so far has been relatively mild! "We'll find a worker's party to hit later- so take your time!"

During the time PR-ing I'm chuffed to spot Face and he comes straight over to introduce himself to Leila.

"He's nice!" She comments and I smirk telling her;

"They all seem nice Leila! Who knows what secrets he's hiding if he's anything like the others- which I suspect he is! Best to firmly friend zone them and keep them on side!"

"Well I didn't mean it like that anyway!" She defends herself bashfully. I don't push her on this subject, plenty of time for that.

Finished we head back to freshen up and get ready.

"I'll treat us to dinner!" I tell her fanning my cash. I have stashed my rent aside and have plenty to spare.

After dinner we dot in and out of bars and clubs slowly heading in the direction of Blush. From Chrissy's porch opposite I watch the PR's for my place of work manhandling girls into the bar. At one point Ryan fireman lifts one screaming over the veranda and inside leaving her friends no choice but to hopelessly follow her in.

"It's brutal!" Leila observes and although she's taken aback by the rowdiness I recognise the fire dancing in her expression. Proudly I note her admiration and awe for the strip as though I am solely responsible for it.

Well, I kind of am. If it wasn't for me, we wouldn't be here!

Finally 11pm rolls around and we exit our seats strolling over to begin the shift.

"What the fuck do you think you're doing Jodie?" Heather barks approaching me. "You can't drink in *that* bar!" She spits the words indicating to Chrissy's where we'd been only moments before. I'd thought nothing of it!

I feel Leila shrinking beside me feeling the same intimidation I used to around her. To some degree I still do but I refuse to cower the way I previously would have. Watch it boss girl, I'm in your league now!

"I didn't know it'd be a problem." I shrug apologetically.

"Of course it's a problem." She rolls her eyes exasperated as if I'm completely thick. "Blush is going under and you're spending money at rival bars!"

"I'm sorry!" I try again embarrassed at my naivety, I thought I knew all of the rules and now I look ridiculous in front of Leila. "I didn't know!"

"You will be sorry if Tony catches you." She says coolly. "And don't let me catch you again else I'll make sure he finds out."

She stalks away and I have to blink away the sting of humiliated tears.

"What a bitch." Leila says comfortingly from my side and my stunned senses begin to return.

"Don't worry about it," I tell her staring at Heather's back. "She's just jealous."

Gemma who witnesses the whole showdown explains what I wasn't to know. The owner of Chrissy's used to be in partnership with Tony hence a deep-routed conflict between them.

"But she's not bothered about that. She's pissed off you're selling 4 euro shots!"

"Really." I'm not at all surprised by this.

"She loves lording it over us and now you've waltzed in and managed the same!" Gemma loves it and is happy for my success. "*She* says you're cheating! She's a daft cow for not doing it herself!"

I feel bad my lewd ways have caused tension but Gemma is right. There is no rule against exposure for money, encouragement if anything. *And* she's hardly struggling!

There was no need for the thinly veiled excuse to show me up. She's sharing her crown now and obviously finding it a bitter pill to swallow. As she already threatened, I'd better not give her any other ammo to sway my position with Tony. I know not to count my chickens.

Leila is being chatted to by a lad nearby and I loiter by her side waiting for my opportunity to pounce. There are 4 of them, Italian, the one who is speaking is a looker and doing all of the talking. He explains how the others can understand English but are too shy to try talking. I wonder if this is the case or if it's just easier for them to let him take the lead. He introduces himself as Gabri and agrees to buy a round of cheeky vimtos for us all.

"My pocket." He holds out a hand in request to his friend. I watch curiously and he's handed his *wallet.* I can't help but smile at this cute error.

"My pocket is always out!" He brags and I get the impression he is a bit of a show-off, a ladies man displaying his wealth and perfect smile.

I have 2 shots left now but Gabri's *pocket* is far from empty.

"Gabri," I interrupt him mid-flow as he animatedly charms us with stories about his college days. "How about you treat me and Leila to this last shot so I can restock?" I bank on his showy manner compelling him to agree and not lose face.

"How about we exchange a kiss." He smirks audaciously and I grin in return. He is handsome and has plenty of money in his *pocket*!

"It'll cost you more than a shot." I inform him slowly as though I'm mulling it over; he doesn't know this is second nature to shot-girl-me. "Twenty euros and you can have both of the shots and a kiss."

"My pocket." He demands it again and I giggle amusedly. Keen to show he is flush he sifts through numerous crisp notes. It's a good job I'm not Heather, I think on my high horse, it'd all be gone! At least I'm doing *something* to earn it!

"Thank you!" I say curtly in return for a twenty. "Kiss or shot first?"

"You and Leila take the shots. I need only the kiss." He replies smoothly. He might be good looking but he is complete cheese on toast. I snigger and clunk the plastic bulb with Leila's gulping down the sweet, sickly drink before puckering up.

He kisses me tenderly as though it is the result of a mutual spark not a sales agreement. It is slow and tantalising but he is far too cliché to ever really woo me.

I restock and clear another tray inside, showing my boobs to sell half of them, before restocking again and returning outside. Tony sits at the bar and gives me a nod. The craved nod of acceptance; a sign I'm still in the good books.

But for how long? I'm hot on the trails of last night's sale success and Heather could throw me under the bus for the Chrissie mistake at any time. Tony however is a wise man. He will surely not let a feud over a failed business hinder the profits of a new one.

As long as I maintain my selling prowess there's nothing to worry over.

Back out on the veranda the Italians are getting ready to leave.

"Jodie," Gabri approaches me and kisses me gently on each cheek. It hurts me in the cringe and I stifle another snigger. "I want you to take this."

He plucks a bobbly chain from around his neck pulling a pair of silver dog tags from under his shirt.

"I am a military pilot." He explains. "These are how they recognise my body if I was shot down."

Ok, that is dramatic! Firstly how had he resisted mentioning his occupation before! And secondly, do I need something to help recognise a dead body!

"I want you to have them and remember me until we meet again!" He holds them out to me. I feel a little ashamed of my assumption about him being a complete show-off, there is some substance behind him I can see that now.

"I've given him your name for Facebook!" Leila interrupts the moment which has rapidly gained status. It's a touching (if not a bit morbid) gift and I'm stuck because I can't really say, keep them you might need them!

He presses the smooth, warm metal into my palm. "They'll keep you safe, keep them close."

I wonder how much Leila has told him about me and how much real psychic ability he possesses as his hazel-brown eyes search mine.

A lucky charm won't go amiss I think feeling strangely comforted by it. I feel a bit emotional suddenly and my feelings towards him shift into a genuine realm.

"Well thanks." I look at him in the refreshed light. I bet he looks good in uniform!

"And when we meet again, I want to see that you still have them!" He tells me with a strange intensity that makes me believe it's possible. "You can visit me, or I can visit you in London."

I'm not from London but I don't want to ruin the moment. Why me? Was our shared kiss so special? He'd *paid* for it! Or maybe he has numerous copies of these dog tags which he is regularly giving out along the strip.

We bid farewell and I turn to Leila feeling speechless.

"They're going on mopeds!" She exclaims astounded by something completely different. "They've got a 40 minute drive to get back to where they're staying with their army mates!"

So she already knew their profession.

"Tonight was the only time they could come to the strip- *and* they had a curfew! Can you imagine?"

"Oh!" Is all I manage. A sudden potential opportunity of a trip to Italy then! I take one last look at the name engraved into the dog tags- Gabriella Adesso- before slipping them into my pocket. I will keep them with me, to remind me of Leila and everything connected to this place so far.

Boats, Ibiza, pilots, Italy, seriously whatever next!

Leila pretty much enjoys a standard night out despite accompanying me to work benefitting from free drinks she helps me and the others, well not Heather, to make extra sales. Heather has secluded herself not only from me but from all of us. Stevie assures me not to take it to heart. She's insecure she tells me intuitively.

It's no wonder really. She just doesn't have the approachable character or sex appeal of the others. And probably there's a colourful past which has affected her, moulded her, just like us all. I feel sorry for her, my intention was never to upset her.

But if she wasn't ignoring me I'd happily bring her into the sales we're gaining. She is yet to learn a valid life lesson- she won't always get her own way!

We decide to hit a worker's party that Beth knows of. Leila frets about not being allowed in but the we reassure her it'll be fine- Gemma rolls her eyes saying only the lads get questioned! By 4 o clock we're suitably drunk to blend in with the rabble of revellers, eventually leaving the strip and climbing a steep side road.

The first person I notice when we arrive at the venue is Ben. It has a large outdoor space which overlooks the strip below and is filled with tanned arms full of bangles and wristbands.

I go over to him and introduce Leila. She is still feverish over being 'let in' and flaps her hands at her sides spying him eagerly.

It worked to her favour that she was with a large group of worker girls as we passed by because her manic expression was as giveaway as her pasty complexion! But the bouncers had only batted an eyelid at our combined attributes as we passed.

Stacey and the others head on to the bar whilst Ben instantly hits on Leila as I knew he would. And then he comes on to me as well!

"What do you say, we could have a threesome! And then when J comes home you could both bang him too!" He suggests it as though it's a genuine possibility.

"No way!" I reply firmly more fussed about the thought of Leila with Justin than anything else! "Not after what you told me about the pictures." I use my own thin veil to cover the excuse.

Undeniably it was the original motivator propelling me over here in the first place. I was planning on defying him for details that would eliminate or confirm J's innocence. It shouldn't matter; he should be eliminated from my mind! But Ben's counsel has given him away. I suspect the photograph story is merely a banana skin designed to slip Justin as he races along the prolific track.

"Chill out." He reaches out and touches my breast. I recoil instantly. "What's the problem? Me and J share *everything*."

"Not *me* you don't." I stand my ground. Either my fanny looked inviting on the photo or he's lied to score a point over his friend. "Did he take those photos or not?"

He finally caves laughter getting the better of his throat.

"He's told me about ones he's seen. That other people have taken! I just thought it was funny!"

He shrugs. Yes, very funny. I don't laugh.

It's always apparently. Always what somebody has told somebody! So much for boys not twisting things, I knew it!

"Seeya later." I end the exchange instead. "Come on Leila, let's find our friends."

"Well!" Leila exclaims as we head inside. "That's a turn up isn't it! So how do you feel *now* about 'Justin'?" She sings his name teasingly as I give her a mock glare.

"He still called me a slag Leila!" I remind her. She's been happily carried away by Magaluf, its goings on *and* Justin. Much more easily than I'd thought!

"So what mate! You already said how you're behaving is slaggy!"

I laugh at her summary of my liberal speech regarding my choices versus society's standards. It's only slaggy because I'm a girl!

But let's not get into that battle!

"Yeah but look at how Ben behaves. At Max! That's why workers are out of bounds." I tell her as we snake our way into the crowds hunting down Stacey

"Face seems nice!" She exerts the previous observation and I briefly revisit the possibility of Leila sleeping with somebody. But not a worker!

"That's exactly my point; I haven't complicated my relationship with Face!"

We find Stacey and Stevie. They have a pint of something each for us.

"Where's Gemma and Beth?" I ask them to which they nod. I look in the direction and find them chatting to a group of guys and girls, I recognise some of them.

"Shall we dance?" I ask Leila and she nods enthusiastically. We take to the dance floor with gusto and watch others dancing, those grinding in dingy corners and bodies as they mill in, out and around.

"Oh my god, Leila!" I cry. "She's there, it's her! The old woman girl!"

And sure enough it is, maybe it's the alcohol and half-light but she doesn't look so haggard. Still rough but in a scary way; an I'll-beat-you-up-at-the-drop-of-a-hat way.

She's with 2 guys, a rose between 2 thorns! Except this rose looks more like the stem towering over both associates.

"Bloody hell Jodes! When you told me about her, I felt *sorry* for her! Jodie! Stop looking at her!" I look at Leila instead finding her eyes wide. "She is scary mate!"

I nod appreciating her assessment saying almost to myself. "She looked so vulnerable. So, lost! Like she needed genuine help!"

"*You'll* need genuine help if you keep staring at her like that!" Leila quips and I laugh thinking perhaps I got my assessment all wrong!

Leila's right she looks completely in control of her situation barking unheard words at them about things I clearly know nothing about!

To our dismay we don't see her again but I notice this is a reoccurring theme. Many workers come and go there is a constant turnover of faces, including 'nice' Face who greets us but can't stop talking to his profusely sweating companion long enough to come over. Gemma and Beth have long gone and Stacey and Stevie talk to Carl, India and a friend over by the patio doors.

The atmosphere has a hubbub of chitchat resonating above the music- which is different to that of a club like BCM. This is a sneaky insight for Leila, behind the scenes of an industry I'm still myself learning so much about.

We leave at half 6; clean-up will have begun so it isn't unsafe and abandoned. The huge trash truck stinks as we pass it, the screeching and clanking deafening as teams of men in hi-vis scamper to tidy and wash the pavements. Stacey stayed behind telling us she will crash at Stevie's so I can use her bed tonight, bonus!

We let ourselves in and I'm surprised to find Andy lurking in the corridor.

"You see Carl?"

I'm even more surprised that he addresses me and I barely feel any recognition towards his voice.

"Yeah." I shrug telling him truthfully and confused I go to push my bedroom door open.

"Where is he?" He enquires further stepping into my path and I remember the 'fuck off' I'd heard Saturday morning. Did they have a fall out?

"At a worker's party at..." I frown trying to visualise what the place had been called.

"Trixie's? Trio's?" Leila tries to help.

"Who was he with?" He asks me now and I wonder how deeply Andy's control issues run.

"Stacey, she still hasn't got a key so they've had to stay together." I have a dig but he doesn't seem to notice.

"Just Stacey?"

"And Stevie, India, somebody else that I didn't..."

But Andy has stalked away leaving me nonplussed.

I look at Leila and we shrug at each other not needing to say anything. Friendship telepathy: very odd mate!

Climbing into separate beds I spread out as much as is feasible in a single and quickly forget about Andy and his odd ways. We sleepily discuss the night and giggle about old woman girl before falling asleep.

A DAY OF REVELATIONS!

My alarm chimes at 10 meaning we got around 3 hours of sleep. I turn over and watch Leila's eyelids flickering as she navigates her dreams before returning to my own.

At 11am I drag myself toward the shower leaving Leila to snooze. Stacey isn't back and I wonder if Carl returned. It seemed like Andy had been waiting for him when we returned, but why? They've had a disagreement; I wonder if Andy is jealous of the little friendship which has blossomed between Stacey and Carl? Perhaps the issue was over having another key cut because another still hasn't materialised.

In the shower I douse my overactive mind and turn instead to today's plan. I want to do something fun with Leila, something she can remember the holiday for. I know she's already had the best time! But she goes home tomorrow and I'm genuinely gutted. A tiny part of me nags to entice her into staying too.

I know that she loves it here! She's told me enough times already and we haven't stopped laughing! But Tanya had described me as being ballsy for doing it. My best friend is loads of fun, a fabulous candidate to showcase this lifestyle to! But not ballsy enough to stay, not *crazy* enough as she called me!

She reminds me of Stevie- who was only cajoled through months of meticulous planning and prep for the plunge. And she still doesn't always look completely comfortable with the goings-on.

The thought of Leila leaving makes me think of my own departure. I am past the halfway mark now. Only another week or so and it will be my turn!

I change my thinking, what daytime activities have I seen advertised? Coach and boat trips, the quirky museum Katmandu? Water sports, jet skiing? I know, a pedalo! Yes! We could hire a pedalo. I've had my eye on the large swan, the only one amongst the regular colourful versions. I've watched groups of girls posing and laughing as they set sail, taking photos within their majestic vessel. It's perfect!

I've washed my hair but I plait it instead of drying it. Hopefully this way it will have a beach wave effect by later on.

Back in my room Leila is awake and scrolling through her phone.

"Look at the pictures I've got so far!"

I sit by her side and look at a dozen or so shots; beginning with scenic through-the-plane-window shots of a rich blue sky and deteriorating to sweaty unfocussed faces and blurred blobs of light.

"They're crap!" She complains laughing. "Nothing I can really shout about on Facebook!"

"Well," it's the perfect introduction to my plan.

"I'm not having any photos next to you! I'll be as white as the swan!" She reacts initially to my suggestion inspecting her fair arms.

"Well at least you're not burnt!" I applaud her good sense of skin protection which comes with being a natural ginge.

"What about our phones on a pedalo though?" She fusses. "And what about the jellyfish!" She asks worriedly.

"You and those bloody jelly fish! Don't worry we don't have to go *in* the water. And it's not going to capsize!" I hope! "You and your phobia!"

She laughs insisting that she doesn't have a jellyfish phobia but still doesn't look convinced at the idea of taking her phone.

"Ok so if you don't want to take your phone on the swan, let's have a quick shoot on the balcony first!"

The view will make for an amazing backdrop!

I did show her on Saturday afternoon, after I'd settled her stomach! But I think the true squalor of what we existed in completely stole any proper attention to the balcony view. She was more concerned about showering arrangements, disgusted in fact. No she definitely couldn't stay!

Sliding back the patio door we step outside, breathing in the delicious warm air. More appreciatively than before, Leila stares at the ribbons of gold sand and sapphire sea to our right; the turquoise sky arching over a snapshot of Magaluf's bars, buildings and mountains in front of us.

"Wow." She says and takes out her phone for a snap. "Stand there, Jodes."

She directs me and I take centre place of the scene behind spreading my arms and smiling inanely.

"Wow!" It's my turn to involuntarily express when she shows it to me. Not only is the view breath-taking but I look, like, *really* different! Good different!

I am an even golden brown all over; my body is verging on muscly having surpassed its toned stage. My eyes are bright and teeth white compared to the dark face I barely recognise as my own.

"Let me take one of you!" I say and she takes up my former position; thumbs up, then remembers to act cool she says, "Take another!" Changing to a 2 finger 'peace' sign! "And another!"

I know already she won't be forthcoming with self-appreciation even though I think she looks mega-fit and should splash them all over Facebook immediately.

She eyes them scrupulously and then says. "Ready?"

I nod and she adds. "Take your phone on the pedalo if you want? I'm not taking mine."

Being the more daring- or the less sensible I agree. I need more evidence of myself whilst I look this good! You know to show any prospective kids- this is *before* mummy had you and ruined her figure!

Down at the beach we approach the wooden stand surrounded by life jackets, scuba diving equipment and a selection of inflatables- a banana boat, rubber ring, flat wide 'sofa' and several colourful pedalos with steep slides, all resting at the water's edge alongside the coveted swan.

"Hola." The attendant greets us. He is muscular, not much taller than me and his olive green eyes look straight into mine. "Beautiful eyes!" He states hypnotising me with his own stare.

"We'd like to rent that pedalo!" I tell him pointing to the swan and looking away from him.

"Ah ok, the swan! Your majesty the Queen!" He tries to convey a plummy English accent which makes me and Leila howl.

"Beautiful English girl." He directs at Leila now and I let her revel in the attention- I can't say I haven't enjoyed it in the past!

"How much?" I ask causing him to stop undressing her with his eyes her cheeks now quite pink.

"20 euros for 1 hour- but you have it 3 for 50."

"How about we buy 2 hours and get one free? 40 euros." I tell him and flash the cash temptingly. He takes the bait and stares at us both lustily before handing over a ticket to mark payment.

After he's *too* helpfully manhandled us aboard he drags us into the water wading up to his thighs before blowing us a kiss.

"Have fun!" He calls. "Beautiful!" And he returns to his post.

"Jodie you're so confident!" Leila gushes to me. "I so wish I was more like you, you just completely took that in your stride!"

I can't help but feel a well of glee at succeeding to exude my new self-assurance.

"Trust me," I tell her. "It hasn't happened over night!"

It's happened over a succession of nights; like swinging across monkey bars- I've overcome the urge to give up, the fear of falling. I'm gaining momentum with each rung although now I can see the finish line- I don't feel any compulsion to get there more quickly. I want to prolong the experience, enjoy the effort.

We have taken our positions in the front of the boat a set of pedals at each of our feet. Our belongings on the bench seat behind us.

"Right, let's go then!" I cheer and we begin to push the pedals round. It is very, very hard. The swan weighs an absolute ton and we barely move forward as the initial shove we'd been given slows and our giggling weakens attempts further.

"Wow, this is hard!" Leila cries waggling her arms in the air. "Help us, we're beached!" She cries giving up.

"No we can do it! Look at those!" I point to a streamlined pedalo zooming effortlessly ahead of us. Determined I count us in. "Come on. Ready? One, two, three, heave!"

It's tough but we manage to get the pedals turning and it slowly picks up 'speed' getting a tiny bit easier.

"My thighs are killing!" Leila puffs no longer pink, but bright red.

"Need a hand?" A friendly voice says from my side making me jump. It's now I realise we're still no deeper than an average man's waist.

"No, no we're fine!" I chirp even though my face feels hot from the exertion.

"Yes, yes please! Give us a push!" Leila happily calls over me.

"I'm Paul." He grins at her and leans over me clumsily with an outstretched hand. I'm pinned by his wet bulk to the seat and seawater soaks me.

"Uff!" I exclaim as Leila replies.

"I'm Leila and this is my friend Jodie!" I can feel his body jiggling as she shakes his hand. "She's a worker!" She tells him proudly. "She works at..."

"Ruby's!" I shout the first name that pops into my head. "I work at Ruby's." I say pushing him off me and back into the water. I give Leila a sharp look that tells her not to say a word. "Come on then Paul, if you're going to give us a push. We've only got an hour on this thing."

I hear Leila take a gulp of air ready to correct me and throw another look her way. She looks at me bewildered;

"What?"

And I giggle in reply shaking my head. Let the damsel in distress work her magic first!

Paul lunges to the back of the boat causing waves powerful enough to rock the whole swan before placing his palms on its tail and surging us forward.

"Quick pedal!" I instruct Leila, we need to harness this power and she does as I say.

"Bye bye!" Paul yells from behind us and Leila turns to wave as we're finally reaching a depth swimmers rarely venture to.

"Why did you lie to him?" She asks me now as we finally come to rest amid some other small boats and pedalos.

"I didn't want him tracking you down at Blush! I know what your beer goggles are like and he was just your type!" I rib her playfully. I've tried not to refer to it too often since the original reaction I'd received. I don't want to put her off snogging completely! But I do suspect it takes getting hammered to build up the courage to do it and then her choice becomes impaired!

“Don’t remind me!” She says sternly but giggles before adding. “I don’t know what’s wrong with me!”

“Erm, your eyesight?” I joke.

“Yeah but Jodes, you go for these amazing looking lads and I can’t even talk to them! And they’d never fancy a girl like me anyway!” She continues. “At least with the plain Janes I know they’ll give me a chance!”

“Leila!” I cry. “Don’t be ridiculous you’re beautiful. That Spanish dude said that himself! And *he* was fit!” I can’t stand the thought of my best friend selling herself so short.

“And to be honest,” I add. “I definitely wouldn’t be following my lead when it comes to choosing guys!” Casting my mind back I smile wryly. “Looks aren’t everything! But trust me; the lads out here are generally just looking to have sex! And the tourists actually appreciate you for it!”

“I’m not going to be having sex with anyone!” She says reprovingly but giggles again.

I reach for a can of cocktail each and pass one over. “You don’t have to do anything you don’t want to my lovely. But I know you enjoy a snog- so let’s get you wasted and kissing some of these gorgeous boys tonight! For a start.”

She grins and shakes her head. Then says;

"I mean it about you though Jodie. You inspire me, you always have! I know what happened with…" She trails off not wanting to say his name. "But you know, first the new job and now… look at this!" I'm busy looking, it is amazing. "I'm going to put that picture on Facebook, the one of you on your balcony, rub it in about ruining things."

"You've still got him on Facebook?" I snap indignantly.

"Only so I could keep an eye on things-"

"I don't want to know anything!" I interrupt her sternly. "I can't believe you kept him on there!" I stop to think only for a moment and then repeat. "No! Don't tell me anything at all!"

"Jodes there's nothing to tell. Nothing's changed!" Just like Tanya said! "I just want to show him what he's missing. He'll be as sick as a pig when he sees you looking like *this*! In *Magaluf*!"

Ok, so I have pictured a number of scenarios involving the news reaching his ears- the expression on his face, the thoughts and feelings it will evoke. I wanted the news to spread through the grapevine. I am undoubtedly having the last laugh with this response.

"Ok, fair enough!" I accept Leila's decision to not follow suit and block him when I did. "Let's get another few, for good measure!"

We go on to spend 3 quarters of an hour posing with and for each other, using my phone to capture more pics and then spend a further 20 minutes deciding which one has my best side.

Our merriment is interrupted by a cry,

"Hola! Hola sexy!"

“Not again!” Leila laughs still not used to the regular barrage of attention. We eye up the canoe gliding by, 4 fabulously formed Spaniards flashing huge white smiles.

“Hola!” I reply gleefully and instinctively reach for my phone. “Como estas?”

“Muy bien!” They reply happily and when they realise that I’m taking a photo of them begin flexing their muscles in a number of poses. I click away and one stands up showing his full glorious six pack.

We girlishly squeal encouraging another to do the same. This is too far for the little boat and it upsets toppling him in. I manage to capture the water erupting in sparkling splinters as he disappears beneath the surface.

The photograph proves exactly why I choose taking risks over being sensible.

After his friends have finished laughing and hauled him back aboard they paddle away waving and calling;

“Good bye, adios! Have fun!”

“See!” I tell Leila gloriously. “Men galore, and at your disposal. Tonight my lovely friend we’re on mission: ‘Pull-A-Fitty!”

“Ooh!” she squeals delightedly and I feel a rush of love for her. She hasn’t dated in ages- the deterioration of her last relationship taking its toll on her nerve. It’s something I’ve worked on before to no avail and maybe I’ll approach the subject once we’re both back in England. Especially now I am once again in the same proverbial boat!

"We'd better head back. It's probably going to take us an hour!" I exaggerate. "*And* I'm hungry, I want to eat before work."

The water splashes rhythmically as we once again work up a sweat progressing slowly toward shore.

We're greeted by the same fit attendant and he drags the swan up onto the sand. I jump off first and Leila lets him lift her down, his hands wrapping around her hips.

"Leila!" I gently chastise her. "I know I said all that about upping your confidence but seriously- workers! No, no!"

In the busy square area near Burger King we stand side by side waiting for the button we've pressed to beep; indicating we can cross the road. I lightly scan the crowds and spot old woman girl almost opposite. She's moving her arms and body, dancing enthusiastically to an imaginary tune.

"Hey Leila..."

"Look! It's..."

We notice her at the same time and burst into giggles. I'm not worried about her anymore; I no longer believe she is homeless! She's just crackers! But just then my phone starts to ring interrupting our laughter and I'm pleased to see it is Stacey.

"Stacey!" I greet my Maga-bestie grinning at my bestie-bestie.

"Oh Jodes, where are you?" She yelps and my heart turns cold. Something's wrong.

"We're in town, getting food, Stace what's happened?"

"We're at the beach. At the usual spot. Can you come to us? Now?"

"What's up Stacey?" I say to a dead line because she's rung off. My heart beats a panicked pace and I guide Leila back to the beach where we'll find her and whoever 'us' is. I randomly trace through possibilities, could it be related to me and Heather? Would she want an out of work showdown? She's bolshie yes but violent? I seriously hope not! I deduce it is most likely related to Carl and Andy. But I don't let up on the marching pace until I spot Stacey. She's with all of the shot girl's minus Heather and all of the PR's minus Amy. India is there too.

As we get closer I can see angry scratches in India's face and a faint trace of bruising around her eye.

"What the hell happened?" I ask her shock replacing a well-mannered approach. My mouth hangs open and I can't help but stare, she looks a mess!

"That fuckin' psycho Amy!" Carl answers before she can explain. His voice is subdued but tinged with rage. "And Andy, the prick. I'm gunna kill him!"

I quickly assume there's been a fight between the girls but how is Andy involved? Poor Leila she must be even more confused, probably frightened. It's certainly turned my tummy over seeing her like this.

"Sit down." I say to Leila and we both join the huddle on the towels. Stacey looks like she's been recently crying; she still has her tiny balled fists stuffed into her mouth and Stevie looks equally shaken.

"Calm down." India is telling Carl soothingly despite being the one who has been attacked. "So Andy told Ryan I was having it off with Max. Amy heard about it she flew at me this morning- doing this. I got a few on her but she took me off guard!" She's recounting it like its run of the mill stuff and yet again it is 'he said-she said' informing belief.

My stomach clenches what if Andy had said it was me with Max! He quite easily could have seen us leave together the other night. What if Amy had seen us? Could I have ended up in this position!

"Truth is Andy's just bitter that me and Carl are together now." She continues. "He's been having digs at you all week hasn't he babe? I just can't believe how childish he's been!"

Pieces of the puzzle fall into place! It explains so much! And I got it wrong about him and Stacey.

"It's bang out of order. I'm fucking moving out of that shit hole. Sorry girls." He flicks his eyes to her then me. "I'm sacking Blush off too."

"Amy's been sacked." India tries to calm him again. "You don't need to leave."

"With that prick Andy still there? Just because he's Jamie's brother he gets away with behaving however he wants! It's bang out of order. You fucking watch, they'll happily let me walk. PR's are replaceable!" He thumps the ground next to him angrily.

"He's a pathetic fat-boy!" India spits. "Don't let him win, let him *see* us together every night!"

I wasn't completely off the mark about Andy's jealousy then, just mixed up on some of the details! It makes sense why he said *India* was with Max, not me. He was slinging his own banana skin for Carl;

except India has taken the fall accidentally. I bet Andy feels devastated at the consequence and no wonder Carl is furious.

"I'm sorry babe. I can't do it. I'll punch him and get sacked anyway. There are jobs at Tokyo Joes. I'm going there now to speak to them." Driven by pent up frustration he jumps to his feet, kisses a spot on her cheek which isn't maimed and stomps away.

"I knew that Amy was a jealous cow." Beth breaks the lull.

I did too! I realise and run my eyes over India's face feeling horribly guilty that I'm glad it wasn't me. It could've been. And I hadn't even considered her a threat. If anything I was bothered about whether Heather could be violent. But I wasn't even giving that serious thought- she would do nothing to jeopardise her job!

And as for Andy. Spiteful git!

He should never have risked India getting hurt, especially if he likes her so much to induce the tactic in the first place! But perhaps he isn't bothered, pleased to have punished her too for spurning him!

"They aren't deep, the scratches." India is so composed. "They look worse than they are."

Far more so than I would be! But then she's far worldlier than I am! What I've experienced, in retrospect, is probably small fry in comparison to her past. "It's a good job Tyler pulled her off when he did. I was just starting to win!"

I try to laugh with her but inside I rumble with what ifs. If I had gotten into a fight with her would there have been someone to intervene, someone to pull her off? I think of Max taking enjoyment in hurting me- would he have gone that far? He treated Amy badly;

not that it justifies her actions, but I could've learned from it- avoided that incident. And Andy has rocketed to the top my dislike list!

Stacey decides to come for food with me and Leila and we tell the others we'll see them later before sniffing out a pub offering cheap, hearty grub. I need to let this new event settle in my mind.

"I can't believe I go home tomorrow!" Leila whines after we've polished off lasagne and chips (I advised against garlic bread due to our pursuit for totty tonight!)

"It hasn't put you off then?" I refer to India's fight.

"No! Well I wouldn't *stay* here! As much as I absolutely love it! But it's been an amazing experience and I'm feeling excited about facing the world again! I think I need to make a few changes!"

She says the last part mysteriously and as suspected it's a no-go on the 'staying' front- but maybe, just maybe she's referring to the dating game and convincing her to play won't be so difficult after all!

"There's still tonight to go!" I torment her. "I want to know what changes you're talking about!"

This makes her blush and I know I've hit the nail on the head.

"You're definitely in the right place if you decide a shag *is* on the cards after all!" I push.

But before she can tell me off;

"Yeah as long as it isn't you Jodie!" Stacey squeals hooting at her own joke. Leila is saved from embarrassment by the reference to another of Andy's fictitious tales.

Except that one only resulted in amusement, not malice.

When we arrive back it is clear Andy has become waiting in the hallway, again. The moment we open the door he's there beadily eyeing us.

"What do you want?" Stacey isn't afraid to make her feelings known.

"Carl's moved out. So you can have a room each if you want."

"Oh." She is taken aback by the suggestion as am I. I like sharing with her but then it would make it easier to, well, have sex at the apartment! It is quite nice of him to suggest it and not to let the room to somebody else. Plus she'll get her key now!

"Thanks Andy." Stacey regains her composure neither accepting nor declining. "I'll just talk to my *friend* about it!" She stresses the word highlighting his sudden clear lack of any and I can't help but feel a teensy bit sorry for him. I doubt he meant for it to turn out the way it did.

"So what do you think?" Stacey asks me behind closed doors. "Would it be better I take it than somebody else? I mean I've got used to Carl, I'm not sure I want to risk getting another Andy!"

Point made and we agree without further persuasion.

"Well at least you can take his key!" I add.

"Come on, let's check it out!" She trills. We scuttle back out into the corridor to spy on Stacey's new room.

It's smaller in here but not by a lot. In trend with the rest of the flat, a clothes-rail runs the length of one wall filled with vests of all colours. Remnants from Tony's failed partnership with the owner of Chrissie's maybe?

One thing is for sure, Andy and Amy's behaviour will have well and truly taken any limelight from my own blunder of drinking in there last night! Heather's motive to derail my job has itself been derailed. Tony is 2 PR's down now- that's two less wages to pay!

There is a desk with mirror, one single bed and it looks relatively clean. Stacey is happy and bless Carl, not all Maga workers are scruffs then. I hope he has managed to find a job to go with his new set up- where ever it is. Who knows India might have moved out too- moved in with him even. It was clear how protective he felt over her. They're not *all* bad eggs.

"It's ok isn't it?" Stacey grins.

"Yeah, it's nice!" I tell her and chance. "Why are there so many clothes everywhere?"

Well she spends more time speaking to Carl than I do, maybe it's been mentioned!

"No. Fucking. Idea!"

Andy is loitering in the hall way again and he mutters something.

"Sorry, are you speaking to us?" I ask him genuinely unsure.

"I said the clothes were an investment. Me and my missus…" He breaks off. "It didn't work out."

So there it is, not only a definitive explanation of the jumble sale but also of his bitter, moody demeanour. It sounds like it was a tough admission to make and maybe even an explanation, an attempt to apologise for some of his behaviour?

"Too bad." Stacey cuts him down killing the moment.

"Why don't you sell it?" I suggest positively. But he shrugs, discouraged and leaves. I feel a tiny bit bad for him again. But then, all of us standing here right now have experienced heartbreak, he is in no way vindicated.

After sweeping her belongings into her case she has dragged it from the room leaving me and Leila alone to spread out.

"What a day!" She gasps.

I agree, the incident with India is awful, but at least she has taken it in her stride. Fair play to her!

"This place really is mental Jodes! I think I need a little siesta before tonight!"

It's a good plan and we take a bed each. I set an alarm for 10pm and realise I only had to share with her on the first night. From having a spare bed, to Stacey, both of them, now just Leila again; and soon it'll be back to being a spare!

I drop the melodrama, Stacey's virtually next door. But I think about how quickly circumstances here change. I've had to learn to take things in my stride. I haven't had time to wallow in any event, have been forced to drop reservations, worries and what ifs quicker than ever before. Go with the flow!

I smile, Leila loves it and I love it as I slide into a deep, relaxing sleep.

LEILA'S LAST NIGHT

What day is it? Does Leila leave today? I momentarily panic before realising it is still Monday; we've had our nap and now have her last night to come!

I help her to decide on a slinky simple black dress and we scrunch her masses of hair into abundant ringlets. Coupled with smoky eye makeup she looks sexy and bold.

"You are *definitely* pulling tonight!" I tell her happily.

"Stop putting so much pressure on it!" She bleats tugging at her hem.

"Oh be quiet. You'll be snogging mingers the moment I take my eyes off you anyway!"

She tuts but laughs and I can't help but giggle. I've got plans for you girlie!

I'm thwarted by Blush being quieter than usual even after midnight. So far there has been slim picking on the male front. Finally though I spot 2 guys, perfect! They are both attractive and I approach them with Leila by my side.

"Have I got a treat for you!" I announce us theatrically.

"Yeah?" Blue eyes grins at me.

"Oh yes. For ten euros each, you get a shot each and a kiss from my friend here, Leila. It's her *last* night, I'm trying to cheer her up." I daren't look at her but I feel her tense up and hear her uneasy giggle.

"Last night! You poor thing!" Blue eyes says. "I've got a girlfriend, but Henry hasn't!"

Henry is smiling delightedly.

"Perfect! You can still buy a shot though!" I smile at blue eyes. "And one for me! I want to toast you for being a lovely, loyal man!"

Yes I'm conning him out of a drink, ahem professional shot-girl at work here, but I genuinely mean it about the loyalty aspect. Between the men I have met so far, I have almost built one whole 'perfect' man. And now I've found the allusive quality I was seeking any evidence of. I feel like I've found proof of God!

I hand out the glasses knowing Leila's mouth has possibly gone as dry as a bone. He's definitely her type- a David Beckham lookalike. And for all the death stares I have received already, I know she will thank me for it in about 10 seconds time.

"To being loyal!" I toast.

I have realised I am in no way looking for another relationship quite just yet. But this sampling of what is on offer has proved a worthy experience, rebuilding my expectations for the future.

I watch as Leila goes in for the snog, with Henry- who is not only gorgeous but has also paid for the pleasure! Yes it could have gone horribly wrong- I think about my feelings towards Alexa when she set me up in the sex game! But just like that it has gone fantastically right! And it will hopefully serve as a catalyst as it did for me.

If Leila hasn't got the balls to jump for herself, well I've just given her a little shove!

"Oh my fucking god!" She's breathless as we walk away and I know I have given her an experience close to how I felt kissing Justin.

"Did you enjoy it?" I ask not needing the clarification.

"I fucking loved it!"

I was right about the drama with Amy and India clearing any residue of other feuds. Heather is back on talking terms with us, well not me really but the others at least. I'll be gone soon Heather, don't worry! I never did tell her my planned leaving date after she intimidated me with talks of 'back-dooring it'.

Out on the strip the PR formation lacks force, 2 posts empty. I just hope they can make up for the loss. Tony will get his just desserts if by saving wages he loses custom. It comes through steadily enough now though and;

"Hey, go and talk to those guys!" I instruct Leila singling out a group. "He's fit on the right."

"I prefer the one next to him!" She giggles at her newly spawned courage.

"So go over there and strike up conversation. I'll talk to this couple. Use me as cover, say I've sent you first and I'm coming to sell to them next!"

Sneaky! A decoy for us both. I'm throwing her in like a fishing hook whilst I tend to the tiddlers.

She agrees and I'm delighted for my selfish reasons, as well as hers! If Heather thought I was cheating before- she's definitely going to now!

Leila trots over cautiously and from where I sell I observe happily as they welcome her in and she begins her easy stream of banter. She's likeable, laddish in her humour. It's a good job I'm *not* a lesbian else I'd be snapping her up myself!

"I see you've already met my gorgeous friend!" I saunter over now. "And have I got an offer for you! If you're single that is!" I intrigue him and yet give him an opt out before revealing the offer. Quickly checking out the others I decide to include the one I originally picked out for Leila. What was it that Alexa had said? Darling, when the waters are so rich, eat!

Another kiss under her belt, and one for myself to boot!

By 3am she is simmering with exhilaration her eyes glassy. She animatedly tells me *again* about Robbie- her second illicitly achieved snog who she exchanged details with. I'd left her chatting to him, continuing my rounds, popping back across occasionally to make another group member buy a round.

When I ask Leila to hit on another group;

'I don't want to snog any others!' She'd exclaimed obviously smitten with Robbie.

'You don't have to!' I used her instead purely to create bread and butter sales bolstering those I make quickly, cheekily, alone. It *is* a touch quieter I concede but I don't struggle and at 4am I'm excited to find out I sold 15 trays! I can't believe it!

Even Max is gobsmacked and he loses the characteristic coolness he's adopted of late calling to Tony. "Fucking 15!"

Leila, Stacey and Heather are also privy to it, Tony, Max, Leila and Stacey beam at me; Heather stomps off in a huff.

"She tried to say it was quieter tonight!" Max flicks his head in her retreating direction. It was though wasn't it? Her pride has been severely dented and this evening's sales tactics using Leila will have hindered her further. She is not a happy bunny!

"Where shall we go?" I ask her now I'm finished, wondering if she wants to head off and find Robbie!

"Could we just go back to yours, and have a little drink on the balcony? Look through the photos and reminisce as the sun comes up?"

"Of course we can!" I laugh at her stricken expression, obviously expecting me to tell her off.

She didn't go for the full 'bang' but it's the perfect ending to Leila's last night. She came, she saw, she did and I know she is taking a new attitude home with her! It won't be long before she feels confident enough to dip a toe in the pool- who knows maybe she'll meet up with Robbie back in the UK.

We've looked through the album on her phone which has grown considerably since this morning oohing, ahhing and laughing considerably. Tonight's escapades finally exhausted conversation turns to the tedious subject of tomorrows arrangements.

"When are you coming back Jodes?" She asks me.

I gaze out to the pale pink sky reflecting in the rosy sea and sigh. It reminds me of the sunset duvet I have at home. Home! "I don't know. Soon I suppose."

I am most definitely going to need a recovery period before embarking on my new school job. That would mean leaving by Tuesday at least- so one week left maximum.

"Cat's been struggling with Esmay a lot! And Glenda has been kicking off at Chris again! Poll's got a new bird and Bill..." She stops and wrinkles her nose. "Well, just so you know, everyone's missed you Jodie! It's been crap without you."

I'm touched that I've been missed and the mundane sameness of our everyday life back home doesn't seem quite as dull as it had done. I almost crave monotony. Almost! I *never* thought I'd say that!

We sink our final alcopop and get ready for bed.

"Night night my Magaluf worker friend." Leila says padding over to me at the dresser and giving me a squeeze.

"Night night. Thanks for coming to see me!"

"Don't be ridiculous. It's me who should be thanking you! It's been the best!"

She climbs into bed pulling the sheet up to her chin. "Just be careful Jodes, I want you back in one piece next week!"

EVERYTHING CHANGES AGAIN

From the moment I wake up I have a lump in my throat. It should be the other way round I think as Leila chats happily over a tapas lunch. She has to get in a taxi in one hour. She's back to work tomorrow!

"I feel like this trip has changed me!"

"I'm not surprised!" I laugh picking at the olives.

"I feel more-" She searches for the word and I know any number could complete the sentence; confident, motivated, attractive!

"Alive!" She finally decides.

"Good for you!" I grin at her warmly and feel happiness at assisting with it.

"See you soon!" Leila's voice is captured inside as the taxi driver shuts her door, striding round to his own side. I swallow hard several times to dislodge the rapid onset of emotion and wave until it is out of sight.

It's almost 4 so I have 2 hours of work to drag myself through before I can go home and cry my eyes out. Ok, so it isn't that bad but I do feel pretty low.

It's a shame my working hours have changed because I could really do with another night on Tanya's balcony getting high! I type a text out to her for the sake of something to do. She soon replies suggesting we have breakfast tomorrow.

Ok ☺ I reply.

The shift drags and it's a real effort to muster up the friendly banter I need. Some people completely ignore me, this is nothing new but today it grates on me.

"No we're fine thanks!" I loudly answer my own question of 'fancy a drink?' The couple in question look back over their shoulder startled by my voice. Oh you hear me now don't you!

As 6 o clock rolls around I return to my old routine of shop bought sandwiches and other comfort items retreating to my bedroom and the magazines left by Leila.

Thoroughly caught up on the latest celebrity gossip I waddle into the living room and blankly watch nature documentaries. Leila messages to say she's home safe and Stacey and Andy leave for work. After another hour it's time for me to get ready before doing the same.

I stroll to Blush in a daze. My vibe is only temporarily snuffed. It'll come back I'm sure. Just wait until I'm back having fun with the girls.

I arrive to find Gemma looking unusually ruffled, her complexion is blotchy. Beth is at her side also looking glum.

"What's happened *now*?" I ask them because it's obvious something has, at which point Stacey looking positively distraught bursts through the doors.

"Jodie! It. Was. Horrid!" She screams. What now? Worse than India having her face scratched off?

"Tony sacked Stevie!"

"What!" I reel to Gemma for confirmation. "Why?"

Stacey continues, "Because he's a horrible mean old man!"

"They wanted *me* to PR!" Heather is upon us, this being the first thing she's directed at me since she laid into me that night.

"So? What's that got to do with Stevie?"

"She didn't sell enough." Gemma answers me now and I still don't get what the connection is here.

"I refused. I'm not going anywhere! So they got rid of the girl who sold the least instead." Her chin lifts defiantly and Gemma stares at her disgustedly.

"You could've taken one for the team! It wouldn't have even been for long!" Gemma tells her angrily.

"There is no team!" Heather bawls throwing up her arms exasperated. "And anyway, Jodie should've been asked to do it! She was the PR after all!"

I feel bad for Heather, it probably *should've* been me, and even sorrier for Stevie.

"I, erm will do it?" I offer resolutely thinking of the damage that has been done to the friendship group. After all I'm leaving in less than a week- if I'd already gone- or had at least been honest about my departure this situation might have been avoided.

"He won't let you Jodie!" Stacey cries. "He said himself; you're the best shot girl he's got!"

He did? I smile and almost ask for more details before noticing the look of hurt on Heather's face and I wince for her.

"It's all your fucking fault!" Gemma lashes out at Heather and looking further affronted she stalks away taking her Jagerbombs with her.

I actually feel like it's all *my* fault but cowardly this isn't something I'm forthcoming in admitting.

Instead I trudge inside to fetch my tray feeling truly awful for everybody and wait at the bar for my shots. Tony gives me 'the nod' but I don't feel anywhere near as happy to receive it. Stevie has lost her job. And I'll be giving it up in less than a week. I'll have to tell them soon!

And how will the girl's feel about me then?

The blame will be shifted from Heather to me instead; which is not entirely unfair. This is a lifestyle for her. She's here to earn her living not make friends; which is probably a good job because she's done a great job of both!

Back out on the veranda we are all depressed. Unhelpfully the bar is quiet again and our punctured happiness is palpable. By 2am I've sold 4 trays. It's like my first night all over again. I don't think the others are having much luck either, Gemma is barely trying.

We have pulled back on the reins an unspoken decision to subtly punish Tony for punishing Stevie so unfairly. Other than Heather of course, who is back to her brassy self and laps up every opportunity quite unperturbed.

I hand over the money for my 7th tray at just before 4 o clock. Less than half of last night's record. Tony looks over the list taking notice of how many we have managed.

"Jo-die." He grunts. "You try harder. Tomorrow! I want more." He warns me.

I want gets nothing I want to retort sarcastically but I'm torn between loyalty to my upset friends and my own needs.

I plod home. I was trying to get to grips with the notion of leaving soon and now Stevie has been sacked! She has lost out to girls prepared to do things that she (and most normal people) find outrageous. I wonder if it was the same for Jess too, is that why she was always complaining about Tony? Magaluf operates like the circle of life; nurturing souls, helping them to grow, but recycling them when the necessity arises.

Stacey has come back as well. The party spirit had no chance tonight. We bid each other goodnight and go to our separate rooms. I climb into bed looking forward more than ever to seeing Tanya in the morning.

BREAKFAST WITH TANYA

"Soo!" Tanya maintains the excitement that I seem to have misplaced. Maybe Leila accidentally packed it and took it back with her. "What's the goss with Justin?"

Wow! So much has happened since I last saw her- Justin is old news! Almost!

I tell her, anyway, about the suspected photos and how they turned out be a tactic to get me into bed with Ben. I thought she would be staggered but;

"Oh god, *old* PR trick!" She says instead. "When I had the emergency phone once, this girl called to say she was shagging in the toilets and a PR had leaned over and took a picture of her!"

"Not quite the same!" I appeal but laugh all the same.

"Yes well she had a boyfriend and they wanted money to delete it!"

"Woah!" I gasp. "Not the same at all!"

It's an amusing story and an interesting money spinner! Well, she shouldn't have been doing the dirty should she? Good job Ben didn't know about Cassie's status!

This brings us conveniently to an update on Cassie- who is newly single and Alexa who is madly in love- yet again. Tanya rolls her eyes as she tells me about *another* man she is adamant is the one.

"I mean how many 'worlds' can one girl have? She's built a whole bloody universe just this year!" I splutter with laughter and know Tanya loves the girl really. "So have you seen Justin since?" She probes returning our focus to the original subject.

"No." I admit. "I'll see him tomorrow- he's working on a bar crawl which comes to us."

"So work is going ok then?" She instigates a fresh topic. This opens up a whole new can of worms- one that takes the best part of eating to unravel.

"Fucking hell!" Tanya finally concludes, for once surprised. "Well you know you can come and stay at mine if you just wanted to get out of there!"

"What do you mean?" Up until now I'd envisioned giving them some notice, telling Tony or Jamie that I'd booked a flight. Telling the girl's when my last shift would be. "Like back door it?"

It occurs to me that I could, as Heather put it, backdoor it. Run away to Tanya's; quit Blush, before going home a few days later.

"Well why not? You don't have a contract."

"I know that but the girl's, I can't just leave!"

"So tell the one you live with, what's her name? Explain to her and do one."

She makes everything sound so possible and when we part ways I thank her for the offer. I'm not taking her up on it. Yes I felt down when Leila left and last night was an uncomfortable turn-up. But I'm happy to go with the flow until the very end!

I'll face the music, soon!

After enjoying a lazy afternoon at the beach I learn that Stevie has found a new job already. She's doing bar work and gets a stable wage which she says suits her much better!

That night I throw myself into making sales only partly motivated by Tony's looming presence and the girls are in better moods. It's going to work out ok, I'll leave, Heather can go back to being top shotter and Stevie prefers her circumstances now anyway- all's well that ends well as they say! And it isn't ending yet!

Blush isn't the busiest it's been but there are enough people to sell to. I feel sure I can keep Tony happy and improve on my 7 trays of last night! And I even sling Heather a sale, an olive branch which she takes. Whether she appreciates it, is another matter but I am appeased.

"Ay love can you get us any coke?" I'm asked after completing a sale. I pass over Face's number how he asked me to do.

"Tell him Jodie from Blush gave you it." I tell him.

"Cheers darling!" He calls to me after a short phone call and gives me a thumbs up as he heads off, presumably to meet the Maga-strip dealer. I feel accomplished that I can help him in his quest.

Gemma, Stacey and I go on to meet Stevie after the shift, keen to show our support.

"It's been fab I've honestly really enjoyed it!" Stevie reassures us after we bombard her with inquisitive questions about her first shift.

We head up the strip together at gone 5, Stacey and me leaving them at the alley to finish our journeys.

Once back I fall asleep reflecting on all the things that have happened so far. I have got to think about booking this flight; as I much as I want to put off the affirming deed, I need to book it definitely by the weekend!

There have been so many highs and plenty of lows. But even the worst of it leaves me with no regrets- and the slight feeling of impending worry at the thought of going home settles lightly across my chest.

ENJOY YOUR TRIP?

It turns out the Germans have been playing football this afternoon and at 5 o clock the strip provides a drip feed of extremely pissed fans. They lost. Cue: hysterical, howling men meandering fed up and lost. It would seem nationality is irrespective to how the loss of the country's team is handled.

"Do you want to come party?" I am being propositioned now in broken English, spittle flying from his wet mouth. "With me?"

"The party is in here!" I bluff but really can't wait for them to move on. He's sozzled and stands way too close for comfort.

"I already have a drink!" He informs me holding a pint of something orange so close to my face it blurs.

"Yes I can see, well…" I'm just about to side step them- role reversal! When he swoops down and grasps me around my waist with one arm. My only reaction is to take the pint from him allowing him to steady his hold. I hate being picked up, fearing I'll be dropped.

But before I can demand that he puts me down immediately, he begins lurching unsteadily across the road.

"Max!" I call out. "Help!"

A few people turn to stare but the scene isn't really that out of the ordinary.

"Put me down!" I plea realising nobody is coming to my rescue. Suddenly he's falling. I fucking knew it! We're both falling! And with a crack I'm slammed into the road. Pain sears from my thigh, elbow and shoulder having taken the full brunt on my left side. Fuelled by adrenalin I jump to my feet examining the pint glass which is empty but miraculously intact, I could've thrown it all over myself but I don't notice as I dart to the pavement.

I see coaches rumble this stretch regularly enough to know we are both in danger of being squished.

Taking a deep steadying breath, I look down at myself to assess the damage. If there's blood I'm going to faint!

My thigh is red and scuffed; this pattern follows the whole length of my leg. I instinctively reach down to brush any remaining gravel out of my skin and feel a sharp jolt from my elbow.

It's swollen and as I carefully twist it this way and that to check for cuts- negative- I can hear a low moan and it rises in volume, snatching my attention.

Spinning around I spot the German still sitting in the road- his head is bright red with blood.

Fuck! I feel bile instantly rise in my throat and my vision jerks violently. I can't even see where the wound is there is so much wet redness; it is literally dripping off him onto the pale grey road.

His friend is by his side, there are people scrambling towards him, one with a huge roll of white tissue paper.

"Get… out... road!" I croak virtually incoherently.

"Don't you think you've done enough damage?" Somebody shouts to me.

I can only focus on the injured man- my eyes drawn against my will. He's grinning lopsidedly trying to stand. His face is smeared with blood and his friend is trying to continue wrapping a thick crown of paper to stem it.

"Come and party!" He slurs completely unfazed! In his state it'd be hard to recognise signs of concussion.

I am no help in this state and have no choice but to stumble onto the veranda in the direction of the toilets.

I barge past Max who is standing in the doorway observing the scene.

He doesn't ask if I'm ok, doesn't even look at me just stares mutely over my head at the gory commotion.

I am going to pass out! And I can't do it out here in front of *any* of these people! I'm not even hurt in comparison to him. I got off so lightly!

This thought only intensifies the hollow swell in my stomach. My skin boils icily and I pour with sweat, but at least it isn't blood!

My palm is clammy on the rail leading downstairs and it takes all my effort to stay focussed enough to get to the loo.

Thankfully there is no toilet attendant at this time of the day and as I lose vision I guide myself along the cold tiled walls before slumping to the floor.

I am conscious but barely and completely paralysed in an egg position. Then I begin to dry retch which makes me feel better loosening the boulder in my stomach and I finally relax my body. After a long minute concentrating on my rhythmic breathing, I shift position. Placing my cheek against the cold tiled wall the feeling begins to lift.

I sit up right leaning my back on the cool wall now. My vision is back and I blink a few times to make sure it's not going to turn off again. That was really scary. A few more moments and I clamber upright. I go over to the sink, splash my face with cool water, pat it dry with some tissue and stare at my expressionless reflection.

I am pale even in this murky orange mirror. Blood has made me feel funny twice before this- it's when it involves a shock and I haven't eaten much that day. I recognised the impending feeling instantly. I shudder. It's an awful, uncontrollable reaction.

But forget me, that poor guy! I feel sick again. What an idiot though! Typical alcohol induced, I'm-superman-syndrome. He could've cracked *my* head open!

Back out on the veranda Max is serving a couple in their 60's. I'm curious to know what the outcome is and flit my eyes over the road expectantly. It's empty!

"Here she is!" The lady calls out and for a moment I wonder if I know her. "Are you ok dear? We saw what happened! I said to Roy we must go over there and check that poor girl's ok! Quite a fright it must've given you!"

Roy nods along and adds. "So *are* you ok? We were worried, weren't we! Joy nearly came to look for you!"

I feel so overwhelmed by this act of kindness I almost burst into tears. Sweet Joy and Roy!

"Erm, yes! No!" I answer suddenly remembering my elbow. I look down at it, there's going to be a bruise but that's all. I look at my leg and the redness has already virtually disappeared. If it wasn't for Joy and Roy (and the substantial blood stains on the road) I might have thought I'd exaggerated the whole thing!

"Looks like you were one lucky lady!" Roy comments taking in my appearance.

Max has gone inside and it's just me and them.

"Where is he? Is he ok?" I ask them. People thought it was *my* fault! Like I'd been asking for it to happen somehow! I feel a stab of anger. How could I have predicted that? Like most things before this it wasn't an average occurrence. As if I would want to endanger myself like that-and him! He had looked in a bad way.

"Has he gone in an ambulance?" I manage to ask.

"No, no. He'll be sore in the morning!" Joy says warm eyes twinkling.

"Just a nick." Roy points to a spot on his head. "They always bleed more. They always look far worse than they actually are!" He tells me reassuringly. I probably look completely spooked and I am actually really glad for their presence.

"Far too much to drink lovey." Joy continues. "He wanted to carry on with his 'partying'. What does that tell you? You should carry on with yours!"

She quotes the word partying and accompanies it with a tinkling laugh- as if our generation have no idea about partying and I realise- I actually believe her. Her last sentence resonates with me too. I've brushed myself off, almost fainted and all in all he's ok. I should carry on with mine!

"Silly buggar got no less than he deserved. Picking you up like that, just thank goodness it wasn't *you* who got hurt!" She says firmly sitting back with her hands in her lap.

Max returns with a tray. He serves Joy and Roy before passing me a drink.

"Thought you needed something *stiff*." He smirks. I can't decipher his tone *or* his eyes. They're neither nasty nor nice but the drink is very welcome. "Sit down Jodie. Take a break."

I look at him. It's a considerate offer considering he didn't come to my aid when I shouted him. I know he would have heard me.

Courteously accepting I pull up a chair with Joy and Roy. They chat to me about the 60's and 70's, turns out they were not only partial to marijuana *and* LSD but also sex parties (yes! I am talking swinging and groupies with grandparents). Only in Magaluf could I find senior sex pests!

It's a delightful contrast with the majority stuffy pensioners I was used to meeting through my restaurant work.

I glance at the road every time I see movement; it's a knee-jerk reaction not wanting to miss any custom. And I keep reminding myself I'm allowed a break.

Looking up yet again I'm stunned with surprise; and like a rabbit caught in head lights stare straight into the haggard face of old woman girl. I'd almost forgotten all about her and here she is looking straight at me.

"Did you split a German's head open?" She demands to know and I stammer. What the fuck do I say? Is he her boyfriend? Oh shit!

"*She* didn't split his head open!" Joy tuts.

"He did quite a fine job of doing that to himself!" Roy elaborates. This feels dramatically worse to the feeling of falling an hour or so earlier.

She lurches towards me and slaps my shoulder. "Good fucking on ya!" She congratulates me and I just continue to stare. I don't know *what* is happening but, oh I wish Leila was still here! Even if just to tell me to stop bloody staring at her!

"That cunt stole my money. I heard he'd been seen here, some PR girl knocked him clean out. Followed the blood, BOOM! Fucking found him! Got my money!" She smiles goofily. "I owe you sister!"

I'm overcome and Joy giggles with glee not at all phased by the language.

Max comes out now cautiously watching us.

"What you drinking mate?" She asks me and I pull myself together but Max answers for me.

"She don't keep company with the likes of you. Now sling your hook you sket!"

Her bloodless lips stretch across stained teeth and she narrows her eyes at him. Nobody speaks and she turns abruptly shouting.

"FUCK OFF!" As she leaves.

I turn to Max.

"Why were you so *rude*?" I scold him feeling sure Joy and Roy will agree.

"Jodie, she's a druggy and a thief. Do you not know she set fire to somebody's hotel room?"

"What!" My mind reels more than it already is.

"And that she burgled a workers apartment the other day? Don't you know anything?" He shakes his head in disbelief and my mind whirs with my own.

No, as I regularly realise, I obviously don't know anything! If only I'd just asked somebody about her!

It certainly explains a lot.

And, shit, I'm on her radar now! She called me sister! I'll have to spend the rest of my time *hiding* from her. How ironic, I have been actively looking for her up until now! Not that she'll likely come back here thanks to Max.

Was he looking out for me? He didn't save me from my fall but has he saved me from something far worse?

2 more brandies plus the couple's easy going nature soothes my frazzled nerves. I can't take any more of this life! I think dramatically as I traipse home at 6.

I am definitely benefitting from my new no dwelling standpoint. Both of today's events could have been much worse! The 'trip' and then druggy, thief, arsonist old-woman girl! But they weren't and I won't sift through pointless internal dialogue about what could have been.

Back at the flat I check Stacey's room, she isn't there. I go to my room and sit on my bed staring at the wall and then I decide to take a nap.

I awake at my 9pm alarm- starving! Joy's wise words linger with me. Carry on partying! I feel a small buzz of welcome excitement. Perhaps today's adrenalin has jumpstarted my system back into action!

I choose a boob-tube to wear with my skirt. They're handy garments! Justin should be there when I arrive too- there's nothing wrong with looking nice and it's nothing to do with him!

The strip is fairly busy and as I approach our PR territory Ryan calls;

"Enjoy your trip did you Jodie!"

I give him a sarcastic smile. No thanks to our barman!

And Jamie approaches me now. Don't you joke about it as well!

"Max tells me that Wendy was in here earlier. Don't fucking get involved with her mate, she's *bad* news!"

"Yes I know Max said." I tell him sincerely. I don't get the impression this is a he said, she said tale.

"He did you a favour telling her to fuck off Jodes."

I nod and head to the veranda cursing Max for worming his way back onto 1 page of my good book.

As always, the pub crawl has taken over inside, bodies dancing wildly, reps tipping Sambuca into their open mouths. I spot Justin but he doesn't see me. I take a lingering moment of appreciation whilst he isn't alerted. Yes, I'm so over it!

Fetching my shots I go back outside and do what the rest of the girls do- wait for them to leave.

I get a casual wink from J as they do and I pack away my disappointment it wasn't more. Probably for the best!

Spirits have firmly returned amongst the group since Stevie is happy in her new job. Gemma reports that she prefers it because there is no constant pressure to sell. All guilt is alleviated and I sensationally explain to them about my ordeal today showing off the bruise on my elbow and pointing out the bloodstained road.

CHOICES

At half past 1 I am going back for my fifth tray- not too shabby in relation to the custom we have had since the bar crawl.

The loss of Carl and Amy is definitely more noticeable as the nights have gone on.

Tony beckons me and whilst Max tops up my tray I go over to him.

"More." He growls bluntly. I look at him ready to disagree and raise an arm to signal the lack of custom. But before I can reason with him he leans closer and grunts. "You can do more. They touch you? You sell more!"

I am aghast and step backwards to look properly at his face. It is closed and hard. I think I've understood his message correctly- and I don't like the connotation one bit.

Max has set me up a new tray and Tony nods to it shutting down any opportunity to appeal. But what can I say? I know my choices, follow orders or leave.

I down a brandy and coke and retreat to the veranda with my tray.

"Tony threatened me! He wants me to sell more." I complain to Beth and Stacey.

"For fuck's sake." Beth rolls her eyes. "He's a tight git! But you can sell more Jodes, get stuck in."

She doesn't know the suggestion he's given but after opening and closing my mouth a few times I decide to withhold it and return her smile instead.

"Yeah, I can do it!" I say.

What's the point in complaining, look where it had got Jess! Although at least if I got sacked I couldn't be held accountable for leaving them in the lurch! Which is more cowardly, getting the sack on purpose or back dooring it? I'm not considering either really but it is a delightful, blame-free musing.

"Do what you gotta do." Beth tells me with a smirk and watches as more custom comes our way.

Paying for extras is rife, normal it would seem! Gemma virtually admitted to doing something, fanny flashing by all accounts, does Beth let them touch her? I'm not about to let anybody touch me though. I know I thought that about flashing my boobs too! But seriously this really is one step too far even for ballsy, crazy me.

My work experience here is hardly going to make it onto my CV- role responsibilities: expose myself for sales! But even so 'sexual contact for cash' isn't going to be added to my mental record.

"Evening boys. Fancy a shot and seeing my boobs?" I grin at a group of 3. "10 euros each. I get a shot, you get a shot and then I'll flash me baps." Smiling I feel the familiar indulgent buzz when they look at each other amazed- can't believe their luck- and begin to hand over the cash.

This way I get rid of 6, have the added bonus of drinking 3 myself- and it's all over quick time! I raise the blue and black bulb chinking his before swallowing it down.

Eugh! What is that? Because whatever it is, it's not cheeky vimto! The guys look untroubled and I shake my head. Maybe my taste buds have been singed off, my tongue permanently damaged from the vodka. I thought switching to brandy had made me feel better but now I'm not so sure.

They'd tasted fine up until now!

"Thanks guys!" I head for the next table bewildered. They are wide-eyed waiting for a similar offer.

"Cheeky vimto?" I ask a little less confidently. That was not cheeky vimto! What's changed?

"And teets?" He asks with a Norwegian accent. I nod,

"Yes, 'teets' and a shot 10 euros." I have 4 left, one each for these and I'm a tray down in 20 minutes.

"Blue W. K. D and port, no?" His friend asks taking one and inspecting it. "Cute cup!" He states.

I wonder if they will be able to taste the difference but nod anyway. "Yes, cool nice eh?"

"Yes, yes." He takes out a ten as do the others. "And we see your teety?" He checks it's for real one last time and I beam proudly.

"Yes, and teety!" I echo amused.

Shots done I'm about to pull down the boob tube and;

"That's not cheeky vimto!" He frowns and shakes his head confirming what I had hoped to blag. He looks to his friends and says something in Dutch, they too shake their heads.

"It's not cheeky vimto." He tells me again now and just as I think he's going to ask for his money back he says;

"Teety?"

I watch Max refill the next tray and realise I am victim to yet *another* cost cutting technique. He uses a splash of vodka mixed with soda and blue curacao filling the bulbs almost to the top before adding the smallest amount of port which sinks slightly, barely creating the usual black bubble on top.

They aint cheeky vimtos no more! I look over to Tony who gives me a patronizing thumbs-up. I no longer want his approving nod and this is somehow worse.

I take my brandy and coke with me; I'm not completely avoiding Rushkinoff then! Back out on the veranda I approach a large group- counting 10- perfect!

"How are you boys?" I ask them but they ignore me continuing their loud chat.

"Do you wanna see my tits?" I shout brazenly which gains me the attention of those closest.

"Yeah, but we aint paying for it!" One calls gleefully and flies forward hand stretched out toward my boob tube.

Not so fast you little shit, I anticipate his move and lurch backwards leaving him to grasp a handful of air.

"Behave." I tell him firmly. "Else you won't be seeing anything. You naughty boy!" I add for good measure getting into the swing of my upcoming teaching role (bad joke).

He has managed to gain me the full attention of his group and I let the laughter subside before telling them;

"Ten euros each. A shot each and I'll flash my boobs."

"How long for?"

"3 seconds." I answer without hesitation; I'm surprised how frequently this is asked! They nod in approval united in their decision.

100 euros tucked away I beadily eye the cups I've given out. So far I have avoided any 1 euro fines for them going missing and I'd like to keep it that way.

"One! Two! Three!" The group rapturously calls whilst fixating their eyes on my naked breasts. It is a feeling of despicable magnificence.

"Eugh!" A couple of them begin to comment on the imposter shots.

"They're shit, that's not cheeky vimto!"

I won't be able to get away with reselling to any tables once I've hit them once. Nobody wants a repeat performance of the inadequate concoctions and they don't *need* another flash of my tits. I'm now limited to one sale per table.

Just gone 2 o clock, tray 6. I need to carry on at this rate to get firmly back into double figures which is where I reckon Tony is expecting us all to be.

I look around inside, weighing up possibilities whilst Max mixes up more rancid versions of cheeky vimto.

How dare Tony cut corners and then pile on the pressure at the same time. He is pushing me to do more, hoping I'll succumb and this makes me feel very uncomfortable around him.

"Are we going out tonight?" Stacey asks me when I'm outside again and I grin.

"Yeah why not?" *Carry on partying!* "Where shall we go?"

"Beth says there's a worker's party at Mulligans. We could go there? I don't think anyone else is tonight though."

"Well, we can still go can't we?" I say looking into her cute, round face which smiles widely and nods.

We hit the next large group to enter together. Between them and another couple another tray is cleared, another tray fetched; another brandy and coke gone and another few shots for me.

But then it slows even more. And by half past three I have limped towards tray number 9. I know already Tony won't be happy but I really have tried my hardest. I have 2 'cheeky vimtos' left and I don't want to sell them now because then I'll be given 10 more!

As if conjured by my thoughts Tony appears on the veranda. He signals for me and Gemma to go over.

"You 2- sell another tray." He tells us to my disappointment. "I want you on 10." And then he stomps back inside being swallowed by dry ice.

"This is starting to piss me off!" Gemma cries and I wonder if she's being subjected to the same pressures as me. Heather swaggers by.

"*I've* done 10." She calls breezily and spitefully I can't help but wish I *had* rubbed my previous successes in her face.

"Oh fuck off." Gemma mutters under her breath and I feel exactly the same about Tony *and* the grenade!

What used to be fun and indecently naughty rapidly becomes tiresome and ritualistic.

12 shots in 30 minutes! I'm not a magician! Not only are the shots bad tasting, makeshift versions but there's hardly more than 12 people here to sell to.

I haven't made as many tips tonight, choosing instead to drink plenty of the shots in lieu myself; main focus to make sales as rapidly as possible. I hand one of the 2 left over to Gemma.

"Come on, have this and let's show him what we can do!"

She takes the shot from me with pursed lips murmuring.

"Thanks." And necks it in two large gulps. "Eugh!" Her lips recoil from her pearly white teeth. "That's awful! What is it?"

I completely forgot to warn her having almost got used to the replica myself.

"Oh yeah, sorry! Forgot to tell you. Another cost cutting method!" I reel off the new ingredients and she shakes her head.

"Fuck you Blush." She makes a weak attempt at our private joke but then concedes. "I might leave. This is a joke!" And she marches inside to top up her tray. Wow, leave Magaluf or leave Blush? Surely just this place, at this rate there will be no staff left! Then will Tony be happy!

Back inside I catch India's eye and smile at her whilst waiting for Gemma to be sorted. She was right about healing quickly, her scratches are fading already; that or she's using some good cover up tricks! Either or, it puts into perspective my own experience earlier. I came off nowhere near as badly as her.

Once I'm reloaded I try those dancing and loitering by the bar knowing Tony is watching me like a hawk. Successfully I sell 4 feeling self-conscious when I flash my boobs for them. I tried and failed without the offer- as is often the case. My boobs have been out so much tonight the staff have already had an eyeful anyway! No point feeling embarrassed now.

As I head to the veranda already scanning the tables and knowing my chances of selling 6 are slim Gemma strides back inside followed by 2 guys. I watch curiously as she takes them down the stairs towards the cellar and toilets and can only imagine what she is doing.

My assumptions are definitely along the right lines. This is not a coincidence! But resolutely I know I'd rather buy the remaining shots myself than go further than I have already. I don't regret what I have done so far, and I don't want to risk pushing it into the realms of another mistake.

Heather is standing by one table, noisily demanding they buy another from her. She's so happy to be back in top shot position, she can bloody have it!

2 of these tables I have already sold to- they know it isn't 'cheeky vimto' and are a no go.

2 girls sit hunched together and I decide to pray on them. You know. Girl-to-girl! This is a tactic I have relied on previously- chat to them about the PR's and their wayward behaviour, recommend the best places to go. And then casually drop in how I only earn 1 euro per shot (tiny lie because most of the time I earn at least 2), in the hope they'll be kind enough to part with some cash. Chances are they are drinking for free a majority of the time anyway! And shame-on-me it usually works.

They are nice girls, very young- barely 18 I'd guess. First time here and completely overwhelmed with the seedy nature. They instantly latch on to anything I can tell them- I warn them about keeping their bags close, recommend they rent a pedalo, but to keep an eye out for jellyfish, encourage them to have fun but don't let the workers have fun with them. I feel like a big sister but in sibling fashion I have to take advantage slightly;

"So you lovely ladies gunna help me out and buy a shot?"

"Cheeky vimto?" Charlotte presumes. "I love them!"

I cringe and then break.

"I'll be honest, they're not even proper cheeky vimto's. You'll find that most bars water them down!"

They giggle at this but it doesn't deter them! Yes!

I have 4 left now.

"Hey girl's, where are you headed next? You can come out with me and my friend Stacey if you like?"

"Yay!" They agree.

I'm finished here- for tonight. Let's carry on partying!

The last 4 will just have to come out of my wage. There is literally nobody left and it tastes like absolute shit. I'm lucky Charlotte and Kim subjected themselves to it!

I know somebody else who will subject themselves- free alcohol after all!

"Stacey!" I call to her. "Fancy helping me to clear up!"

I warn her they aren't 'real', we drink 2 each and I introduce her to the girls. She's as happy as me to escort them to a worker's party- we'll give them an eye opener tonight.

The 4 of us head to Mulligans. Tony's gratified and I'm rather pissed and listen grinning inanely as the tourists babble about what they've seen so far.

"She was sucking it! *Actually* giving him a blow job in the middle of the street!"

Not so shocking to me anymore.

We tell the bouncers that our friends have just started working with us- they're easily convinced and we head inside. I notice and recognise some of the PR's from down here- and there's Carl!

"There's Carl!" I shout to Stacey over the music. Her head pings up at the name and she darts immediately towards him. Must have missed him! I think but after a quick exchange she's heading back.

"Shall we get fishbowls?" She asks nodding to a 5 euro fishbowl sign.

I assume this is a direct attempt to change the conversation and allow it nodding along with the other 2. Stacey and I push ourselves to the front of the bar and I hoist myself up making it clear I am waiting to be served.

When I turn ready to pass the bowls backwards as they're handed to me Stacey is nowhere to be seen. I quickly scan the crowd and signal for Charlotte to come and help. Where is she? Charlottes takes her and Kim's and with mine and Stacey's bowl sloshing in my hands I see her now. She bounds towards me grinning, takes the fishbowl and we head to the dance floor. There's a raised area to my left which is packed with gyrating bodies and I watch them whilst boogying ourselves. One couple are fully going at it, hands wandering all over each other's bodies completely unfazed by the heaving commotion surrounding them.

I look at Stacey whose eyes flicker around the place- she's dancing distractedly. Charlotte and Kim jive by our sides and I observe the astonishment on their faces as they too watch the passionate couple. Their hands now inside each other's clothes.

I'm surprised it still shocks them- they've seen their fair share already by all accounts but I enjoy watching their stunned glee all the same at the distasteful behaviour.

"Isn't that…" Stacey is calling something to me but I can't hear her above the pounding music. Ironically Jason Derulo chants 'daylight comes and we don't wanna go home!' And I happily sing along, meaning it and shrug in response to Stacey.

"I can't hear you!" I call to no avail.

It hasn't got the casual vibe of the workers party the other night-it is loud and rowdy in here.

"Jodie," Stacey is trying again. What's up with her tonight? "Isn't that…"

I don't have time to ask her to repeat it for the third time because at that moment a hand cups my bum and a familiar voice says;

"Fancy seeing you here." Hot breath tickles my ear and I spin around to face Justin. He is so dazzlingly gorgeous. I have only been kidding myself if I thought I was remotely 'over' him.

He pulls my hand towards him, snaking it around his waist and I relish the feel of his warm, hard body under his vest. The oxygen in my lungs leaves me with a jolt and loosened by the alcohol I just for a moment enjoy the contact between us.

Grimacing I remove my hand and give his chest a push.

"Fuck. Off!" I mouth to him and slowly turn away. I don't want you to fuck off!

Inner voice: fuck off!

"He's fit!" Charlotte yells in my ear and I shake my head. The music is far too loud for me to explain. Kim also throws me an approving look and I roll my eyes.

He's back, pressing his scratchy cheek into my neck whilst speaking directly into my ear.

"Come outside with me." He winds his hands around my waist and I let them linger on my own sculpted stomach.

Let him see what he's missing, I think boldly.

"Come outside with me." He repeats and he smells so good I can feel myself thinking where's the harm?

"I'll be back!" I shout to Stacey who is barely paying us attention anyway and let Justin guide me through the crowds. I indulge in the admiring glances he attracts, delighting in other girl's wishing they were me; the one being led by the hand of this beautiful boy.

We step outside and a bubble of music escapes into the warm night air with us before Justin shuts the door trapping the din inside.

"Why you being so cool with me Shorty?" He addresses me and pulls a cigarette out of the box offering it to me.

I decide to take one because why else have I come with him otherwise. Yes, Jodie, why else indeed!

"You made it this way." I tell him flippantly and wait for him to hand over the lighter. I used to be a full time smoker but have given up- except for the odd special occasion. Like when it involves weed, I muse. Or Justin evidently!

"Come on girl, I'm just playing around with you." He says smirking, looking up from under his eyebrows sexily.

Don't cave Jodie. He might be *the* fittest boy in the universe but there'll be more. There are more!

"Ben told me you about you being a pervert!" I exaggerate for my own benefit. "Pictures of girl's privates whilst they sleep, really?"

But he's undeterred and throws an arm to his face letting out a loud laugh.

"Sly bastard!" He exclaims now eyes wide, face open and candid. "He *tricked* you babe! It's our private joke you know? When we fancy each other's bird it's we tell them the other one does something weird!"

"Ok." I know this but; did he just refer to me as his bird!

"You called me a slag!" I try again and he maintains my eye contact taking a long draw on his fag. I realise mine has burnt down without me taking a pull and defiantly put it to my lips. You are so divine! I want to yell at him plugging them with the butt instead.

"But you are just a slag really babe." He laughs wickedly eyes flashing. "We *all* are. It's only *natural.*"

Yes the comment is shameless but no it doesn't shock me. It *is* only natural, isn't it? And I am a 'slag' for it. He's only stating the conclusions I already derived for myself.

Digging deep I find a scrap of willpower. I drop the cigarette to the floor and grind it into the ground.

"No thanks J." I force a smile. Then turn on my heel to re-enter the club.

For fuck sake, I push the door that needs pulling.

"Pull." Justin says amusedly.

"Really?" I retaliate. "I was going to try and lift it from the bottom!"

That isn't my own joke! I heard it somewhere and still finding it highly hilarious burst into hysterics. Insane, well done! Played it so cool there…

But I did it!

And do I feel proud? I'll be honest, no not really. My mind has fallen out with me, big time! What have I done! And my body is set on sabotage igniting a tormenting tornado of unspent desire.

Stacey spots me instantly, still scanning the crowd whilst two-stepping. Charlotte and Kim still stare agog at the spectacles on offer around them- the girl now has her leg wrapped around her partner, thrusting herself against him. They literally could be having sex in front of our very eyes and probably are.

"What… he want?" Stacey shouts to me. Conversation is going to be extremely stilted and I resort to good old fashioned finger gestures, to "do it".

"….going to do it?"

I shake my head. And use my hands to show 'no way' for good measure. Charlotte and Kim watch from the side lines trying to understand.

".. going...shag him?" Charlotte yells making my ear ring and not just with the shitty reality of it.

"No!" Another 'no way' signal. She looks perplexed.

"Why… fuck not!"

Yes Jodie 'why fuck not'!

I can't win. I try to do the right thing and it doesn't even feel right!

I resolutely get back into the dancing. Rihanna is cooing 'where have you been? Are you somewhere in the crowd?' The base drops, the lights flash and I try to enjoy myself. *Carry on partying!* This time next week I'll have had my first day in my new job!

A guy I don't recognise sidles up to us. He's wearing a flat cap, short with a handsome face. For a moment I think Stacey has pulled a random PR but to my surprise she winds a hand around his waist and gives him a deep kiss!

"Wow!" I can't help but stare. She kept that quiet! Charlotte and Kim pat my arm and clap happily. Their wide grins glow under the strobes.

Stacey doesn't have to bid us goodnight it is pretty clear there's only one thing on her agenda! I wonder who the mystery man is as they melt into the crowds and I lose sight of them completely.

Charlotte, Kim and I continue to bop and I feel immaturely disappointed. Why didn't she tell me? She's supposed to be my Maga-bestie!

Justin reappears now with a fishbowl for me holding it out like a grand prize. My heart skips a beat. He *is* the grand prize.

I laugh and take it from him. Should I be worried it's spiked? Probably a bit late in the day to be thinking about that but I hold it between us, pushing a straw towards his lips. That's how to check isn't it; see if there'll drink it themselves.

His full, smooth lips! I remember exactly how they felt the first time. The *last* time! He purses them round a straw and I do the same, our foreheads an inch apart. I know he is staring at me but I can't bring myself to look up from the ice cubes bobbing in the bowl. Icy shivers escape from my gut outwards as I gulp, and my whole body tingles.

We have completely emptied it, I have avoided brain freeze and I finally look up into his delicious face.

"Your place or mine?" He cocks his head and I wave unapologetically to Charlotte and Kim leaving Mulligans with J.

In a *million* years I did not think this would happen!

We are lying on my bed facing each other. Justin has paid me all the compliments in the world and not just about my sexual ability but how I make him laugh, how naturally beautiful I am, he loves my *sexy* eyes! Like serious gushing! In all areas, ahem!

His fingers have been lightly tickling my body and it doesn't matter where he places them my skin greets his touch with explosions of delight. I feel like I'm on fire with his energy.

Finally his hands investigate under my skirt. He kisses me all over my mouth and neck. I slip my own hand down his shorts. I am overcome with desire finding his huge, hard nob hot and throbbing in my hand. I firmly pump my fist up, down, up, down. I slide the wetness from his tip over his shaft with my thumb shuddering myself when he exclaims in pleasure.

As he urgently finds my slimy clit and begins pressing on it, rubbing it, burning prickles of pleasure erupt deep inside of me. I use my other hand to tug his shorts down and slip between his parted legs cupping his smooth balls, massaging them in return.

This is so freaking hot! I'm going to cum!

Just then he breaks away from the rubbing inserting his fingers easily inside of me. This is still great but I can feel the orgasm leaking away, the intensity gone.

I need to get a condom! I think distractedly but then as if sensing the change in my body J's fingertips return to my slippery and bulbous clitoris.

Fuck, my breathing is heavy, I am sweating. I can feel his dick twitching and he pumps his hips into my fist, grinding his pelvis pushing his balls flat into my hand.

"Argh, shit!" He gasps and I too feel the rush of climax overcome my bucking body. We are cumming together- it must be love!

The bed is a mess! I'm a mess! There's wet and white globs splattered across my skewwhiff clothes and the sheets between us. My inner thighs are completely soaked with my own as is Justin's hand and he examines it now looking a little bewildered.

"That was good!" He says excitedly, more to himself. Roughly pulling his shorts up with 1 hand he jumps up and strides from the room. For a split second I think he's leaving then I hear the bathroom light being switched on and a running tap.

"Alright mate!" He says as he appears back in my room a handful of tissue for me. I frown enquiringly and he thumbs towards the door shrugging. Andy I assume, lurking in the corridor again, he seems to be making a habit of that.

After dropping the tissue beside me he begins to put his trainers on.

"Aren't you staying?" I ask him eyeing the cleaner bed next to mine.

"Nah." He replies and doesn't look up from tweaking his laces.

"I'll see you Saturday then?" I say referring to the bar crawl. "I'm leaving next week!"

He hesitates slightly and my heart skips hopefully, I wouldn't have minded a cuddle but even more so, round 3- yes please!

He walks to the door though and finally meets my face.

"I'm off." He smirks and with that he's turned and gone.

Oh ok. I feel crestfallen as I hear the soft thump and click of the front door shutting behind him.

So I was perhaps a little silly to allow myself to believe his spiel. But he seemed so genuine! Of course he did, being a grade A player! There have been plenty of red flags. I've just chosen to ignore them all. I only have myself to blame for that!

But this really is one of those situations where I'd have regretted *not* doing it more than I regret doing it! I couldn't have closed the 'Justin' chapter in the way that I satisfactorily can now!

He just said whatever it took to get his end away; and all over my clothes and bedsheets at that. But I got mine away too as it were and I loved every second of it. I was hardly going to get into a relationship with him out here, or anywhere! It's not even what I'd want (honest)!

'I'm off' soon anyway, and 'I'm off' to a brilliant new start.

Stripping off properly I put a tee-shirt on before climbing into the spare bed. I won't allow myself to feel upset over Justin's obvious lack of respect for my feelings but I will fall asleep smiling about the compliments and the feel of his skin under my fingers. He came, I saw, we did. And I'm happy about that!

VILE PIG

I really need to book a flight today. Ideally I want to leave on Monday; and that's only 3 days away!

There's an internet café down the road. Once I'm ready I'll head there and, deep breath- *book* something!

To be honest I'm half tempted to book something sooner. The thought of another shift like last night! Tony bearing down on us and shots that don't taste anything like the real thing. And I've accomplished what I ultimately stayed to do-have another passionate night with Justin!

It's a soft, warm day and I stroll down the street. I'm going to miss it! I'm going to miss it all so much!

There are 3 computers free in the small, stuffy café. I take a seat at one and drop a few coins into the attached meter. I type 'flights from Magaluf to UK' and press enter. A list of sites professing cheap flights instantly fills the screen and I click onto Sky Scanner.

Flights today- no way too soon! But maybe it's what I need to do, like ripping off a plaster- painful but quick.

No!

Ok. Flights tomorrow, Sunday, Monday, Tuesday; they are as regular as buses to town from my village back home. I narrow the search to Sunday or Monday and to arrive at East Midlands. Or maybe Tuesday?

I start my new job Thursday- I have to relocate my inner voice of responsibility- which has remained dormant for almost a month! And both mum and Leila have Mondays off, either one could pick me up.

So Monday it is.

But now that I hover the cursor over the 'book' button I feel my heels dig into the ground. I slowly tap my card details into the relevant boxes. The last couple of weeks bats through my mind's eye like a flick book and finally I am confirming a midmorning flight on Monday.

Well, that's it!

A few more nights at work doesn't seem so bad now. I'm determined to enjoy what is left! Go out with a 'bang' and all that!

I actually feel really emotional! But I don't want to cry. Not again and not here!

'Flight Booked' I am informed, 'a notification has been sent to your email address'.

Well, that's that! I slip my phone out of my pocket and draft a text to send to my nearest and dearest- *I'm coming home Monday!*

I text Tanya as well to let her know the news; hopefully I get to see her once more before I leave.

I order a toastie and nibble on it replaying all of my best and worst memories. Despite any of the heartache I only have positive feelings towards Magaluf and about my decision to stay. It has been exactly the tonic I needed.

Tears averted I decide to hit the beach for a few hours. I'll avoid the others for now; I'll have to break it to Stacey later on. I'm inquisitive about her mystery man from last night- but I'm already dreading her reaction to this news! Her Maga-bestie is leaving her!

Hopefully this new man of hers will keep her suitably distracted. I wonder why she hadn't told me. Maybe I'm not her Maga-bestie and won't be missed after all! Her behaviour had been sketchy last night but I'd had no idea!

Once 4 o clock arrives and I am at Blush I feel happy after a day of chilling. I can't believe it but a part of me is *excited* about going home! I look and feel amazing- there'll definitely be a trip to the local pub on the cards now. To show off! There'll be no more hiding away for me.

Not only does everything that happened on the lead up to Magaluf feel irrelevant but so does a majority of what has happened here. The experiences with Max and J, the shagging of random boys, taking part in sex games, flashing my boobs and kissing lads for money! It's all being left here. Other than in my mind's eye, it exists nowhere else once I land back in my sleepy, sheltered village. I have learned so much, grown beyond recognition; I refuse to regret *any* of it.

And I also have a new start to look forward to!

I've always worked at that restaurant. I have maintained the same friendships with people who worked there with me, lost some of those friendships too.

So not only is this a fresh career opportunity but also the chance to meet new people. And ultimately move forward with my life. Coming to Magaluf has given me hands-on practise at navigating friendship forming in the most extreme of realms!

Andy strides purposely towards Blush and I ready myself to nod to him. Since his 'ex' admittance I've tried to remain impartial. He walks straight up to me and I almost back up thinking he's going to collide right into my face!

"Like ya blacks do ya?" He sneers.

I barely process his words and he laughs, turns and heads inside.

It hasn't registered. I feel like I've been slapped. Did he really just say that?

Like his term 'dike' he says the word derogatively. That's racism isn't it? And it's an attempt to insult me; which it doesn't because I like who I like! I don't care for people's opinion on skin colour- or their sexuality!

He saw me with Lee- and he's white. So he has said it purely to insult me; which does insult me because it's racist! I can't tolerate racism. It's just the lowest form of idiocy.

I instantly regret every inch of sympathy I felt towards him.

What a vile pig!

It's disrespectful towards Justin! Yes, he has been disrespectful towards me- sexist player. However I'm not blind to society, Justin has probably, unfortunately, been privy to prejudice before. He has no control over negativity based on his skin colour so I won't indulge it further by telling him.

It is wrong Andy has said it- and he deserves some form of comeuppance but it's not Justin's quarrel. It is undoubtedly me Andy is aiming to offend here.

Vile pig.

My mind reels, I'm caught up between anger and shock. How dare he say such a thing! And to think I've been giving him the benefit of the doubt! It seems I have got to accept that some people are nasty and spiteful.

How far does, 'he doesn't know any better' stretch? He's a fully grown man, in Magaluf for fucks sake the ultimate clash of colour, sexuality, cultures and nationality's!

He has learnt nothing at all from his experiences, never mind those of late! Until he can learn, feel, understand and be kind he doesn't deserve company.

I think it's time he forgives his ex for whatever she did and gets over his jealousy of Jamie. If he doesn't put his resentment to bed he will have a bitter, lonely future. Maybe he should sell those fucking clothes, move out and get on with his life!

Suddenly his lording it over the flat seems very pathetic indeed; almost laughable when it's in such a state too.

Chris Brown can be heard now blasting from inside. He'd certainly get it too! I think defiantly. He happily makes a living playing music made by black people doesn't he!

I feel like marching in there and saying this to him. But then that would only fuel the ridiculous comment. And it's *me* he is insulting- *my* actions- I knew he was judging me.

Out here I've followed my heart. I will always risk being held accountable for my actions by somebody else's standards. J labelled me a 'slag' and Andy is also referring to my promiscuity.

That is part of life; at home and here in Magaluf. I won't be letting it put me off this journey though. Being true to myself has made me so happy. I won't always behave so brazenly, especially in public! But just the knowledge of everything I have done makes me feel empowered and bold. I know I *can* if I *choose* to and that's what counts. So who knows where next, Ibiza! Italy?

My hand reaches for the dog tags that I have resolutely kept in my *pocket*. Have they bought me luck? Maybe! I didn't smash my head open yesterday after all!

But I've definitely learned that you can make your own luck.

When I broke up with stupid prick I thought my luck was out. Only I had been responsible for taking that route, my 'luck' was only a reflection of the choices I made.

Then I sacked him off, got my new job! And said yes to the holiday! And since then I've said yes- or rather jumped feet first- into all kinds of things I could never have imagined existed. Never mind contemplated I'd *actually do them*!

I *feel* lucky. That's what counts. I feel positive and excited for my future.

And I must make sure that includes actually jumping off a boat!

Because since then I have taken every opportunity presented to me with both hands and learned from it. And mostly enjoyed it all!

When Andy leaves half an hour later I watch him coolly. I don't waste energy feeling anger or resentment towards him. He doesn't even look over. Does he possess any understanding of how he makes other people feel? Blinded by his own feelings and needs. Everybody can relate to being selfish at times, but it isn't an excuse.

When I finish at 6 I take a stroll along the beach and call my mum. It's the first time she has a huge grin in her voice as she demands to be the person picking me up from the airport.

When I hang up the call I have a message waiting from Tanya.

I'm off tomorrow night! Backdoor it and stay with me till Mon x

The words float in my mind and I stare out at the horizon.

Stay with Tanya Saturday and Sunday, it is very tempting. Leave Andy, leave Blush, Tony, the shitty fake shots.

But what about Stacey? She might be pissed off I'm leaving so soon as it- what about if I quit *and* leave the flat. And what about the other girl's? Heather. We might have had our differences but I still owe her some respect- she got me the job, taught me the rules. And she hates 'backdoor' workers!

I'd have to hide! I realise now as familiar rebellious pleasure twinges. Hide from Wendy and Blush! My last 2 days would have to be undercover. But that wouldn't be so hard to do. I know everybody's work patterns. I could stay out of the way of the 'Blush area'- be on high alert for Wendy!

I don't know. So I decide to eat.

And then I sit on the balcony reading, pausing now and again to stare at the view in front of me.

It is my life, I remind myself over and over whilst I shower and get ready for work. It is my choice. *If* I want to leave, take Tanya up on her offer of rest-bite before leaving on Monday then I will!

There is no *if*; I know what I want to do.

THE LAST TIME

I still turn up to Blush determined to complete my last working day here. I take a long and sentimental look at the scene I have become so accustomed to; Jamie, Kristie, Sam, Ryan and Bex doing their best to drag punters into the bar from a selection of rampant party-goers. The strip in just some of it vibrant glory- this is only such a small section of it. The worn wooden veranda and backlit pinkish sign: Blush.

Beth and Gemma are leaning on a table and smile to me as I pass them in my reverie.

The last first tray of shots from Max; who at first glance I fancied and now think suffers from a split personality-so I only fancy half of him. India who I admire for her beauty and wonderful stories of travelling but who also fell victim to Andy's vicious tongue and Amy's jealous temper. Her pretty face is almost restored and I'm glad for her.

The last time I won't care about receiving 'the nod' from Tony who I gained and lost respect for in a pretty short space of time!

Taking the tray of phonies I think I'd rather be selling tequila again!

I have to tell Stacey. I know that. But I'm not risking Heather finding out now.

Instead, I'm just dying to know about this mystery man having not spoken to her all day. So I sidle up beside her.

"*Sooo*! Tell me about *last night*!" I probe her.

"What's there to tell!" She smirks coyly, she knew it was coming!

"Erm, the mystery? Why didn't you tell me before! I mean when did this even happen?"

She giggles girlishly before admitting. "I didn't want to jinx it! I mean the stories I've heard about workers! You know what I mean!"

Yes I do! Am I going to tell her about Justin last night? Am I going to tell her what Andy said to me?

"Jodes, he could turn out be an absolute nob. But I don't think he is! And I didn't want to say all this and then be proven wrong! Again!"

Her hesitation is understandable and I don't harbour annoyance at being kept in the dark. I've hardly been forthcoming with every detail, ahem Max!

"Well, you've got to take a risk sometimes! They're not all nobs, I don't think! So what's he called?" I inquire. "How did you meet? Where does he work?"

Turns out Carl introduced her to Todd one day at the beach and it stemmed from there. Messages passed back and forth using Carl as the connection. No numbers ever got swapped and then with the drama and Carl suddenly walking- the link was severed.

When we saw him that night in Mulligans he called Todd and told him we were there. So it was a night of reunions for both of us then!

She's gleeful after her first proper night with Todd. He's only the second since her relationship, her first with Jim and not being that great! Todd however has ignited a furnace within her and she glows with it. Hopefully he'll seek to take her mind off me leaving after all.

Almost half way through the shift and I hit jackpot with a large group of Italians. They clear my tray twice meaning I'm sitting comfortably on tray 5. I can sense the tension from Gemma and Beth. The bar has been relatively quiet and to their dismay the Italian boys had specifically wanted to buy my shots. I'll be gone tomorrow girls! I wish I could tell them. It will help with their sales!

I'm chatting to another group now, trying to convince them to buy me one. I'll play my trump card soon but for now I'm enjoying the banter.

"Ok, so let's strike a deal!" I tell them finally. "You pay me 30 euros, we all have a shot and I'll show you my tits."

They agree, like so many before them, amazed by the offer. I take their money and we do our drinks and then I whip up my top.

The guy closest to me leans across. I think he's going to try and grab my boob and quickly put them away but instead his hand slips straight up my skirt and grasps a clumsy handful of arse.

"What the fuck!" I react hotly. "Don't just grab me!"

"We paid you!" He retorts blasé.

"Not to touch me you didn't!" I tell him crossly and slam the cups back on my tray.

"How much to touch you?" His mate jokes oblivious to the nerve he's hit.

"I'm not f…!" For sale. I can't complete my sentence because in retrospect I actually am. "Forget it." I tell them and stomp away.

What leg do I have to stand on! I'm taking cash to see my body. He took liberties but why wouldn't the lines be blurred. And there's definitely nobody I can complain to. In Tony's eyes and probably that of the girl's too I already should've offered a grope.

I stand with Gemma and Stacey quietly at the edge of the veranda. I feel grotty but it's my last night anyway. I watch the bodies being pulled along the strip by an invisible current and a string of boys trot happily past us.

"Hey!" They call to us drunkenly, waving and grinning.

"Hi!" We smile in return hoping to do our part in luring them in.

I am distracted from my mood eyeing up one particularly attractive face in the line when I catch sight of another approaching me in my peripheral. Before I can stop him he plucks a shot from the tray and scampers away.

"Oi!" I retaliate furiously but I haven't made a move before he is scuttling into the distance. Ryan clocks what has happened and gives chase. Jamie grabs hold of one of his mates by the neck.

The scene unfolds so quickly it is all I can do to follow what is happening. Ryan comes back within seconds, empty handed, the perpetrator long gone. Jamie has the boy round the throat. He looks petrified as Jamie raises a wide open palm bringing it down across his face in a hard slap.

I bet that made his ear ring!

"That was for your shitbag mate! Fackin pussy!" He roars. The strip impossibly pauses, all eyes on Jamie and the boy with a bright red face. Some of his mates laugh nervously others hurl abuse from a suitably safe distance and they hurry on their way.

I feel sorry for the lad who took the punishment but glad for the knight in shining armour act!

I'm 5 euros down now, thanks to him taking the cup too. I'd nearly made it without losing 1. What a tosser!

Oh well. I'm leaving first thing for Tanya's; she has work at 9am so I want to get there before she goes. All of the issues- the cost cutting, sales pushing, sly behaviour- it doesn't matter anymore.

At least one thing is clear. That guy disappeared into the tide of people with ease. I will have no issues doing exactly the same if needs be during my last weekend.

"PEPPER SPRAY!" Jamie is roaring snatching my attention to the present. The crowds are dispersing, dashing inside and all the PR's rush toward the veranda. I heard what he said but amid the ensuing chaos I'm confused!

Then a deep burning sensation begins to fill my throat and my senses ignite. Before my eyes can begin to fully stream, I too scamper to safety indoors swept along with the impromptu crowds.

"What the…?" I gasp.

"Security just started spraying it!" A tourist to my side says.

“There was a fight!” Another spouts. “They were trying to break it up!”

The excitement soon dies down as does the peppery fire, but the spray never really had chance to take hold. I have wondered before how pepper spray feels and I’m glad my encounter is so brief.

We head back outside now that the air is cleared. The pressure is off to sell shots tonight and it is fun once again, a game not a living. When I’m told no, I no longer resort to my offers. If Tony sacks me, it makes no difference to my plans. My pride remains intact either way, I’m happy.

It is half past three now and the girls are making plans for after our shifts. There’s no way I’m saying anything now. If it gets back somehow before I’ve actually left, Tony, Jamie- or worse, Heather could turn up the apartment!

“I’ll stop at Todd’s if you’re not coming out.” Stacey tells me. “Andy still hasn’t handed over Carl’s key!”

I shouldn’t feel surprised at this but I do.

“He is such an idiot!” I shudder.

“I know but it’s been the perfect excuse to chill at his so much!” She giggles before chirping. “See you tomorrow Jodes!”

I guiltily resign to leaving her a note on her bed confessing where I am. I’ll leave her my share of the rent to hand over to Jamie too. I can meet up with her anyway before I actually leave for England.

At 4 o clock I turn in 8 trays. Neither Tony nor Max says a word as I pay for my last tray ever. And I wonder whether Tony would have even sacked me or if he was just pushing to see how far I'd go.

It's just another shift over for the staff as they wind down and head on. But not to me, it's yet again, just the beginning!

I leave Blush knowing I will quite possibly never step foot in the place again! Maybe once I'm 30 I'll dare to return.

LMFAO, Sorry for Party Rocking is playing: sorry not sorry!

Back at the apartment I repack my case for like the third time- new clothes joining those I brought along. I mull over tomorrow, and Sunday; it will be so lovely to end this whole thing almost how it first began.

An impromptu holiday relaxing in the sun by the sea; it's just what the doctor ordered after almost 3 weeks solidly working.

THE 'BACKDOOR'

My alarm chirps at 8am and my eyelids are as stiff as cardboard after just 3 hours of sleep. I can sleep once I'm at Tanya's! But now I need to write this note.

I retrieve the travel insurance documents from my hand luggage where it has been since my mum put it there! 'What to do in the event of: an injury, food poisoning, a cancellation'. I pick the sheet detailing robberies thinking of our near miss on the strip and sitting at the desk, try to make my groggy head think clearly.

Just be honest, you'll see her again soon! After a long hard think I begin.

Stacey, I have decided to run away and stay at my friend's place. I leave Monday. Can we meet up before then my Maga bestie? I will miss you!

I re-read it. And then add,

I'm leaving the rent for Andy in the living room. Can you make sure Jamie gets it please? Thanks, Jodes. P.S. Can you tell G, B and S I'm sorry I didn't tell them either! xxx

And then I take the food poisoning sheet neatly scratching;

I hope one day you wake up and grow up! You pathetic twat. Here's the rent. PS- sell these fucking clothes and clean the flat, it's vile!

I know I said I wouldn't stoop to retaliation but this is advice. He can do with it what he wishes.

I count out 250 and have about the same amount left over. That's not bad. It will definitely see me through and buy a few souvenirs.

It's not even half 8 when I slip onto the balcony for one final time. I take a quick snap of the view knowing I will remember it forever anyway.

I take one last look around the squalor I have been living in whilst quietly clearing a space on the coffee table for Andy's note and the rent money. Then I leave Stacey's note on her bed, along with my key as a parting gift. I shut her door behind me.

Goodbye horrid bathroom. Goodbye my bedroom, the bag with the condom in it still hangs on my door handle. Let it set the scene for the next person who arrives here. You can have your fun but be safe and be tidy!

I don't want any tell-tale rumbling suitcase wheels to alert Andy and lift the case along the hall way.

Unlatching the door I take my last step out of the flat. I even take the stairs still. My legs are much more accustomed to them now.

I avoid the strip completely and instead turn left. I know if I head this way, choosing left again I will walk parallel to it and evade Blush.

Now I'm out here I'm full of fresh exhilaration. If I saw Tony now, or Jamie I think I'd just leg it! It's done, I've done it! I've quit the job and flat I'd hankered after so anxiously and now I'm going to enjoy another (mini) holiday!

Finally I put my suitcase down and tug it along behind me. The first time I did this we'd exited a taxi moments from a hotel entrance. I was fresh and unsure but looking forward to my impending girls break. Then, I was happily skipping toward my first day at Blush; full of anticipation and intrigue. And now! 2 days ahead of me and a promising future to fly home to on Monday.

I am almost at Burger King now having successfully re-joined the route I know. The streets are clean and virtually empty. One girl stumbles along- she's holding her heels, her hair is plastered to her head. Foam party maybe, or skinny dipping? Bless her; there is no stride *or* pride going on here!

It's ok! I want to tell her. Go with the flow and be happy!

But then I'd at best look like I've been on some of Face's gear for the night so I keep my mouth shut.

The streets begin to open up as Tanya's place nears. Getting wider and brighter, the buildings better kept and restaurants and beauty salons instead of bars.

I distractedly glance at the moped which slows as it passes me. The guy sitting upright wears a helmet and he peers at me as if he knows me.

Oh shit!

The penny drops. It was Don! But he's passed now. His face was obscured by a slim black helmet but I have placed his familiar eyes now. And he definitely recognised me! Well the cat's definitely out of the bag now isn't it!

I feel gutted I couldn't say bye to him. But at least he is the one to find out first; he plans to do the same soon anyway although I'm sure he'll do it properly!

I quicken my pace just in case I have misplaced trust in Don and he has alerted Tony immediately! And arrive at the safety of Tanya's block within moments.

She opens her door greeting me with a huge smile!

"Hello! How are you?" She laughs. "Come in, come in!"

I follow her into the homely apartment. Another of her team is in the living room and she introduces me to Claire.

"I've got to shoot now Jodes. But you can tell me all about it later! I'll be home by 7."

"Ok cool. I'll treat you to dinner, to say thanks for having me!" I suggest.

"Ah babe, you don't have to do that!" She flings a few last minute items into her bag.

"I want to!" I tell her eyeing up her bed.

"Well, if you insist!" She grins from her doorway. "That'd be lovely. I know just the place! I'll see you later; help yourself to whatever you need! Bye"

She leaves and I go over to push her door closed. Before I do anything I need more sleep.

Tanya's bedroom has the same comforts and more of mine at home. Books, stationary, framed pictures and fairy lights. I lie on the bed surveying it; it will so soon be my own bedroom. I close my eyes and drift off into a welcoming sleep.

It's midday before I rouse. I lie still for a moment then check my phone. Will Stacey have read my note? Will Andy!

Maybe Don has already broken the news that he saw Jodie with her suitcase a fair way from home.

Well it's done now, I've back doored it. Time to have a shower, and then hit the beach! Why not?

Tanya's bathroom is like a dream in comparison to what I've been used to. Not only is it so much cleaner but every nook and cranny houses all manner of products. The result of 4 girls sharing; shampoos, conditioners, exfoliating creams, scented shower gels in abundance. I decide to wash my hair and have the most satisfying shower I have had in a month.

I head to the furthest end of the beach, far away where the other workers hang out. Hopefully I'll hear from Stacey- I hope she isn't mad with me!

I spread out my towel and arrange myself ready to read and relax.

"Hiya!" A voice rings out. I'm safe, I don't recognise it! "Hiya!" I hear again and look to find a guy ambling towards me.

He plonks himself cross legged on the sand next to me. He has shoulder length dark hair and green-grey eyes. "How you doing?" He asks me like it's the most natural thing in the world.

"I'm, erm, great thanks!" I reply hesitantly. "How are you?"

“Me? I’m smashing!” He smiles broadly his eyes twinkling. “So you’re here on your own?”

“Yes.” I wonder if it’s a dangerous thing to admit and backtrack. “Well no actually I work- worked- here. My friend is at work now, I’m waiting for her to finish.”

“Ah, that’s grand.” He replies kindly. “I’m Aaron.” Has he literally just ambled over for a chinwag!

“Oh, hi, I’m Jodie. So how about you, who’re you with?” I feel impelled to return his small talk.

“I’m with me mates, over there.” He points an arm adorned with tattoos. I spot a magic 8 ball and poker cards amongst other inked images. “I live in Spain; they live in Manchester where I’m from.”

My interest is slightly spiked by this information. He can’t be a Maga-worker he’d have already said. And although he’s got the right quirky look for the job, plus the sense of confidence he seems much nicer.

“So where abouts in Spain do you live?”

“Barcelona.” He tells me. I’m impressed. He seems too young to be so far away from home.

“And what do you do in Barcelona?” I enquire further.

“I’m working in a bar but I’m studying to teach English over there.”

“Nice!” I nod. There’s an idea! Could I transfer my impending teaching career abroad?

"Yeah it's great. I've been there 4 years."

"Gosh, how old are you?" I ask bluntly.

"24." He smiles. "How about you?"

"25." I tell him. He looks younger than that but then training to teach English in Barcelona seems mature beyond any 24 year old I know back home!

"Fancy a dip?" He indicates the sea. I think of Alexa, Cassie and me doing just that on our first day. It looks inviting, but now however I have a jellyfish phobia!

"There's jellyfish!" I tell him thinking this will put him off.

"Argh, they're only tiddlers! I'll piss on you if you get stung!" He offers genuinely.

I laugh out loud. "Surely that doesn't work!"

"Of course it does!" He replies laughing along with me. "No I'm only kidding it doesn't. But vinegar does. And I promise if you get stung I'll fetch you some from that cafe. Although weeing on you would be much more fun."

He winks at me cheekily.

"Why are you talking about it as if it's going to happen? I'm not going in the sea!" I shake my head.

"Stop being a wimp Jodie! Of course you're not going to get stung, look at how big the sea is!"

I giggle at his logic and feel tempted because one thing I'm not is a wimp! Especially not after everything I've been through. Plus I wouldn't mind continuing with this easy-going conversation with Aaron.

"Ok." I agree. "But what about my bag?" There was a time I didn't think twice about leaving it unattended but again my knowledge has expanded on that subject too.

"You can leave it with them." He thumbs towards his mates who keep looking over, obviously checking on his progress.

Bag dropped we head toward the sea.

"Race ya!" Aaron says gleefully and begins to bound into the surf. "Come on!"

I go for it and chase him into the frothy cold waves. He waits for me to catch up and before he can take pleasure in splashing me I immerse myself quickly.

"Ah that's nice!" I say breathily as my skin temperature rapidly adjusts.

Just then something bristles on my shoulder blade. I frown and for a moment think I've been stung! But I pass it off as seaweed or other debris, that's one thing I dislike about the sea, being touched by something unknown! Aaron notices my expression.

He chortles. "Whassup? Not been stung have ya?"

"No!" I giggle but my shoulder continues to feel irritated. "I don't know! I thought I felt something!"

"Paranoid!" He teases me.

I stand up freeing my upper half of the water and realise yes my shoulder is definitely prickly.

"Is there something there?" I turn slightly, allowing him to view my back. He roars with laughter.

"Well knock me down with a feather! You have an 'all!"

"No! No way!" But try as I might I can't see the offending area. I don't think he's fibbing though the area is tight and burning.

"Come on!" He begins jokily tugging at his shorts.

"Piss off!" I retort and we laugh at the pun.

"Well, I did say I'd get you some vinegar!"

We exit the sea and pass his friends. Aaron cheerfully reporting;

"She's been stung!"

We dart into the closest café and I check out the white lump and surrounding puffy red circle in the bathroom mirror. I can't believe it! I really have been stung!

Well what does that tell me! That I should heed my own warnings more often? Aaron presses a square of napkin doused in vinegar on my shoulder and after a couple of minutes the sting subsides. It reminds of a particularly bison wasp sting, and isn't as bad as I imagined.

"They only small eh." The waitress tells us watching in amusement. "It hurt, no?"

I shrug, "Nah not really."

"Big ones do!" She tells me knowingly.

Well that settles it. Aaron said they were only small! If I'd known the sea was full of big ones I wouldn't have gone in. Calculated risks and educated guesses- that's the best I can do!

I spend a little longer sitting with Aaron and his friends. Two of them disappear and when they return a short while later they are sporting new tattoos. This isn't the unusual part having seen cling-filmed body parts already. But the location- on the inside of their bottom lip! They pull it downward in turn to reveal the black words etched into the red flesh.

Alex's says 'Tara', His girlfriend's name. How romantic, I think? And Kevin's reads; 'CUNT'. Brilliant!

"So what are you doing later on?" Aaron broaches the subject as he and his friends get ready to leave.

"I'm seeing my friend," I say honestly feeling a teeny weeny bit disappointed. "But I'm free tomorrow. It's my last day!"

"Do you want to give me your number? We could meet up if you wanted to?"

"Yeah, why not." I look at him smiling brightly and wait until he is ready to type the digits into his phone.

"Cool! Well I'll bell you tomorrow then! Bye!"

"Bye!" I bid farewell to the group and they retreat kicking up sand as they go with their large feet.

I check my phone and I'm relieved to read a text from Stacey saying she will meet me tomorrow- her and Todd have plans for today-

and that she saw my note to Andy discarded in the bathroom bin. 'LOL'.

So much for dwelling on my 'advice' then!

I can't wait to tell Tanya I got stung by a jellyfish! I can't wait to tell Leila! How hilarious, I hope she isn't sick again! And what about Aaron? He's unusual and cute, perhaps one final holiday romance for the road…

And Barcelona to boot! Yet another potential opportunity to add to my future prospects, if all goes well tomorrow.

Laying back on my towel I close my eyes and relax letting the crash of the waves lull me into peaceful daydreams.

Back at Tanya's I shower again and lather myself in somebody's thick, flowery moisturising cream. My body is deeply tanned in the places that have been privy to the sunshine; my boobs look whiter than ever. I put on a comfortable playsuit, tie my hair in a topknot and apply only a lick of mascara. It feels lovely to not care about layering on the makeup and to have no cares about how many shot's I'm going to sell.

Don't worry boobies, you'll be staying covered up this evening.

Tanya comes home shortly after 7 and finds me sitting on her bed reading.

"Hey! How was your day?"

"Don't ask!" She rolls her eyes. "How was yours?"

"I got stung by a jellyfish!" I tell her and shift the back of my top to reveal a pinkish area with white dot in the middle.

"Did it hurt?" She asks me and I shake my head.

"Not *really* bad. It felt like a wasp sting but worse."

"Well! That's one thing I've never done, been stung by a jellyfish!"

I laugh, wow, I've excelled! And then she says;

"I'll get myself ready, and we'll go yeah? I'm starving!"

I am too I realise as she swans off to have a shower. And tonight I know for sure I will be indulging in aioli- the extremely garlicky Mediterranean dip I've had to steadfastly avoid whilst holding down a job which involves kissing! I can't wait!

Completely content after over indulging in a range of tapas dishes we're curled up in a cushioned bench each on Tanya's balcony. It makes a nice change sipping lime Bacardi Breezers to the continuous harsh spirits I've been used to.

Like last time Tanya rolls a joint and lights it inhaling deeply.

"Wow that feels good." She smiles lazily. "So are you looking forward to going home? I bet you've missed everyone!"

"Yeah." I agree non-committedly. "I do. I was in no rush to go home before! But now, I'm actually looking forward to it."

"I tell you what Jodes. Nothing ever changes with that place. Every time I go home, it's the same old people doing the same old shit. Don't ever be afraid to get yourself out there. You're not missing anything there! And they are missing everything! Sometimes I wonder if people even think about how the big world is. You know, that there's so much to see and try, and instead they're so caught up in petty drama."

I take the spliff from her and let the message wash over me. It is so true. I bet in 10 years stupid prick will still be in the same position and not just with his life, but literally the same position at the end of the same bar- whereas for me! Who knows? The world is my oyster!

"So do you want to do some more travelling?" She queries now and resolutely I know the answer.

"Yes, definitely." Hopefully this is all just the start of many adventures!

"You'll have to visit me again next summer, who knows where I'll be posted!"

BOMBSHELLS

Tanya is off to the airport to do another pick up. Tomorrow it will be me heading there! My stomach swirls with a mixture of nerves and excitement. I feel like I have been here forever!

I'm on my way to meet Stacey. We've agreed to meet at Bar Sixty because it is right at this end and therefore a fair distance from Blush! I can't wait to see her but I feel apprehensive about what she might have to tell me about the others' reactions to my speedy departure.

"Jodes!" She squeals and embraces me as though it's been weeks. "You naughty girl!" She apprehends me and I lower my eyes.

"I'm sorry I didn't tell you sooner!" I explain. "But I didn't get the chance and..."

She doesn't let me finish her eyes bulging indicating she can't wait to tell me something.

"*Well* have I got some news for you! You. Will. Not. Believe!"

She holds her palms up between us and I can barely contain myself. This is big I can tell!

"What? What?"

She quickly checks we don't recognise anybody in ear shot before leaning forward and whispering. "Gemma found out she's pregnant!"

"What!" I shriek causing a few people to turn and stare. "What the fuck!" I holler and this gains me a disapproving loud tut.

I don't care! I was like so not expecting that! It can barely sink in. I was thinking perhaps something to do with me leaving or Blush itself.

"What…? When…? Who…?" I flounder for the words to complete any of the questions rapidly forming in my mind.

"Well she missed a period but she wasn't worried because she's on the pill! Then she missed it this time too but with Stevie getting the sack she pushed it to the back of her mind. She decided to take the test yesterday, I suppose now things have settled down again. And yep, positive!"

I'm shaking my head in disbelief remembering her comment about leaving. "So what's she going to do? Does she even know whose it is?"

Stacey shrugs slurping her drink through a straw keeping her animated face locked on mine.

"She's going home; she and Stevie are booking their flights as we speak- which Stevie says she's actually relieved about. She reckons she'd had enough ages ago! But yeah Gemma, she has no idea about the dad! Well, she knows it *could* possibly be one of 5. But until she gets proper dates and that. And she doesn't know if she'll keep it. So, she's leaving anyway! At this rate I'll be looking for another job too. Plus, I do not want to live with Andy on my own!"

"Oh yeah, god Stace I'm sorry!"

"Oh don't be daft! *Anyway*, I've not even told you the best bit! But before that, what the fuck was the note all about?" She enquires.

"What note?" I'm confused thinking she means my note to her, still dazzled at the news about Gemma. Pregnant! Poor thing; I mean she was using contraception! But maybe she'd missed a couple, been sick; these things can make it ineffective. I recall my own pill packet, I have dutifully taken every single one and I look forward for once to seeing my period- you know just to be sure!

"Oh, erm let me think!" She jibes sarcastically. "Duh! Grow up and clean the flat or whatever it said!"

"Oh! Yes!" I titter self-consciously. "Well he said something to me, really horrible and I couldn't just leave without saying something in return!"

"What did he say to you?" She noses like I knew she would, I'd do the same! So I give her the low-down, Justin and the comment I received about him. She doesn't care about the fact I went back there with J, but her reaction about Andy is every bit as disgusted as mine was.

"What a prick!" She evaluates the scenario. "So, I didn't feel bad for him anyway, but now even more so!"

"Bad for him why?" I cry. This is what I thought the initial bombshell would be and I'm physically on the edge of my seat.

"He told Jamie you went without paying your rent! He's a serial fantasist Jodes. Did he think Jamie wouldn't mention it to me? Never mind that you already asked me to check! Did you think he wouldn't pass it on Jodes? Did you do it on purpose?"

"I don't know!" I realise now although it had crossed my mind; I hoped deep down he would do the right thing. "I can't believe it!"

Stacey raises her eyebrows.

"Ok, I can believe it. But how do you know? Has he paid it now?"

"No! Well it's sorted don't worry! I took the note to show Jamie just now. He couldn't stop laughing." She informs me and I giggle now too.

"No way! So what's he going to do?"

"Well he was actually pretty pissed off with him. Said it was about time someone called him out. He's gunna tell him he can pay up today or he'll take it out his wages. *And* he's going to dock his wages too. Apparently Tony's been pushing for a cut but Jamie had been fighting his corner. Everyone knows he was responsible for India being attacked and the loss of 2 PR's have obviously affected trade! And now he blames him for losing you too!"

My mind is totally reeling. Do I feel sorry for Andy? No, not really. I haven't actually made any of this up- unlike him and his wild stories. He's getting his just desserts. He would have happily let everyone believe I not only back-doored it but didn't even pay my rent before going!

"Plus Jamie thinks selling the clothes is a good idea. He's going to ask Andy about selling them through Blush, split the profit somehow."

She shrugs and I feel completely vindicated. Revenge was never my intention when I left the note and hearing this news that Andy could maybe have a shot at a fresh start is good. And as an added bonus he's given my departure the perfect excuse. Eliminating me from any hard feelings. Almost!

"And what about Heather?" I query now not sure I actually want to know.

"She's glad mate."

"Oh!"

"Don't take it personally! She was jealous, Tony was furious he'd lost his 'best shot girl'!" She imitates his thick accent and I giggle, his 'best shot girl'. Well I knew it didn't I? Even if I only held the title for a few days!

"She was pissed off about that. But then sold 12 trays and was. Well. Happy! Like ridiculously. And then with Gemma leaving too, she'll be even happier! More trade for her."

"And Beth? What is she doing?"

"She was on about seeing out the season and going somewhere with India and Carl come October. I think she wants a work permit. And I reckon Tony will sort her one now! There'll be nobody left!"

It's all turned out pretty well, other than Gemma's unplanned pregnancy. Who knows though, it could turn out to be a fantastic thing for her- she has to make her own decision there! Blush is nothing how it was when I first came, just like that the sands have shifted yet again and everything has changed. It helps with leaving it behind. I don't feel that pang of FOMO (fear of missing out)!

I do feel some envy that Beth, India and Carl are off on their travels but then I know it's on the cards for me too one day. With a buddy would be nice, Leila perhaps? I can't wait to see her again! I already have so much to tell her- and she'll be able to put names to faces which is even better!

So much happens here on a daily basis I reckon I'm going to be feeling a little underwhelmed back at home!

Stacey goes on to tell me all about Todd and I listen contentedly. She's told him she only plans to stay another fortnight herself and that she doesn't want to get too close in that time because they live so far apart back in the UK.

"I like him but it is way too soon to be considering a relationship! If I really miss him when we're home then you know, we'll see. But what's the point in worrying and wondering? What will be will be! If it's meant to be it will find a way! Do you know what I've realised Jodes?"

"What's that babe?" She's been learning her own lessons about herself and I wonder what understanding she has come to.

"Love isn't meant to be hard work and painful. It's meant to be fun and natural. And I'm in no rush to find one great love." She stops to think and I let the words reside with me. "Just. Go. With. The. Flow. And fall in love with lots of people along the way!"

"Well said Stacey! I'm happy to raise a drink to that!" I don't think I could have put it better myself and it's just what I intend to do! "Cheers darling, to going with the flow!"

It's going to be so much fun!

Before parting we agree to meet up once we're both settled back in the UK. And even if we don't we're 'Facebook friends' and we will always be Maga-Besties!

And speaking of going with the flow, after a day of bouncing from café, to beach, to bar with Stacey I am now on my way out to meet Aaron.

I feel happier than I have ever felt before. I am free in the knowledge that I am not tied down to anything or anybody. That I have a choice and I can choose my own path.

The path I'm on now leads to Burger King where I've agreed to meet him. I can see him up ahead, his hair tied up into a pony tail. It alters his face almost beyond recognition highlighting strong high cheekbones. But then he gives me his broad smile and his warm friendly eyes instantly remind me of his good company yesterday.

"Hey!" he greets me gently and gives me a causal hug. "And how are you today? Sting gave you any grief?"

"No, no!" I reassure him. "Can barely see it now! How was last night? Go anywhere good?"

"Bounce?" He states.

"Yeah I know it, good music if I remember right."

"Not my thing but it was ok!"

"So what *is* your thing?" We chat easily and having made him aware that I must stay away from the central area of the strip we're heading to Plaza where his friends already are.

I recognise one of the PR's and he nods to me as we enter. Chances are I could still get away with asking for worker discount prices- but I won't push my luck! I've spent the day beaming since finding out that I not only got away with back-dooring it scot-free but I also inadvertently managed to ensure Andy paid a price for actions *and* helped present a chance to better himself. Maybe I am too nice, but I hope that he does.

"Jodie!" I hear and turn to see Ben coming over to me.

"What are you doing here?" I ask him. "Shouldn't you be at work?"

"This is work!" He replies. "I work here now!"

"Oh ok." How can I be surprised it's part of the community; job swapping and moving accommodation at the drop of a hat. "What happened at Club Twenty One?"

"Ah nothing. Lost my roomie didn't I? Dan over there had a room and there was a job opening so I just thought fuck it! Fancied a change." He continues adding details about pay and perks but his words- lost my roomie- ring in my mind. His roomie is Justin.

"Hold on!" I stop him. "So what happened to J?"

"He left mate, Friday. He owed somebody money or something. He *was* a dodgy fucker Jodie!" He says trying to justify the photograph lies.

So chances are when he said 'I'm off!' after I told him I was leaving he meant like, off home. Off for good! Within 12 hours, he would have been gone and I was none the wiser.

Well! Yet another turn up for the books! If he knew he was leaving, he chose to hunt me down on his last night. I can't help it, I feel smug about that.

Ben fetches us a round of fishbowls to share, earning me credit amongst the group.

"Glad we met you!" Alex is saying.

"How's your lip?" I ask after the unusual tattoo.

"It's ok. Kev's struggling though aren't you mate."

Kevin rolls his eyes and I notice that his lower lip does actually look swollen but he doesn't look in the mood to talk about it. Alex continues for him.

"Didn't follow instructions did you pal!" The group guffaws and finally Aaron elaborates.

"He licked some bird out last night! And it's swollen up since. Don't think that's quite the salt water you shoulda been swilling is it mate!"

"She was a beast as well!" Alex heckles.

"Well we were playing pull a pig!"

"Pull a…!" Actually, I don't want to know. Lads will be lads- I'm under no allusion thanks to being so close to my brother and Micky. The things they talk about! I'll certainly have some topics for us to dissect when I'm home. Tomorrow! Yay, I can't wait to see everyone!

As the night progresses we make a small triangle with the bars we visit. I am pleased the lads are happy to accommodate the limitation because they are good fun.

And I admit I fancy Aaron more and more- he's different, confident and funny. But I'm not going to 'bang' him I've decided. If that's going to happen it will be when I'm visiting him in Barcelona!

We're in Sinky's now and dancing daftly to their cheesy selection of music. S Club 7 has just finished and now Vengaboy's has started up. Aaron has got some moves and I tease him about this music evidently 'being his thing'.

I nip to the loo and stare at myself thinking this is it, my last night done. And it's been great. It's all been great! I take a quick selfie and check the time.

Almost 2am. Tanya has text to say she's home and has left the key under the doormat for me. Bless her, what a legend. I have to be up and out by 9. It's time to leave the strip for one last time.

I head back to Aaron on the dancefloor where a lucky, lucky man adorns him with flashing bunny ears. He's handing over his cash and when they see me approaching he begins waving the bucket of single red roses under Aaron's nose.

Aaron doesn't hesitate and plucks one from the selection paying for that too. He shyly holds it out to me grinning with his lips closed.

"Ah, bless. Thanks!" I coo to him its sweet of him and now I've got to tell him I'm leaving! "Aaron, I've got to go! I've got to be up early and…"

"I'll walk you back." He says immediately.

"You don't have…"

"It's fine. Honest, come on."

We leave the dark club and head into the darker night. It is much quieter around Tanya's area and we walk in a silence loaded with tension.

“I wonder how much money lucky, lucky men make!” I wonder aloud thinking about the rose that I still have in my hand. I am desperate to chat, ignore the nerves that come with an impending first kiss.

We reach the steps of Tanya’s building.

“Thanks for walking me back.” I tell him politely. “I can manage from here.”

“No problem.” He steps towards me and reaches in for a hug. “I’ll add you on Facebook, soo if you fancy a trip to Barcelona?” He peters out.

“I’d love that!” I say honestly.

“Ok, well. Safe journey tomorrow! It was nice meeting you.”

He gives me a kiss on the lips but refreshingly doesn’t push it further. We smile at each other one last time and he strolls away from me.

I wonder if I will see him again and I wonder if it will be in Barcelona!

I skip up the stairs, take the key from its hiding place and quietly let myself in. I head to the kitchen and fill a glass with water to put the rose in. The girls can enjoy it before it wilts.

After doing my teeth I quietly slip into bed with Tanya. And close my eyes to fall asleep in Magaluf for the last time.

FAREWELL MAGALUF!

My heart has been hammering since the moment I got up. Tanya apologises she can't drive me there herself but I don't mind. To be honest my mind is racing and empty at the same time. I can't make conversation.

I thank her for having me and promise I will see her again sooner this time.

The taxi driver doesn't try to talk to me which is fine. It's only a half an hour ride to the airport and it isn't long before I'm in the vast, air conditioned check-in lounge.

Whilst waiting I watch other tourist groups chatting together and feel a pang of lonesomeness. Not long now and I'll be back on familiar turf and there'll be plenty of people to talk to! I think about Gemma and Stevie doing this whole worker thing together and wonder how different of an experience it would have been if Alexa or Cassie had stayed with me.

Ultimately I'm glad I did this alone. I have grown so much in confidence. I feel like I could face any challenge that's thrown my way. I've missed having support around me in the form of my family and friends- but it's made me appreciate it all the more. And I realise they will always be there for me regardless of where in the world I might be.

3 hours tediously creep past. I browse the selection of shops, purchase souvenirs and then sit on the uncomfortable chairs trying to immerse myself in reading and I am finally now boarding the plane.

My heart is heavy and my throat thick with emotion.

"Welcome to Ryanair!" The stewardess chirps as I pass her.

I have a window seat and I hope whoever is next to me doesn't eat with their mouth open, smell or fall asleep on me. Aeroplane seats are way too close for comfort and right now all I want to do is wallow in the memories of the past month, undisturbed.

I smile at the 2 ladies who take the seats beside me. I have my book on my lap in case I need to feign that I am deeply engrossed but they're happily chatting to one another anyway.

It is a short flight home- 2 and a half hours.

Well, this really is it. We are rumbling towards the runway. The engines begin to power up, a roar which increases in volume and then with a lurch the plane begins rapidly picking up speed until it floats slightly and we gradually climb up, up, up into the air.

Bye bye Magaluf, you wonderful, crazy, wild place. You will always hold a special place in my heart! I watch the grey crisscross of roads as they grow smaller and wispy clouds begin to blot the island out. As we continue our route all I can see now is a vast rolling blue ocean and I sit back in my seat with my eyes closed trying to hold in the tears.

"Thank you for choosing us today ladies and gents. We are just coming into East Midland's airspace now. We're a little bit ahead of schedule and should be on the ground within 20 minutes. Local time is just after 1pm. Weather is clear and sunny, 17 degrees."

The pilot signs off and the lady next to me clicks her teeth.

"17 degrees!" She comments. "Take me back to Spain!"

I glance at her and smile. She's right about the temperature; it's going to feel considerably cooler than the late 20's I've been used to. But at least the sun is out to welcome me back. And even if I was given the choice I wouldn't have the plane turn around and return. I don't want to think about it, but amongst many other reasons- I need to book myself in at the sexual health clinic!

I look at the carparks, the cars resembling toys and we descend further. My mum's waiting for me somewhere out there!

I swallow the lump that's reformed in my throat but tears leak despite my best efforts and roll down my cheeks.

I don't know why I'm crying. I'm tired in general, gutted to be home, glad to be home, relieved and devastated to have left Magaluf behind. I'm proud and pleased with myself, I feel like I have a whole new head on my shoulders. I've missed my mum and family and friends more than I'd cared to accept and I know these tears are going to return again when I see my mum in the flesh!

I think I am in part crying for the girl who flew out there and didn't return. And I am crying with happiness for the girl who is coming home today. This is not the end, Jodie. This really is, only the beginning!

Printed in Great Britain
by Amazon